— THE CHAIN OF —
LACODERE

— THE CHAIN OF —
LACODERE

A STORY TOLD TO

R.G. SOMMER

EDITED BY

JOHN MYLES

authorHOUSE®

AuthorHouse™
1663 Liberty Drive
Bloomington, IN 47403
www.authorhouse.com
Phone: 1-800-839-8640

Published by AuthorHouse   08/17/2012

ISBN: 978-1-4772-4411-1 (sc)
ISBN: 978-1-4772-4410-4 (hc)
ISBN: 978-1-4772-4412-8 (e)

Library of Congress Control Number: 2012912624

PREFACE

It would appear, and sometimes with a note of downright good faith, an author is prompted by moral justification or sheer fright, to begin his story with a preface or prologue; or perhaps, conclude with an apologetical epilogue. In either event, the author wants to say something over and above what is mentioned in the body of the theme so as to acquaint the prospective reader with a semblance of truth not necessarily found or detected in the story itself. In this respect, I can't claim divergence.

So, I'll take the thrill out of reading the Chain of Lacodere from the very outset by telling you it reeks with fallacy and greets truth in any shape or form with a passing wave. To my knowledge, the characters are, in toto, a figment of the author's imagination. The plot could only find solace in the comforting recesses of musing make-believe and artful fantasy.

Making the main character of the story a Benedictine monk shouldn't cast a shadow of disdain on the wonderful order of priests founded by Saint Benedict, any more than the holy Jesuits should raise their intellectual brows in disgust upon learning that they educated a mythical soul. And, if some Dominicans happen to possess pot-bellies, it shouldn't detract from their greatness one farthing. Making mentions of the Christian Brothers of La Salle should be a source of free publicity in their faithful interest in the education of the American boy rather than lead some to believe to the contrary. If there exists an abbey in the State of Georgia, I'm as surprised as the Governor of Louisiana would be upon learning of the town of Lacodere within the confines of his historical state. It should be quite conclusive, then, that both are purely legendary.

In treating the moral question involved herein, let me make haste to assure the reader I presented situations that could exist without attempting to read the latest books on Moral Philosophy and Technology as a medium of safeguarding my conscience. In short, with respect to morality as such, I graciously disregarded all degrees of inhibition. Social, moral, and, indeed, spiritual errors are in the majority today; the fact they appear boldly in the ascendancy in the sphere of our present century should better the position to reason their causes in this treatment. However, in no way did I attempt an emulation of Guy de Maupassant or try to act out a drama of the Moliere character and fashion. Herewith is the story of a strange situation, prompted, no doubt, by circumstances that were never meant to educate, nor even enlighten the mind, but to entertain rather than sharpen.

With all due apologies rendered, as the author is at rest in his conceited conviction that nobody on earth or in Heaven should feel hurt because of the Chain of Lacodere, let us undress our intellectual minds and walk boldly forth with only a desire to be entertained by the joys and sorrow, the pangs and jubilations, and the intimate heartaches of Timothy Patrick O'Shea, American Boy!

Nemo me impune laces sit!

R.G.S.

"Years mature into fruit so that some small seeds of moments may outlive them."

Robindranath Tagore

CHAPTER ONE

It was close to the midnight hour when Father Kevin O'Shea placed his book on the desk, walked over to his window, pushed aside the soiled curtain, and gazed into the starry heavens, admiring the twinkling jewels that surrounded the moon in all its majestic glory.

His eyes focused themselves in the direction of the Novitiate building beyond the main Abbey, and he thought to himself how wonderful it was to be able to sleep with a deep restfulness like the thirteen novices who made up the nearly closing Novitiate year. He thought of his own Novitiate made in that very same building nineteen years previous. His hand released the curtain as it closed the scene, and slowly he walked to his desk. His heart was heavy and sad. Nothing seemed to matter to him now. His priestly duties failed to have the appeal and zeal of former years. His mind was obsessed with the past. A past that knew very little joy and contentment. There was a void within his breast that yearned to be filled . . . filled with the happiness that should be in the breast of a priest so learned and highly regarded in the Benedictine Order.

Father Kevin's desk was a literary mess. Papers of recent examinations given, but not corrected, books on various problems of psychology, notes taken in his own studies made so many years ago. He picked up several sheets of examination papers only to toss them back on the desk with utter disinterestedness. He walked over to his combination radio-phonograph and turned the switch. Within a few moments, the strains that yielded the immortal Debussy love song usurped his mind. He returned to his desk and sat down. How many times he listened to Clair de Lune that night he wasn't able to determine. Each time, though, he thought his heart would burst, and it was with manly restraint he pushed back the tears that would surely flow unless checked. This time, the music was too much for him to bear. He buried his face in his hands and sobbed like a child. A certain release of this inward sorrow often managed to clear the mind and enable one to regain lost ideals, but to Father Kevin, no such release rewarded him.

His mind wandered back to his boyhood days; days filled with much happiness and all the bliss that comes to youth; days that admitted little of responsibility, less of moral burdens. He was only recalled back to the realities of his cell and its monastic surroundings when he would lift his head from the nest-like rest of his hands and look about him and fasten his eyes on the many papers to be corrected.

There wasn't too grave a difference between May 29th, 1946 and the same month and day twenty years past. The locality was now Georgia, while in 1926, it was Lacodere, Louisiana. He was now a priest in the Abbey of Cassino under the Rule of Saint Benedict. Then, too, a great World's War was fought and won by the United Nations that wasn't even heard of in 1926. He, in those days, wondered if Al Capone would be caught and apprehended along with his many cohorts of those wild Twenties. He was busy then, with the same thoughts that many seventeen year olds in 1946 entertained. In 1926, he was the pride of Lacodere Prep and the apple of the Hesuitical eyes of the institution. In 1946, he was the professor of Psychology and newly appointed Dean of Men at Cassino College in the heart of the peach country of Georgia.

Yes, Father Kevin had much to be thankful for in 1946, and in that very same year had a great deal more to divorce from his mind if he was to be the success all the Abbey's faculty thought he should be. Even tonight, the twentieth anniversary of his high school graduation, he must start to forget all that preceded and look in the direction of the future for that ray of hope and consolation that comes through the veins of activity and the avenues of diligent labor. He must forget Madeline Turrell forever. He must break the recording of Debussy's classic. The strains of sadness that usurp one's soul while listening to "de Lune" must be forever purged from within by new thoughts, clean and healthy thoughts, thoughts that make one awaken in the early morn with situations to conquer, mountains made into little hills for those tired limbs to climb with ease, studies made simple only through clear lectures, love to find its way into the heart where hate finds contentment only for the belligerent. All this Father Kevin must do for his own betterment and for the many young men who will look upon him as their guide and Father-Director. Therefore, he must put aside his own grief and past misgivings to supplant in his own Irish heart the happiness that must be always apparent on the glowing countenance of one who is free, yes, free from the shackles of those days in 1926 and the more horrible nightmare of 1944.

The present is the best time in the world for reconversion. After a rest throughout the summer to follow, he will find the fall filled with important appointments—new faces in his psychology classes—new students to enroll in the preparatory department of the College, and the usual run of freshmen with their "know-it-all" expressions in speech classes.

Why not dry up those tears and prepare for the great advent of tomorrow, wherein lies new hopes, new loves, greater zeal, and look with determination into the prospectus of tomorrow with the ointment of salvation for the many students who will look to him for the encouragement so vital in an age of uncertain scopes?

Why not close the pages of yesterday forever, place the thoughts of Madeline in the void of oblivion—the grotesque horrors of that siege on the beach of Peleliu in the history of that September 15th? But, no, he wanted to recall the smiles and joys and laughter of his own Novitiate. He wanted very much to relive these decades, if only for tonight. He wanted to remember September of 1941. Yes, there were sad days intermingled with the joyous ones. Tonight he would take a trip back and recount the time spent. Tomorrow it would be over—his passion, scourge, crown and death, with his resurrection, a new and different Father Kevin would emerge forth to tackle tomorrow's problems tomorrow. But, for tonight, he must sit back and think.

Father Kevin got up from his seat and turned the switch that silenced Clair de Lune. He returned to his easy chair in the corner of his cell and sat down to prepare for a nocturnal reminiscence. One last gesture—he slipped his hand between his tunic and shirt, unfastened the clip, and released the Chain of Lacodere from around his neck. It fell gently into the palm of his hand. He closed his hand tightly around the gold chain and medal, leaned back in his chair, adjusted his head on the uppermost leather cushion-back, and closed his eyes—to think!

Chapter Two

September 18, 1909, was a happy one for Timothy Patrick O'Shea. During his noon meal, the nurse called from the hospital to announce that he was the father of an eight pound baby boy. She wasn't able to determine who the boy resembled or what features he possessed, because she was very busy at the time, and if the father of a newborn baby was really interested, he could come to the hospital and see for himself.

The birth of little Timothy, (he was baptized just two weeks after the eighteenth and given his father's name) left Margaret O'Shea in poor health. Doctors advised Big Tim to move to the South—perhaps Florida or California as the damp climate of Seattle, Washington was anything but healthy for Mrs. O'Shea.

It was a hardship for Tim to leave Seattle. He lived in the great Northwest for nearly five years. An occasional trip back to Alaska to visit the scene of his acquired fortune was his only leave of absence. To move South would probably make him forget the snow and ice he loved so much in the desolate Klondike region around Nome. But, if the doctors wanted Margaret to go South, well, South they'd certainly go.

In October of 1910, the big and roomy house on Fontaine Street in Lacodere, Louisiana, finally saw its completion. Margaret designed the whole house according to her own tastes. It was the year that her sister, Elizabeth, came to live with them from Ireland. Big Tim sunk quite a sum of money in this large stone house. It was easily the biggest place the native of that southern town had ever seen. He bought anything and everything Margaret wanted. If she desired some rare piece of furniture manufactured in the Chicago area, he'd be off to get it, remembering to pick up something on the way he thought she'd like. If he couldn't get what she suggested in Memphis, he'd take a trip to New Orleans. Often he and Elizabeth would leave Margaret and the baby and take a jaunt to New York City or Boston in quest of chinaware or rugs or silver pieces. Big Tim thought the world of Elizabeth and confided his business deals and personal ailments to her understanding confidence.

Despite the wonderful treatment Margaret received for some unknown reason, she never really recovered from giving birth to Timmy. In the afternoons, she would retire to her room to rest. In the evenings, after the supper hour, Margaret would read or write letters to friends in Ireland. She spent little time with young Timmy. All the duties and cares of the child were left to Elizabeth or the servants. She loved the baby well enough, but it was he who caused her to lose all sense of duty. She just wasn't the same sweet Margaret Big Tim married in Killashander that lovely May morning in 1891.

At the suggestion of Doctor Jereau, the newly acquired family physician, they should take a long vacation to Europe and leave Timmy in the faithful hands of Elizabeth. This met with two-fold agreement. Big Tim could return to Erin after so many years of absence, and Margaret could see those many friends she corresponded with each evening she spent at her desk in the library. It was mutually agreed that the trip would be made in the Spring of 1911, and they would sail from Boston's harbor in early May. Leisure trips to New York could be planned so as to make the necessary wardrobe purchases and little gifts for all their Celtic friends procured at the numberless stores in the East. There was a marked improvement in Margaret's outlook after the plans were formulated and settled upon. She completely forgot about Timmy and Elizabeth. She regained strength to visit New Orleans more often. Sunday Mass as taken in with religious fervor, whereas before, she was either too ill or too tired to dress so early on Sunday morning. Or, maybe she wanted to get back into the swing of things Catholic so she wouldn't shock the relatives on the Ole Sod.

Timmy was growing into a beautiful child. When Elizabeth would take him for an outing in the carriage, people would stop to admire his beauty. He never cried when people would pinch his fat little cheeks. He seemed to enjoy the attention. It was sort of a precaution that he remain in his buggy, because he was able now to walk a little, or, at least, operate a kiddy-car. He learned to say "Liz" before "mama," but this didn't bother Margaret. She was glad of the shifted responsibility. If Elizabeth took delight in taking Timmy to church in the mid-afternoons, it was perfectly agreeable with Margaret.

As the months rolled along, the day of departure arrived. Both Big Tim and Margaret were ready. They were ready weeks before the date was set. Timmy didn't cry when his mother bent low to kiss his cheek—Elizabeth did enough crying for both. There seemed to be a glow of happiness in Margaret's every expression. Her orders to Elizabeth were simple. She could do whatever she pleased. There was no need to render instructions concerning Timmy. All the past year, she was his constant companion, nurse and mother. In fact, she was happy to have him stay with her rather than make the journey across the ocean with his parents. Big Tim gave a few financial instructions and in a laughing gesture, told her there was enough money in the bank to take care of her needs the rest of her life, that is, if she didn't live more than fifty years longer.

They were off! Last goodbyes, kisses and tears were soon an echo of the mind and a pressure too hastily passed along. Elizabeth saw Big Tim's smile for the last time as he waved from the carriage and ordered the driver to hurry along. Little did they realize their second honeymoon was to end in disaster.

Christmas arrived in Lacodere with Easter following in early April. Timmy was growing into a fine little lad of nearly three. He could carry on, in his own little way, a conversation that consisted mainly of questions. His "Auntie Liz" patiently answered all his inquiries. She never tired of Timmy, yet, she couldn't be held guilty of spoiling him. In the afternoon walks, they would make a visit to the Benedictine Church where young Father Joseph could be seen making the Stations of the Cross.

Timmy like Father Joseph. He would lift him high in the air and pretend to leave him suspended only to release him when the boy would scream with laughter and ask for a second and third lift to the heavens. The big German priest often held Timmy close to his chest and carried him to the side altar where together they would touch the burning taper to every vigil lamp before the shrine of the Virgin Mary, and never insert a coin in the container. This made the child very happy. His little eyes would beam as he watched the blue, red and yellow lamps flicker. But Auntie Liz remained in the pew at the rear of the Church praying for her little nephew and her sister and Big Tim. She had received very few letters since they departed. Did they plan to remain in Ireland another year? Certainly nine months away in Europe was enough vacation and rest.

It was the ring of the postman that made Silba rush to answer the door in March, 1912. When she opened the door the fragrance of early magnolias greeted her. It was late in the month, and was the first letter in several weeks Elizabeth had received from Ireland. When Silba returned to the kitchen to finish the dishes and laugh and play with Masta Timmy, Elizabeth went out on the sun-porch to read Margaret's short note. She hesitated and reread the paragraph that mentioned their return:

> "Tim has reservations of some description on the wonderful ship called The Titanic. I'm so thrilled about sailing on this magnificent ship. It's her maiden Voyage, and Tim was so fortunate to get space assigned. We'll be home around the end of September. Timmy must be a very big boy, and I hope he's been a good boy since his mommy left. Miss you very much. Kiss my baby for me."

When Elizabeth told Timmy his mother was coming home, he showed little emotion. He looked at his Auntie Liz in a strange way. Their little vacation would soon be over. His years wouldn't permit him to rationalize in the direction of any other possibility. Had he but known that this was only the start of his real life in Lacodere, Louisiana.

Much preparation was in order about the O'Shea household. Jordan, the colored houseman, gardener, chauffeur, and story-teller must renew his efforts to have everything in readiness for the return of the travelers. Silba would start that very day to give the house a thorough going-over. Time would fly with all hands working diligently, all with the exception of Timmy's. He wouldn't cooperate under any plea or stress.

CHAPTER THREE

The last couple left the living room of the O'Shea house. All had expressed deepest sorrow that Margaret and Big Tim went down with the ship the builders had promised "even God couldn't sink." Old Mrs. Turrel, who did the shirts and fine linen, came to offer sympathy and condolences. She had her only child, little Madeline, by the hand, now a big girl for two years, and with long, silken-like, coal-black hair. She was an unruly child, due perhaps because her father wasn't around to administer the strap when occasion demanded. Madeline's father was killed in Memphis only three months previous to the great sea disaster, when the Rock Island's freight train pinned him between two cars. Mrs. Turrel had her hands full with little Madeline, and a recent cough the old lady developed seemed to hinder her from doing as much laundry as she should to provide substantially for herself and child.

The ever-talkative village plumber was there to tell everyone about the headlines which boldly retold what was on the lips of all the nation. The ship was cursed. Why should an iceberg appear when no previous report was noted? Other ships had crossed that very route only a few hours before and certainly would have given a warning signal. What could have been in the mind of the ship's master with such a notable passenger list? He was accused of being drunk and had abandoned his post. But then, lots of people make as many accusations about others with little or no foundation or basis for proof. Indeed, sorrow reigned throughout Europe and America. It found a path to the heart of Elizabeth, the new mistress of the house on Fontaine Street. But, for Timmy there was no understanding of the tears that fell for days after. All he could manage was a pained expression because his auntie was sad.

The attorney assured Elizabeth Connelly that she was financially secure through the wisdom and prudence of Big Tim's knowledge of trusts and the benefits derived from good insurance policies. All Tim required of his sister-in-law in the event that either he or Margaret should pass along, together or separately, was to have a continued devotion for Timmy. The Will provided for everything of a material nature. Mr. Marlowe's final words were directed at Timmy.

"You must be a good boy, Tim, and do what your Aunt Elizabeth tells you to do. We are all your friends, son, and want you to grow to be a fine man like your father."

Just how much the lad absorbed from this parlor oration remained in the sanctuary of his innocent silence. The only expression Mr. Marlowe could grasp was a faint smile of assent.

As the years passed along, the sadness of that September in 1912 went with them. Timmy was growing into a strong and healthy boy. He was learning very fast to play little tricks on Jordan and Silba. Even, at times, he would tease Aunt Liz until she had to laugh at his devilish mischief. All was not play for Timmy, though. He had his prayers to learn and little chores about the house to accomplish. He no longer had the baby-room. This was converted into the sewing room, and the odds and ends collected in the course of Silba's travels throughout the house were deposited there. When anything was wanted and found not in its proper place, all one had to do was look in the baby's room. Timmy now occupied the master-bedroom and on cold nights with the wind howling a weird tune the little fellow would crawl into Liz's bed and beg her to tell him stories about Ireland and the "little people." She always told a story with a moral attached. If a man happened to be bad in her little story, she always made him suffer for awhile and then come out in the end as a glorious figure. Timmy loved these stories and would hug his auntie's neck till she promised to tell another and another. Often she would awaken in the early hours of the morning and un-tackle little Timmy, who had engaged in a one-man wrestling match with his arms and legs gripped about her as if he feared she was going to depart for some distant country and leave him behind. She couldn't restrain her impulse to brush aside his waves of blonde locks and kiss him gently on the forehead or cheek. No mother loved her child as Liz loved her Timmy. Her whole life and being centered itself around the boy.

Another September rolled around. It was Timmy's sixth. He was now in the second grade at Our Lady of Lourdes Academy and easily won the nomination for the honor of being Sister Mary Immaculata's pet. Who wouldn't love a child with golden wavy hair, bright blue eyes, with a pink and white complexion? Sister Mary Immaculata never wanted a baby of her own till she saw Timmy come to her classroom. She was contented with the virginity of the convent life. Her Mistress of Novices told her time and time again that men were deceitful and cunning cousins of the very devil—that is, all with the exception of Jesus and Joseph and John, the Baptist, and, of course, Saint Dominic, their holy founder. There were a few more, too, who were very nice, but they were dead now and in God's Heavenly

Palace. But, she often admonished the sweet young novices never to look around in church, and if a father should happen to come to the school to see about his child, instead of sending his wife, as any respectable and decent man should do, the good sister must never look him in the eye lest he try some diabolical trick on her coveted innocence.

Sister Mary Immaculata wasn't the only sister at Our Lady of Lourdes who liked Timmy O'Shea. Other nuns gave him holy cards and scapular medals for just being a sweet little boy. It was on this sixth anniversary when Auntie Liz pulled her surprise party for her champion. The invitations were sent out weeks in advance, and the acknowledged receipts were totaled up so that she could count on a table for six. Father Joseph would be most happy to come for ice cream, cake and candy. So would Madeline Turrel and Doctor Gerard's little boy, Gibby; and Sister Mary Immaculata would secure the necessary permission from Mother Superior and take her feast day habit out of moth balls for the occasion. Mr. Marlowe's impish Mary Ann would come too, and the party would be complete when Skeets Malone, of the fighting "Second" would show up to duel anyone at the party—boy or girl in the six-year old class. There would be no accidents at this festival feast. All were friends of the honored lad. All brought little presents to show their admiration. All went away still singing, "Happy Birthday, Dear Timmy," and hoping his seventh September would find them together eating ice cream, cake and candy.

Father Joseph said six years was awfully young to make one's First Holy Communion. But, exceptions could be made in Timmy's case without Papal approbation. So, Sister Mary Immaculata started in January to prepare her pet for his first Confession and Solemn

Holy Communion. She introduced him to the Baltimore Number One Catechism and with all the pedagogical tools in her mental briefcase, she trained Timmy to know God, and to love God with all his little soul and body and mind. He was an apt pupil throughout the course of instruction. If Sister Mary Immaculata said the Baby Jesus was born of the Blessed Virgin Mary through the power of the Holy Ghost, that was dogmatic evidence not to be disputed. When she told him he grew up to manhood and suffered cruel agony at the hands of unjust persecutors, and finally was hung on a crude cross to atone for all little boys' and big boys' sins for all time, Timmy registered shock that dug deep into his little heart. Sister Mary Immaculata taught Timmy all she knew and understood about the Sacraments and Sacramentals, the Commandments of God and the Precepts of the Roman Catholic Church. She was determined to make a junior theologian, if not a moral philosopher, out of her little charge.

Because Skeets Malone was seven, Father Joseph saw no canonical impediments in the path of receiving the wild lad into the Eucharistic fold. He would keep his fingers crossed, though, when the little Irishman with the Dublin brick-layer's disposition came to confession. Next to Timmy O'Shea, Father Joseph loved Skeets Malone. They were now inseparable youngsters and daily ate their lunch together either at Timmy's house or Skeet's home. But, Father Joseph thought Skeets would make a better Southern Baptist as far as learning the truths of Catholicism were concerned. Sister Mary Immaculata often complained to Father Joseph That Skeets preferred to entertain the class with his wild tactics to the more necessary task of acquiring religious knowledge. She had her own personal complaints, too. Wherever the youngster found the names to prefix to the holy nuns his parents could never find out. His own dear Sister Mary Immaculata, he called Sister Moody Mollie. The ancient member of the Community he called, Sister Moldy Martha. He had others, too, but less respectful and more stinging than his pets of the above classification.

Complaints sent homeward either didn't reach their destination or failed to be delivered in the truth of the sender. He learned at that tender age the value of a well thought-up lie—it's effectual advantages as well as it's consequences.

Despite all protests from the nuns at the Academy, the First Communion Day arrived with all applicants accounted for. The holy women objected to at least three of the Communicants, but were overruled by the Teutonic voice of Father Joseph. "How dare these veiled daughters of Dominic trifle with the demands of the parish priest?" Who were they to deny these little ones to 'come unto Me'? stormed Father Joseph. Anyway, he thought ten was a nice number and would permit them to walk each with a partner and evenly fill the first row on the Blessed Virgin's side of his church.

Timmy's partner was Madeline Turrel. She was like an angel in her little white dress with long cotton hose of purest white. Her long black hair with the curls falling with dignity down her small back were not hidden by the veil held in place by a crown of littlies of the valley. She was a child gifted with rare beauty that shone forth in her every expression. Her eyes twinkled like stars of silver as she slowly walked beside the companion of her silent dreams. The pace they took was solemn and unlike the usual dancing and prancing feet of Madeline Turrel. Once in awhile, she would look from the corner of her eye to see if Timmy was still beside her. Another pair of eyes strained to see the sight from the rear pew—those eyes that watched the growth of a boy. Oh, how Elizabeth prayed that morning for her

Timmy! Oh, how she wished he could remain forever in his sixth year! There were no thoughts then of an association between her Timmy and Madeline Turrel. God forbid such a match to take place either in heaven or on earth.

When the choir sang, "Oh, Lord I Am Not Worthy," at the signal from the priest's words, "Domine Non Sum Dignus," all was quiet in Saint Mary's Church. Many were the tears shed by the adult members. Many were there in Saint Mary's Church who recalled their own First Communion Day. Many were there that morning who wished they retained their First Communion innocence. But, all were happy in Saint Mary's Church that Maundy Thursday in the year of our Lord, 1916.

CHAPTER FOUR

The talk was now the conflict in Europe. Would we be forced into the awful fracas? Speculation was high in favor of the affirmative. Father Joseph entered the subject via his Sunday sermons. The colored folks had their sessions, and the white folks their forums. Everyone capable of reading the newspapers followed the activities of the nicknamed "Huns-of-bitches." Poor Father Joseph defended the rights of the German war lords, President Wilson seems, at the time, less worried about acute possible war threats to the United States. Auntie Elizabeth was even less concerned. She had a great trial to carry in January of 1917 that was as mountainous for her as the prospects of a World's War seemed to the United States. Her little Timmy became desperately ill.

January 15th, 1917, was the worst day recorded in the history of Lacodere, Louisiana. It was miserable and cold. Snow and slush covered the streets and walks. Children played vigorously in the uncommon mess only to report home with runny noses and chills all over their bodies. Parents kept the village doctors in constant attention giving them little time for personal relaxation. Skeets, Gibby and Timmy were not excluded. They were all regular boys and loved the excitement snow brings. Because of the unusual amount of snow and rain that January, school hours were either shortened or dispensed with altogether. This further troubled the parents who possessed lively youngsters. It may not be regarded as flagrant violations of the Fourth Commandment to run out in the snow and return home with wet feet and aching muscles, but it certainly borders on gross disobedience. On the seventeenth of that fateful month Timmy went to his room without the customary greetings to Auntie Liz and Silba. He was tired and complained of a sore throat. Liz unleashed all the harsh words in her vocabulary in the direction of Timmy.

"Why must you do things that only hurt yourself? Don't think for one minute I'm going to sit up with you all night and nurse you back to health. I'm sick and tired of telling you time and time again to be careful and dress properly when you go out to play. Maybe if you would listen to your Auntie Liz when she tells you these things, you wouldn't have to go to bed and take castor oil for your supper."

These were hard words to take even when one felt good. They were even harder words to force one's self to utter, especially, for someone who loved another so dearly. But duty does beget love oftentimes.

Timmy rolled over in bed and hid his eyes in the covers. He was cold and miserable throughout. Auntie Liz left the room to call Doctor Jereau for consultation. He prescribed the usual dose of castor oil, fruit juices, and no solid food.

"Keep him warm and don't let him leave his bed till I can get a chance to see him. I'll come just as soon as I finish my supper."

Either Dr. Jereau was too busy or an emergency call came in from the hospital, but he failed to come to the O'Shea house until Liz called a second time around two in the morning. Timmy was crying bitterly when Liz came to his room. She went over to the big bed and bent over the little figure all curled up in a human knot.

He was shaking and complained of a severe pain in his throat. Liz was worried. Her scolding before supper returned to her with all the force of a gun's backfire. Yet, could this little fellow be acting in hopes of sympathy? No, he couldn't do that at such an hour! Doctor Jereau promised to be over in just a few minutes.

"Have some hot water ready and plenty of towels. Whatever you do, don't go near him till I get there," were his final words.

Doctor Jereau may know medicine through and through, but he didn't comprehend love in the same degree. Liz disobeyed his orders and lifted Timmy in her arms and held him fast. She felt his arms and hands clasp her neck and the tears trickle down her throat. She couldn't restrain her emotion any longer. She, through her tears, whispered softly in his ear that she was awfully sorry for speaking so roughly to her little baby. If he would forgive her this one time and get better, she'd never scold him again. Timmy's answer was a tighter hold on her neck.

The door of the bedroom blew open and a cold gust of wind whistled through the room. Liz bent low on the bed and forced Timmy's release. She covered his body with the warm wool blankets and kissed his lips that seemed so dry and hot.

The front door closed with a terrific noise as Dr. Jereau rushed up the stairs. He was familiar with the house and in great strides was at the bedside of the sick child before anyone could register a greeting. He pushed aside the covers and sat next to the boy on the big bed. After the preliminary temperature and pulse had been taken, he looked into the lad's throat. He couldn't help the startled look in his face. He got up and turned to Liz with wrinkled brow and sharp words that rung deep in her memory as he wrung his hands, "This kid should have been in a hospital hours ago. If my calculations are in any measure or degree accurate, he is a diphtheria patient."

Liz couldn't hold back the hysterical scream. Silba put her arm around Liz to comfort her. Neither woman heard Dr. Jereau mutter something about the bacillus and the throat coated with a false membrane. Their excitement was too great to reason along medical technicalities. Liz pictured in her mind the horrors of death again striking the O'Shea household. Timmy was leaving forever! She screamed, "Oh, God, can't something be done for my baby?"

Doctor Gerand was called in for consultation the next morning. All through the night, Doctor Jereau and Liz sat side by side waiting for some reaction to occur. Around ten in the morning, Timmy began to cough and spit mucus. Only a few minutes later he began to choke. The two doctors set up an emergency operation table, washed everything they were about to use and set out to perform an operation on the boy's throat in order to permit him to breath. A silver tube was inserted in an opening in the throat which was to serve as a medium for easier breathing. Yet, if he should in any way block this artificial channel, he would surely choke to death. The thought of such an accident rang through Liz's mind. If he should die, she didn't want anything of life. She lived not for herself, but for her Timmy.

In these hours of trial, Silba acted as nurse to the best of her ability. She was always attentive when the doctors were present and didn't have to be told what was needed at just the exact moment. She attended the sick many times before in her numerous years in domestic service. She was drawn closer to her little patient, because she sensed a personal responsibility in time of dire necessity.

Timmy progressed very nicely for a few days with his new tube. Although his arms were tied to the side of the bed to prevent his touching the infected throat, he wrestled and turned to free himself. The doctors visited him every two or three hours in the course of the day and night. He would soon be able to have his silver tube removed, and in a short time, resume his school days. At least, that was a promise made to him if he continued to be a good boy.

On the 21st of January, a storm was brewing all day. Close to evening it became worse. The thunder and lightening played havoc with the telegraph poles and lights were replaced with candles. The ferociousness of the storm increased towards the late evening. By midnight, it sounded like all hell broke loose, and God was sending his wrath on the people in the form of thunderous threats. Liz was frightened. She sat in Timmy's room watching his restless body move to and fro under the sheets. Once, in the dim light, she thought she saw the apparatus move completely over to the side of the bed, and she quickly ran to the bed to make sure the wires and steel girders were in place. All these mechanical contrivances held the tube in Timmy's throat at the proper angle. To move it many inches would cause certain destruction. But, she was wrong. It hadn't moved. Her nerves were tense that night, more than usual because of the storm. She sat rocking in the chair very close to Timmy's bed. Silently, she said her Rosary beads, asking her Heavenly Mother to make Timmy well and happy again. Then, as she neared the Third Mystery of her beads, Timmy started to cough and choke. Liz let the beads fall to the floor and hastened to his side. He was fighting vigorously to free himself from the bonds. It was like a man struggling in the middle of the ocean to avert drowning. His little white and greyish face was drawn with pain. Beads of sweat oozed out of his pores. Liz could stand this agony no further. She screamed like a woman possessed with the evil spirits . . . and ran to the door for Silba.

Silba was coming up the stairs two at a time. When they met at the summit of the staircase, Liz ordered her in a hysterical voice to get the doctor. At that moment, she didn't know whether she told Silba which doctor to call. Those moments were Liz's hell on earth. She couldn't control herself for an instant. She was beside herself with grief. If there was a God in heaven who bestowed mercy on the created, where was His infinite mercy? He was there, there in that very room waiting for the moment for Liz to compose herself and ask for His help. She did call on God and His Son and all the saints in heaven to help save her Timmy. She knelt down by the bed during that horrible ordeal and begged God to forgive her, "And would you please save my baby?" There were very few favors she asked of God for herself, but this one she just had to have answered.

The idea came to her while she was still kneeling beside Timmy's bed. If he was going to die from chocking, at least, she could relieve the pain attached to such an agonizing torture by removing the silver tube. She ran around the bed so as to be closer to his frail body, and with a quivering hand, slipped the tube from the insertion made in his throat, asking Christ to help her, to help her through his situation and let the child die in peace rather than suffer such hellish torments. Timmy gasped once, then again, and turned his head with a faint sigh. Liz quickly turned his head back to stop the combined mucus and blood that was slowly forming at the wound. She thought sure he smiled at her, but she was too nervous and excited to let it register. While she still held the gauze over the opening, Doctor Gerard entered the room unbuttoning his overcoat.

There was no exchange of greetings between Frank Gerard and Elizabeth Connelly; no words, just occasional expressions with the lips and eyebrows. There was work to be done, and time was at a premium. Liz sat in her chair at the far end of the room. Silba assisted Dr. Gerard as best she knew how. Numberless Hail Marys and Our Fathers stormed heaven in the space of time Doctor Gerard started to work on Timmy until he left three hours later. A few Creeds and Acts of Contrition were included in Liz's three hours of agony. Her prayers were rewarded. She was overcome with emotion when Doctor Gerard walked up to her and whispered in her ear that Timmy would be up and at 'em within a very few weeks. And she could thank God, too, while she was about it, for granting her the presence of mind to remove that infernal tube that blocked the lad's track. Liz just couldn't speak. She cried with joy. It would be months before she completely recovered from this ordeal. She was oblivious to the doctor's departure.

At one o'clock the next afternoon, Gibby and Skeets came to call. They were of the opinion that Timmy should be ready to come out and play in the tree shack. They had added an additional room on their club house of the air and wanted to show Timmy their handiwork. Silba answered the door, but wouldn't let the visitors enter.

"Land O God, ain't yo all got all yo senses in them heads o yors? How yo all think Masta Timmy figas to git his poo, sick body up outa that big bed o his and come down to fool with yo young 'uns? Ah really an truly think yo is serious 'bout Timmy comin' out to play, too. Yo take yerself on along home befo yo catch yo death o foolishness."

Gibby and Skeets were a little bewildered and turned their backs on Silba and walked slowly down the path leading to the wooden sidewalk like two spanked pups. Skeets took a healthy kick at the stone near the gate only to bend down and rub his shoe vigorously to ease the self-inflicted pain.

Inside the big house, Silba reported to Liz the recent callers and asked permission to go and see Masta Timmy herself. She didn't wait for Liz's answer, but went directly up to the sick boy's room. She tip-toed onto the soft carpet and slowly walked to the bed. She gazed on the sleeping face with hands folded behind her back like someone looking over at the side of a dock on the waterfront. She wanted to say, "How yo all feelin'?" But, she knew it would be wrong to awaken his peaceful slumber. She just stood there for several minutes and watched him breathe in and out at regular intervals. According to her silent and unprofessional diagnosis, her little Masta Timmy was going to be running around the house and upsetting her cleaning and cooking within a few days. Then, and only then, would Silba laugh her hearty laugh again.

Weeks later Timmy was allowed up. Although he was told not to come down to the first floor, he begged Jordan to carry him to the large fireplace in the living room. When he made his entrance, Liz nearly fainted from surprise. She was about to tongue-lash poor Jordan, who only followed out his "bosses" orders, when Timmy started to cry. That was all he had to do to melt Liz's heart into subjection. She took him in her lap and wrapped the blanket around his body, carefully seeing to it that even his feet were not left exposed.

The lights in the living room were dim but the fire provided warmth and some light to the spacious room. Shadows danced with glee on the walls rendering weird and grotesque fantasies. Two figures sat in lonely silence before the crackling fire, too absorbed in being together again to utter a word.

Timmy broke the solemn silence by asking Aunt Liz a question that made her Irish heart leap for joy. "Would you be mad at me if I grew up to be a big man and be like Father Joseph?"

"Mad?" Her heart was overwhelmed with pride at his suggestion put in the form of a question. What mother or auntie of an only son, or nephew, wanted her offspring to grow up and find a new love? If, on the other hand, the new love was the priesthood, pride replaced envy.

Liz's answer came, at first, in the form of a stronger hold on her bundle of love. She was overcome with the suddenness of this admission. From whence did it originate? Timmy hadn't talked with Father Joseph lately. He was too young to read of the priestly life with its allegorized hardships and spuriously advertised sacrifices. Was she holding a little saint on her lap that night? Hardly! When he was well and happy about the great house, he was more like the devil's advocate.

"If you want to be a priest like Father Joseph and say Mass every day and visit the poor and sick, and once in awhile pray for your old Auntie Liz, well, you'll make me happier than I have ever been in all my life."

They both looked at each other for the longest time, and when his little head fell gently on her breast, she knew he was tired out, and it was time for one little future Anselm or Benedict to be tucked away for the rest of the night.

CHAPTER FIVE

Timmy continued to grow as the years sped merrily onward. Gibby, Madeline, Skeets, Mary Ann and Timmy graduated together from the eighth grade at the Academy. The World's War was over and the fight to safeguard Democracy seemed to be past history in the minds of the villagers. Even Father Joseph was returned to his church by his Abbot at Cassino Abbey. He forgave the people of Locodere for petitioning for his removal due to his sympathy for the Germans during the heated months prior and during the war.

The Jesuits, at the request of the Bishop, accepted a track of land in 1920 on a knoll near the Academy and built a large school to answer the needs of the immediate community and the surrounding towns. It was, at first, to be called Central Catholic High, but the Provincial of the arrogant sons of Ignatius thought Lacodere Preparatory School sounded a little nicer, and would, in all probability, demand a higher tuitional dig at the local pocketbooks. By 1921, when Timmy, Skeets and Gibby were ready for Algebra, Latin and Ancient History, the Prep School was an institution of considerable importance.

Even the humble Benedictines, who felt the sting of the Bishop's snub, rather than admit facility at sucking the ecclesiastical treat, smiled their approval and admitted the "Jebbies" had a fine school. Lacodere Prep boasted an enrollment of close to four hundred students in 1921. Their faculty was composed largely of young Jesuit scholastics doing their three-year "hitch" in the classroom prior to their final trot in the heavy heat of Theology. These young men, still in their own collegiate knickers, made a big impression on the little boys, who were used to the gentleness and the holy-card-passing of the coy nuns.

The little ladies of the town attended Our Lady of Lourdes Academy on through their high school years. Madeline Turrel was still the mischievous lass of the Freshman class. She took music lessons twice a week from the time she was in the third grade. The nuns saw in her a brilliant career and forced her to practice on the piano for hours at a time. But, she never lost that carefree and listless attitude towards life. All seemed to be a time for acting. She refused to settle down to the arduous task of deep thought and concentration in studious matters. Mrs. Turrel apparently lost all sense of maternal control over her daughter. She wasn't slow to admit that she was a failure in this regard.

Timmy and Skeets were still the closest of friends throughout their four years of high school training. Although Skeets wasn't a bit reluctant to lose his books and skip classes, he could never entice Timmy to trod the same path. They played football together in the fall and both starred on the first team. During the winter months, they were experts on the basketball court. In the spring of the year, Timmy pitched and Skeets caught on Lacodere's unbeatable nine.

In their last year of high school, Timmy, Gibby and Skeets went just about everyplace together. They pooled their assets and bought an old wreck of a car. It was September 18th again, and the year was 1925, when Timmy was in his senior year at Lacodere and celebrating his sixteenth birthday. He was a tall, good-looking boy. He was heavy enough to hold down the fullback's position on the school's football team. In two contests, he made six touchdowns, which elevated him to the highest honors the students of the underclass division could place a fellow—Timmy was a star! The Jesuits liked him, too. He led the class in Greek and Latin and aimed for that coveted gold medal and chain, which in the eyes of the holy sons of Saint Ignatius, was the tops in scholastic attainment . . . the Chain of Lacodere.

Football prevented Timmy from seeing much of Madeline. Yet, after the local games, he would take her to a movie or recital or just to the park. The wrath of Skeets and Gibby came to the front when Timmy preferred Madeline to them. Even Liz was jealous of the youthful Madeline with her dancing eyes and soft voice. Timmy didn't stay home more than to take his meals, study his trigonometry and Greek and sleep. He was restless at this age and found a certain peace in Madeline's companionship. Very few were the visits made at Father Joseph's rectory, less at the Church of Saint Mary. Was he forgetting that he wanted to devote his life to God at Cassino Abbey? He didn't even discuss the priestly life or serve Mass every morning like he used to. In his mind, he was struggling between two loves—Cassino Abbey and Madeline Turrel. It was either sacrifice, recollection and severe mortifications, or, the temporary beauty and flesh of the dancing eyes and musical voice of a girl who grew rapidly into daring maturity. Timmy knew in his heart he was being drawn into a strange newness of life. He was beginning now to feel the true meaning of growth.

The big charity game of the season was to be played in Memphis on Thanksgiving Day. "Praise" notices ran in the Southern newspapers from late October through the month of November. Sports editors of nearly every "rag" in the Tri-state area, plus Louisiana's contribution, claimed Timmy O'Shea as the greatest fullback in Southern Association football. He was compared to the great Illinois star of the same year, Red Grange. Although Grange played college ball, Timmy compared favorably when the consideration was made as to ages and systems of play in their respective leagues. Timmy was fast, a good blocker, a splendid kicker, and excellent when tossing the "pigskin" for accurate yardage gains on passes. People wanted to see this game between Central High School of Memphis and Lacodere Prep of Louisiana. Mainly, they spent good money at the sport shops for reservations because this Southern Irishman was going to spark up a small school's team.

Liz never did approve of football. She hated rugby when her brothers played at Blackrock College outside of Dublin. Therefore, she refused to go to any of the games. She really feared the other eleven boys on the enemy team would single her Timmy out for the direct kill. She just sat at home and worried.

Gibby Gerard was the mainstay on the line. At least he was the brightest guard Lacodere had that year. Skeets called signals in the quarterback's "slot," and once in awhile jumbled his numbers to the extent that nobody could determine what play he intended to execute. He used to laugh and make funny remarks in the huddles. Sometimes he would carry the ball for a yard or two of gain, but more often, it resulted in a loss for Locodere. But, his antics were forgivable considering his keen sense of humor.

Timmy had to go to the front for him in more than one predicament. Just before the team was due to leave for Memphis, Father Quinn, the Senior Religion teacher, refused to let Skeets represent the school. During his Religion class, the old Jesuit was giving the students some pointers on the art of fair play, both on the gridiron and on the field of life. Most of the boys thought the discussion rather dull and relegated his ideas of morality to their grandparents' era. Skeets turned to Timmy, and what he sincerely thought was in the confines of subdued whispering, but clearly caught in the sound waves that floated up to Father Quinn's desk, said, "What does that phoney know about life? Things have changed a lot since he went through his menopause back in the Civil War days." Timmy couldn't help laughing out loud. Skeets was told to leave the classroom and not to bother to report back again.

No one could sell himself to the highest bidder like Timmy. He had the rare quality of pleading a case before the Jesuits that forced their pompous egos to take a step downwards and stay subjected till he finished his defense. On many occasions as president of the student body, he was able to get things out of the members of the faculty no other student would dare think about trying to get. It wasn't that he was bold. He was very clever in melting the holder of the apple until the poor individual had to relinquish his hold to a more deserving soul. With Father Quinn, it was on a matter of playing up the old man's ego. Timmy was a past master at the art of "polishing the apple."

"Father," he said, "Skeets is really very sorry he cut loose with that crack in Religion class today. Why, would you believe it, Father, I saw Skeets making the Stations of the Cross just before I came up here? He's just excited about the game with Central. Please retract your penance and let him back in your class. As far as the game goes, it means a lot to him. But, getting back in your religion class is far more important than any football game could possibly be. I know, too, he doesn't deserve your consideration, but in the same breath, I know you're too big a man to let a matter as grave as it is to stop a careless fellow from continuing his religious course of study under the Jesuits. He made a mistake—a big mistake—but Christ was able to forgive men who persecuted Him and finally put Him on a cross to die. This to me doesn't seem as weighty."

Bringing Christ into his argument threw the priest for a loss. He smiles. Timmy knew he won the battle. All Father Quinn could muster up was a nod of assent. He rubbed his eyes to thwart the possibility of a tear rolling down his cheek and waved Timmy out of the room.

When Timmy entered the lavatory, where Skeets was waiting for him in the end booth, the culprit came out with a cigarette in his mouth. "How did the old bastard take your prayer-meeting session, Brother Timothy?"

"That's one sure way of expressing your thanks, Skeets. Do you realize you were sitting right on the edge of the can and Quinn all set to push you right in?"

"I never did like that old reprobate. Why the Jesuits ever took him into their gang baffles me," said Skeets in disgust.

"Well, I told him you were going to apologize, so you'd better get the lead out and drum up your saddest look. For God's sake, Skeets, don't get sore and tell him to go to hell or laugh right in his face. You know, all the Jesuits aren't stupid! A few like that may get into their army just to make the big shots conform to humility. Anyway, if you make a false move with Quinn, he'll blow a fuse even the Pope won't be able to repair for you."

"Okay, pal, you're the only one who can move priests and old women. I do pretty good in that league myself. Say, by the way, how are you and Madeline making out? That business is working into a pretty good deal! How far have you gone with the little French bitch?"

Timmy looked straight into Skeet's eyes. He was burning inside. Skeets knew it was time to depart and left on the double.

CHAPTER SIX

It was nine-thirty and the big bonfire that closed the rally in the rear of the school was slowly dying into extinction. All the fellows and their girls were singing spirited songs in anticipation of a victorious fight over Central on Thanksgiving Day. Many of the parents left after the talks given by the Principal, Father Joseph, and the team's ever-popular captain, Gibby Gerard. Timmy said a few words. Even Skeets got up and entertained the boys and girls. He was a born clown, and nobody competed when Skeets started his comedy. He was a one-man show, and it didn't cost a dime to take in his humorous wit. Sometimes, it was a bit tainted, but the general conversation of the youth in those wild Twenties was regarded as slightly on the fast side.

Several parents and students remained on the campus till the last spark of fire left the once glowing bonfire. In the distance could be heard the laughter and songs of mixed voices of Lacodere boys and Our Lady of Lourdes girls. Timmy and Madeline remained in the shadows silently holding hands and watching two Jesuit lay-brothers pour water on the ashes. It was a cool night, and after such a grand fire, two young romancers found it difficult to remain standing—and so far apart. It was Madeline who drew her lean body up to Timmy's and pressed her shoulder gently into his chest. This was the first advance Madeline had ever made, and Timmy enjoyed its thrill. He was satisfied just to watch her dance and play the piano, and throw her head back and watch the beautiful black hair, fall-as-it-may, down her back. Now it was different. He touched her as other men touch the women they called their own. Slowly, but with cautious hesitancy, he placed his arm around her shoulder and felt her head come close to his. He looked down on her, and his heart began to thump with a furious beat. She must have felt this delightful pulsation and quickly turned her head so her face met his. She closed her eyes and ran her hand up the front of his sweater to his chest, finally resting itself around his neck. Timmy could withstand the impulse and sensation of her closeness no longer. His lips met hers in perfect formation—the first time he had ever kissed a girl or wanted to be in such a position. The sensation seized his body, and he quivered under its delightful spell.

There was no thought of the priesthood, of the Thanksgiving Day football game with Central, of the Latin and Greek, or of the big write-ups in the daily papers. He was thinking less of his tremendous popularity in Lacodere, and his Auntie Liz didn't dare enter his mind at this pleasant rendezvous. He tasted of the chalice of love and wanted to drain the sweet liquor then and there. But, Madeline withdrew from his embrace and asked him to look at his watch. It was only an excuse to have him beg her to return to his arms. His innocence failed to cope with the wiles of feminine intrigue. If she was playing the ancient game of "hard-to-get," Timmy wasn't aware of its rules.

"I'm sorry, Madeline, but I couldn't help myself. I guess it's the thought of going to Memphis and our big game and everything,"

Timmy's voice blurted out. "Oh, take me home, Tim, and let's not forget tonight ever!" was her quick response.

They parted at the gate that led to her modest little home. No light was awaiting her return. Madeline either didn't merit someone waiting up for her or didn't want anyone to know when she arrived. There were no delayed good-byes. Timmy ran all five block to his own gate where the light on the porch was burning brightly. He placed his two hands on the gate and jumped completely over, landing on his feet on the inside path.

In his room, before the mirror, he looked at himself while he removed his sweater. The big "L" on the front needed a little sewing. Without a moment's delay, he went to Liz's room and burst in without bothering to knock. Liz was in bed saying her Rosary beads. He showed her the sweater and asked if it could be fixed before they left for Memphis. Liz looked at Timmy with a strange expression in her eyes. She asked about the bonfire celebration and if there was a big turn-out. All questions received a curt two letter answer—just O.K. Then, as Timmy was leaving the room, he bent down to kiss Liz's cheek and bid her enjoy the sweetest of dreams. Liz caught Timmy's arm and, for a second held it tightly against her head. "You're getting to be a good, big boy, Timmy, and I'm afraid just a little too handsome for your own best interest," was Liz's goodnight address. Timmy didn't say a word, but turned and walked slowly to his big room. He didn't realize he left the material evidence of Madeline's affections on his upper lip.

Once again, he returned to the mirror and ran his hands over his face. Still no signs of an approaching beard. When would that awful down graduate to masculine bristle? This was a nightly occurrence with the young lad and a source of much annoyance that nature moved, in some respects, so snail-like. But, tonight he found the red, waxy lipstick traces and gave out with a guilty whistle. He removed his shirt and pants and threw them over the chair in the far corner of the room. The same chair Auntie Liz occupied during the awful sickness that nearly took Timmy through the portals of eternity.

He sat down in the middle of the room to take off his shoes and socks. He stood up and put one shoe under his arm while he took a basketball player's stance, and with his right shoe, shot a perfect "basket" in the tin wastebasket in the corner by his desk. With his left shoe, he took the same stance and tried a "push-shot," but fell short about six inches from the target.

His next nightly pastime was to lay outstretched on the floor and lift his body up and down on with his arms. After about thirty of these sweat provokers, more commonly regarded as "body-lifts," he would turn over on his back, lift his legs high in the air, and make them go 'round and 'round as if he were riding a bicycle down a hill. After a few minutes of this exercise, he would stand erect before the mirror and place his hands on his hips, with his feet close together and bend down and around and up again. This went on for quite a few minutes. By this time, his body was a mass of perspiration. His last exercise before his quick shower was the touch of the toes without bending the knees.

Timmy looked at his watch before winding it for the night. He placed it on the night stand and unbuttoned his shorts letting them fall carelessly to the floor. With one sweeping kick, they flew in the air, and he ran ahead to catch them before they reached the far end of the room. He deposited his shorts in the hamper in the bathroom and started the water running full force for his shower.

After a few minutes under both hot and cold water, Timmy returned to his room and knelt down to pray. Tonight his prayers seemed ever distracted by other thoughts. This had certainly been an unusual evening for him, and try as he might, he couldn't arrest his thoughts from his mind for the short duration of his night prayers.

A quick Sign of the Cross, a running leap, and Timmy was in bed. The light cord above his bed served to switch off all lights in the room. Tonight he wasted no time in pulling the cord. It had been an exciting day and a glorious night, especially close to the end!

Before sleep finally caught up with Lacodere's star ball player, he tossed and turned in restless anxiety. He couldn't forget Madeline and the way she gazed into his eyes. She left an imprint on his mind and a desire for her love in his heart. He felt again and again the sensation of that kiss vibrate throughout his whole body. He was feeling the results of becoming a young man in every sense of the word.

CHAPTER SEVEN

It was beautiful in Memphis when the boys arrived from Lacodere to play their classic tussle with the highly favored lads from the midtown school. Little did anyone realize the Prepsters from Louisiana would suffer a blow before they actually faced the foe on Thanksgiving Day.

A section of Overton Park was reserved for the visitors to enable them to practice in semi-secrecy. All their coach required of his boys could be summed up in a series of running plays void of any blocking and attempts at real football. They were advised to merely run through plays as a medium of freshening up and limbering their bones.

During one of these plays, Gibby Gerard ran head-on into the frame of a fellow ballplayer and remembered nothing till he was returned to Lacodere. He was rushed to Saint Joseph's Hospital with a brain concussion and slept peacefully through the greatest game in the history of his school. His parents were notified of the accident and rushed to Memphis to be at his side when he regained consciousness.

It was a severe blow to the Lacodere Prep, and the boys on the squad felt the loss keenly. Much ran through their youthful minds, but nothing seemed more important to them than a cutting feeling caused by the absence of their Gibby.

The matter of selecting a captain for the great game caused no end of deep concern. Speculation ran high among the boys now that Gibby was out of the starting lineup. It was the common talk from the moment the accident happened till they were rewarded with the news from the coach. A condition, which is supposed to have found its origin at Notre Dame University, was copied at Lacodere Prep by Father Pete; that is, the captain of the team should be a lineman. Perhaps it was to share the honors around the team. The backfield men carried the ball and smiled with satisfaction as the fans in the stands shouted their names in congratulatory praise. The poor "dogs" on the line made the holes for the halfbacks and received nothing but a lot of tough treatment. So, even if Notre Dame University didn't originate the idea, Father Pete showed his appreciation for the expended efforts of his linemen by naming one of the seven to the coveted "slot" of captain.

Few people knew Joey Roys like Father Pete knew him. He was a lad who didn't mix too much with the other boys. He was poor, and he knew it. His father drank too much and his mother worked too hard to supply the food and clothing for himself and the two other younger brothers. His only hobby was the present craze of modern youth. He wanted to fly for the Army or Navy or anybody else who would teach him the dangerous art. So, his spare time was devoted to making model planes and drawing designs for miniature motors. Because Father Pete liked Joey and knew of his sad situation at home, he was determined to make him as prominent on the field as the best of the linemen representing Lacodere that year.

Back at the Peabody Hotel, Timmy and Skeets sat in silence eating their dinner. They were oblivious to the smooth music of the orchestra that was filling an engagement at the Plantation Room.

Even when the leader dedicated a number to him, the best Timmy could do was stand awkwardly and smile his thanksgiving. He was thinking now of Gibby and Madeline and Liz. His mind was all jumbled in a state of confusion. When the waiter received a telegram from the headwaiter and delivered it to Timmy, he thrust the wire in his hip pocket and nodded a thanks without the slightest thought of a gratuity to the waiter in the form of a piece of silver.

After dinner, Skeets got up from his place and told Timmy that he would leave the tip if he, in turn, would take care of the check. It was agreed. When it came to spending money, Timmy inherited many of his father's spendthrift traits. He had an account of his own in the Southern National Bank of Lacodere and could write checks up to a sizable amount. He had half the student body of his school "on the cuff" for small loans. None seemed to worry about a pay-off because Timmy was a poor collector. He didn't worry either.

"I'm going over to the Catholic Club and shoot a little pool with the city slickers," said Skeets. "I'll be back before nine," were his parting words.

"Wait a minute, and I'll go over with you as far as the club," replied Timmy. "I'm going to make a visit at the Dominican Church and then run up to the hospital to see how Gibby is getting along."

As they left the hotel's lobby, two men came up and asked them how the game looked for them without their running guard. Both boys sized the men up and figured they were "tin horns" from South Main Street. Anything they might say to them wouldn't matter too much one way or the other.

"Why naturally we'll miss one of our best players and buddies" said Skeets, winking at Timmy, "if you won't breathe a word of this out, I'll let you in on a hot piece of first-class information. The coach is getting a haircut and close shave tomorrow and playing in the right guard position."

The two boys walked slowly up Third Avenue till they reached the Catholic Club. En route they discussed the probable outcome of tomorrow's tussle. Timmy wasn't sure how it would work out for Lacodere. Skeets, on the other hand, thought it would be a breeze, forgetting about Gibby and basing his confidence on past performance. Of course, knowing Skeets, one can readily understand his attitudes and his carefree ideas on life and people. It was in the sack to knock over Central tomorrow. It was a snap to wisecrack in class and take it on the lamb for the afternoon. Life was just one big playground for Skeets. Nothing in this life seemed to bother him. He felt because he was Skeets Malone, it licensed him to say or do exactly what he so desired.

"I'd like to go over and make a visit with you, Timmy," said Skeets, "but I fail to see where I'm to become any holier than I am right now. You go over and pray for both of us. While you're in there looking at the Lacodere's statues and watching the pot-bellied Dominicans go through their ritualistic gymnastics, you might say a prayer for Madeline's salvation or conversion. I've got a pretty good idea of what you're after. I don't blame you, Timmy. I'm just envious as hell that she's selling it your way instead of mine. She's the kind of a babe all the boys wanted to pepper her with stones in the Gospel. Now with me, it's different. I'd like to throw her . . ."

"Shut your dirty mouth, Skeets," said Timmy with burning indignation. "For your information, you foul-minded dope, Madeline and I are just good friends. I like the way she plays the piano and, what's more, I like her company. Beyond that, well, we're just good friends! See?"

Skeets burst out laughing and cracked, "that was more than piano playing you two were doing at the bonfire last night, O guiltless one! Or were you playing a duet together? And since when do 'just good friends' become so cozy in the dark? I'm just warning you, O'Shea, that 'pigeon' is out for one thing, and it ain't your autograph!"

Hardly able to contain himself, Timmy replied, "Suppose you mind your damn business and let me take care of my own affairs!"

"Well, pal, don't come to me with a heart as heavy as a bucket of hog livers when she tosses you aside for somebody with a little more fire in his furnace," he said as he turned into the main entrance of the Catholic Club.

Timmy went across the street and entered Saint Peter's Church. Inside he heard the organ playing a strange piece. It wasn't church music, and he sat in the rear pew to try and recall where he'd heard that music played before. There were a few old ladies making the Stations at various distances from one another. One old man, poorly dressed, knelt in prayer before the tiny shrine of Saint Anthony at the rear of the church. Other than the few old ladies, the elderly man asking "Tony" for a lift and the organist, the church was in a deserted and forsaken state that night.

Timmy watched the flicker of the sanctuary lamp in the distance. The haunting refrain from the choir loft and the stillness of his surroundings made him lonely. He wished he had joined Skeets in a game of pool. But, he quickly forced those ideas from his mind and once more concentrated on the beautiful organ recital he was privileged to hear. Finally, the organist ceased playing, and Timmy heard the door shut and the heavy steps of a man descending from the gallery above his head. Lacodere's star athlete also got up from

43

his place and walked out to the vestibule of the church and nearly bumped into the organist as he came down the stairs.

"That was sure pretty music you were playing up there," said Timmy.

"Well, now, young man," the old gentleman began, "are you by any chance a lover of Debussy?"

"I've been accused of being a lover, but I never thought they called it Debussy," said Timmy smiling.

The old man laughed with a peculiar squeaky noise. "You and I had better go back up to the organ, and I'll play the number for you again," he said, still laughing.

"Gee, mister, that would be swell," said Timmy with a note of real interest.

As they returned to the choir loft, the old man asked Timmy his name, where he lived, how old he was, and what attracted his attention to music. Timmy answered his questions to the best of his ability excluding the all-important reason for his Memphis visitation.

He turned to the old man as he helped him adjust the music on the rack and asked him if there were words to this Debussy classic.

"Do you always have mere words when your heart sings of love?" he said. "Haven't you sat with someone," he continued, "and just listened to some beautiful music afar off without the aid of lyrics—perhaps the birds in the distant trees adding their voices to blend in harmony with the strains of the melody? And, hasn't it been more peaceful and restful to be with somebody who shared your contemplative thoughts of sincere silence with only the moon to enlighten your heart and show forth the true path of real friendship—if not love? Oh, I'm sorry, Timothy, I didn't stop to realize you are a boy of sixteen and hardly concerned about the depth of such subjects as love, the moon, and the sweet song of the thrush."

"Oh, I don't know about that. I sort of go for a piece of music that hits me a little on the sweet side. Just because I'm sixteen doesn't mean I haven't the same . . . oh, let's skip it!" said Timmy running out of words to express the meaning he wanted to convey.

"The piece that hit those tender heart strings and in all probability recalled some sweeter memories is called *Clair de Lune*. Translated into literal English, that should add up to "Clear of Moon," or as we would say in our own humble way, plain, old moonlight. But, then, let me play it for you again. It sounds much better on the organ than if I were to give you a lecture on its tone qualities," he said smiling up at Timmy.

The old man played *Clair de Lune* with great zeal and facility. Timmy's eyes wandered around the grey old church, but his thoughts went further—on down to Lacodere and the sweet memory of last night with Madeline. The old man smiled as he caught Timmy dreaming. That far-away look in his eyes was clear evidence the music he just finished playing made his mind drowsy for a dreamer's paradise. He could see clearly that Timmy was more than sixteen in his thoughts, and the soulful expression indicated the boy was harnessed to the pangs of a youthful lover. The organist tapped the boy's shoulder to indicate the end of *Clair de Lune*. Timmy was embarrassed when the man asked him if the music made him lonesome for someone.

As they walked down Adams Street, Timmy asked his companion if he would mind directing him to the hospital. When he learned how close he was to Saint Joseph's, he regretted leaving the church so early.

"Obviously you're not a Memphian," the old man drawled, "or you'd know where Saint Joseph's is located."

"I told you my home is in Lacodere, Louisiana," Timmy snapped back.

"So you did, so you did," was his only reply.

"One of your relatives sick up there?" he asked with a note of concern in his voice.

"Not a relative, Sir, but a classmate of mine from Prep."

"Don't tell me I'm walking down this street with one of the ballplayers who will be playing against my grandson's team tomorrow?" he said breathlessly.

"Does your grandson play for Central?" asked Timmy.

"Yes, I guess when you said 'play' that it hit it perfectly," was his answer. "You see," the old man went on, "I wanted him to go to Christian Brothers College, but all his friends went to Central, so he followed the herd."

"They tell me the Brothers at C.B.C. slug first and talk afterwards," said Timmy smiling.

As they turned on Jackson Avenue, the old man pointed to a large, red brick building with a statue of Saint Joseph standing on the green lawn, and told Timmy to go to the main desk and ask the nurse to give him the number of the room. He bid him good luck in his game and hoped that the piece he played for him would often return to give him pleasant memories. Little did the organist realize that Wednesday night, on the eve of Thanksgiving Day in 1925, that Timmy would carry that self-same Debussy love song in his heart the rest of his life—not as a reminder of Memphis or the Dominican

Church or even the old man, but of a grave and serious incident yet to follow in his youthful life.

Gibby was doing well, but the nurse refused to permit visitors until Doctor Gerard approved. If Timmy wished, the nurse would call Dr. Gerard down and let him tell the athlete personally. No, that wouldn't be necessary, but he would appreciate it a lot if the nurse would inform Gibby or Doctor Gerard that Timmy O'Shea came up to see the sick teammate. The nurse beamed her consent and gave Timmy a wink that could be construed to mean most anything. Instead of blushing, Timmy winked back at the nurse and walked out the front door of the hospital with a smile on his face.

As young O'Shea approached the Third Avenue entrance of the Peabody Hotel and was about to enter the lobby, a smoothly-dressed, slick-haired, shallow-faced man of about forty walked up to him and asked if he was staying in the hotel. It was the way he placed his hand on the boy's shoulder and let it drop to his hip that caused suspicion to race through his mind. He had never been warned of the men who wander through the world lacking virility, but craving it in others. There was something revolting about his solicitude for a young and good looking boy alone in the large city. At least, Timmy thought him very repulsive. When he looked the stranger in the eyes, he couldn't help feel a chill run through his body as he noticed his eyebrows and traces of makeup on his face. Timmy waked faster and shook the unwanted hand that had lodged itself around his waist with a sharp turn of his body. Under no circumstances would he consent to yield to his last question which came as a shock to the young football player. The bait question of this loathsome degenerate was typical of his confreres in the profession of perversion. If Timmy was in need of companionship, this man's room would be the last hole in the world he'd want to be seen dead in, much less alive and active in! The pervert stood a few steps beyond the swinging door and enviously gazed on the body of the rapidly departing youngster.

Alone, and behind a locked door, Timmy sat on the bed reading the telegram from Aunty Liz received during dinner. She wished him the very best of luck and assured him of her constant prayers during the big battle of Thanksgiving Day. He laughed heartily when he read the line asking him to be very careful and stay away from anything that looked troublesome. Little did Liz know of the recent escapade in the lobby.

Skeets returned to the hotel room as promised around nine o'clock. He found Timmy in bed and well on his way to sleep. Skeets was in a talkative mood, but Timmy failed to cooperate with him. There was nothing left for him to do but undress and crawl in beside his pal.

Timmy awakened to greet Thanksgiving in Memphis around five thirty. It wasn't the way he wanted to awaken in the morning, either. Skeets had all the blankets pulled around him, leaving Timmy's body exposed to the cool morning breeze from the open window. Skeets lay quite contented by the side of his partner, all curled up and unmindful of Timmy's distress. Timmy pulled the covers in one grand sweep and with his free hand, slapped Skeets on the bottom. The war of the blankets was waged at five-thirty-five that Thanksgiving morn by two of the closest of pals.

Neither Timmy, nor Skeets heard the pounding on the wall during their little bout. They continued to wrestle on the bed and finally rolled together onto the floor. The telephone rang. Both boys stopped abruptly. They looked at each other and waited silently for the second ring.

Skeets started to grab Timmy around the neck only to be interrupted by the second announcement from the telephone. Timmy got off the floor and dashed to the receiver. The clerk in the lobby informed Timmy he had received complaints from the surrounding rooms on his floor that a murder was being committed in their room, and it would please the management if they would refrain their slaughter until after nine o'clock. Timmy tried to convince the clerk that they were only engaging in a friendly little tussle. The clerk snapped back that if it was all the same to him, would he kindly abstain from starting his football game until he got to the field that afternoon. Timmy was about to apologize when the irate clerk banged the phone with a loud noise.

Skeets was all in favor of resuming his match for the supremacy of the blankets, but at Timmy's request, arranged them in orderly fashion on the bed. Both boys jumped on the bed in unison and covered themselves in preparation for the remaining hours of sleep before taking their breakfast.

Around nine o'clock, Skeets opened his eyes and looked at Timmy. His friend's arm was around his shoulder in fraternal affection. Skeets slipped his hand through the wedge and ruffled Timmy's mass of curly hair. Close to his ear, he whispered softly, "I hope we'll always remain pals, Timmy, and don't be sore at me for those words last night in front of the Catholic Club." This was the first and only time Skeets expressed a note of outward affection that sunk deep in the heart of young O'Shea.

Timmy opened his eyes and smiled at Skeets. There was an exchange in their expressions that didn't need words to show their strong bond of childish love. It was then and there that Timmy and Skeets shook hands and vowed everlasting friendship. A bond that lasted with gilt-edge security until the summer of 1935 when Skeets turned moral advisor.

Skeets lost the flip of the coin for first crack at the showers. It was the first and one of Timmy's rare chances to get the edge on the Locodere comedy man. While the fullback was washing and singing loudly in the bathroom, Skeets ordered their breakfast to be brought up to the room. Boys approaching seventeen and ardent sportsmen eat heavy in the morning as well as the other two sittings each day. The room service clerk asked Skeets how many men and their Saint Bernard dogs were participants in this particular repast. As usual, the witty boy chimed in with some inane answer.

While Timmy was dressing, Skeets took his shower. Before either of the boys were finished, a loud knock came to the door. Timmy answered its summons and in walked three of the Lacodere footballers from the Gayoso Hotel. Skeets, upon learning who their visitors were yelled out so he could easily be heard in the hotel's lobby, "throw those ten-cent vultures to hell out. This ain't Malholahan's Lunch Wagon."

Timmy called the room service clerk and asked to be connected with the dining room. He then asked the head waiter to double up on the previous order just given from Room 1418. He received a gasp in response.

Over their ham, eggs, sweet rolls, milk and coffee, the five boys laughed heartily and discussed the afternoon's prospects. They were all happy and highly confident boys. Joey Roys, and Howie Forest and Buddy Feeley talked football all morning in the hotel room. The only disturbance to their little athletic conference was a special delivery letter to Timmy from Madeline. It came around eleven that morning, and Timmy read the note hurriedly and returned to his teammates. Only Skeets looked somewhat dismayed or registered any degree of personal hurt when Timmy took time out to read the brief words of encouragement and continued love and affection.

At noon the five ball players left the hotel in the company of their respected coach, Father Pete. They went by cab to the hospital where Gibby Gerard was still holding his own. They talked with Dr. Gerard, and he told the boys to go out and play for a win, not only because it would make his Gibby really happy when he came to, but because the spirit of Lacodere and the pride of Lacodere must be held up by those sturdy men who called themselves her representatives.

Chapter Eight

Over twelve thousand men, women and children packed the stadium to cheer their team to victory. The Catholic Schools of Memphis formed a rooting section of their own and made considerable noise when Locodere's purple and gold roared on the field in perfect formation. The Glee Club from Siena College and the Knights of Columbus band provided music. Lacodere never played before a more appreciative audience. The thirty odd boys in their brightly colored jerseys ran through several plays down the field. Timmy kicked a new football to Skeets and Joey Roys practiced centering the ball back to Tommy Collier. After about ten minutes of this practice session, Lacodere's squad left the field to permit Central's large outfit to take over.

In the stands, little boys could be seen milling through the crowd selling souvenir programs and banners. Everyone seemed to be full of happiness and anxious for the game to start. An announcer called off the Lacodere lineup and told, in a few words, the absence of Gibby Gerard was due to a serious accident in yesterday's scrimmage and left the visitors shy the services of one of their outstanding players. While he was still telling the public to patronize the youngsters selling hot dogs, candy and peanuts, a tremendous ovation was heard at the far end of the field. It followed through the whole Central

High School section of the stadium. Central's Indians in their red and white jerseys ran full speed onto the field. People stood and stamped their feet with wild joyous screaming. No college club in the whole South received such a welcome or promise of support. The Indians looked as smooth as silk on the field as they ran through a few plays. They had Pop Warner's Stanford University system down to perfection. A certain grandson on the field passed the "pigskin" to another teammate with accuracy unparalleled. Each time he threw a pass, it sailed between thirty-five and forty-five yards. The feminine members of the Central rooting section would gasp in uniformity when the ball would fly across the field. If Johnny Moore wasn't the most popular young man in Memphis that day, at least he was the object of every girl's affection in Central High School. And, the beauty of it all was that he knew it too.

Again, Lacodere's eleven ran on the field followed by the substitutes. Joey Roys reported to the umpire and met the great public school star, Johnny Moore, for the first time. They shook hands and listened to the instructions and ground rules. Joey won the toss-up and elected to receive. All men were in their respective positions. A last checkup by the two quarterbacks and the game was about to get under way.

The whistle blew a shrill call to play. The ball was kicked high in the air and headed directly for Tommy O'Hara, right end on the Jesuit school's team. O'Hara made the catch and ran up to the forty, to the fifty, and was finally brought down on Central's forty-five yard line by two big Indian linemen. The first action in the huddle was a quick Hail Mary and a Sign of the Cross led by, above all people, Skeets Malone. He called for play forty-two, right through center with Timmy carrying the ball. The shift was to the left, as

Father Pete had taught them, and the ball snapped back to Tommy Collier, who, in turn, slipped it to Timmy in a spinner play. Timmy dove through the line for a gain of four yards. He felt, though, the strength of Central's powerful fortress. Those boys were not playing marbles. They were out for keeps. Again, the Catholics were in the huddle. They were going to attempt a pass. Skeets didn't figure they had anything to lose by trying a surprise attack via the air lanes. He was a good judge of his opponent. The ball went sailing down the field right into the arms of little Teddy Barry, the right halfback. He ran an additional ten yards before he was tackled on Central's ten yard stripe. Skeets took the ball on the next play over right tackle and brought the team closer to the enemy's goal by five yards. The next play was another line plunge over the center with Howie Forest handling the ball and Timmy and Feeley running his interference. Howie was tackled hard on the line of scrimmage and dropped the ball. Central's right guard made the recovery.

There was a time-out called by Lacodere while Howie was carried off the field and a substitution made. He received a big ovation from the stands, but Howie never heard it. He never even heard the final score. Death, instead, scored en route to the hospital, caused by the terrific jolt the lad took when he made the fatal plunge over center. The autopsy performed the following day showed a broken neck and a severe concussion of the brain.

The spirit of football lives long despite the cruel accidents that befall the youthful participants. Only the parents of these modern gladiators live to curse the sport of the Fall season.

Time-in was called and Jodi Broussard made his first attempt at filling a backfield position in a major contest. He and Howie were the best of friends. Father Pete knew this and told him to play in there for his pal. He did play. Jodi played superb ball. All through the remainder of the game his French blood was boiling, yet he never lost control of himself and did much to assist his club through the trying minutes that remained.

It was half-time before either club knew it. There still remained no score. Father Pete gave a Rockne pep talk during the half. He had spirited music by the Columbian band in the distance to add zest to his oratory. He told the boys that Gibby wanted them to win, that Howie would expect to hear of their win when he came around again, and, in fact, all Lacodere wanted their boys to bring home a winning team. "Now, get out there and win because YOU want to win."

The big Jesuit priest left the dressing room to the boys and the Brothers, who acted as rubdown men. With a bottle of alcohol in one hand and a rough gardener's hand, the Brothers went around rubbing legs, backs and necks. They were a tired group of fellows as they lay stretched out on the floor and benches. None wanted to talk because there wasn't anything to talk about. They were still behind until they had that first important six points on their side of the ledger.

Again both teams were on the field. This third quarter went nearly as fast as the preceding two. Still no give-in from either side. It was the closest and most contested game Memphians ever witnessed. The fourth and last quarter brought the desired results. Timmy intercepted one of Johnny Moore's sure-fire passes and nearly raced the length of the field for the first and only touchdown of the game. The try-for-point was made by Jodi Broussard around right end. He seemed to have no opposition as he ran the few yards. He placed the ball on the ground, and in a voice most of the players could hear, said, "That one's for you, pal." Those who heard Jodi's few words and saw the tears form in his brown eyes knew what his heart spoke.

Central High tried everything in the proverbial book of football tricks to make the score at least even up. It was too late. The gun sounded a few short seconds later and ended the game.

CHAPTER NINE

There weren't happy songs or street dances when Lacodere's team returned to their home town. The boys were sick at heart. They learned that Howie had paid the supreme sacrifice. Gibby was still in the hospital in Memphis, and the Jesuits ruled football out from that day forward in their Lacodere institution.

Liz was waiting for Timmy in her bedroom. She was happy to see her hero, but it was with a forced smile that greeted him. Liz was confined to her bed by Doctor Jereau. They talked about his trip and the game and the pleasant visit to the Dominican Church. They also spoke softly of Howie's grand personality and his cheerful outlook on life. When Timmy mentioned Gibby and how he met his fate during the Wednesday scrimmage, Liz turned her head and cried softly in the pillow. Timmy went to the other side of the bed to console his aunt with a pat on the head. She looked up at him with sorrow deeply fixed in her eyes.

"It might have been you, Timmy," she said, softly.

"Now isn't that a helluva thing to say?" he said. "After all, Liz, I would much rather it be me than one of my best friends."

"You'll always be that way, too, won't you, Timmy?"

Timmy didn't answer. He looked on his aunt with a strange and bashful smile.

Liz turned her head and attempted to raise herself and lean against the back of the bed. It was too great an effort. She slipped back on the pillow and closed her eyes. Timmy walked over to the bed and asked his aunt what was wrong. At first, she didn't want to talk. After prodding her with appealing questions, she opened her eyes and told him she had to go away for awhile.

"Away? Awhile? Where are you going, and why are you leaving so suddenly?" he asked excitedly.

"Timmy, I'm not so sure I can tell you. Even though I'm not your mother, I'm sure if I were I couldn't tell you."

"What kind of chatter is that?" asked Timmy. "Did you knock off the Southern National or put the bite on Father Joseph's mite box?" he said with a laugh that echoed throughout the room.

"No, I didn't rob the bank or steal from the Church," she said with a forced grin on her face. "I, like all women, must go through the portals of transition. I don't think it fair to you to burden you with troubles, my troubles in particular, or the pitfalls of womanhood in general. Do you?"

"Of course, you must remember, I didn't find romance in the women's section of the Montgomery Ward catalog, you know. I may look like a hayseed, but it stops right there. I've been around a little, and I've looked through one of Doctor Gerard's books with Gibby on several occasions. I'm not bragging, but I regard myself as a minor authority and quite familiar with women's disorders. So, don't be afraid to tell me the ghastly details. Why, I'll run down to the drug store and get old Hopkins to 'rassel' you up some medicine," Timmy said with a note of earnestness in his voice.

"You dear boy," said Liz, as she extended her hand to grasp his, "there are some ailments one can't cure with medicine. I realize you and your pals know a lot about subjects mothers never dream enter your heads for investigation. And, I know in the South, youngsters grow a little faster for their years then they do in New England or out West. Why, as I look at my little boy now, I can see how you've grown just in the past year. But, I don't think you're old enough to sit with me and discuss my illness. Let's give Doctor Jereau's prescription a fair trial and follow his instructions.

"Whatever you say, Auntie Liz, is okay with me. You know that, don't you, honey?" Timmy said, still holding her warm hand in his.

Elizabeth Connelly would leave for a long and much deserved vacation as soon as she was able to get up and manage the arduous task of packing and preparing for an extended rest period. Perhaps by January or February she would leave for Southern California or Arizona or Miami Beach and relax her tired mind and rest her weary body. In the meantime, though, she must be encouraged to eat and regain her lost strength to better qualify for the promising vacation—the first since leaving Ireland in 1910.

CHAPTER TEN

C hristmas that year was happy and delightful. The Bishop approved of midnight Mass in the churches of his diocese, and the priests and people were eager to take advantage of the afforded grace. Saint Mary's never looked more beautiful with hundreds of poinsettias in profuse array on the three alters. The sisters from Our Lady of Lourdes spent Christmas Eve scrubbing and cleaning to make the church radiate with the sparkle of cleanliness. The soft lights and pine trees in the background of the main alter lent further beauty. The replica of the Christ as a babe with Mary and Joseph hovering over Him attracted the young as well as the old. Little children hardly able to walk wanted to climb in the manger to feel the Infant's face and pet the animals in the distant hay. The air was filled with Merry Christmas and everyone was happy.

At the big house on Fontaine Street, Skeets and Timmy were putting the last touches of tinsel on the tree that stood in the center of the large parlor. Gibby, now healthy and fat from lack of exercise, sat on the piano stool tapping out, *Silent Night, Holy Night.* Once in awhile, he struck the wrong note, but nobody really cared. Liz was coming down as soon as the boys gave her the signal that all was in readiness. She was as happy as a school girl with her first new silk ribbon. If missing Mass that Christmas Eve was a hardship to be accepted with her other cross, at least she could enjoy the birthday of Christ in her own home with the boys making her heart light and burdenless.

Mr. Rosario called from the flower shop while Timmy was admiring the tree. He wanted to close his shop in a few minutes and go home to all the little Rosarios. After all, hadn't he paid "five dolla" for a "Santa da Close" suit and his "a kids" were waiting for the big, fat, jelly Saint Nicholis? Timmy snapped his fingers and told Mr. Rosario he'd be down to the shop quicker than the old Italian could say his Confitior. Timmy excused himself and yelled up at his Aunt Liz that he'd be back in about half an hour. As he was going out the door, he told the boys in the parlor not to let his aunt come down till he returned.

It was only a matter of minutes till Timmy walked breathlessly into the florist shop. He took the wreath that was wrapped in green paper and paid Mr. Rosario's daughter with two five dollar bills. She called him back for his change, but he waved it aside and bid them enjoy the merriest of Christmasses. He was still laughing when he turned the corner on the street leading to the cemetery and walked into the arms of Madeline Turrel.

Timmy hadn't seen too much of his heart throb since his homecoming after the victorious football game in Memphis. Occasionally, they would meet in the library and sit and talk instead of study their outside-class reading assignments. Maybe two Fridays out of the month they could be seen in the very last row of the Rialto Theatre holding each other's hand and gasping at the feats of wonder a certain Valentino was able to exploit with women on the silent screen. But as a whole, Timmy stayed close to home and waited on his aunt with all the devotion and experience of a trained nurse.

"Hi ya, Madeline," Timmy said excitedly. "I'm going to the cemetery to put this on Howie's grave. Come on down with me. I want to talk with you about something—about us."

"Okay, you big, blonde lady-killer," she said with a tang of the deceitful in her voice. "I'd go any place with you—anytime, too—even to a graveyard."

Timmy didn't appreciate this greeting, but took her arm and walked down the dark street that led to Mount Calvary Cemetery. Each time he was with Madeline, his heart would beat faster and seem to turn somersaults in his breast. This time was no exception. He was happy to be alone with her again.

At the cemetery, they both knelt for a minute or two. Timmy knew the De Profundis and recited it in silence for the repose of the soul of a great little friend. Madeline knew her prayers, but her thoughts never seemed to run along that line of mental exercise or spiritual rendezvous. She was thinking of someone else and something vastly incongruous with prayer.

After Timmy placed the wreath on the humble marker that read:

HOWARD PATRICK FOREST
December 24th 1909—November 27th 1925
REQUITE IN PEACE

He took Madeline's hand, and together they slowly strolled down the path that led to the outer gate.

"He was sure one fine fellow," said Timmy. "It's too bad there aren't more like Howie around."

"Have you ever been kissed in a cemetery on Christmas Eve, Timothy?" said Madeline, boldly and perfectly unmindful of what he was talking about.

"Can't say that I have, sugar, nor that I'd want to be kissed in such a desolate spot," was his quick retort.

"Well, I want to be kissed, and by nobody else but you," Madeline said teasingly.

Timmy ran his lower lip between his front teeth. He pretended not to hear this last request. They walked on through the gate and back up the narrow sidewalk leading to the heart of town. As they were talking about Christmas and midnight Mass, they heard a low whistle with three variations. It could be none other than Buddy Feeley, who adapted this means to announce his appearance on the scene.

Buddy was a tall, young man with pleasing features and a happy disposition. He and Howie were inseparable before his friend's untimely death. He felt the absence of Howie keenly within his breast. Outwardly, he gave no evidence of his loneliness. As Timmy was to Skeets, so Buddy and Jodi were to Howie. Together they went swimming and hunting, and when not in a general crowd of boys, they would take in the local movie or just sit at home and work in Howie's workshop in the basement. They seemed to be happy when they were together, whether it be playing or listening to the radio or working out their "Trib" problems.

"Hi, Maddy. Who's the ugly looking 'goof' you're hanging on to? Seems I've seen that face someplace before," was his greeting to the pair.

"Speaking of people being ugly! Did it ever occur to you that you're a dead ringer for Lon Chaney? I saw that unwholesome looking character last week at the Rialto and couldn't help thinking of you. By the way, 'knot-head,' are you coming to the house before Mass?"

Madeline didn't acknowledge Buddy's burst of foolishness and gave facial indication that she didn't approve of Timmy's time spent in repartee.

"As a matter of fact, repulsive, I was on my way up there right now," said Buddy, ignoring Madeline's obvious snub.

Timmy bid Madeline goodnight at the corner and told her he'd meet her at the entrance of Saint Mary's about a quarter to twelve. She didn't answer, but turned sharply and ran down the street.

"Ain't women the craziest squirrels God ever created, Timmy?" said Buddy, shaking his head.

"Maybe you have reference to that buck-toothed hippopotamus you're running around with lately. Where in the hell did you ever resurrect that load of feminine brutality?" said Timmy, laughing.

"Well, how do you like that? So, you call my dream gal a hippo, huh? Me that picks 'em strictly for class and culture."

They both laughed heartily, and Timmy wrapped his arms around Buddy's neck and pulled him over to his chest. He released him quickly when Buddy jabbed his thumb in Timmy's ribs.

At the house, Gibby and Skeets were arranging packages under the tree. Silba and Jordan were making preparations for "Tom & Jerrys" in the kitchen. Liz was sitting in her room awaiting the signal from the boys in the parlor to come down to see the tree. It was to be a gala Christmas party with the climax coming after Mass when all gathered around to open the gifts. Gibby, Buddy and Skeets would celebrate their own family Christmas on the morning of the 25th in their own homes, but for tonight, the boys were together, singing their hearts out and happy in the mood of Christmastime.

Timmy was at the entrance to Saint Mary's long before a quarter to twelve. But Madeline wasn't there to meet him and wish him her greetings. Knowing Madeline's peculiar temperament, Timmy didn't bother to wait beyond the appointed time. He went around to the sacristy where Skeets, Buddy and Gibby were vesting for High Mass. Skeets tossed Timmy a red cassock and silently he put it over his head and let it drop loosely over his body. After adjusting the large white cincture around his waist, he put the lace surplice on and was ready to assist Father Joseph at Mass. All four boys made an impressive showing on the altar. They recited their Latin responses in clear tones and their every movement was a prayer to behold. The choir sang beautiful hymns announcing the birth of the King of Kings.

The little boys in their bright red cassocks formed a guard of honor around the crib. They resembled little angels with hair so neatly combed and hands clasped reverently before their breasts. One little angel had to look around to smile at his daddy, who watched with pride the son he loved so dearly. The sisters trained the little ones with unfaltering patience. They knew when to kneel down and adore their Master and go forth to receive Him into their lily-white hearts. Much was the time spent with these baby souls. More was the joy when Sister Mary Immaculata watched their every motion during the long mass.

Father Joseph spoke a few words to his congregation about the birthday of Jesus. How He came to be born in lowly circumstances and live for so short a time, preaching and doing good unto others and subjecting His Devine Will to that of His Heavenly Father's.

Father Joseph loved Jesus and loved little children. He turned slightly to the tired little boys by the improvised stable at Bethlehem and told them they must always love the baby Jesus as He surely loved them with all His heart. He told the mothers and fathers and uncles and aunts present that early morning that it was his intention to accept their Christmas offering and distribute it to the poor of the parish. He closed his short sermon by wishing all his people the Christ Child's choicest blessings on their souls, and may they enjoy now and forever the happiness of Christmastime.

It was nearly one-thirty when the boys arrived home to again wish each other a Happy Christmas. Liz was in the living room before the big fireplace. It was warm and comfortable by the fire, and Liz watched the dance of the flames as they merrily ran up the chimney. Jordan entered with a tray of sliced fruit cake and a large silver bowl of "Tom & Jerry" mix. He passed it to Liz and the others. It was a happy gathering with gifts for all.

Jordan passed out the presents from under the tree to Liz, who looked at the name inscribed and passed it to its rightful owner. Even Silba and Jordan had their presents under the tree and were permitted to share in the fun of opening them with the rest of the group. There were big boxes and tiny packages. Everyone received at least three. Liz seemed to be the honored guest with four to her credit. Each to their own chair or corner they went to open and admire with awe the new piece of clothing or book or nick-knack. Screams of, "look what I got," resounded throughout the room.

Liz told Jordan not to bother to clean up the tissue paper and string the boys carelessly threw about the room. It could be taken care of tomorrow. Each of the young men came to the big plush chair where Liz was seated and gave her a kiss on the side of the head. As the last withdrew to return home, Timmy came up and sat beside his aunt and looked deep into the roaring fire. Liz ran her long fingers through the boy's hair. It felt good to be near the one you loved and feel that love circulate through your body. He looked into Liz's eyes and asked her if she, too, were happy.

"Being here alone with you, Timmy, makes up for any sorrow I may have had in my life. If you should ever leave me now and never return to my side, I'll be happy in my thoughts, knowing I had you as long as I did," was her sweet message of love to her Timmy on that early Christmas morn.

Timmy undressed and went directly to bed. Outside he heard in the distance soft music and singing. He jumped out of bed, threw his robe about his body and went to the window. Down the sidewalk came the members of the Salvation Army Corps returning to their station. They had been singing since early evening and still had songs in their hearts. They would only stop at the houses where lights remained burning. Timmy's light shone forth over the trees on the side of the large stone house. The carolers sang sweetly as if it were their first number of the evening. The beautiful strains of *Oh, Holy Night* rang forth in the still night. Timmy knelt by his window and looked out over the trees and gazed into the dark blue sky. He thought he saw one star that was larger and more resplendent than all the rest in the heavens. The end of the hymn was a signal for Timmy to dim his light and close his tired eyes for the Boy Emmanuel was soon to come.

CHAPTER ELEVEN

Nine o'clock wasn't too late to rise on Christmas morning, especially when one went to bed so late. But, there were a few errands to make and much preparation before the big feast. Timmy jumped out of bed when he heard Silba knock on his door. "Yo all ain't got time to lay there a-dreamin' way yo time, Masta Timmy," the old mammy said through the door. "Yo gotta help old Jordan and me fix them dishes fancy-like, and set that there big table like real 'ciety folk fix 'em. Ah you all lisnin' to yo Mammy Silba?"

Silba receive a faint reply from within the confines of the master bedroom, but she left unconvinced that her words carried much weight, especially Christmas morning.

After a quick shower and an even quicker dressing, Timmy joined Aunt Liz in the library for coffee and poached eggs. Liz was an ardent reader and spent all her free time in the well-stocked reading room. Through force of habit, she took her breakfast in the library instead of the dining room. She, Big Tim, and Margaret would sit in the library or the long sun porch for their first meal of the day. Since Big Tim and Margaret passed away on that frightful voyage homeward, Liz remained the only one to perpetuate the custom of eating in the "book-room," as Big Tim called it.

Planting a kiss on Liz's right cheek and wishing her another Merry Christmas, Timmy sat down to enjoy a steaming cup of coffee. He refused the offer of sweet rolls claiming they may interfere with his dinner that afternoon.

"In as much as you have taken care of the dinner arrangements, and thoroughly instructed the help as to service and the setting of the table, would it be too much to ask of you if I might be included in some of the details?" said Liz with a twinkle in her eye.

"And just what details do you feel you've been excluded from?" said Timmy, not even looking up from the sports page of the Commercial-Appeal.

"Probably the most important," said Liz, "and please put that newspaper down until you have finished your breakfast. You're not in a Thompson Café, you know."

Timmy folded the paper slowly and gave one last look at the headlines before throwing it on the center of the table.

"And, now, dear Auntie Lizzie, what do you regard as the most important details of our big dinner party?" said her nephew, as he reached for the silver sugar bowl.

"If you'll ask for that, I'll be only too happy to pass it to you," she said, making an attempt to pass the bowl.

"What about the important details you're 'beefing' about?" he said, unmindful of her corrections.

"Who besides Doctor and Mrs. Gerard, did you invite to this affair?" said Liz, slowly becoming exasperated with Timmy's cool attitude. "Of course, I realize this will be a big affair, and you've taken pains to make it such, but I fail to see why you have inserted the element of secrecy that only creates suspicion rather than surprise."

"Auntie, have you ever been on the stage? You certainly read your lines well," said Timmy.

"I can't imagine what reference you have to the theatre and this long, drawn-out answer I'm waiting for," was her reply.

"You know, Auntie Liz, there really is something of the dramatic in you—a tiny bit of Cornell, a dash of Hayes, a speck of Barrymore and even a slight sprinkle of either Gertie Lawrence or Jane Cowl. Why don't you give vent to your talents and romp the legitimate boards of the ancient art for the sake of dear, old 'moola'? I dare say our Southern belle, Miss Bankhead, would be envious of your performance and future reputation," said Timmy, laughing.

"All this inane prattle of yours," she went on, "only spells a deceitful medium of evasion. Will you or will you not settle down for a moment and tell me who is coming to this house this afternoon for dinner?"

"If you're going to be insulting," he said, still laughing, "I, in my own, selfish, little way, will abstain from any further conversation with you until such time as I have successfully eliminated the last drop of this vile and opaque mixture, commonly referred to as coffee, by those who have utterly no qualms of conscience."

"If the coffee is all the nice things you say about it, why in heaven's name did you take a second cup?" was Liz's answer.

"Please, Miss Connelly, don't take the stand in defense of this liquid and arsenical potheen. The fact that I take a second cup, yea. Even a third cup may have meritorious design attached. I may choose this means of doing penance for your sins and mine, rather than don the mild scourge of sitting in front of Saint Mary's in sackcloth and ashes," Timmy said, still laughing.

"I must say, in all truthfulness, you're incorrigible," said Liz.

"Now, Elizabeth, down deep in your heart you really don't think that I'm that—whatever you just said—all you want to know is who shows for dinner today," said Timmy. "What do you say, Liz," Timmy went on, "if we call the whole thing off and go up to Memphis and feed the polar bears?"

"By the Lord God, Timmy, I really think you're losing your mind," said Liz with a serious look on her face.

"Am I to understand you dislike Memphis, or the idea of feeding poor, hungry, polar bears?" was his sarcastic reply.

Without waiting for any further condemnation, Timmy pulled a list from his hip pocket and started to read aloud the names of his dinner guests. Liz nodded her approval with each one until he mentioned the name of Madeline Turrel.

"Well, why don't you 'blow a fuse'?" he said seriously. "I know very well you dislike Madeline. Skeets doesn't like her, and Gibby makes wise cracks about her, and all the other kids around town call her 'Jezebel'. What for? What has she done to you or any of the other people of this town? I like her and see no reason why she should be excluded from the party. She can act the part of a lady with the same casual distinction as any of the other female guests who consented to come to the dinner. Go ahead, throw in your dime's worth of slanderous diatribe with the others. If Madeline isn't permitted in this house today, well, I'm making myself scarce for the rest of the day," Timmy exploded fiercely.

Liz was too shrewd and tactful to argue with Timmy when he assumed this stance. She knew he'd be around within the hour to apologize and put his arm around her neck. Even though he'd leave the table without finishing his breakfast, she was sure his contempt was only temporal in duration.

Timmy left the table and went to his room. He stayed only a few minutes when he slammed his door behind him and ran down the stairs two at a time. He stopped at the library entrance and looked at Liz for a moment before telling her he was sorry. He waited till she smiled at him before going out the front door.

Liz picked up the list left on the table. She scanned it hurriedly. There was: Doctor and Mrs. Gerard, Mr. and Mrs. Malone, Mr. and Mrs. Marlowe, Mr. and Mrs. Feeley, Doctor and Mrs. Jereau, Father Joseph, Mr. and Mrs. Forest, Skeets, Giby, Buddy, Joey Roys, and the infamous trouble-baiter, Madeline Turrel. She put the list under a plate and left the library to see how Silba and Jordan were progressing with the Irish linen tablecloth.

Timmy's first call enabled him to assemble himself and regain his happy disposition. He knocked on Madeline's front door. Old Mrs. Turrel answered the summons and forced a smile on her tired face. She always managed a smile for Timmy no matter how low she felt or disdainful her outlook of the future might be.

"Merry Christmas, Mrs. Turrel!" said Timmy with a note of gusto in his greetings. "Was the old fat man with the red monkey suit good to you this year?" was his second burst of greetings in the form of an interrogation.

"Same to you, son, and many, many more for you and your Auntie Liz. If I had my health, I think I'd be happier than anything else in the world," was her reply.

"Is my pretty doll home? I didn't see her at Mass last night, so I figured she went to Saint Mary's this morning," said Timmy, walking into the front room. He continued, "I brought her a little something I thought she might like, and then again, she might not! But wait, here's something for you from Auntie and me. Sure hope it fits. If it doesn't, you can exchange it at Saks Fifth Avenue next time you're in New York."

Both laughed heartily. Mrs. Turrel never saw Memphis, let alone New York City.

Timmy sat down and awaited Mrs. Turrel's explanation to follow.

"Madeline went to Mass a few minutes ago, Timmy," she said, "but it's a low Mass, and I'm sure she'll be home in a little while. There's something I'd like to tell you, Timmy. But, please promise not to tell Madeline. She becomes provoked with her poor mother when I talk to others about her."

"It's a deal. What is it, Mrs. Turrel?" asked Timmy, bending over to grasp ever word of her low-toned conversation.

"Madeline isn't a bad girl. In fact, she sometimes gives me much pleasure, especially when she plays on the old piano over there," pointing to an upright piano that took the greatest amount of space in the humble room.

"My sister in New Orleans answered my letter of a few weeks ago, and Clare said that she'd let Madeline come to her home and live with her. I thought the change would do her good. And, Clare is so interested in music, I just know she'll encourage Madeline to practice longer hours and make something of herself."

"When is Madeline supposed to leave Lacodere, Mrs. Turrel?" said Timmy enthusiastically.

"Sister Miriam Josephine told me yesterday that Madeline could finish her semester's work by March or April and receive her diploma. Then, I think, if Madeline wouldn't balk at the idea, she could go and live with her Aunt Clare," said Mrs. Turrel, "where her advantages would be a little better for her."

Timmy couldn't help registering surprise. He had a few ideas for the future that didn't include Madeline, but at the same time, he didn't feel he wanted her to leave so soon, at least not from Lacodere!

There was no use waiting any longer. She'd perhaps stop off at some girlfriend's house and not return to her own home for some time to come. Timmy handed Mrs. Turrel a small box wrapped with red and white ribbon. "Give this to Madeline for me, will you, Mrs. Turrel?" he said as he started out the door. When he got halfway down the stairs, he turned and shouted back, "Tell Madeline that dinner is at two o'clock—on the dot."

Timmy had a few stops to make before returning to the house on Fontaine Street. One very important visit was to be made at the crude old house by the Southern Railroad's tracks. At least once a week, he went calling on Mrs. Duseauault and her seven little French children. None of the little ones were very healthy looking, but they had an appeal for Timmy. They would run to the window and throw back the sugar sack curtain and scream for joy when they saw Timmy come up the dirty path.

The oldest child was thirteen and a very pale-looking girl. Timmy never could remember to call them by their proper names. They would laugh at his blunders when he called Annette, and Bernadette would come to his side. He would feel strange when they would climb all over him to see who would be the first to kiss his cheek. Never would he scold them or command them to wash their faces. Even when the baby came running to him with diapers filthy and heavy, he would pick the child up in his arms and run his hand through his little head of hair. He loved all seven of the children, but somehow he was attracted to Robert, who was just turning eight. There was something about Robert that appealed to Timmy. It wasn't because he was the nicest looking of the seven, or because he had some sense of cleanliness about his person, but it was the way the little fellow came and held on to his sweater or coat as if he wanted to be with him always. The others would pay their juvenile respects to their adopted big brother and then scamper off to other sections of the ill-kept house. Robert, though, would remain like a puppy dog that fears it may be left behind. Once, Timmy took Madeline with him on his weekly visit, and she gave all evidence of being bored. The children, too, were very quick to notice her reaction and formulated a sudden and lasting distaste for Timmy's girl.

The older children had a tree set up in the very center of the main room. There were no rugs or carpets on the floor. The tree, thought Timmy, would have been much better off had it remained in the woods by Lake Tahoo. A few holy pictures, with finger marks that soiled the representations, adorned the walls. If these were not hung by the devout little members, there wouldn't have been wallpaper in the house. All the children slept in two beds that were joined together so three blankets could cover all their frail bodies. There was no husband to look after the repair of the home. At least, if the husband did live, he didn't make it a custom to hang his hat in this humble dwelling—not for the past year or more, anyway. He went West when his wife was carrying Imogene, the last of the unfortunate crop.

When Timmy walked into the front room, his first move on Christmas Day was to count heads. Yes, all seven were accounted for. Where else could they go or be? He asked them if Santa paid off yet, and they answered him in all sorts of ways.

One said, "He's so loaded down that he's late coming to our house."

Another said, "He just plain done forgot us this year."

"You're all wrong, kids," said Timmy, winking to Mrs. Duseaunault, "the old fat man with all the hair on his face told me he had a terrible cold, and Mrs. Santa wouldn't let him go out after eight o'clock last night. So, what do you think he did?"

Not one would dare break the solemn silence. They were looking at this professional Irish liar with open mouths and awe-inspired looks of bewilderment. Timmy's word with these little ones was dogma.

After a quick and whispered, "God forgive me," he said, "WELL, I'm going to tell you." Looking at each little face with serious determination, Timmy continued, "Santa came to me very early yesterday afternoon while I was in my room, and he told me to give each one of you an envelope. Here's exactly what he said, 'Timmy, do you know all the little Duseaunault children?' And I looked him right in his good eye and said, 'I sure do. They're my very best pals. And Santa, just between you and me, Robert is my very, very best pal!' I asked him what he had in the envelopes, but he was so busy, he couldn't even wait to tell me. He just said, 'You be sure now, Timmy, and give one of these envelopes to each of my little friends at 21 Sinite Avenue.'"

The children were wild with excitement. They jumped all over Timmy in their eagerness to show their appreciation. He handed each outstretched hand an envelope. To Mrs. Duseaunault, he gave a check that made her sleepy eyes bulge with a radiance of joy. Each child took his envelope and went to a corner or secluded spot of the room to open it. Timmy picked Robert up in his big arms and hugged him close to his chest. He whispered in his ear that he had a special gift for him in his basement, but it was too big to carry, and he would have to come up and help him down with it sometime. No, not today. Maybe tomorrow or the next day.

They all took the money out of the envelopes and made a comparative study of the bills. Timmy released Robert and the little fellow ran to the bedroom. The others were laughing and comparing the sizes and denominations of their gifts with one another. Timmy watched their expressed exuberance from a vantage point in the center of the room. In the distant room, Timmy could hear the sniffle of his little pal. He walked, unnoticed, into the bedroom to investigate the motive for tears shed on Christmas Day. The little boy was outstretched on the bed sobbing as if his little heart would break. Timmy knew these were not tears of joy or jubilation. Something was wrong with the little French cher. He sat down on the soiled blankets and placed his hand on the child's back. When Robert felt the hand rub his back, he turned his head in the direction of Timmy and turned away quickly to hide his tear-filled eyes.

"Now, what did I do to bring about these big raindrops?" said Timmy. "If you don't stop crying, I'm going home to Auntie Liz," he continued.

The little boy turned again and faced him. This time, he buried his face in Timmy's waist.

"Here, here! I don't go for that line of music," said Timmy, patting the little fellow's head gently. "If you're going to be my pal, I don't want you to spend your time washing your eyes out."

Robert wiped his eyes and nose with the sleeve of his shirt. It was his Sunday shirt, too. He looked up at Timmy, proud that he could be called his pal. Fully over the sudden and unaccountable cry, he turned to Lacodere's star ball player and said, "Would it be a sin for me to love you more than my big sister or any of my other brothers or sisters?"

Timmy gulped on this question. In all his life, he never had one thrown at him that made him stop and reflect before answering. His reflection was short-lived. Robert had another that curved the plate low and inside.

"Do you love me enough to let me come and live with you in your big house and teach me to play football like you do?" was his innocent inquiry.

"Sure, I love you, Robert. I'd give anything in the world to have you for my little brother. We could have so much fun together. But, so does your mama and all your brothers and sisters," said Timmy, wondering what to say next. He continued, "If you came to my house, your mama would miss you and blame me for stealing you away from her."

While Robert was thinking up an objection to thwart this logical syllogism that threw his hopes of moving into the awful darkness of despair, Timmy continued by saying, "I'm not home nearly as much as I used to be, either. We couldn't play with all my toys in the basement, because I have to practice basketball every night after school starting the day after tomorrow. But, just you wait till summer rolls around, and we'll go fishing with Skeets and Gibby and have our lunch out in the boat in the middle of the lake. Now, won't that be swell?"

Robert was all smiles at this proposition. He opened his envelope and took out the bills and looked at George Washington's picture. He wasn't too concerned with money problems at this early age. True, a couple of dollars was more than he ever had in all his life up to this Christmas Day, but the thought of being alone with Timmy and just to be able to sit by him and gaze into his big blue eyes was sufficient to gratify his every desire.

"Will you teach me to swim, too, when we go to the lake, Timmy?" he asked with a frown on his little face. "And not let Skeets or Gibby or Buddy 'duck' me over my head?" he continued, before Timmy had a chance to answer his first request.

"I sure will, Magnus Robertus, and you'll be the best swimmer at Lake Tahoo when the summer is over. And, maybe, if you and your brothers and sisters are real good this winter, Auntie Liz will let you and your mama have our summer cottage for a whole month during the hot weather. But, don't you dare tell anyone, yet. Okay?" said Timmy, getting up to leave.

Before he left the bedroom, he bent over and kissed Robert and said, "That's because you're my little pal, and I love you very much."

In the front room the other children were still busy making comparative studies of the numbers and letters on their bills. Timmy went to each one and either pinched them gently or patted them on the head. He saw Mama Duseaunault sitting in the only rocking chair in the room with a tired little girl in her arms, who still clung tenaciously to a big red and green envelope in her little hand. She thanked him in French for his gifts and asked God to bless his charity. Timmy blushed. Not because he didn't understand French, but because he had to be thanked for something that made his heart leap for joy, the something that gave him pleasure to be able to perform for the less fortunate that God's created.

They didn't want Timmy to leave. They never did when he made these weekly calls. But, he had a few stops to make before returning to the house on Fontaine Street. He told them all to be real good children, and if heard any bad reports, he'd never return to visit with them again. After that little speech, he uncrossed his fingers.

They all promised to help their mama and be that source of joy and comfort all children should be to their mothers. He walked off the porch waving goodbye to his seven little adopted brothers and sisters. Then, he forgot a very important announcement. It was the movie at the local theatre the following Saturday. He quickly returned, opened the door and yelled, "Guess what, kids? Doug Fairbanks is coming to the Rialto in the 'Adventures of Robin Hood' this Saturday! How would you all like to come with Skeets and me?" There was a unanimous approval with the usual yeas in that little crowd of youngsters. Even the baby "goo-gooed" something, with a tiny smile beaming on her little face.

Timmy found Buddy home, and they looked over the many gifts he received from his parents and relatives. His younger sister came down to show off her new dress. Buddy's sister had a soft spot in her heart for Timmy, but knew well she didn't have a chance while Madeline was still in the running. The way she said hello to Timmy when she made her grand entrance should have been sufficient indication the girl was carrying the torch of love, not in one hand, but both fists! But, Timmy was a blind as the proverbial bat. If the lovely Vilma Bank fell in front of him begging his love, he'd spurn her affections for the wink from the eye of his little wild Madeline.

The trio looked over the green Christmas tree with its adornments glittering in the light from the electric bulbs. Mr. Feeley came out to announce that he decorated the tree all by himself. The fact that this was a gross injustice to Mrs. Feeley's efforts meant little to Mr. Feeley.

Timmy didn't stay long at Buddy's house. He had still another stop to make. He bid them all a Happy Christmas and told them not to hold up the dinner that afternoon. He departed, receiving the best wishes of all the Feeleys.

Every place Timmy went, whether it be Christmas, Easter or the Fourth of July, he was always welcomed with cordiality. The people of Lacodere loved their football hero, who to them had higher qualifications than to punt or pass a "pigskin" all over a field at a charity game in Memphis or on the home field. It was that perpetual Irish grin on his face that captivated the hearts of the Louisiana folks. The blacks were happy when he came out in the field to join in with their quaint, but haunting melodies. The poor and the rich white people opened their hearts and doors whenever he came on the scene. He was easily the most popular boy in town. If he was ever guilty of a sin that possessed grievous characteristics, he couldn't be held responsible in toto. As in the final words of the Shakespearean tragedy, when Othello, the noble-spirited Moor killed Desdemona, his loved one, Timmy could well cry out with Othello, "I loved not wisely, but too well."

Timmy laughed when Skeets told him he had changed all the tags on the Christmas packages before retiring the night before. His mother received his father's underwear, and his father pulled out his grandmother's fancy corset. But, Skeets was like that even on Christmas morning. Together, they went to Skeets' room to look over the selection of scientific books he received. It was all he asked his parents to give him, and they came through with flying colors.

"You know, Timmy, I didn't have to twist dad's arm beyond the elbow to get him to buy these books," he said laughing. "The old boy came through like a ton of bricks rolling down a hill."

Timmy would have stayed longer to listen to his pal's foolish chatter, but he inwardly felt an urge to get back to the house and assist Silba and Jordan. There was that possibility, too, that Jordan may get into the cognac if his own supply of cheap gin ran out. So, rather abruptly, he told Skeets he had to leave and urged him to be sure and have his folks at the house on time. The clown made some remark about his father's table manners and appetite, but Timmy missed its point.

Faithful Gibby was waiting for Timmy when he ran up the front stairs of the big house on Fontaine Street. He had something to tell Timmy that required the privacy of the master bedroom. Up the staircase the two athletes ran jabbering as they went. Timmy took his sweater and hung it in the closet. Gibby followed him talking as fast as a parrot with a sports announcer's vocabulary.

"While you were out, Madeline called on the phone," said Gibby, all excited. "She wouldn't talk to your aunt, so I don't know what she wanted. Don't worry, she'll be here! That much I got out of her. What do you see in that babe, Timmy? Oh, I admit, she's plenty sweet on the old blinkers, but you can't tell me her piano playing is the thing that attracts you. Come on, what gives?"

"Honestly, Gibby," Timmy said, walking slowly over to his desk and arranging the many gifts he received from friends, "I wonder myself what Madeline has that makes me dizzy when I'm around her. You know, Gibby, and God pity your worn-out carcass if you breathe this out, I'm going to become a priest when I graduate in May."

"A what?" cried Gibby, holding his hand to his head. "Now I've heard everything!"

"That's right, a Roman Catholic priest. One just like Father Joseph. Oh, maybe not as good a priest as Father Joseph, but a Benedictine Father."

"Do you think for two shakes the hold Jebbies are going to let you slip out of their Ignatian clutches?" asked Gibby, laughing. "Anyway, when did you decide you were going to take the big leap into the river of sanctity? This is something new, isn't it?"

"It may be new for me, but fellows have been going away to seminaries or monasteries for generations," Timmy dug right back.

"What does Aunt Liz think about all this?" Gibby asked.

"When she finds out, she'll probably start a new series of novenas to her favorite Irish saint," said Timmy, still laughing.

"What about Madeline? How serious have you and she become, Timmy? Most of the kids think you and she have . . ." Gibby broke off his statement when he noticed the pained expression on his friend's face. All he could blurt out was, "I'm sorry, Timmy. I didn't mean to hurt your feelings. But, you know yourself, when a fellow goes as steady with a 'broad' as you've been doing, they automatically claim they're 'shacking-up' together. I don't claim this, but many of our so-called dear friends are willing to bet that kind of money."

Timmy didn't say a word in defense of himself. He looked at Gibby in such a way that his friend wanted to make a hasty departure. Instead, he jumped right into the question of the priestly vocation further.

"Timmy, are you really serious about all this? You know what Father Joseph said Novitiates were like. And, living in a monastery isn't exactly my idea of a picnic. Maybe you have more than just seven holes in your head," said Gibby with a serious look on his countenance.

"Let's forget the whole thing, Gib, we'll talk about it later. It's nearly one-thirty, and I'm not dressed for dinner. God only knows whether Silba has the turkey in the oven, yet," said Timmy, starting to undress.

"What robes will you choose to wear, O holy monk?" said Gibby, going over to the closet to select a suit.

"Okay, wise guy, cut the jargon and hand me my blue serge suit. I think it's the one I got back from the cleaner's last week" said Timmy, pointing to the third suit from the wall.

"Yes indeed," said Gibby, fumbling through an array of sport coats, overcoats, tweeds and suits. "I'm sure blue serge bring out the true mannish features and makes the wavy, blonde hair show up in all its distinctive beauty. You wouldn't settle for this oxford grey sketch, would you?"

You can forget the plugs from 'Vogue' and hand me the suit. I'm nearly freezing here without my pants," said Timmy, impatiently. "Of all the profound muttonheads in this world, you're runner-up for top honors."

Still in the closet and knocking pants and coats off hooks and hangers, muttering like a mad man, Gibby emerged half-way from the closet to announce the moths must have eaten it.

Timmy walked into the closet and immediately picked the desired suit off the hanger and turned to Gibby and said, "This, my favorite knot-head, is what is commonly referred to as a blue serge suit. Now that you're fully educated in gentlemen's apparel, you may sit your can down in that chair," pointing to the one nearest the window, "and remain there in complete silence until I'm respectably clothed," said Timmy, grinning.

The two boys walked down the winding staircase laughing over their foolish antics of a few minutes previous. Both made for the kitchen to investigate the bird in the oven. To their satisfaction and complete approval, they found the turkey in readiness to be served. All else in the domestic department was in fine style. Jordan was sober and Silba was working like a Trojan.

"Where is Auntie Liz?" asked Timmy, addressing Silba.

"She's done gone up to dress fo dinner, boy. Don't yo all relize dinner am at two THIS aftanoon?" said Silba brushing the sweat from her forehead.

The boys walked into the dining room to inspect further. Everything seemed to be in order and met with fastidious tastes cultivated very suddenly in two young American boys. From the dining room, they walked militaristically into the living room to await, first, Miss Connelly, then the seventeen other guests. Their wait was brief. Madeline was first on the scene.

Chapter Twelve

Madeline walked with ease into the living room. Gibby stood erect when she entered the doorway. They both nodded as if they had met someplace before and took seats at extreme distances apart. After some conversation, Gibby asked to be excused. Timmy stood up as his friend left the room for the library. Alone together, Timmy and Madeline made a striking couple. Her long black curls and his blonde wavy hair didn't tend to clash in the brightly lighted room.

She walked around admiring the gold tapestry from India and the jade ash trays from China. She felt her foot go deep into the Persian rugs with every step. Timmy watched her rhythmic movements and drank in her beauty with every turn of her body. In one sweep, like a graceful swan, she faced Timmy who was caught in the act of gazing intensely. They embraced, and his hand ran down her back as their lips met. He pulled away when he heard footsteps coming down the staircase. It was Aunt Liz, dressed as she had never dressed before.

"How do you do, Miss Connelly?" said Madeline, void of any feeling in her voice.

"Merry Christmas to you, Madeline. So happy you were able to join us today," was Liz's reply.

"Look what Timmy gave me for Christmas? Isn't it just beautiful?" said Madeline, moving closer to Liz. "And to think that I wasn't able to give him anything in return, but a sweet little kiss on his pretty mouth," she said with a twinkle in her eye.

"I can't see very well without my glasses, Madeline. What is it?" said Liz bending down to catch a glimpse at the object Madeline held between her fingers.

"Why its Timmy's gold football he received for winning the game in Memphis last Thanksgiving day. I never thought he'd love me that much to part with the Charity Game trophy. And, look, Miss Connelly, he had a little diamond put right in the center of it. Oh, I just love him for it," she said excitedly.

Liz didn't say a word. She was filled with envy and scorn for the creature who won Timmy's heart to the extent that he'd part with the prize of his possessions.

Only thirteen footballs of solid gold were awarded in the whole Southern Association by the vote of the newspaper writers. Each had the player's name inscribed and the position he played. Timmy's read:

Timothy P. O'Shea
FULL BACK
Lacodere Prep
1925

After Timmy received his award in early December, he took it to the jeweler's shop on Second Street and had Mr. Fenton put a diamond in the center. Naturally, he wouldn't tell a soul about it. Let Madeline show it off on her breast with all manner of feminine pride. Yes, she conquered Timmy with the age-old tools—beauty, charm and personal mannerisms that burn deep into the heart and soul of impetuous youth and enkindle the fire of desire to burn more ardently in the mind, the stigma of which not even Tim can erase.

The guests were arriving steadily. To come to a two o'clock dinner at three didn't find its origin in the South. If many of the Southern people lack culture and refinement, they make up for this deficiency by their sincerity, generosity and good—naturedness. To be late to a function sponsored by a friend showed signs of lack of interest and concern. This was not a trait in Lacodere's society.

Timmy excused himself to greet the first of the arrivals. It was Doctor and Mrs. Gerard. Timmy took their wraps and handed them to Jordan. In the living room, a heated session was in progress between Liz and Madeline.

"Despite any protestations you may make to the contrary, Madeline Turell," said Liz with an air of authority, "I'm fully aware of the designs and methods you are employing to snatch all the goodness that is in Timmy. Either you voluntarily unleash your hold on him, or I'll seek a means befitting the type of character I think you to be. Have I made myself quite clear, my dear?"

"Miss Connelly, don't you think you're being a bit mid-Victorian in your attitude?" said Madeline, dryly. "After all, neither Timmy, nor myself, have any other designs in mind than to remain very good friends. I know you dislike me. I'm quite certain I know what prompts that dislike. I assure you, and I don't think I'm obligated to do so, Miss Connelly, Timmy is quite safe, and, I might add, somewhat on the dispassionate side, even chaste so far."

"This is hardly Christmas conversation, ladies," said Timmy, entering the room with a worried look on his face. "Let's reserve any misunderstandings to a later date, a much later date."

A few minutes later, Doctor and Mrs. Gerard entered the room with their pride and joy, young Gibby. Glad Gerard went into verbal ecstasy over Liz's dress. It was soft, black velvet, with a snow white Belgian lace collar and a large diamond brooch set around twenty-five little diamonds neatly placed at the center of her bosom. On her left shoulder, she wore not one, but two beautiful Isle of Capri gardenias. Her hair had a sheen that glistened with a lustrous brightness. Yes, Liz was most beautiful!

Mrs. Gerard wore a gown that surpassed all other guests of the day and evening. It was of light blue velvet with a trimming of fine Alaskan mink. Gibby, with a little assistance from the good doctor, gave his charming mother a platinum necklace with a gorgeous sapphire that hung regally around her neck. The doctor told the other guests Gibby won it on a punchboard to antagonize his wife.

The last of the eighteen invited dinner guests arrived promptly at two. It was a happy gathering in the living room. Any previous misgivings were quickly forgotten. Jordan passed along the room asking each one if he or she would care for a tidbit. He couldn't, or refused to say hors d'oeuvre. Some accepted, more refused. Jordan left the room as mysteriously as he had entered only to return trayless, announcing, "Dinner is ready," instead of the rehearsed, "Dinner is served."

There was no doubt in anyone's mind that Liz had the finest linen in Lacodere. She vied with the other ladies of the town for the best in silver, too. Her china was picked by careful scrutiny at the time Big Tim and Margaret occupied the house. There was one striking difference in the O'Shea dining room that made everyone take particular notice. Throughout the house, there were numberless oil paintings and gold framed miniatures. Some were originals bought by Big Tim; some very fine and expensive reproductions. In the dining room was an original of the Last Supper, by d'Vaneree. This was the prize of the household. If Jordan didn't do anything else in the course of his lazy day, he was commissioned to see that this painting was dusted and no direct sunlight dare fall on the canvas with the thirteen characters so exquisitely painted by the celebrated French artist. Once the Provincial of a French branch of the Jesuits visited Lacodere and the O'Shea home. He tried to get the painting for his House of Studies back in France. Of course, he told Liz how appropriate it would look in the Jesuits' Theocolate. Then, when this crude, but usual appeal failed in its attempt to find fertility in the soil of his logic, he offered her two thousand dollars. Liz just smiled.

The beautiful deep maroon velvet background added much to enhance the cultural effect of the masterpiece. A bronze shade with a long light globe lent museumistic stimulation. Everyone passed laudable remarks about the painting. It was another way of starting conversation at the table when some were prone to remain in the sheltered background of reserved silence.

If the painting failed to yield some long-winded oratory, surely the beautiful Dutch candelabra situated in two places on the long table would start someone off on a dissertation of unique silver pieces.

The flowers were of the season. Huge, sacred-red poinsettias with their bright yellow dots smiling in the center. Everything was spotlessly clean and radiant. There was nothing gaudy because the occupants of the house on Fontaine Street were not showoffs. If they had an abundance of money, they were quick to tell you who amassed the fortune. They were humble people who loved life and those who could share the same love.

The dinner was well-served and equally well-prepared. A real Christmas feast. Fruit cocktails were served in Russian silver cups with a dash of orange bitters and ginger ale. They seemed to lull over their courses and leisurely talk on and on. Poor Jordan was beside himself waiting for the guests to finish, so he could bring in the next dish. He was nervous, too, because Liz gave him very definite instructions as to the care of her cherished Belleek from County Fermanagh. Few Irish have so many pieces when they come from the Old Country. Less have the means to buy a complete dinner set of the precious pottery. Liz valued her Belleek beyond any of her household affects. The smooth, cream-colored material with the dainty shamrocks curled at various stations on the plates and cups, made the ladies envious. Its texture was as rare as its weight. The practicality of the pottery never enters the mind of a connoisseur of quality.

Much laughter ran through the dining room that day. Even Madeline entered the conversation and joined with Doctor Jereau in a story a trifle tainted. Jordan heard the bell nearly before it was rung by Liz. He cleared the table of the cocktail containers and brought forth the oxtail soup. Timmy pinched him as he passed by, and Skeets attempted to trip the old man as he round his corner. Poor old Jordan! If he didn't love these youngsters with all his heart, he couldn't have undergone the constant petty abuses inflicted by them.

The main course was served in regal style. The turkey, with a coat of gold brown, lay prostrate on the silver platter. Little spiced crabapples with eyes made from cloves surrounded the enormous bird. King Tom was wheeled into the gourmets on a mahogany pushcart. All eyes focused their attention on the twenty-five pound fowl. It was the custom to wheel the bird, that gave up the ghost for so noble a feast, around the table so all could admire its beauty before it underwent the carving of the surgeon.

It was nearly four o'clock when the last of the mincemeat pie was demolished. Timmy gave thanks to God for the delicious meal as all stood at attention by their places. There were audible belches from Doctor Gerard and Mr. Malone. But, these common notes of congratulations were forgivable under the circumstances.

Three tables were in readiness for bridge and a fourth could easily be set up if any desired to play contract or auction. None seemed overly anxious to sit and concentrate with thirteen cards staring them in the face. They sat around and talked in little groups, laughing and joking with one another. Doctor Gerard told a story that usurped at least fifteen minutes of the lazy afternoon. It was an experience too few could boast of, nor many more would want to undergo. It didn't take a great deal of persuasion on the part of his listeners to come to silence. When Doctor Gerard told a story, one could hear a pin drop. Before the physician started to clear his throat, his wife asked him not to tell the Pittsburgh experience. "It's entirely out of place here, Frank, and anyway, that story leaves me with a frightful headache," she said, turning to Liz.

Doctor Gerard waved aside her protests and asked the crowd if they'd enjoy listening to the most horrible and gruesome experience that could befall a young intern in his first year out of medical school. They all answered in unison that the story was in order. The doctor winked at his wife as much as to say, "You played your part to perfection." He drained the last drop of demitasse and placed the tiny cup and saucer on the tray by the beaming fire in the grate. He accepted the cigar and light offered him by Jordan and sat down to unravel the most unique situation ever to befall a man in Pittsburgh,Vicksburg, or Hoboken, New Jersey. He had the best audience a storyteller could wish for. They were comfortable, relaxed and filled to capacity with the finest food in all the Southland.

Timmy was quick to notice a place next to Madeline on the sofa. He quietly tiptoed across the room and sat next to her. They both smiled graciously at each other and faced the speaker. Skeets, who was sitting next to Gibby with his big arm around his friend's shoulder, watched this transition with disgust. He turned to Gibby and said in a whisper, "The only difference between that beautiful bitch and Mary Magdalene is that Maggy repented!" Those were brutal words coming from a boy who inwardly had nefarious designs on Madeline and knew they could never be enacted with mutuality.

"When I finished Temple's Medical School course in 1899, I left Philadelphia for a year at Pittsburgh's General Hospital," said Doctor Gerard, starting his story. "For a youngster coming from the foothills of the Ozarks to the historical city of the Quakers, it was quite a transformation. I found it very difficult to adjust myself to the customs and mannerisms of the staid Easterners. I made some friends in Philadelphia, but they were few and far between. While at Pittsburgh General, I made even less. It was all work and no play for Mrs. Gerard's little man, Frankie." Here he stopped to wink at Mrs. Gerard, who was watching him intently.

"It was a very cold afternoon in late March of 1900 while walking down Forbes Street, in the heart of downtown Pittsburgh, that my experience started. I was in no particular hurry, yet I walked rather briskly due to the extreme cold weather that was very biting. I had my heavy overcoat around my white blouse, because I didn't have time to change, and I knew I was going back on duty at the hospital at four. During internship, afternoons that one is lucky enough to fall heir to are a rarity. Most student doctors hit the hay instead of wandering the streets of a large city looking for trouble.

"Mine came in the form of a very beautiful woman. As I said before, I was walking down Forbes Street taking in the sights of the town with some stress placed on the windows which displayed the latest in styles for spring creations, both masculine and feminine.

"I noticed a very gorgeous creature walk past me in a mink coat. When she passed me, it dawned on my sleepy brain that I met her someplace before, but where? I stopped suddenly and looked around as I'm wont to do, even on the streets of Lacodere, when I can't place someone who has taken the time to greet me in passing.

"Lo, God and behold, this female charmer also stopped to try and figure where she met the passing face half hidden in the collar of an overcoat. Both of us found ourselves standing in the middle of the sidewalk looking back at each other. Normally, this would be very embarrassing had it not proved I took her to a dance at Temple University in my sophomore year of medicine.

"I walked up to her and asked, rather sheepishly, if she were Geraldine Arnold, from Frankford Avenue in Philadelphia. She said she was, working a strange smile on her face. Confirming this to my satisfaction, I asked if she remembered me from Temple, and earlier, from Blytheville, Arkansas.

"She agreed she was as guilty as I for not recognizing a friend immediately and begged forgiveness with reverence and sublime humility. Who was I to dicker in a situation like this?

"Because it was very cold and people were constantly bumping us as we stood in the center of the thoroughfare, I suggested we enjoy a cup of hot tea in the dining room of the very smart Schenley Hotel. In fact, we were right in front of the hotel that is located on Forbes Street. Together, we walked in and located a table in the far corner of the room, where we could sit and talk over a pot of tea and smoke a cigarette or two with some degree of privacy.

"'And what brings you to Pittsburgh?' she said, starting our little conversation off. 'How stupid of me. Of course, you're doing your internship here.'

"'Not to be too much of a copycat, may I ask what brings you to this smoky town?'

"She was hesitant at first, but then cut loose with enough talk to make me wish I had never asked her to delve into her private affairs. She started, and I failed to get a word in edgewise till we were about to depart."

"'You recall back in Philadelphia last year when Jimmy Burke and I announced our engagement and the plans for our marriage at Visitation Church? Well, you also remember, I presume, how mother sent out invitations and took me to New York to fit me out at B. Altman's.'

"Of course, I didn't really know whether she went to B. Altman's or Franklin Simons. She could have gone to Best's for all I knew or cared. I did recall, though, the local papers gave her quite a spread in their society pages. But, I nodded as if I personally assisted her with the selection of her trousseau."

"'Then,' she continued, 'the very day of the wedding, with all preparations made, relatives and friends waiting at the church, Jimmy runs out on me. Mother passed away last month, never getting over the terrible shock and humiliation. I was the laughing stock of my set, and, I guess, all Philadelphia.'

"I asked her, like a damn fool, why she came to Pittsburgh, and she told me in startling revelations, 'I heard yesterday that Jimmy was here in Pittsburgh, and I've come over to see him!' was her quick reply.

"'What do you intend to say to him if you do see him?' I said hesitatingly.

"She said that she'd be willing to forgive and forget the whole matter and start anew if he was of the same mind and character. If he refused, well, she couldn't be held responsible for what she'd do. 'After all,' she said, 'he killed my mother by his conduct, and . . .' here she broke into a sobbing spell. 'He's slowly killing me.'

"I didn't know what to say. I tried to comfort her by patting her on the arm. No matter what I would have said either in defense of this rascal and condemnation of his rotten attitude might be taken in the wrong light. Dealing with women with turbulent psychoses isn't always a pleasant pastime. Treating a woman with a definite neurosis isn't as simple as putting a bandage on a scratch."

Doctor Gerard drew a laugh from his tense audience. It was just a breather, though, for things to follow.

"I told this luciferous blonde that caught the eye of many a man in the dining room. I should be off to the hospital." She was gracious enough to forgive my anxious retreat and inquired what department I was assigned to at the "butcher factory". When I told her I was a flunky in the psychiatric ward, she laughed, the first decent and human emission of this nature she enjoyed in our conversation.

"I urged her not to do anything rash irrespective of what the outcome of meeting Jimmy might give vent to." She smiled in response to this tidbit of friendly advice.

The air was brisk as I walked along the sidewalk and continued up to the hospital. I had to check on Mrs. Falconi by four-thirty. She was locked in a private room on the seventh floor under strict observation. The day before, she had slashed the wrists of her three-year old Maria and took the youngest of her brood of ten into the bathroom, a boy of two months, who siffered from an abscessed condition of the rectal tract, and was gradually working its way into a nice fistular abscess, and bashed his head against the bowl of the toilet, throwing the gory remains in the hamper near the wooden bathtub. Her only explanation for this two-fold slaughter was the shake of her head and the inane excuse, 'They just a wouldn't stopa crying!'

I unlocked the door leading into the ward and walked directly to the private room of Mrs. Falconi. When I walked in, I locked the door behind me and looked around the room in one glance for Mrs. Falconi. To my horror, that one glance revealed a big question mark. Where in the hell was Falconi? I noticed the windows were still shut so she couldn't have disappeared. On second observation—I always do better on the second look, I found her stretched out on the floor underneath the bed, without a stitch of clothing on her big, fat Italian body and prayerfully running her Rosary beads through her dirty fingers.

"Around nine-thirty that night everything seemed quiet in the hospital. The grey, smoky sky of the afternoon played tricks on the poor unfortunates who had to be out on such a stormy night. In the afternoon, although it was bitter cold, there was no immediate evidence that a storm of such fierce velocity would brew up to such proportions by nightfall. The windows in the old General Hospital gave a weird rattle as the wind whistled a vehement sound. I was glad I wasn't out on ambulance duty that night.

"I can't remember whether it was eleven or ten-thirty when old Mrs. Hodgekiss, the night superintendent of nurses, came to my room. I remember I was reading Dickens instead of *Applied Surgery* as I sat in my chair with my legs stretched out on the iron bed.

"You're wanted on the phone, Doctor Gerard, and I think its an emergency of some kind or other!' she shouted, and without giving me a chance to inform the ugly witch that I was not on outside duty that night.

"I went to the phone cursing Doctor Steve Twehy for his negligence in handling the night stuff.

"The party, on the other end of the line was very excited. He asked if I was Doctor Gerard and a friend of Miss Arnold. When I said I was Gerard and knew Miss Arnold, he told me I was to come to the William Penn Hotel as soon as possible. 'Miss Arnold need you, Doctor Gerard—she needs you at once!'"

Without bothering to change into civilian attire, I threw my overcoat over my arm and ran down the seven floors to the basement entrance. I asked Rafferty, the driver of the ambulance, a horse-drawn affair, to take me to the William Penn. The poor fellow thought it was a hospital case and obliged without a murmur.

"As I ran through the swinging doors of the town's main hostelry, the largest and most elegant I had ever been in to date, I was met by the night clerk, a young man of questionable looks and character, who directed me to the second floor. Breathlessly, he jabbered something about Miss Arnold acting very queer and repeatedly calling the desk for liquor, cigarettes, and finally me. Up the marble staircase I ran, passing the mezzanine floor and ascending to the infamous second. I found the room number. I remember quite clearly now, it was 249. I knocked on the door gently. No answer! I knocked again, this time more pronounced!

"'Come in, please!' was the feminine command.

"That, ladies and gentlemen, I should never have done," said Doctor Gerard.

"Boy, were you ever stupid, huh, Dad?" said Gibby, excitedly.

"Yes, son, I was about in your class in that respect," said the doctor sarcastically.

"Anyway, I walked into the spacious suite and beheld before my startled eyes this beautiful blonde in a state of tumult and confusion. Her hair was disheveled and the transparent, black, lace negligee was loosely drawn about her body. She looked frightfully uneasy, and her face lacked the beauty of the afternoon's meeting. It wasn't makeup she needed, it was rest and peace of mind.

"I said to her, 'My God, what on earth is the matter with you? You look like you've seen a ghost.'

"'Worse than that, doctor,' she said burying her head in her hands. 'I've seen Jimmy!'

"For the first time in my life, I felt lost for words. I did manage to work out a very weak question which only proved I was deeper in the mire of my own cesspool.

"'Well, when you saw Jimmy, what did he say?' I asked her, rather sheepishly.

"'He gave me two hours to get out of Pittsburgh!'"

At this juncture, the guests in the living room let out a grand, "Oh, my God! While some, with even more devotion made the Sign of the Cross. But, Doctor Gerard never let down the tenseness he created and continued his story just as he knew the people in that cozy living room would expect him to do.

"I gasped for breath before fumbling out the next question. 'What did you say to Jimmy when he told you to exit?'" I said, biting my lip.

"'Look under the bed, and you'll see my answer,' she said coldly.

"I walked over and bent down to lift up the spread that covered the double bed, and found to my amazement the body of Jimmy Burke, his head saturated with blood, and lying in a pool of the solidified substance."

Again the ladies in the gathering let out an unrestrained scream as the doctor proceeded to demonstrate by looking under one of the sofas in the living room.

"I dropped the spread as if it were something red hot. Turning to the killer, I asked her, excitedly, 'For Christ's sake, and I don't mean irreverence how in the hell did you ever come to let yourself do this horrible thing?'"

"'Jimmy drove me to it!', she said, walking over to their chair to pick up my hat. 'I'm getting the hell out of this place and quick!'

"I started for the door and stopped suddenly when I heard the tone of her command.

"'You move out of this room, and I'll make it two,' was her order, with a small automatic to give her words that necessary assurance."

"Why, you're mad! You wouldn't dare shoot me for no apparent reason.' Then like a flash, I thought of Mrs. Falconi. She didn't bother about reasons when she polished off her two little children.

The only difference here was the fact that Miss Arnold wasn't fat, nor ugly, nor an Italian.

"I wouldn't suggest pressing a trial in that light, doctor!' was her cool and collected answer.

"I chose to agree with her, knowing full well if I didn't, I'd be equally as stiff as my confrere under the bed. At that time, I love life for all it was worth."

"'What do you propose I do about all this?' I said, swinging my arm in a grand sweep that ended very dramatically in the direction of the guest under the bed."

"'You, doctor, will be most useful in assisting me with the disposal of Mr. Burke's remains!', she said curtly, still pointing the gun at me, and with no degree of care.

"'Goddamit, I didn't have anything to do with this. Why drag me into your filthy mess?' I asked her."

"'Please, doctor, let's refrain from the abusive language and remove this body immediately!' was her fiendish response to my question.

"'Listen to whom? What objects to abusive language!' I said. "How am I supposed to assist you?'" I asked, trying to act the part of an uninterested accomplice.

"'In a very simple way, doctor. I purposely engaged this suite of rooms on the second floor and near the delivery entrance that leads to the alley. Would you suggest that I draw you a further picture?' she said, cunningly.

"If some here recall, back in 1900, the flood waters of the Ohio River did considerable damage to property in Pittsburgh and, in spots left deep canals, even in the heart of the city. It was just such a canal that ran in the rear of the William Penn Hotel. It was this murderer's intention to haul, or better yet, have me haul, the body out of the room, down the corridor and let it slide down the temporary delivery chute, and, finally, into the swollen water of the Ohio River that was temporarily lodged in the back of the hotel.

"I was to do the heavy work while she directed the nefarious deed with the aid of her Cold automatic—handbag size, as a teacher's pointer."

"I had difficulty lifting Jimmy from under the bed. He seemed to weigh close to twice his normal weight. She gave no assistance of a physical nature. After some little expended effort, I managed to get him out of the center of the room. He was in a ghastly condition with his eye wide open and watching every move I made. She opened the door, looked up and down the hall, and ordered me to bring him through to the corridor. On up the long hallway, past the fire exit, around another bend in the gloomy corridor and finally to the delivery chute."

"'Now, Doctor Gerard, pick him up and let him slide into the water below!' she said.

"'God, but you're sinister!'" I said, trying to catch my breath after the long haul.

"I lifted his legs onto the chute and then his torso. His back lay on the chute, but one arm hung over the side in obstinate resistance, preventing his body from freely sliding. It was she who unloosed the arm as I bent over to see the body swiftly skid its way to the water. While watching his departure, a great gust of water flew up in my face as he landed in the canal below . . . I'm so happy it did, because I work up then, and that good-looking Doctor Steve Twehy was over my bed with the rest of the glass of water, smiling in his usual carefree way. And to this day, friends, I must admit it was the most terrifying dream I ever had."

Doctor Gerard received the usual amount of "boos" and sighs after his story. He was used to them. But, he wasn't ready for his own son's question that left him without words. It proved to all present, though, that Gibby had a very alert mind and capable of finding the slightest error in a given set of facts.

"Dad," said Gibby, winking to his mother across the room, "how is it you were able to walk around so freely on the streets of Pittsburgh if there was high water everyplace.? And, when you were in the hotel room . . ." here he broke off into a hugh laugh, but didn't finish his second question. His mother gave him the old high sign lest the doctor show a little homelike wrath.

The question threw the eminent doctor for a loss for explanatory words. But, he good-naturedly laughed along with the others who failed to detect the slightest fallacy in his story.

Skeets stood up and demanded the floor. He wanted to tell a dream story of his own concoction. He sat down with a crimson face when he heard Buddy say in a loud voice, "you're dreams don't bear repetition in mixed company, Skeets, if they're anything like the one you told us about a few days ago in the gym.'

Timmy took the floor and asked the happy crowd if they'd enjoy listening to the music of their talented fellow-guest, Madeline Turrel. Naturally, no one dared voice their contrary opinion against that of the honorable host. They all knew of the accomplishments of Madeline Turrel and were anxious to have her contribute to the festive occasion.

She walked to the piano with a sense of ease and sureness. She didn't bother to ask for requests, but sat down as she was want to do on several occasion at recitals and started to play. She had a command of music that came from the very soul of her being. On three different public appearances in the course of the past year, she won gold medals for playing symphonies. There was the medal for Beethoven's Fourth Symphony, another for Brahams' Third, and the final award for her rendition of the difficult Scotch Symphony by Mendelssohn. This evening she would stay clear of the above-mentioned and play excerpts from Liszt, Tschaikowsky and the ever-applauded Johann Strauss. She opened her little concert with the Symphony in D Minor by the celebrated Cesar Franck. It was welcomed by heartfelt applause. Then came a short selection from the pen of Vincent D'Indy. Nobody seemed to recognize this, but rendered the same graceful hand. From D'Indy, she gracefully moved into the Fifth Symphony in E Minor, a Tschaikowsky classic. She played several Strauss waltzes and ended, for a brief spell, her magnificent repertoire with a beautiful arrangement of the Faust Symphony by Liszt.

She was playing for well over an hour before she took this brief respite. It didn't require much coaching to get Madeline to return to the piano. She loved to play because she loved music. It was her very life, and her soul was wrapped in the deep, mellow notes she played so well.

The second and last part of her concert were requests from the audience. Some wanted dreamy Southern folk songs. Others wanted Shubert and Mozart selections. They all were rewarded. But Timmy wanted Debussy! When he requested this lovely piece of inspired music, Madeline looked at him with a deep and longing desire in her heart. It was her favorite, too!

The fire in the fireplace was growing old, and the evening of the day was slowly drawing to its close. The many happy guests of the O'Sheas' were tired from laughing and singing. They sat in silence and contemplative meditation as Madeline played 'Clair de Lune.' Some present couldn't help noticing the expression on Timmy's face as he watched the girl at the piano! It was an expression of hungry yearning that yielded an insight into his innermost thoughts, thoughts that would catapult into strong desires because of the inspirational sweetness this haunting piece produced in the flesh of two young children.

Her soft white hands moved over the keyboard with true and professional rhythm. The lights seemed low and the hearts of all present in a receptive mood for the inoculation of a love song unsung. Two in that room were together in their thoughts. Madeline played 'de Lune' as she never played before. She was grateful for the chance to make Timmy closer to her own cherished dreams. Love would surely flow through the realms of music if by no other means. Yes, Timmy's heart needed no melting as he watched Madeline play so magnificently. His burning desires seemed to pound heavily and forcibly against the portals of his heart, producing his Irish blood to labor through his youthful, usufruct in the channels of united love.

Liz watched this whole scene, too. She wasn't jealous, she was hurt because she feared someone else might be hurt that meant everything in the world to her.

It was difficult for all to leave such a comfortable home with its atmosphere of devotion to one another. But the hour was late and no bribe could keep them beyond nine o'clock. They had a Christmas long to linger in their hearts.

CHAPTER THIRTEEN

The New Year was ushered in at the home of Gibby Gerard. That is, as far as the younger set were concerned. The living room was converted into a large ballroom with many youngsters dancing to the waltzes and fox trots provided by the phonograph. Timmy danced every number with Madeline, while Gibby saw to it that Buddy's sister was well taken care of throughout the evening. Skeets Malone watched Timmy and Madeline with jealous eyes and never heard a word Mary Ann Marlowe whispered in his ear. He tried in vain to pawn her off on Tommy Collier and Feeley, but they were too fast for the comedian.

The year 1926 was the most eventful in Timmy's collection thus far spent. He made rapid strides on the basketball floor despite losing the championship to a small school in Mississippi. He proved the brighter light in his studies with Gibby running a close second. He paid greater attention to the matter of fostering his vocation. Trips to see Father Joseph became more regular because he began to realize he was advancing in stature as well as wisdom. Liz was to leave in late January for an extended vacation to regain her health. Timmy would rule the house on Fontaine Street, and the greatest error a youth can make would be committed there through lack of corporal vigilance and moral restraint.

Liz was two weeks packing and preparing for her mysterious vacation. The mystery lay in the fact that nobody knew just where she intended to go, not even herself! She thought about a trip to Cavan in the outskirts of Dublin. She gave some consideration to Hot Springs, Arkansas, because it was closer to home. She had booklet material on Miami Beach, Florida. Hollywood, California loomed once or twice in her mind. On the day of departure, she told Timmy she would seek rest in Providence, Rhode Island. There she had a distant cousin who lived on Gano Street—the better side of Gano Street, and she hadn't seen this cousin in ever so long a time. Hence, the trip to Providence served as a two-fold purpose. The change of tempo and her own good health were of prime importance to her at this delicate period of her life.

On the 28th of January, Liz kissed her Timmy goodbye with tear-filled eyes and mental remorse. She gave the self-same instructions any good mother might give her son. But, Liz left for the city of historical culture with some doubt in her mind as to just what Timmy would or would not do if the occasion arose. She promised to pray for him every day and asked him to do likewise for her. In late April, though, Liz must have relaxed in her promise.

Directly North of Lacodere lays the Windy City. Of course, one must go some distance Northward before actually arriving in the city of Chicago. During this period of Timmy's life, hell seemed to open its gates and permit some of its worst inmates to wander into the very heart of this great metropolis. One, Al Capone, arch czar of criminal tactics, ruled a kingdom composed of whores, pimps, perverts and uncouth madams. Lieutenants in various sections of Chicago paid homage to their commander and were rewarded by estates that comprised lucrative stipends from illegal booze, dope and general gambling resorts. All America underwent the sting of this "wop's" force. Girls were transported from far and near to satisfy the trade and demands of the curved mouthed madams who entertained the lower element of Chicago.

The world at large was moving swiftly in the direction of moral degradation. At least, Father Quinn thought so and constantly preached to the Senior Class to refrain from reading secular newspapers that brought these facts into prominence. Despite all his sermonizing, the boys talked of Chicago and Al Capone. Bank robberies were followed with the same intensity as a rape case in Alabama. The usual grouping took place behind closed doors where students, young and old, could discuss the current wave of debauchery. Timmy, Skeets, Buddy, Joey, and Gibby were not excluded members in these sessions, irrespective of their association with the Sodality of the Blessed Virgin Mary to foster cleanliness of soul and body. There were office holders in the Sodality, but they also held office in the lavatory in the basement whenever opportunity availed itself. They read the papers and commented on the events that took place in the Northern cities.

Intersectional basketball games were in vogue more out of necessity than pleasure. The boys of Lacodere found little competition in the neighboring towns, so were forced to look elsewhere for stronger opposition. Trips to Clarksdale, Mississippi and Monroe, Louisiana and Memphis, Tennessee, and as far South as New Orleans were not uncommon. In those days, a tournament was played to determine the sectional champions.

The school that managed to come forth victorious played in some specified locality. This memorable year, the finals were played in the Delta town of Clarksdale, on the banks of the Mississippi.

Clarksdale High boasted one of the fastest quintets in the Southern Association. They played every school in the section in superior style. Vincent Brocato, who laughingly claimed kinship to the late Chris Columbus, of navigation fame, was the dynamo that sparked Clarksdale to consistent wins, later proved one of the finest attorneys in the State of Mississippi and judge of the City Court in his home town. Brocato had tricks for every game that baffled the enemy to such an extent, they would have preferred to call it quits after the first quarter. He drove Skeets nearly mad with his deception and finally saw to it that three of the stars from Lacodere were ruled out on personal fouls. Lacodere succumbed to their might along with the other teams. Father Pete knew when he sent his five on the floor, the outcome would be slaughterous. The final score favored the Delta boys by a margin of at least thirty-eight points. Some local businessmen thought of the idea of sending their team to Madison Square Garden. They were fully justified in their expressed faith that an exhibition tussle with one of the New York City teams would pay off in local prestige as well as render a financial return. Subscription on this proposal fell through and the idea was abandoned to the disgust of Brocato and his aggregation.

The tournament between the two runners-up, Clarksdale High and Lacodere Prep was played early in March. Prior to this fateful game, Lacodere sent twelve boys to Memphis to engage in a free-for-all on the maple floor of Christian Brothers College. This school, commonly referred to as C.B.C., despite the fact it was only a high school, had boys attending and playing on their team who rightfully belonged in the confines of the reformatory. Yet, the good Brothers, who work diligently in the vineyard of salvation, refused to relax in any degree the measure of discipline they felt was so important to good Christians and noble-minded citizens. The Brothers certainly didn't make the boys bad. They were such from lack of parental correction and jurisdiction. They did all they could with the boys to make them follow in the footsteps of Christ in the short time allotted in the course of a school day.

The game in Memphis in late February resulted in a 58-37 victory for Timmy and his teammates. After the game, they were instructed to return directly to their homes in Lacodere. Skeets and a few more decided to forget this insult and remain over Friday night in the big town. Skeets heard from some of the defeated members of the C.B.C. team that liquor could be purchased in a shack down near South Fifth for a fair "chunk of clink." He conveyed this information on to Timmy, Buddy, Joey and Gibby, who admitted that it wouldn't be too bad an idea to see what the stuff tasted like. In reality, liquor in those days looked very much like it tasted. It had an odor similar to a public toilet in downtown Birmingham, and when it finally went down the throat, you were sure it came from the bottom of the Mississippi River and boiled to a fair-thee-well.

The boys pitched in and rented a room in the Claridge Hotel, too close, thought Skeets, to the city's local "piki." After putting their bags in their room and indulging in a hurried shower, they met in the lobby to plan their course of action and the evening's entertainment. Skeets suggested that they all go out and locate the town's prettiest and most respected prostitutes and proceed in the direction of getting them, "goggle-eyed," and ultimately, submissive, on some of "Uncle Tom's Favorite Belly wash." The boys knew Skeets all too well. He'd suggest most anything to shock Timmy and Gibby, but this time, he gave every appearance of being sincere. The boys laughed as they got into the cab and ordered the surprised cabby to take them to South Fifth Street, the three hundred block!

Gibby was surprised that a whole bottle of spirits could be purchased for a dollar and sixty cents. His father paid over six dollars for his liquor, a lot less in quantity, too. But, Gibby was relieved to know, when the man with the heavy beard assured him, that the stuff had to be good because it was imported all the way in from West Memphis, Arkansas, a distance of about six miles.

The boys took their bottle and went out to the waiting cab and ordered the driver to head in the direction of Adams Street and the Claridge Hotel. All the way back to the hotel, Skeets kept insisting they should do a little "cat-hunting," a term unbeknown in his grandfather's day. With the exception of Joey Roys, his appeal met with frustration.

Back in Claridge Hotel, the boys ordered a ginger ale mix, glasses and ice. Each took a substantial "slug" mixed with ginger ale and very little ice. Skeets was determined to get Timmy in a condition to make the rounds with him that night. Gibby took his drink like a veteran of old and went out of the picture like a novice. He sat on the side of the bed talking rapidly and without much concern whether anyone agreed with him or not.

Within a very short time, he began to turn a dull greyish color. He rushed into the bathroom, a very sick young boy. Timmy called the desk and was able to secure another room on the same floor for his sick friend. While talking to the clerk, he took his second drink without the ill fate of his friend who was forced to call it a night and retire. The Stag party proceeded merrily along its path.

Joey and Buddy introduced songs they didn't learn in choir practice at Saint Mary's Church. Soon the quartet finished the bottle and were ready for most any eventuality. Skeets wanted to visit Beale Street. It seems everyone wants to visit Beale Street sometimes long before they realize Memphis has other streets of greater show and beauty. Timmy and Buddy staggered into Gibby's room to inform him of their plans only to find the lad with one shoe off, his shirt tossed on the floor, and the rest of his unconscious body restfully sleeping on the bed.

The boys wandered down Main Street looking into the windows of Gerber's and Goldsmith's, but failed to make out anything that even resembled anything. They were bewildered and forsaken. At least, the liquid in their blood streams made them feel they were outcasts of society. On down Main Street they staggered till they arrived at Beale Avenue. Skeets asked a man on the corner in front of a pawn shop if he knew where Lauderdale was. That was like asking the colored boy where "heben" was located. He pointed in an easterly direction, and the boys walked down Beale brushing shoulders with the black folks till they came to the corner of Lauderdale. Skeets knew what he wanted, but his partners seemed in a physical and mental fog or dilemma. He pulled out a piece of paper and went over to the street light to determine the address he had written earlier that afternoon. All it had on it was, "The Big House off Beale and Lauderdale." They walked up Lauderdale and back down the other side. About two or three houses from the corner, they heard a voice calling. Timmy and Buddy stopped short. Skeets asked in a loud voice if Emilia lived there, and when he received his answer, he took Timmy by the arm, and they both went up the stairs. The "lady" said she didn't have any Emilias there, but there were plenty of pretty names just the same. As if the name characterizes the quality!

None of the four boys were sober or could operate without the help of the other boy at his side. They stood on the porch and noticed the little red light in the inner hall that illuminated the porch. A large, fat-faced woman came to the door and greeted the boys with a forced smile. She asked them what color they preferred, and the boys stood on the porch in dumbfounded amazement to learn that one made selections of this nature by color. Skeets made the first signs of possessing a tongue and asked if the "ladies" were busy and if they'd mind coming up to their hotel with them. The hard-faced and gaudy-clad woman laughed at the innocent proposition and told the boys that the girls never left their rooms because they were decent whores! The very mention of this name impregnated a hurt through Timmy's veil of drunkenness.

Up the stairs the four adventurers walked, led by the fat, old matron with a long red dress that had stains of black here and there and a few small holes made by sparks from cigarettes. She introduced them to several women who were lounging around on sofas and large easy-chairs. They were, for the most part, country girls "citified." There were blondes and red-headed girls, young ones and those mature in their peculiar sales talents, rotund and frail girls. Timmy though he saw a thousand girls in the incense-filled room. In reality, there were only eight harlots and their godmother with the red dress, ready and willing to help these youngsters spend their developed fecundity.

The boys were hesitant in their stupor to make the initial advances. They sat around like bashful boys waiting to see who would suggest the game of "post-office" at the birthday party. But, this wasn't exactly "post-office" as far as the "ladies" were concerned. It was a cut and dried business proposition that only admitted of an affirmative or negative response that would ultimately lead to an invitation to come in or get out. To the boys, they were the Eight Wonders of the World, and the other seven could easily be by-passed for an insight into something that was neither novel in origin nor edifying to behold.

The girls looked on them as their younger brothers and awaited the signal from their madame to charge or retreat. Some felt it a useless enterprise to advance, others, hardened to the practice of their employment, a hopeless one. If the libidinous pictures on the wall, and the lecherous tapestry hanging in visible evidence, coupled with eight semi-nude, totally unchaste women within elbow's reach, couldn't lure four virile and handsome boys into thoughts of sensuality, then it was sheer folly to remain in the same room to have their wares insulted by complete and total abstemious youths.

The madame instructed the four most potential inmates of her den of ill-fame to investigate the merits of her newly acquired guests, and ordered the others to resume their vigil for future prospects in another section of the brothel. She closed the door of the parlor and dimmed the lights to an immodest low, only permitting a faint ray of blue light to shine forth on eight figures closely bound in human oneness.

The tricks of the profession seemed ever to fall short of their desired end. The reception of a big, fat blonde on the lap of Buddy Feeley caused him pained uneasiness, and he pinched her unmercifully until she slapped his face and joined her sisters in the far end of the house. Timmy, mindful now of nothing, fell fast asleep in the stuffy room, and unaware that his head was being curled through the fingers of Memphis' most notorious prostitute, a woman who threw forth her chest in pride and boasted of her accomplishments with Machinegun Kelly, Babyface Nelson, and the arch crime-master, Al Capone. Timmy was dead to all devices of her artifice; she knew it; he never became aware of how she knew it! She left the high point man of Lacodere's basketball quintet to sleep in self imposed loneliness. Buddy watched from his station in the far end of the room until the woman left her temporary charge. He walked over to awaken him. It was of no avail. He adjusted Timmy's clothing where the whore had worked without reward and helped him to his feet. He was a mass of dead weight on Buddy's shoulder. The madam came quickly to render assistance to the door. It wasn't a good policy to permit guests to exit without at least the usual cordiality and a "hurry back" invitation. Skeets, who felt his few drinks in a different manner, joined forces with Joey and left for the darker room beyond the parlor.

It was nearly an hour before Buddy was able to bring Timmy around to normalcy. Up and down the street they walked. It was difficult to manage Timmy because he failed to give any signs of revival. Only when Skeets and Joey arrived on the scene did they successfully manipulate in the direction of the hotel and an uneasy night of sleep.

Saturday night five boys lined up in the last row of Saint Mary's Church to tell their story to His representative. They were not just a little backward and ashamed to walk into the confessional and make a thorough report. It wasn't the easiest task in the world to enter the dark curtain-veiled box and talk to Father Joseph. No need to conceal your voice from one who knew you from the time you screamed at the baptismal font and watched you grow from the year one. But, Father Joseph knew boys, knew them better than the Jesuits thought they knew them. He would understand and absolve them in the name of Christ after taking patient moments to talk to them, leading with them to forsake illicit thoughts and desires and replace them with those of their dear Lord's Passion and death. He would create sorrow in their boyish hearts by his kindly words of admonition. He could call each of them by their first name, but he hid his face in his handkerchief letting them believe their identity was a deep mystery. They would leave the confessional and slowly walk to the front of the church and beg forgiveness and say the penance. Even Gibby, whose sorrow and contribution was made in that bathroom in the Claridge Hotel the night before would feel a tear roll down his cheek in admission of his culpability. Timmy, next released, could hardly contain himself. He heard the whole story from Buddy en route home the next morning. He retold it to Father Joseph, several times breaking down and telling his confessor that he'd never do such an evil thing again. Skeets came forth still acting the clown. He pretended to wipe his brow of the imaginary perspiration and walked down to Buddy telling him something bout his goose being well cooked. Buddy, like Timmy, wanted to become a priest. He felt so unworthy of so high an office, but through the kindness of Father Quinn's talks, he made up his mind to be a Jesuit. Like his two friends at the rail, he poured forth his heart to the priest. By this time, Father Joseph must have thought his whole congregation patronized Memphis' houses of ill-repute, and indulged in drinking "imported" whiskey in fashionable hotels. Each of the four boys named the house on Lauderdale Street and all five confessed drinking in the Claridge Hotel. None failed to admit they were sorry and would try very hard to avoid the occasions of such incidents in the future; even Skeets, and this time, he didn't have his fingers crossed.

The boys left Saint Mary's Church feeling much better, if not complete relief. Even Gibby was happy after his ordeal of the night before. However, none wanted to take in the relaxation Harold Lloyd offered at the local cinema house. All parted a few blocks from the church. Timmy went to see his little family of Duseaunault children. There he was received as if it were Christmas Day again. Where else could he find innocence in such explicit profession? When 'ere he felt the pangs of loneliness creep over him he would walk to the humble little house to see the seven children and hold Robert on his lap. Always he felt relieved of that pressure that bears down on the soul of an adolescent. Some his age found that escapement in the darkness of the theatre where they would watch others laugh and be entertained by the antics of the artists of the screen. Some took to books or games or music, but Timmy had to have human companionship. He felt one day he would make a fine community man in a Religious Order where recreations were taken in common and all shared each others' joys and sorrows. Or, at least, that's what most Rules or Constitutions are supposed to aim at!

Each day the postman brought word from Liz. Words of advice and shavings of news about herself and those she met. She remained five weeks in Providence, Rhode Island, on Upper Cano Street. She and her cousin frequently went to the grand city of Boston to shop or just visit. The snow and frosty trees appealed to her sense of the beautiful. She told Timmy she would bring him a nice present from either New York City or Miami Beach. Her doctor in Providence told her she needed the sunshine and warmth of the ocean breeze before returning to Lacodere. In March and April, she remained in Miami and wrote glowing accounts of the hotels and the friends she made in the famous resort city. She also told of the terrible havoc

that was wrought through the hurricane of the previous year. But, her quarters were most comfortable, and she never registered a complaint. On Easter Sunday, the first Sunday in April, she visited the ancient city of Saint Augustine and attended High Mass at the Cathedral. Her letter was a source of inspiration to the boy who one day aspired to offer the Holy Sacrifice.

It was close to the middle of April when Lacodere Preparatory School awarded their annual medals. They chose the 15th because the Provincial kindly consented to come up from New Orleans on that day for the occasion. Timmy was called to receive the coveted Chain of Lacodere, a solid gold chain with a gold medal of Saint Ignatius of Loyola on one side and the inscription:

TIMMY PATRICK O'SHEA
FOR EXCELLENCE IN LATIN AND GREEK
1925-26

on the opposite side. Timmy received a thunderous applause. Gibby was rewarded for his knowledge of Religion and for a theme written on the subject: "The Eucharistic Congress, Chicago, Illinois, 1926." Skeets was as surprised as everybody else in the auditorium when his name was called for excellence in science. He really was an exceptional student in Chemistry and showed signs of pronounced knowledge in Physics. On his way up to the stage, he had to cut loose with his usual line of comedy, "I suppose now," he said laughing loudly, "the damn Jesuits will expect me to join their outfit and become a priest like old featherhead Quinn."

There was no danger of the Jesuits inviting Skeets into their militant ranks. As a general rule, it isn't the Jesuits who make the

first approach in that regard. It's the student who begs admission. In Skeets' case, he has no fear to entertain concern. Every "Jebby" on the faculty would throw him the black ball.

Gibby Gerard was called to the stage to receive the medal for mathematics. Finally, Timmy O'Shea was called for his second award. It was a difficult task for the Jesuits to select the winner for the conduct and application medal, but the votes seemed to favor Timmy. As in all things, Timmy would have preferred to see his friend take a third medal rather than even appear to vie for the tie score. Never once did Gibby feel his friend wasn't worthy of the preference and was always first to offer his sincere congratulations whether it be on the athletic field or in the classroom.

Chapter Fourteen

Madeline told Timmy on graduation night, April 28th, her own private graduation, that she was leaving for New Orleans to continue to study her music. Timmy, in turn, told her that he was leaving in the Summer for Cassino Abbey to study for the priesthood. If Madeline froze within, she never showed it exteriorly. When Timmy made this confession, something snapped in her heart. She never really wanted Timmy before this admission. Now, she had to have his love. Her beliefs mattered little, the mode of her conduct less. She might have known Timmy was destined for the Church. She could easily have won Skeets by a different line of approach. There was that unexplainable something psychologists fail to cope with in their analyzation that urged Madeline to want something she knew was never meant for her. All would agree Timmy had charm, kindness, and a wholesome character. Other girls of less beauty and talent tried with their own meager instruments and devices to win his favor. He was generous and kind to all of them. But, they knew they lost the race before it started. However, Madeline was determined and refused to give up. Somewhere, someplace, he'd weaken. He was still only Timmy O'Shea, boy of sixteen.

Madeline was there the night Timmy was awarded the gold chain and medal. It was the most beautiful chain anyone had ever seen. It was passed around to all his friends, and that included the whole auditorium. Madeline put it around her neck and asked Timmy how it looked on her. He told her it fitted her graceful neck with the regality of a queen. She handed it back to him, and he thrust it in his pocket with unconcern.

The night Madeline graduated, there was no pomp or show. She received her certificate in private, and all was over within a few short minutes. Father Joseph congratulated her and wished her much success in her musical life of the future. Somehow he made a strange little prediction that failed to register at the time of its utterance. He didn't know himself why he ever said it to her. "Madeline," Father Joseph said, holding her firm, white hand, "never go near the water, it'll be your fate."

"What on earth do you mean by that, Father Joseph?" she said, laughing with a queer expression on her face.

"My dear," he said, "I can't for the life of me understand why I said that to you just now, unless, perhaps, it was because I once knew a very beautiful and talented girl, about your age, back in Germany, who met her untimely end off the side of a fishing wharf. But let's not worry about that. Forgive me for saying such a thing, won't you?"

The matter was forgotten, and Timmy asked if he might walk her home. She consented and quickly drew him close to her. They started out as any young couple, filled with a burning desire to stay young and always happy, who might choose to walk homeward in the cool April evening. Near her home and in the darkness of the shadows of the tall trees, he stopped suddenly, and with both hands drew her close to his chest. His head bent low as hers came up to meet his lips. He held her long, and neither wanted to quit the tight embrace. He whispered softly in her ear that he loved her with all his heart. Nobody else would ever find the same place she now held. Yes, he promised many things in his ecstasy of love. Too many things never to be fulfilled. Too many things that would reap the harvest of heartaches rather than joy for two young people.

"You like my chain, and I want you to have it and wear it always," he said, putting it around her neck. "It will bind us closer together, and if I ever receive it back, I'll understand without a multitude of explanations necessary."

She held the medal in her hand and then kissed it passionately. Before they parted that night, Timmy told Madeline again and again how much he loved her. He had never been so expressive in all his life.

"Liz will be home soon, Madeline. Will you come to the house for supper this week, and we'll spend an evening together, and you can play for me—just for me?" he said.

"How could I refuse such an offer, Timmy. Let's make it tomorrow night. I'll be over at eight. Okay?" she asked, running her hand over his smooth face.

"Tomorrow night it is, honey," said Timmy, kissing her lips and cheek before saying goodnight.

He ran all the way home and tossed the empty award box in the bush near old Sturgini's house. He knew the old Italian would find it and be around in the morning to try and sell it to him. When he came to the front door, he let out a whistle that could be heard five blocks away. He wanted to make sure Silba was up and ready for all he had to tell her. She came running in her bare feet with the old house dress loosely covering her body.

"Prepare the best dinner you've ever tackled, Silba. Madeline is our guest for dinner tomorrow night. And we can use some of that fancy wine in the basement, too. And don't come into the living room all evening like you usually do. We want to be alone, and, anyway, Madeline is going to play on the piano!" he said in rapid fire dictation.

"Yes, sa, Masta Timmy," she said laughing. "I'll be the real thing, won't it?"

It was Thursday morning, April 29th, and a big day in the life of the Seniors at Lacodere. In most schools, close to the end of the school term, the graduating class take it upon themselves to sneak away from the routine of Virgil, Solid Geometry, and Physics. They group together and steal away for a picnic or a day in the city. The Lacodere boys planned weeks in advance for their great day, and when it arrived, left the cares of the classroom for the freedom of Lake Tahoo and the summer cottage of the O'Sheas. Timmy had three boats and a little dock that could be utilized for moorage as well as diving. Poor Silba had worked incessantly to ready the cottage for their arrival. Jordan saw that the boats were fit for fishing and cleaned the cottage to its usual luster. Each boy provided enough food for three so as there'd be no shortage of vital intake material. Silba couldn't be on hand to serve because of her instructions for the evening dinner party.

Fifteen boys can create considerable noise. There were no restrictions placed on them. They had the complete run of the place, and because they knew they were alone on the lake, acted accordingly. They might have shocked their parents had they seen their sons running along the lake front void of clothing. But, they were boys all the way through. Some took to the raft in the center of the lake to sun their bodies, others piled in the boat for a cruise around the lake to admire the beautiful little white and blue cottages in a setting of springtime loveliness. Still others enjoyed the cool, clear water on their bodies as the sun beat down on their heads and shoulders. Everywhere, voices of joyous youngsters mingled with the Song of Spring in a happy symphonic arrangement of gladness. This would be the last big get together for the Senior Class. The last real chance to be boys before assuming the duties of manhood.

All afternoon, they played and sang and ate the food prepared for a party of at least forty-five. Nature couldn't have been more gracious and generous on that April 29th. Every place the eye traveled, it drank in the beauty of gorgeous flowers, emerald green leaves, and a golden sun shining brightly in the heavens. After an unceremonious luncheon, some took to a meadow a few yards from the cottage to bask in the sunshine and dream as only boys can dream, dreams that refused to admit science and mathematics and languages. The more industrious helped Timmy clear away the refuge and dregs of the noon pastime. There was no formality imposed. They were all free!

It was difficult to get a scrub ballgame started, but all were anxious to oblige the few who engineered the proposal. This was short-lived, because hot bodies wanted the cool refreshment of the lake. Someone hit the only means of conducting a game into the far woods, and to find the ball would mean precious minutes away from the joys of their outing. The game was abandoned to favor the water.

"What is so rare as a day in June?" could easily be changed to suit a day in late April in this paradise of laughter and happiness. It was all too soon drawing to a close. The boys, tired from relaxation, red as New England lobsters, tramped homeward to decline any offers of supper with dad or mother, or the drilling inquisition of a younger or older sister.

Timmy's evening was to be the most eventful in the history of the boy's life. He was anticipating its results from the time he arose in the early morning till he left his friends in the late afternoon. There was much to be accomplished before eight o'clock that night; a shower to take, a table to supervise, a living room to check, final orders to Silba on serving and making quick exits, and the piano to be dusted. Lots of little things most boys overlook entirely or depend on others to be accomplished. This was an occasion for deep-rooted impressions. He wanted everything to go well, as this would, in all probability, be their final rendezvous together.

Madeline was admitted as the great clock in the hall struck the last note of the melodious chimes denoting the appointed hour. Timmy's face beamed as he helped her off with the light evening jacket. He couldn't help fixing his eyes on her curved shoulders so white and smooth. He removed the bouquet of tiny pin roses he sent along to her earlier in the evening and pinned them on the strap of her dress. Together they walked arm in arm into the living room. He held her arm a little more securely as they descended the three steps leading to the sunken room. Her long, blue gown matched the heavy rugs of royal blue, as they walked so stately across the floor.

Timmy was wearing his graduation outfit as an initiation into adult social spheres. From head to toe, he was sparkling with cleanliness. His hair was immaculately combed to give every evidence of time spent at the mirror. His face was smooth and ruddy from the afternoon's sun bath. The white tuxedo jacket, with its neat maroon boutonniere and collegiate bowtie of the same material, the stiff white linen shirt, the neatly pressed black trousers with a satin band running down the side of each leg, highly polished shoes, all proved most appealing to Madeline as she sat opposite Timmy on the spacious sofa.

His eyes sparkled as he looked longingly into hers. There was desire in every twinkle and design, in every look. She was aware that evening as she sat talking over the day's activities with Timmy, that he didn't dress this well at their other meetings. Even on their first major date, he wasn't as resplendent and handsome as he looked to her tonight. She wanted to go over to the large chair to touch him and feel the pulsation of the blood run through her body. But, the night was yet very youthful, and she would force him to make the gesture to conform with mutual and complete harmony.

Silba rang the bell to announce dinner. Two very happy people walked into a room where the fragrance of flowers permeated the atmosphere. They were too wrapped up in each other's thoughts to be concerned with food and decorative sterling. Timmy had that longing look in his eyes and was unable to fix his attentions on anything save his dinner guest. He noticed the Chain of Locodere around her neck shining in the light from the chandelier. It gave an imposing appearance as the medal moved with every rhythmic motion of her breast. Her heart seemed to beat faster when she would look at Timmy and find his eyes focused on her.

Neither ate much salad or dinner, but continued to talk on and on about New Orleans, baseball and the future. Somehow, Timmy didn't want to discuss his future and the thought of that night ever passing. He wanted perpetual nowness to be forever theirs. Just to be permitted to look at her long black hair falling on her snow white shoulders, to look into those eyes and try and fathom the depths of their meaning, to gaze with content on her face and discern the knowledge of that strange little smile, to be able to hold her tenderly in his arms and feel the closeness of her fragile body against his strong chest, to run his long fingers through her fine, silken hair, and listen to her heart chant a lover's refrain with her lips breathing words of endearment into the recesses of his very soul and body.

They continued their meal in semi-silence. Both hunted for words that would be a source of evasion from a topic they dared not discuss. Both, at other times, seemed versed on topics of mutual appeal, somehow, now, they were at a loss for words. At a loss for words in the realm of music and sports and scholastic subjects that should not be replaced or divorced from the minds of youth to favor a pseudo-sophistication.

It was close to ten o'clock when both retired to the living room. Jordan brought in two small glasses of Benedictine liqueur. Timmy offered one to Madeline assuring her it would assist in the digestion of her supper rather than prompt intoxication, but it was promptly refused with a gesture of thanks. He waved aside his own, and Jordan made his exit to the pantry where he and Silba toasted each other in regal style.

There was a note of uneasiness about Madeline. She couldn't remain seated on the sofa for any length of time. She would get up and walk around pretending to study the paintings on the high walls. Timmy went with her explaining each masterpiece and a note about the painter as if they were particular incidents in his life. At the far end of the room was hanging the celebrated painting by Servanni. Madeline stopped to look with intensity at the two figures in the garden clothed only with the garments of fear and remorse. Each tree and flower and animal was a study in perfection. Timmy noticed at once the attraction and hastened to throw the switch on the side of the picture to afford greater light.

"This is Servanni's Expulsion From Paradise. My father out-talked someone in Cleveland and bought it for my mother. Don't you think the colors are beautiful," he said in hopes this might arrest her obstinacy and agitated intractability.

"I think its wonderful, Timmy, but I'm not attracted so much by the art as I am by the subject it portrays," she said, still gazing at the two figures.

"I've always thought, or been led to believe, at least," said Timmy, smiling, "Adam and his gal friend went and put some bearskins or something around them on the trip out of the garden. This Servanni man has them trucking down the local boulevard without even the proverbial fig leaf to shield them against . . ." Here he stopped to look at Madeline before continuing, ". . . against the rays of the sun, for example, or future stormy weather."

Both laughed heartily. He turned off the light, and they walked to the piano. On the way across the room, Madeline turned to Timmy and asked if he really thought Eve's sin was so horrible and merited such a drastic punishment.

"Far be it from me to argue along those lines, honey," said Timmy, with a determined look in his face. "But I always thought it was a joint sin in which both Adam and Eve were involved up to their necks. We all know, and Father Quinn gave us enough lectures on the subject, that sin is relative to situations and conducive circumstances that prompt individuals to become sidetracked. There are a lot of conditions to be carefully considered before one can substantially designate an act of some specific violation as sinful." Timmy stopped for a moment and looked into Madeline's dreamy eyes, and then continued. "You know as well as I do what constitutes sin. Sin in my estimation isn't nearly as bad or odious as lack of sorrow. If sin is a human weakness that is inherent, I would suppose the scale could return to even balance again by sorrow and contrition as a means of future strength that enables a person to regenerate the soul and make it pleasing in the sight of God."

"That's a very pretty oration, Timmy, and your knowledge of Religion should have merited you the Religion medal as well as this beautiful chain." But, she continued, looking into his youthful face with a note of determination, "when I confess my sins, and they're many, believe me, I haven't any real sorrow for the sins. By that I mean, my sorrow lacks one of the basic ingredients and is definitely in a state of imperfection. Sure, I'm sorry I offended God, but usually I feel in my heart what I'm happy about and for what the good or enjoyment it afforded me personally. I love you very much, Timmy, even though I know I shouldn't love you the way I do. Every time I touch you, I want it to be a lasting sensation. You're supposed to be destined for God and his Church. Is that fair to me? Must I love someone who is dead or tied to conventions? Must I sacrifice my desires that burn so feverishly within me just because you want to hide everything that appeals to me? If I can't have you and your love, well, I don't want anything. Go to Cassino and waste your life away in hypocritical prayer and fasting, but, remember, Timmy, you'll always have known me!"

The last entreaty went over the falls without registering its proper effect.

"I think we're pretty young to be talking so theatrical, Madeline," said Timmy, gulping down his words. "You know I love you more than I can ever tell you. But you know I've always wanted to be a priest, and I don't think I'm entering Cassino because I'm afraid to face life. I like kids and stuff, but I still want to be a priest like Father Joseph."

"But, you're going away without having had any of the real pleasures of life, Timmy. Why don't you wait until you're sure that you want to be a priest?" she said, unable to face him directly.

"Gosh, Madeline, I've had lots of pleasures just living here in Lacodere with Aunt Liz and all the fellows." Then he hesitated as he turned her towards him and said, "and with you, especially, honey."

"Why don't you include Silba and that crippled colored man you have around here, and all the newspaper clippings you have stored away while you were here on the ball field. Oh, Timmy, you're so dumb about certain things. Maybe its best you bury yourself in books and that hideous looking black garb and go to that awful monastery," she said sarcastically.

"I always thought you and I were different, Madeline. What the fellows said about you made me fighting mad. Even when Liz told me not to associate with you, I turned against her. I have always liked you since we were little kids at Our Lady of Lourdes," Timmy said, looking down at the medal against her blue dress.

"I can just about imagine what the fellows told you, and it's true! Do you hear me, it's true, every bit of it. I'll even side with your sweet and charming auntie," she said snarling each word in contempt. "I don't want to be good if it cost the price you're paying. I'm bad and always will be bad! Now, honey," she said, smoothing out his hair and running her soft hands over his ruddy cheeks. "Aren't you going to take me upstairs and show me the rest of the house?"

Timmy was frightened. Never before had such a proposition been placed so bluntly and by such means. He sat on the edge of the piano bench bewildered in the canyon of speechlessness.

"Will you play for me, Madeline, like you played on Christmas Day?" he said bashfully trying to evade her direction.

Madeline didn't answer, but sat down beside him and began to play chords at random. It was as if she was trying to concentrate on something specific. She finally smiled in Timmy's direction and settled on the beautiful piece she played at her graduation ceremonies for the nuns. One could almost feel the beauty of "A Luxembourg Garden" as her nimble fingers dashed in endless delight over the keys. Each note rang deep into the long and quiet living room and danced its merry way throughout the rest of the silent house. Timmy sat beside her watching the movements of her lily white hands and the clicking sound of her short cut nails against the ivories. She looked at him with that twinkle of evil still apparent in her eyes. He felt the sting as if she was mocking him. He suddenly felt the surge of an ecstasy rush through his whole body. He wanted, as he looked at her soft white skin, to betray the ideals of goodness and submit to this self-confessed juvenile concubine. Why shouldn't he tear away the mask she accused him of wearing and seize her in his arms and kiss her passionately? She didn't want his love. She wanted him!

Even as she played, the desire became bolder and bolder. As he watched her change positions on the bench, each time coming closer and closer, he lost all sense of what she was playing; lost all sense of where he was sitting. His starched collar became a source of disturbance and the heat of the afternoon's sun bath began to bring forth beads of water to his forehead. He knew a transformation was taking place within and would soon disclose itself from without.

Earlier in the evening, he knew calmness, but now it was close to midnight.

Madeline must have sensed this inward struggle and took advantage of her trump card. She reached out and turned the switch that threw the room into complete ebony. Timmy thought it was romantic to permit only the rays of the piano lamp to show forth until he felt the darkness creep over him. Softly and sweetly she played their piece. The enchanting strains of "Clair de Lune" swept through the air. Madeline played it with deliberate purpose. She closed her eyes as she felt Timmy's strong arm find itself around her waist. His hair mingled with hers as two heads crept closer together. It was as if time suddenly stopped short to permit two young people to grasp firmly the thoughts of this brief moment of bliss. The music penetrated deep in his soul as the hunger of love became stronger and apparent in his weakening spirit. The boundary lines had been crossed, only the consummation remained. Passion engulfed rationality and sexual desire was hailed the victor. Timmy couldn't stand the onslaught and succumbed to the command of the flesh. He drew her closer and compelled her hands to silence her music and listen to the rage of a heartbeat that breathed a savage tune. He found her lips waiting his embrace and felt the vibration of her muscles pressing against his body with every movement of his hand. Something touched her that acted as a signal-bearer of things to follow. They stood up and tried to hunt each other's stare, but darkness forbids the light of consent. A firmer grasp, a tug of closeness, and a moistened hand so soft and white found repose on a face eager to accept her challenge with loving caresses. Admission and consent were made without an utterance.

Two figures slowly walked the winding staircase. Only the constant tick of the hallway clock gave signs of activity. Timmy's heart was beating most audibly as he clung to Madeline's arm. In the darkness, she was smiling, up the first landing and past the bust of Napoleon. In that flash, he didn't regard the famous Napoleon as a hero, but a brother defeatist. They were close to Timmy's room. Then he hesitated! He felt the pull of his jacket and couldn't resist. He wheeled her around and held her fast in his arms. Their lips met in tight embrace. Two souls were joined in one where guardian angels flee in scorn. It was an evil kiss with diabolical assurance.

No words slipped from their lips when they crossed the threshold and closed the door behind them. No lights would burn. Only the "Clair de Lune" showed forth its grandeur in unholy awe and silence. They were alone in the dead and still night—together!

Timmy left his room by daybreak and sought refuge in the room across the hall. He didn't know when Madeline left the house that morning, nor cared. Like all such conquerors, he loathed the vanquished. He was afraid to throw open the shades and admit the morning sunlight. He knew he lost a precious jewel forever in the mud of illicit mire and degradation. He was afraid to reenter his room and hid his face like a blushing child in the pillow. He tossed and turned his nervous body till Silba's voice could be heard at the foot of the stairway.

"Everyone has secrets, Silba," said Timmy, looking into his coffee rather than face the old woman. "You won't give me away, will you?"

Silba knew the faults of men, in a measure, better than those of women. Yet, on her face, as Timmy awaited her answer, he could read the thoughts in her mind through the expression on her face.

"No, Masta Timmy," she said turning to leave the library, "we all love yo too much to hurt yo trust. But, please, Masta Timmy, will she be the same trustin' kind?"

Timmy knew who she referred to and remained silent. In his heart, he hated himself with all the remorse and bitterness of his being. He never wanted to see Madeline again as long as he lived. While he was dressing to report at the school for baseball practice, he wondered what she must have thought of him. He recalled all the reproaches from Aunt Liz and his friends. He thought of little Robert Duseaunault and the childlike expression of faith and love the little boy felt for his athletic friend. How could he ever face this lad who was the essence of innocence with such a mark on his soul? He didn't want to see the boys that morning at ten, nor any morning thereafter, for that matter!

"Boy ole boy, Timmy, you look like somebody beat holy hell out of you," said Skeets in the shower room after practice. "You couldn't hit your hat this morning. And, as far as pitching goes, you might just as well have used a slingshot. What have you and Silba been up to?"

Timmy worked a faint smile on his face. He couldn't hide too much from his pal because he made a practice of being always open and above board. He made a weak effort to excuse himself for his bad playing and told Skeets he wanted to see him that night, after confessions!

"What goes, chum? Are we going to Confession and then throw a helluva big party before Aunt Liz waltzes home? It takes a long time and a lot of matches to burn your place down," Skeets said, laughing and throwing an armful of soap suds all over Timmy's back.

"No," said Timmy, turning his back to the stream of water in order to wash away the newly acquired gift of suds, "we aren't going to toss a party. I just want to talk to you about something. My God, Skeets, do we have to have a party just to have a little conversation?"

"My, aren't we in a rare mood this A.M.? Did you by any chance or stretch of my evil and immoral imagination see Miss Madeline lately?" he said curtly.

"I'll see you tonight, Skeets. Come on over for dinner, even though it is Friday," said Timmy, running out of the shower to the dressing room.

All day Timmy was worried. He wished several times the Jesuits hadn't declared a holiday in memory of the founder of Lacodere Prep. He was glad, in a way, Father Joseph moved Confession day from Saturday to Friday night in response to the Bishop's command that the priest also assist in two other mission churches in the surrounding area. With the consent of his own parishioners, he moved the day of reporting faults and infractions of the "Big Ten" to Friday so he could hear the stories of other ardent repentants on the usual day for spiritual house cleaning.

Timmy worried all day about going to Confession. What would Father Joseph say to him, and, possibly, think of him? That same priest who practically lived in the house on Fontaine Street. The same priest who loved his little Timmy from those tender years when he would lift him high in the air and make his joyous screams resound in the holy house. That same Father Joseph who took his little Irishman to the vigil lamps and watched with fatherly affection each lamp burn forth a prayer made possible by the lovable and carefree child. No! He couldn't go and tell this priest of the mortal stain on his soul. He must go to another; someone he was sure wouldn't recognize him as a fallen angel.

Silba handed Timmy a wire announcing Liz's arrival home on the 1st of May. He thought a minute before realizing the first day of May was Saturday. Liz didn't say just what hour she'd be at Lacodere, but Timmy knew it was up to him to be on hand to meet her after such a long absence.

Throughout the day, he tried to call Madeline on the telephone. Mrs. Turrel was very sweet to him each time he called, but she couldn't produce Madeline. This was a source of worry along with everything else that upset him. He didn't want to call Madeline, but something kept driving him to pick the receiver off the hook and dial her number. Around three o'clock, he left the house and walked by Madeline's little home. In a way, he wanted to see her and then again he didn't. He found no evidence of life around the house so walked up the hill to Locodere Prep. On the way, several people shouted from their porches signals of salutation. He waved his hand, but couldn't look their way. As he approached the campus, he saw the famous missionary all the boys were talking about.

Father Cerveneau just returned from India and was to remain in the New Orleans Province of the Society of Jesus for at least a year in order to regain lost health. He was to give the boys a lecture on the India Missions the following Monday. Several of the young Jesuit Scholastics acted as his praise agents for weeks before he arrived at Lacodere. Naturally, the students expected this holy French priest to haul out ropes and make them stand on end, and tame cobra snakes on the stage of the auditorium. Little did they realize he would talk about the great need for priests and nuns in the Foreign Missions and completely eliminate the vaudeville.

Timmy saw the priest walking up and down saying his breviary. He could nearly see and hear the psalms, lessons and hymns emit forth from the lips of this walking saint of God. This was to be his Confessor, he thought.

"You're the Missionary from India, aren't you, Father?" said Timmy.

"Yes, my son, what's left of me. And what is your name?" said the priest, closing his office book.

"I'd rather not tell you, Father. You see . . . I'd like to bother your office time . . . and . . . and . . . go to Confession," he said, stammering for words. "That is, if you'll hear my Confession, Father," he concluded, having a difficult time getting it all out.

"As you say in America, son, okay," said the priest, smiling up at the tall youth. "Do you want to go right here on the campus or would you prefer to go in a confessional?"

"Right here is swell for me, Father. I think the air is going to do both of us a world of good," said Timmy, trying to be a bit subtle.

"Now, look here, son, you can't tell me a fine, clean-cut lad like you needs that much air to purify the atmosphere," said Father Carveness, laughing.

"That's what you think, Father. You'll probably throw the book at me when you hear what I have to say," said the boy, most serious in his expression of sorrow.

"Let's let old Father Carveneau be the best judge of how awful you are, huh?" said the priest, patting Timmy's arm. "I'll even put this breviary over here, see? Now, I won't be tempted to throw it at you."

Timmy made his Confession with all the sincerity of a true repentant. He was truly sorry for the grave offense against God and

His Commandment. He blamed himself for the weakness that stole his virtue. Tears formed in his big blue eyes. Peterian tears, not of denial of his Master, but the expression of deep sorrow for a sin of weakness. He was ready and willing to accept any penance to atone for a hurt he inflicted and would promise anything to receive the absolution of forgiveness. It was all over in five turns around the front of the large campus. He asked Fatheer Cerveneau if he should continue his plan to enter the Benedictine Order at New Cassino Abbey. The wise old priest gently patted the boy's shoulder and assured him he needn't be concerned that our dear Lord would place him in anathema because of one sin no matter how grave. Hadn't He forgiven the great Saint Augustine? He asked the boy to sever his association with the party that caused him to fall, and to pray fervently during the month of May, and ask the Blessed Virgin to guide him on the path of righteousness. He told him not to ever lose sight of his vocation and during the Senior Retreat in the latter part of the month, he should take counsel with the Retreat-Master. Timmy knelt in the center of the field and looked at the huge bronze statue of the Sacred Heart and received the kindly priest's blessing. His heart was joyous again as he half-walked, half-ran to the house on Fontaine Street.

CHAPTER FIFTEEN

S keets called Timmy around suppertime to inform him it would be impossible to keep their date. However, if he wanted him to come around later that evening, he'd be happy to oblige. Timmy declined his offer and told him that Liz was due home the next day and little things around the house had to be taken care of, or there'd be hell to pay.

Again, Timmy didn't feel disposed to return to the master bedroom. He preferred the guest room and retired early.

Liz was greeted with all the welcome and pomp the household could drum up. Sure, she had been missed. Timmy and she talked for hours about the cousin on Upper Gano Street and the trips to Boston, New York City and Miami Beach. They laughed and were happy again. To all appearances, Liz was again her normal Irish self. The lines seemed to disappear from around her eyes. Rest away from Lacodere cured many ills.

That afternoon, Timmy made his usual visit to see little Robert and his brothers and sisters. He wasn't surprised to find them all clean and awaiting his visit. Jackie Coogan was on the screen at the Rialto and promised many minutes of joy and sorrow to a crowd of seven little children. There were many tears shed that afternoon as the audience watched Coogan run through his part. Jubilation reigned when the curtain closed, and their bob-haired idol found his goal and riches. There was the usual rattle of paper bags throughout the movie as eager children dug deep to get that large piece of peanut brittle that obstinately hid itself under the smaller pieces. With so many youngsters after so many large pieces, it was little wonder older members could find the time to concentrate on the little actor's plight.

After the show, all seven marched into the combination fruit and soda store. Timmy always ordered eight sodas and deliberately held up drinking his till Robert was through with his pineapple mixture. Then, he would ask the little lad to help him finish his because the man behind the counter made it too big for one fellow to drink. Always Robert would look at Timmy in amazement because he failed to understand how such a big man like his pal couldn't find room in his stomach for one little soda. There was never an argument, though. He accepted the drink and learned very quickly the art of winking in thanksgiving.

Timmy was the object of jealous eyes as he walked with his adopted brood down Main Avenue. He looked like Saint Vincent de Paul and the orphan children. But, if ever a young boy was wrapped up in the love of youngsters, it was Timmy O'Shea. He found it difficult to let them return home on time for supper. He wanted their company on through the evening. Yet, home they should be, and home they surely went.

During Timmy's absence, Liz made the rounds of inspection. The least little dust was called to Silba's attention in a sweet, but serious tone. It baffled her to notice that someone slept, or at least occupied, the guest room. She made inquiries through Silba. The dutiful Silba was as mystified as her mistress. On into her own bedroom and thence to Timmy's. Between the two pillows on Timmy's bed, Liz bent down to pick up the object that once burned deep in her soul. It was the gold football with the tiny diamond. Words of hate swelled in her heart and formed on her tongue and lips. What had taken place in this room during her absence? Certainly Silba would know and must talk. She hastened to the head of the staircase and called the colored mammy with a hysterical voice. There was little time for poor Silba to devise a story, even less to hide the pained expression on her black face.

"Please don't lie to me, Silba," said Liz, her face wrought with anger. "I want the truth. Do you hear me? The whole truth and don't spare any of the details. Do you understand me?"

Silba couldn't hold back the tears that fell from her worried eyes. She loved her Masta Timmy just as much as Liz loved her boy. How could she be expected to violate the trust placed in her? It was with difficulty the old colored woman related the incidents of the night before last; that night when Madeline failed to eat all her supper and played so nice for Masta Timmy. Silba told, to the best of her ability, and begged forgiveness for being forced into such a pact. The very pact of betrayal she silently feared would come to pass. She knew Timmy had broken some rule that didn't necessarily bind her race. She knew, though, she had broken a trust, and, to her that was infinitely worse. She cried bitterly in the quiet of her basement apartment.

Liz realized too well what had transpired. It was quite enough for her to know that the girl she so despised had gained the entrance of the front door. That was to her an outright admission to any other section of the house, including the bedroom in Liz's absence. As she sat in the parlor thumping her fingers on the mahogany desk, the whole sordid details, as she imagined it, unraveled itself before her. Timmy and she must have occupied the master bedroom because Silba saw them enter. How many nights Madeline came to call was a source of annoyance to Liz. Certainly, if she came once she must have been there a dozen times while she was on her vacation. But, Liz confined her attentions to the night when she left the trophy on the pillow. That night, in particular, Silba informed her that Timmy removed himself to the guest room close to daylight.

Poor Silba, like all members of her sex, possessed the unhappy faculty of being curious to a depreciative degree. Under the guise of some sort of charity, she felt she must watch every movement of Masta Timmy. Therefore, she was quite qualified to relate an exact accounting of what took place.

Liz went to her room and placed the gold trophy in her locked jewel case. If the owner wanted it, she would have to make claim in person and undergo a full explanation of how it came to free itself from her possession. This hoped-for explanation never took place—in the manner Liz wished! She gained full possession of the trophy football, unhappy as she was in its possession.

It often occurred to Timmy during the summer months that he never heard from Madeline. He felt it wasn't his place to write after the promise he made to the priest in Confession that day on the campus. But she never came into his thoughts as he tramped through the wooded section around the cottage at Lake Tahoo. Gibb and Skeets were his constant companions during the remaining weeks before his departure. Little Robert followed the trio in fraternal admiration.

The summer was moving swiftly by and the thoughts of graduation exercises and the glorious days of Retreat the Seniors made and the four years together were subjects of deep conversation as three young men spent their leisure days under the sun and in the cool lake water. Gibby never talked of the future like his friend Skeets. He had nothing to offer when the conversation was brought to light. He just listened to Timmy tell of the possibilities of entering the Benedictine Order on the 15th of August and the premedical course Skeets had mapped out for himself at Tulane University. He listened to the conversation with concern because he was mentally having a severe debate with his conscience. Buddy had left in the heat of the middle of July for the Jesuits' Novitiate, fifteen years of intensive study and discipline. Skeets thought for sure Buddy had lost his mind when he took his hand and quickly said his good-bye. It was a parting that endured forever! It wasn't Buddy who cried, it was the hard-shelled Skeets who let fly with the parting tears. Now, Timmy was leaving for the monastery. "What was wrong with his friends, anyway?" he thought to himself. Joey Roys, the only sane member of the quintet, left for an early start in June to study about airplanes and their kindred subjects. What had Gibby up his shirt sleeve? Time alone would present itself with an answer.

Down in the sweat-provoking city of New Orleans, Madeline Turrel was beside herself with grief. She had given up her music lessons after the doctor told her the news. She wanted to return home to be with her mother when the baby would come in January. More than that, she suddenly wanted Timmy, but she wanted him to want her. Every letter sent since late May to the house on Fontaine Street received no reply. Slowly her anxiety was turning to hatred. She vowed never to return to Lacodere, never to show herself to Timmy in hopes of extracting sympathy.

143

The letters did arrive at the house on Fontaine Street. They were carefully read and placed in a box with a golden football trophy. If Timmy knew of their arrival and contents, all thoughts of the priesthood would go amiss. Liz refused to permit her prayers of so many years to fall short of the goal she intended her Timmy to attain. If he had made a mistake, it was her duty to rectify the youthful error in the manner she deemed propitious. But, Timmy was never to know that he was the father of Madeline's love child even if it meant breaking a moral obligation to safeguard a Sacrament. The Sacrament she wanted Timmy to receive from the time he was a small child.

The day before Timmy was to leave for his year of silence, the first year of a man's life in the confines of a monastic order, he and Liz enjoyed their last supper together. They talked of every known subject from the great Titanic disaster to high school graduation. He was now leaving her to do what they both wanted to see accomplished, the priesthood. Before Timmy answered the front door bell, Liz held his arm for a moment and asked him one question. The answer of which caused her to smile a smile of victory.

"Timmy, dear, do you ever think of Madeline and wish, perhaps that you and she could one day marry?" she said, looking directly into his eyes.

Timmy stopped short and smiled down on his Auntie Liz. As he turned to leave, he said, "That's all in the past, now," leaving the room with a grin on his face.

Gibby was welcomed by both Liz and Timmy. When he told Timmy to prepare for a shock, as the host closed the front door, Timmy read on his face that he was going to have a companion on his trip to New Cassino Abbey, a companion that would ultimately be closer to him than anyone had ever been from the day he kissed Aunt Liz goodbye on the great feast of the Assumption of Our Lady into Heaven.

Chapter Sixteen

"School must be startin' kinda early this year, huh boys?" said the bus driver, who was quite a loquacious member of his profession, and for the past forty odd miles carried on a conversation more or less with himself. Gibby and Timmy seemed content to exclude him from their own personal thoughts and comments. Yet, they managed to drawl out a "yes" or "no" when they felt it convenient.

"We're not going to school at Cassino Abbey, mister; that is, just yet. We're going over to make a retreat—a long retreat," Timmy told him, winking at Gibby.

"You Catholics do the damndest things I ever heard tell of," said the driver, never taking his eyes off the road. "My wife's cousin is one of them Catholics, and she done gone to work and become a sister in one of them convents where nobody can ever see her anymore. Not that I'd ever spend a few minutes of my valuable time going peeking into one of them convents just to see Cousin Sarah. Her name is changed to something very high and fancy now, though. Anyway, I just feel she is done out in her mind when she left the farm and Mr. Harrington's handsome young-un, Clarence. He's the next farm over and a might smarter boy you never have seen. He has the finest pigs in this section of Georgia. And, next to Cassino College, I reckon he has the finest peaches in this here land of ours. I just can't see why Sarah had to leave all that for the life of a female hermit. Course, she wasn't as pretty as some of the girls around town, but she had possibilities. And, I know she coulda won Mr. Harrington's boy, Clarence. Most people think just because a fellow has a twitch in one of his eyes, it takes away from his handsomeness. That ain't so, boys. This here Clarence could dress as slick as the next fella come Saturday night, and he's always had a jingle of "dingle" in his pockets."

The boys laughed at this quaint character. As the old bus rounded the bend, Gibby grasped Timmy's arm. There before their startled eyes was New Cassino Abbey situated on a huge hill overlooking the valley below. The boys strained their necks to get a good look at their new home as the bus rolled merrily along.

"Well, here you are, boys. I can't get off the main road to drive you to the college. I have a very strict schedule to keep up with, and if I should make any detours, I'd be in an awful scrape for time. You know, boys, people watch this here bus as it passes down the road and set their clocks by my schedule. One man said I was the best . . ."

"So long, Fella," said Timmy, as both boys jumped off the bus and not interested in any further tales of self-congratulation. "Thanks for the buggy ride. And, by the way, we're of the opinion that Sarah is a damn sight better off without Mr. Harrington's Clarence."

Gibby waved goodbye to the driver as he changed gears and moved in the direction of Rome, Georgia. They stood on the gravel road watching the old car kick up a smoke-screen of dust.

"I don't see anybody coming down to meet us or help us take these bags to our new quarters," said Timmy. "We might just as well get the lead out and hike to the main building up there."

The boys walked slowly up the dirt road on the hottest day in August. With two suitcases and a coat over their shoulders, they were sweating under the afternoon's sun. Halfway up the hill, the boys turned their brown faces in the direction of the approaching car and together signaled the auto for a lift. Little did they realize who they were waving at with a thumb to their noses as the car sped by leaving only a cloud of dust in its tracts.

"Ye gods," said Timmy, picking up his suitcases and slowly moving onward, "you'd think in all charity, at least, whoever owns that big 'pot,' he'd give us a lift up this hill. They probably thought we were a couple of tramps the way we look. What I wouldn't do for dive in the 'drink." I sure hope they let us go for a swim when we get up there.

"If my ideas of monastic life are correct, Timmy, we'll be lucky if we even get a bath before next Saturday," said Gibby. "And, then it'll probably be used water in an old wooden tub."

"Now wait a minute, pal. Those hermitical days are relegated to the Fourth Century. We get a bath with soap and towel or my name isn't Timmy O'Shea."

"By the way, Timmy, what name are you going to take when we start our year of silence?" said Gibby, trying to keep up with Timmy's pace.

"From what Father Joseph tells me, and I guess he told you, too, we get three names to select from. I think I'll take Kevin if there isn't somebody registered here by that moniker," Timmy said.

"I'm take Ignatius for my name, Timmy."

"That's a hot one. Do you think the Abbot is going to let you take the name of the founder of the Jesuits? I think you'd better look deeper in the pool for another one, Gibby," said Timmy, laughing and brushing the sweat from his brow.

"I don't see anything wrong with Ignatius. It isn't my fault if the Benedictines didn't have an Ignatius in their outfit. Anyway, it's about time they had one. I'm going to be it!" said Gibby with a determined look on his face.

"Let's sit down over here by the tree and get out of this sun," said Gibby. "I'm almost ready for the glue factory instead of the monastery."

The two sat under a large weeping willow tree that extended out over the road. When they pushed aside the long leafy branches, they found a bench made of crude limbs from a cherry tree. At least, it looked very much like cherry tree wood. Timmy and Gibby didn't care much whether they ever got up to the monastery that afternoon. It was nearly three-thirty when they sat down for a brief rest and close to five when they decided to take the rest of the hill on time for supper. In that period of restfulness, they talked of their plans for the future and what the Order of Saint Benedict had to offer them. Most future priests have many little secrets they tell their closest associates never thinking that at some future date they will be fulfilled. Timmy told Gibby things he'd never think of telling or dare mention to Buddy or Skeets. They didn't fall on deaf ears.

As the two boys emerged out from under the weeping willow, another car was seen some distance down the road. They refused to try and halt the driver for fear they would suffer once more the scorn of refusal. A kindly priest with heavy glasses looked at the pair with a smile.

"And who might you gentlemen be?" asked the priest.

"We're the two fellows from Lacodere Prep Father Joseph sent over," said Timmy, acting as spokesman.

"The two new novices, huh?" said the priest, looking the boys over from head to toe. "Which of you happens to be Timmy O'Shea, the athlete?"

"That should be me, Father; what's left of me after this trip to Calvary. This is Gibby Gerard, and a sweet ball player on any man's club, Father," said Timmy, working a smile on his tired face.

"Jump in, men, I'll run you up to the Abbey, and it won't cost you a thin dime, just a Hail Mary sometime when you can remember it. How is Father Joseph behaving himself? And how did you ever decide to become Benedictines in the face of Jesuit education? Do you think you'll like, or better yet, be able to stand the Novitiate here?" The priest asked too many questions too rapidly for the boy to answer. They just let him continue the conversation while they rested their weary bodies on the hard cushions on the rear seat.

"You know, boys, the life of the Benedictines is one of real trial. That is, for the first fifty years, anyway," the priest said, smiling on the two boys.

Timmy didn't appreciate this priest's wit, nor did he intend to cultivate any great taste for his affections in later life, at least, those were his thoughts as the car pulled up to the front of the Abbey's main building.

"Now, you boys march into the Abbey and pay your respects to Father Abbot, and I'll take your bags over to the Novitiate building. Incidentally, Mr. Gerard and Mr. O'Shea, you'll be seeing a lot of me in the course of the next year. I'm Father Raphael, your Novice-Master."

The two youngsters looked at each other, but didn't say a word. Each could read the thoughts of the other. They walked up the cement stairs and rang the bell. It had a sound like the fire alarm back in Lacodere. A lay-brother admitted the boys into the Abbot's parlor, and they sat for fifteen minutes wondering what they should say when the head of the Abbey came in their presence. They were told by Father Joseph to kneel and kiss his ring when they first met him. It would give a good impression, if nothing else. Then they were told to sit back and let the old gentleman give them a nice talk about the value of a vocation and how wonderful God had been to them to signal or single, whichever the boys preferred, them out and send them to the Benedictines, giving little credit to Father Joseph's "pep talks." Also, they were not to worry about the hardships of Novitiate life. God would give them substantial graces to carry them through. Then he would dismiss them and told them to report at the Novitiate where they would find ten or twelve other young men, equally as bewildered and wishing they had bought return tickets instead of one-way fares, ready to assist them to their cells. Father Joseph assured the boys the old Abbot never changed his welcome address in over twenty years. This, however, didn't alter his sincerity one iota.

True to form, the Abbot walked in. He was surprised to see two young boys with faces tan and hair in complete disorder. His first thoughts, upon seeing his guests, were that they fought each other all the way from home. Neither Timmy nor Gibby remembered to replace their ties and gain some degree of neatness. It was still very warm and the use of a sport jacket seemed out of place even before the holy Abbot who was dressed in his full habit with gold chain and cross and huge amethyst ring. Just as Father Joseph predicted, the

Abbot told them to be good boys and place their faith in the Devine Master and Saint Benedict. He showed the boys a picture of himself as a novice some sixty odd years previous. The picture was old and worn from taking it out and showing it off. Then he turned suddenly to the boys and asked them the meaning of the strange signal he received from them as his car passed them on the road earlier that afternoon. Timmy looked at Gibby for a ray of hope and consolation. But, Gibby found something on the wall that was far more attractive and less incriminating. It was Timmy's turn to get them out of this unwholesome situation.

A bell rang to announce something in the main building. It was the life-saver for the boys. Quickly, the Abbott took them to the window and holding the curtain in one hand, pointed with the other to the Novitiate building a few yards down the path. He ordered them to report at once to the Novice-Master as he would be awaiting them. He assured the young men that they would see him often in the course of their year of silence and labor. He gave them a quick blessing and departed.

Father Raphael was standing in the doorway of the Novitiate building as the boys walked down the path talking a blue streak. They both looked up as they heard their names called. It was the same smiling priest with the heavy glasses. Timmy thought to himself how mean the priest would really look when he finally wiped that professional smile off his face and set out to "give 'em the works."

"This way, gentlemen, your cells are on the top floor. You'll find other boys up there willing to assist you in every way possible. Please make haste as I'm having a conference in the Community Room in thirty minutes."

The priest turned around and walked directly into his room on the first floor and shut the door behind him. He didn't stop to inform the boys that a room in a monastery was called a cell and that thirty minutes wasn't very long to move the suitcases and trunks that stood waiting for a third floor haul.

But obedience was drilled into the lads long before they ever saw Casino Abbey. Father Joseph told them they would be tried many times in the course of the year, and a strict watch would be made so as the Order could determine their fitness for Religious life. Timmy and Gibby would learn as the year progressed that they were no longer regarded as athletes from Lacodere Prep and highly personal figures around the Louisiana country. They would learn very shortly that they were just two young men who wanted to become priests in an Order that was rigid in the tendons of prayer and labor.

A bell announced the proposed conference. One of the lads from Atlanta, Georgia, knocked on Timmy's door and told him that he'd show him to the room. On the way down, the newly acquired friend asked Timmy if he was the boy who played fullback for Lacodere Prep. Timmy answered with a modest nod and turned the lad's attention to Gibby who was coming down the corridor with a redheaded youngster as a guide.

The boys spoke in whispers as they walked down the three flights. It was a rule in the Novitiate that one wasn't allowed to speak to another without permission. Silence was observed, not because there were signs at every step, but because the boys knew it was a violation of obedience to break the rule. The signs were mere reminders, and reminders were of necessity for the young men.

Fourteen young men from the ages of sixteen to thirty-two made up the Novitiate of New Mounte Cassino Abbey. They were a solemn group as they set seven on each side of a long table. The Father-Master sat at the head with a determined look on his face. He seemed to know each man's thoughts as he gazed about the room. He made the sign of the Cross and began his tenth year as Novice-Master and Sub-Prior of the Abbey.

"In the name of the Abbot and members of the Abbey of New Mounte Cassino, I take this time to welcome each and every one of you to the Novitiate and may, with God's special help and graces, you all persevere and take your Vows a year and a day from the start of your retreat," said Father Raphael, with a solemn note that range throughout the still room. He went on to tell the men of their duties and obligations as novices.

"It is only fair that I tell you," he continued, "that each and every one of you will be watched and guided throughout this year. Some of you may fall by the wayside and need extra help. Some may feel in the course of the year that God never meant you to be Benedictines, or any other kind of priests, for that matter. It's for you to decide. That's what you are here for. Test yourself and learn through a year of prayer, recollection, penance and trial, whether you are the possessor of that rare jewel called a Religious Vocation. It's no fault of yours if you have given yourself a fair trial, and you are either requested to leave or do so of your own choice.

Father Raphael's conversation gave every appearance of being directed to one individual rather than a group. In that way, each prospective novice felt the Master was personally talking to him. Being singular rather than plural is far more effective in talks of this character.

"From time to time," Father continued, "you will have opportunities to examine your conscience and disclose such findings to a spiritual director. Just be honest with yourself, and God will give you the necessary help. What you were in the world matters nothing here in the Novitiate. If you were outstanding in social life or business dealings or on the playground, all must be put aside and in its stead you must plant the fruitful seeds of love of God and His All-Important Precepts."

Father Novice-Master looked up from his notes to see that all were taking in the merits of his introductory discourse. He smiled as he watched the serious expressions on the faces of the young men.

"Roughly, I shall tell you of your duties here," he said. "Each day, however, we shall have a conference wherein I shall endeavor to acquaint you more fully with the Rule of Life and duties that shall be yours to follow. To break a rule is most serious. Sometimes it may be so serious that it would involve Confession, such as giving scandal to another member of the Novitiate. Be ever vigilant in this regard as you be tempted to hurt another by your lack of charity.

"Tomorrow night you will start your retreat. At the close of the retreat, you will take your habit of Saint Benedict and start officially your Novitiate year. I say "officially," because Canon Law governs the length and rules of a Novitiate in her Code. You'll learn of Canon Law as you go along, not so much this year, but certainly during your Theological studies. I'll give you a rough sketch of your life and duties now. During this retreat, the Retreat-Master will point out various duties that will be greatly enlarged upon during your year here in this house.

"On the second floor of this building, there are nine young men who are just about to enter upon retreat with you. They are just finishing their Novitiate year and will go on for college studies like you boys will do at the end of your stay in this residence. Their number was fifteen when they started a year ago. Some left, others were told to leave. Please don't carry on any conservation with these men unless you have a very important reason, and, also, permission from me. This is a wise rule and one that I must ask you to obey blindly.

"You will arise in the morning at the sound of a bell at four-thirty. You will have fifteen minutes to wash and dress and be ready to join the group at the main entrance of the Novitiate and march over in silence to the main chapel in the Abbey building. I say in silence. I really didn't mean that in the strict sense of the word. We shall say the De Profundis as we march. What I mean by silence in this sense of the word is that we are not allowed to talk to our partner concerning petty things.

"In the chapel, we shall say a part of our Office in common called the "hours," and then hear three Masses before breakfast. This may seem like a hardship at first, but when you become adjusted, you'll fall in line with the rest of the Abbey. The first Mass is called the Meditation Mass, the second, the Community Mass, and the third is called the Mass of Thanksgiving.

"Then we go to breakfast. This is taken in silence and not at your leisure. You have just begun a very busy day, and there remains no time in the course of the day to permit one moment to go unaccounted for. After you have eaten, you will assist with the dishes and return to the Novitiate for your own duties in this house. They consist in making up your room, or as we must learn to refer to it, your cell, and other cleaning assignments that will be posted on the board in the Community Room. Please remember, gentlemen, there is to be complete silence throughout the house except during recreation periods.

"Your work completed, you will come to this room for a daily conference as well as your various little courses of study. You will bring a notebook and pencil so as to take notes on these conferences, and later in the course of the day, meditate on the merit of the content of these conferences.

"I must hurry through this little talk as I see its getting late. Even though you don't grasp everything in the routine of a Novice, you'll hear of it in these conferences you have every day. As you know, gentlemen, you have entered an Order that has for its motto, Ora et Labora. Those of you who know Latin, and I'm sure all of you are familiar with the basis authors of High School Latin, will be able to translate that ancient motto handed down from Saint Benedict himself. Pray and Labor. Never forget that motto, gentlemen, Pray and Labor. You will have every opportunity to give vent to the principles of this laudable phrase as time quickly passes by. I shall personally see that you Pray and Labor to the very best of your abilities.

"As you know, you will change your names. I advise you to pick a Saint's name that appeals to you and try to imitate his virtues. Select, if you can, a Saint of our Order. You'll have the duration of your retreat to think of a suitable name. If you can't decide, we'll attend to that for you.

"The duty of a true Benedictine is to Pray and Labor. That we have already discussed briefly. The prayer of the Church is the Office. We, here, make it a solemn duty by reciting it in common in the chapel. It takes a great deal longer to say the Office in common than it would privately. But, you can see how difficult a priest in a parish would find it to travel until he found some other priest to recite the Office with him.

"Then, it is our duty to observe the liturgy of the Church to the fullest of its glory. We study liturgy every day along with our little classes in the Rule of Saint Benedict, Latin, and the Constitutions that govern our order.

"I won't keep you any longer, gentlemen. I see its time to go to the chapel for Matins and Lauds. Now, this is the main part of our Office. We say this just before supper during the summer months. Later, we'll say it before retiring for the night. You may follow me to the chapel and watch the proceedings of the other monks. In a few short months, you boys will be in choir chanting the Psalms and Hymns. But, for now, you just watch!"

A lot of what Father Raphael said didn't make much sense to the eager group of youngsters. They were busy thinking of their year ahead and all they left behind. Gibby and Timmy were separated, but their thoughts ran along the same avenue. They thought of home and all they left in Lacodere, Louisiana.

After Office was over, the boys followed the other monks to the refectory for supper. It was a room nearly as large as the gym at Our Lady of Lourdes Academy. The Abbot and a few other priests set at the head table. Somebody got up to read during the meal about some woman who was beaten unmercifully and then tossed to the lions. The reader never smiled, but kept telling stories about other men and women who were thrown to the lions and tigers in the Roman theatres of old.

Often Gibby winked to Timmy with a frightened look on his face. He wanted to be sure that Timmy was with him all the way through this year. If Timmy ever left, Gibby knew he'd go with him. He loved Timmy like a brother and didn't want to suffer alone. Both boys really suffered during the first weeks of Novitiate life at

Mounte Cassino Abbey. Neither would give in, though, and both bore the pangs and heartaches with true valor.

The first night in their new home found two boys very tired as they turned out the lights at the sound of the nine o'clock bell. Two boys in separate ends of the top floor couldn't go directly to sleep the first night. They had to think of home and all they were giving up. They couldn't help the tears that came to their eyes as they lay with arms under their heads looking at the bare walls of the gloomy room. Gibby thought of the kind words of his mother and the doctor. Timmy thought of his first real parting from Liz and the house on Fontaine Street. Robert's smiling face appeared in a passing flash. And, he thought, too, of Madeline Turrel. Only then did the tears flow down his cheeks. Real tears—tears that would come again and again.

CHAPTER SEVENTEEN

The peach harvest was over and the change of seasons commenced. Timmy was now known as Frater Kevin throughout the monastery and a very popular young monk. Gibby received the choice of his selection and proudly signed his name as letters to the doctor as, Frater Ignatius. Both boys were proud of their black tunics with heavy leather cinctures girding their waists. With the complete scapular and cowl, they gave every appearance of being the youngest and most handsome pair of novices in the Abbey of Mounte Cassino. Everyone liked Fraters Kevin and Ignatius. And why not? They seemed to respond to every dictate of the Superiors; the Divine Office came rather easy for them, and they progressed rapidly in perfection along the tough road of Novitiate routine.

There were times when Frater Kevin needed Frater Ignatius' words of encouragement like that day when the Novice-Master expelled two Fraters for gross violations and infringement of the Rules. Both boys pledged loyalty to correct each other's faults before they became too apparent in the eyes of Father Raphael.

Buddy wrote to them once telling them how much he enjoyed the life with the Jesuits. Skeets wrote very humorous letters telling of his experiences in the French Quarter of New Orleans. He assured the two novices that it was merely a biological experimentation and highly recommended for future physicians. Anyway, it was difficult to study day in and day out at Tulane University without some sort of relaxation.

In October, the sound of screaming voices from the stadium could be heard by two ex-football players. It was a source of distraction to meditate on Christ's Passion and Death when they knew Cassino College was taking a terrific beating from some arch rival of the south. Frater Kevin wanted to hurl aside his long black habit and don the robes of the football player. Frater Ignatius felt the same impulse, but failed to let it creep into the light of notice. He knew the Rule of Saint Benedict nearly by heart and with this knowledge and understanding was able to ward off temptations that befall a novice. On the other hand, Frater Kevin could give the substance of the Rule, but failed to render it as perfectly as his confrere.

Letters from Liz always contained a wrath of news that made her Timmy very happy. Little Robert was a constant visitor now that Timmy was away becoming a monk. He helped Aunt Liz around the house and did little errands for her. Often, she would find the little youngster in Timmy's room admiring the trophies of former football battles. She found him one day in the bathroom trying on Timmy's blue and white silk basketball togs. All these little things made Timmy lonesome for Lacodere. He never received news of Madeline Turrel. His monthly letter from home only contained assurance of prayers at Mass and Holy Communion. Nothing could be found that would tend to mar his vocation or aspirations to the High Office.

During the month of the Holy Souls, the football team played a number of home assignments. Never were the novices permitted to witness any of these tussles. In fact, they were never allowed to communicate with either the High School students nor the College men. They were alone in their three-story building set apart just for the novices. In November, because the Church prayers were recited especially for the souls that have gone to their eternal rest, Frater Kevin found his name on the bulletin board for cemetery labor. Each November, the novices must clean the tombstones of the departed priests, brothers and especially former Abbots that are laid to rest in the quaint little cemetery some distance from the Abbey proper. Only one novice is assigned each day to this task that takes him better than two hours of his work period. The chosen novice must not only labor in that cemetery, but also pray a moment at the tomb of his departed brother in Christ.

The news of Silba's death came as a shock to Fraters Kevin and Ignatius. Though Silba never seemed to profess any special belief, she was buried from the Congregational Church in Lacodere. Frater Kevin was sad all day after reading Liz's letter. When work period came, he took his bucket of white sand and another filled with warm water and walked the long path to the gate of the cemetery. He was trying to forget all the amusements that Silba afforded him in his life, trying to forget the secrets that he pressed on her ears. Forget as he might, they constantly came to his mind and tears of real sadness welled in his eyes. He knelt at the large bronze crucifix where three former Abbots were buried. He could hardly read their names on the plaque because of his tear-filled eyes. He dipped the brush into the warm water and then into the bucket of sand. As he was scrubbing the plaque he failed to notice a bent figure come up behind him and kneel a few feet from where his sand bucket was placed. It was the mystery priest of the Abbey of Mounte Casino. The priest everybody saw, but would never dare speak to; the priest who looked at Frater Kevin with warm and friendly eyes in the refectory and chapel;

the same priest that caused Frater Ignatius to blush whenever he was forced to pass him in the choir stalls; the priest who had the ignominy of the whole Abbey on his bent shoulders for the grave sin he had committed as a member of the great Benedictine Order. Here he was, kneeling within touching distance of the young novice he so silently admired. Today, he would break his silence of ten years and talk to this famous athlete the papers regarded so highly. He would warn him as a father warns his beloved child. Then, he would return to the glum silence of his Refugium Peccatorum.

The priest tapped Frater Kevin on the shoulder. If Timmy was startled, he never gave exterior signs to show it. He merely turned and faced the priest with a bewildered look on his face. He couldn't help the tears that remained in his eyes and on his cheeks. He wasn't in the least ashamed of his expressed sorrow.

"I've read a lot about you in the papers, Frater, and have watched you in refectory and choir. Would you mind an awful lot if I took a little of your time to talk with you?" The priest was looking down on Timmy when he spoke these words.

"The novices aren't supposed to talk to you. I mean, to any of the professed members of the Abbey," said Timmy, trying to avoid any conversation with the priest.

"Certainly you wouldn't begrudge me a few moments of your time. I noticed the past day or so you looked worried, and I felt perhaps if you were disposed to talk with somebody, you might feel a little relief," said the priest, still unwilling to look the novice in the eyes.

"We have a spiritual director who looks after our needs, Father. Thanks just the same," said Timmy.

"The needs sometimes fall very short when one must go to an assigned director," the priest said, turning to leave the cemetery. "I'm very sorry you, too, look upon me with disgust, yet, you don't even know me. You're not even interested in knowing me."

Frater Kevin threw his brush into the bucket of sand and ran after the priest. He took the priest by the arm and asked him to forgive his insolence. He didn't really mean to be insulting and to prove it, he was willing to take a walk to the far end of the cemetery where there was a small grove of young trees. There they could each take a tombstone and use it for a chair and talk their respective heads off.

The priest smiled his approval. It was many years back that a smile like he gave Timmy appeared on his drawn face. But, Timmy knew how to win people just by looking at them. There was something in his very mannerisms that attracted the monks and novices to him. Something he was unable to account for, but knew existed.

The two monks sat close together on the large tombstone of some ancient, but not forgotten, member of Cassino Abbey. Timmy waited in courtesy for the priest to give him some horrible account of a past public sin of his life that would cause the Abbot to "Silence" him for nearly ten years and take away the right to exercise any of his duties as a priest. Timmy knew that he must have committed some very grievous fault to cause the Abbot to act so harshly. To take away the privilege of offering up the Mass seemed to him punishment enough. But, never to leave the Abbey or talk to any of its members, yet, report at every exercise of the Devine Office seemed unbearable. What kind of a sin did this man commit? Timmy was taught that any sin was subject to forgiveness. All sorts of possible sins ran through his youthful mind as possibilities for his newly acquired friend to have committed. Timmy was way off the path. Men were weak in more ways than he could imagine. The sin of pride, more deadly than any of the other sins, could easily have been in Timmy's mind had he been exposed to Moral Theology.

"I've watched you ever since you arrived in the middle of August, Frater, and wondered if I'd ever have the nerve to come up and ask you to be my friend. But, I feared what would happen, and it did! You wanted to turn me away like the others." The priest was crying as he finished his opening address.

Timmy reached over in the priest's lap and took his hand. With his other hand he patted the priest on the shoulder. "I'm sorry, Father, I seemed in a daze over there. I really didn't mean to be curt. After all, I don't really care what you did. If you want me for a friend, I'll try and fill the order. Maybe I'll come to you when everyone else turns a deaf ear, and you can be of help to me."

Frater Kevin meant every word he said. If he was noted as a kidder, he also had moments when he was most sincere and serious. There was an expression on the priest's face that burned deep in the boy's mind. An expression of sorrow felt keenly over a long period of time. If only Timmy knew the suffering and humiliation that Father Richard Brady underwent for the past years, he'd be most willing to give the priest the few moments of pleasure he so needed to ease his restless mind; those moments that were costly only to a Rule made by man, a Rule that is broken daily in far more serious infractions by priests, brothers and nuns in the ordinary routine of so-called spiritual life, a Rule that enjoys the elasticity of lax consciences among would-be religious.

Frater Kevin knew it was contrary to the Rule to talk to the professed members of the Abbey. He knew it was specifically outlined that the novices should not so much as greet Father Richard Brady much less engage in conversation with him. But, Frater Kevin knew human nature even better than his Novice-Master, who spent the greater portion of his priestly life in the Foreign Missions of China and Japan. He may not be thoroughly acquainted with Philosophy and Theology, but he did know people, because he loved people with all his heart.

The priest carried on an uninterrupted conversation with Frater Kevin for nearly ten minutes. Timmy listened with sympathetic understanding. When the priest was through talking, he told him not to worry another moment. He would write to someone who could adjust the matter and free the priest of his bondage.

"In 1912, I guess you were a mighty small boy, Frater. I was assigned to a Church in Atlanta, Georgia," the priest began, looking over at Timmy. "In those days, I was a rather young priest to be made pastor of an old worn-out church. The pastor I replaced was sent back here to the Abbey and retired. He was a saintly old man who believed in reaching his parishioners through prayer rather than the awful task of hitting their pocketbooks occasionally. I was told by the Abbot and later on by the Bishop that it was my duty to build a new church in my parish, a church of a certain size and structure.

"Naturally, Frater, I was filled with all sorts of zeal on this first major assignment. I was anxious to have the nicest and largest church in the city of Atlanta. All priests have visions of beautiful churches when they are created pastors. I wasn't any different from the rest of the vast herd.

"A group of men in the parish took it upon themselves to visit me the first night after I was installed. Over a few drinks, we discussed the possibilities of the new church. It meant extensive drives, bazaars, fairs, raffles and every other means of getting money together in a district of these United States where people don't believe in the precept of supporting their parish priest and church.

"After five years of every method known to man, I was able to sleep, happy at night knowing I was well on my way to building a new church. I had in the bank nearly twenty-five thousand dollars of the people's money.

"In the spring of 1917, my cousin from New York City visited me. He was dressed with all the regal attire of a prince. He had the latest in everything including ideas on finance. I should have closed the door on him when I first saw him approach the steps of the rectory. He stayed for dinner and asked me all sorts of questions concerning the proposed church I had written my aunt in New York about. He then wiggled out of me how much I had on hand to start building. If I had been a smart man, I would have withheld certain information from this cousin. But, I guess I figured because he was a member of the house, in a remote sort of way, I was obliged to inform him of my successful collection during the past five years. When I told him I had in the vicinity of twenty-five thousand dollars in the bank awaiting approval from my Abbot and the Bishop to start building, I thought for sure he was going to have a fit on the parlor rug.

"He told me of a clever means, through the stockmarket, of making my amount jump to a double figure, and, at the same time allow him a little marginal return for his speculative ability. It was so cleverly put to me I couldn't see how it would fail. He told me that Anaconda Copper was going steadily upwards on Wall Street, and then in a few weeks, it would take a sudden drop and then rise again. This information came to my cousin from some confederate on the "inside." Somewhere along the line, I just forget the exact details now, although I certainly shouldn't, we were to invest and wait for the drop and sudden rise and clear out with a handsome profit. I believe my cousin said we were to buy it "low" and sell it "high." At least, I have a vague recollection of these infamous terms. He was able to produce figures that would amaze a poor parish priest like myself.

"I invested five thousand dollars of the church's money in the faith of my cousin. He wanted, of course, the whole amount, but I couldn't risk such a withdrawal when three of my parishioners were on the staff at the bank we did business with. I thank God, now, it was only a fifth of the whole sum. I have neither seen my cousin, nor the certificates of Anaconda Copper since. It was a blow I hope to God you never are forced to suffer, my boy. What was I to tell the people and the Bishop and my Abbot? It was quite simple. I told them I loaned the money to my cousin, and he absconded with every red cent of the five thousand. They could hold me responsible in full.

"The good people who praised me to the high heavens were the first to scream for my blood. They wanted me behind bars for the rest of my life with the keys to the prison hurled in the Gulf Stream. My Abbot, at the demand of the Bishop, paid the full sum of money to the parish committee and withdrew me from the parish to the Abbey, where I have been doing penance ever since, a penance that has made me old and hated by all for these many years. Boys like yourself, who don't know the circumstances, go through a year of Novitiate life here and only learn that I'm a bad priest who committed a grave sin, and because of that sin, I'm to be ostracized for the balance of my life, or at least till some Abbot has a merciful heart. This present Abbot isn't built that way. He was procurator when it all happened and the man who dug up the required money at the demand of the Abbot. The real point I'd like to make, Frater, is this: You boys go through a life completely new and entirely different from other lads your age. Your charity courses are built along the lines of Christ's teaching. Do you think Our Lord would want young men to grow in the virtues of Religious Life with hatred in their hearts for one of their Religious brothers? Of course, you'll agree with me now that you know my story, but, how many youngsters like you go through a part of this Novitiate and then decide to leave, never knowing what that strange-looking priest did to receive such a penance. I'm not trying to condone my sin. It's as black as this tunic. But, I like to think, anyway, my soul is a lot whiter than many in Religious Life who are going about with their heads high in the air and concealing from society the hideous and cancerous-eating hearts that weigh their very souls to the eternal pitfalls of a highly deserved hell. Please forgive me, Frater. I should never have said that to you. I'm sorry!"

There was a silent pause. Father Richard spoke a few words before his eyes became filled with fresh tears of sorrow.

"Now, you know my story, Frater Kevin. It wasn't at all like you thought it would be, was it? I'm sure you entertained some very strange notions as I guess many other lads of your age must have done. Through kind friends, I have paid back half of the amount. Someday, please God, I shall pay back every cent and be in a position to ask the Abbot to replace me in my old standing with the Community."

The priest broke down and wept bitterly. It was difficult for Frater Kevin to watch this big Irish priest lose control of himself. It was too much for one Irishman to watch another suffer. They say, and with some degree of truth, an Irishman can watch an Englishman bleed to death, but to see a fellow countryman suffer only a slight hurt, it must be shared! So, Timmy cried with his newly acquired friend. He cried because Father Richard cried, even through he knew he was going to relieve the priest of is burdens in only a few short days.

Timmy stood up and told Father Richard his worries were over. He assured him that his Aunt Liz would make up the remaining amount at his command. After all, two thousand five hundred dollars was a lot of money, but he had many times over that amount in his own right in the bank at Lacodere. He refused to listen to the protests registered by the priest. It was a duty he felt was his to accomplish. The priest was overwhelmed with joy. It was the first sign of hope he had ever received and from somebody he thought too high to even listen to his little story. They agreed, as they walked back to the bronze crucifix, that this was to be strictly between themselves. Father Richard would inform Timmy just as soon as the Abbot made his decision. On the other hand, it was not to be an outright gift. It was to be a loan, a long term loan, one in which Father Richard would try to repay with the little gifts he could secure from people on the outside. No, Father Richard didn't want Frater Kevin to be the loser. It mustn't be fraternal charity between two monks just as it stood. Father Richard must find a means to repay this obligation.

The priest left Frater Kevin with the load of sorrowful years lifted and feeling years younger. It was Frater Kevin who assumed the weight of those years thrust upon him. He enjoyed the burden of new responsibilities. They made him forget his own little indifferences and petty bits at his conscience.

The bell announced the end of the work period. Although Timmy knew he had accomplished very little of a material gain, he was satisfied to tell in the Chapter of Faults, which was held every few days in the choir, that he was negligent during his work period. He would receive the little penance offered him and forget the whole incident. Any infraction of a minor character was told in public and the usual penance administered would be a decade of the Rosary for the suffering souls in Purgatory or some other little prayer for the deceased members of the Abbey. In any event, the prayers novices said never could add up to the number of faults committed.

Before the season of Advent, which is the time set aside for the preparation for the Feast of the Nativity, Frater Kevin received his first callers. They were Aunt Liz and little Robert. The latter was most impressed with Timmy's new garb and wanted to try it on for himself. The check was delivered to Timmy without a word of explanation requested, although Timmy did tell Aunt Liz the whole story and received her wholehearted approbation. There were other things to discuss, and this was to be Timmy's last visit from Aunt Liz until Christmas. The three walked to the cemetery after they had visited the chapels in the Novitiate and the main Abbey.

While walking down the path that led to the cemetery, Liz was trying to tell Timmy what she had rehearsed over and over again on the train. It wasn't going to put anything over on her Timmy, and she wasn't in a very good position to deceive. She was so used to the truth herself, that it became most difficult to arrange a possible situation that may even give a semblance of falsehood about it. If she would come out directly and tell Timmy what was on her mind, she would have a third person on the trip homeward. This, she didn't want, because she felt in her heart the boy belonged to the Church.

As they passed the small lake where the students spent many hours swimming in the summertime, Liz asked Timmy why they cut his hair so short and changed the part so radically. She was surprised to learn that this was just another test placed on the disposition of each novice. The Master requested, from time to time, many little things that he knew would be of disagreement to young men. He had an idea that Timmy was a little proud of his curly blonde hair, so, he instructed one of the novices to cut the waves off and change his part. Timmy only bit his tongue and swallowed his vanity. To show indignation was exactly what the Master was looking for. If the subject was able to take it in the true spirit, he was regarded in a greater light than the individual who wasn't able to absorb this change of physical manner. There were many like trials in the course of the first three months. Many more followed in the course of the next nine; more of a personal nature that found no origin with the Superiors. Timmy, as Frater Kevin, would learn to take these with all the rest.

"I don't know what your reaction will be, Timmy," said Liz, trying her best to grope for the words she felt properly fitted for such a delicate subject, "but, I feel it is only right that I should tell you lest you learn from some outside source before I had a chance to inform you directly."

"Okay, Auntie Liz, let's have the gory details. The house burnt down, huh?" said Timmy, laughing.

"No, Silly, I'm going to have an addition to our house," she said, unable to look Timmy straight in the eyes.

"My God, Liz, have you gone to work and found yourself a husband after all these years of protected maidenhood?" he said, looking over to see if Robert caught this remark.

"No, Timmy, I've invited Mrs. Turrel to live with me because I felt she could help me tremendously around the house now that Silba isn't with me. And, also, I feel very lonely without somebody like you around to "mother." Doctor Gerard and Glad, and, in fact, all my friends thought it a wise move if I adopted a little baby to raise. It would make me feel more like living in that great big house now that you're away. Of course, little Robert here will come and visit with me, but I need someone permanent to put to bed every night and see that its ears are nice and clean and that the child goes to school, and we have Christmas again . . . and . . ."

"Okay, Auntie Liz, we won't have any of these tears," said Timmy, bringing his aunt into his arms and holding her against his chest. "Anything you say goes with me, baby, you know that. I don't know why you felt you had to ask me. It's your house, you know."

The three walked on past the cemetery and beyond the meadow to the orchards. The trees looked barren as they stood so stately in rows too numerous to count. Robert found contentment in climbing the first tree in the orchard. Liz and Timmy sat in the crude loveseat in a quiet section nearby. They talked about everyone who came to their minds. Liz was clever enough to avoid the name of Madeline Turrel, and she left Cassino satisfied that her Timmy wasn't thinking of New Orleans or the girl he once loved so passionately. In a few minutes, Timmy described monastic life as he knew it. He had done the very same in his monthly letters home, so it really was a repetition of his life in verbal form.

"By the way, Liz, what kind of a brat do you intend adopting?" said Timmy, trying to appear interested in the matter that seemed so vital to his aunt. "I certainly hope for your sake it doesn't look anything like me, or you'll really have another session on your hands."

"I hope he does look like you. Just exactly like you, Timmy," said Liz, looking him straight in the eyes.

There was no note of registration. If Liz had a point to convey, it failed to find its mark. Liz was just as happy. It meant that she could work everything with all the success of an engineer who knew construction and mathematics through and through.

Parting wasn't nearly as sad as it had been in August. Liz kissed Timmy goodbye knowing in her heart that he was happy and contented. Nothing would disrupt this obvious happiness that he displayed on their visit. She could go back to Lacodere and formulate her plans as she thought best. With the help of Mrs. Turrel, Madeline should cooperate in the light of reason and what little faith she still possessed in her soul. Nothing under heaven could stop Liz as she held Timmy's face firmly between her hands and looked fondly into his sparkling eyes. No, with the good God's help, nothing will dare happen to hurt her Timmy.

Liz promised to try and come to the Abbey on Christmas Day, but was reluctant to be pinned down to a direct answer. She felt there was so much to do between the first Sunday in Advent and Christmas Day that it would be impossible to get away. Yet, she knew if Timmy insisted, she'd come!

Little Robert had a strange request to make of Liz just before they left the parlor. He asked her to turn her face to the wall as he had a secret to impose upon his big "brother." Auntie Liz was used to these secrets. Often she was forced to ask people to leave the living room as little Robert unraveled some innocent secret that beset his nerves until it was safely intrusted to Auntie Liz's understanding heart. Liz winked at Timmy as a warning to prepare for most anything to follow.

Timmy, in turn, threw his scapular over his right shoulder and bent very low to catch this all-important bit of news. As he waited for the tidings, he felt Robert's arms around his neck, and suddenly, like an unexpected flash from the horizon, the moist lips of his little pal found rest on his mouth. As unexpected as it was, it was received with all due respect. Timmy picked the boy up in his arms and returned the secret imposed upon him and held him for a few seconds before he told Liz she could turn her face towards them.

The little lad was filled with that rare joy that comes only to youngsters who have suffered the longing desire of love, but never received its warm reception. It was enough for Robert to be near Timmy, but to find such intimacy so well received placed him in a sphere heretofore unknown. Timmy pledged solemn secrecy as he indicated to Liz through the sign language that the lad's secret was only a goodbye kiss of an innocent child of eight.

Christmastime in the monastery doesn't admit of the necessity of shopping and worrisome details of the secular. There are decorations on many alters, a crib to build for the newborn Babe and a refectory to be made more homelike, little things that make up the daily tasks of young novices. Tasks they never had to perform as members of the fast moving society in the world. All extra duties were willingly accomplished because they added much to the exterior and interior happiness of all the brethren.

While the great clock in choir struck twelve, the Abbot walked out of the sacristy to start the first of seventy-five Masses that would be offered by the various priest-monks of the Abbey between midnight and noon the great feast of Christmas. Over his left forearm, he carried a black scapular and cowl. He stood at the foot of the main altar and turned to address the priests, brothers and novices. He cleared his throat and asked Father Richard to come to the altar steps. Father Richard knew this meant his restoration had come at last. All eyes in the choir followed the priest as he slowly walked up the center aisle of the chapel. Some could see tears in Father Richard's eyes even through the mist of their own. None could be happier in that filled chapel, as the last sound of the bell announced the midnight hour, save the priest who suffered the loss of his companions these many years.

He knelt before the Abbot and received his scapular and cowl. With trembling hands, he adjusted it about his shoulders. It had been a long time since he had this part of his habit about his body. The Abbot blessed the monk and told him to say his three Masses in honor of the Holy Ghost, the Infant Jesus, and the Blessed Mother. He told him he was forgiven and was once more restored to the position he lost in 1917. The old Abbot then addressed the other monks and told them to be charitable to Father Richard and accept him once more as their brother. He told them to regard the monk as having returned from a long journey and to open their fraternal hearts in the charity of true brotherhood. He told them to rend the kiss of peace before he began his Solemn High Mass.

Each monk-priest, brother and Frater-Novice extended the kiss of peace on the cheek of Father Richard. The poor priest was overcome with joy as each man placed his hands on the monk's shoulders and bent over his stall to permit his cheek to touch the forgiven priest's. It was an impressive sight for Fraters Kevin and Ignatius. They were not in the slightest degree overcome with embarrassment when the priest came to their stalls. When the priest came to Timmy, he bent very low and whispered in the ear of his benefactor, "To you, I owe this." Gibby couldn't help hearing this and smiled to himself.

Returning to the main altar again, the Abbot gave the priest his kiss of peace and told the priest he was happy to have him back in the fold. He shook his hand and assured him the other priests who were stationed outside the monastery would be duly informed and recalled home to render their thanksgiving. It was the biggest Christmas present a priest could receive. It was the kind of gift that made Timmy shine with pride in being able to continue to help another over a difficult step.

Again, Timmy won out. Liz paid her Christmas call on time for dinner in a special dining room set apart from the regular refectory. There, she and the two fraters enjoyed a bit of Lacodere brought to the Abbey. A few little presents were handed over to the boys and in return the novices gave Aunt Liz a spiritual bouquet of Masses, Holy Communions and Stations of the Cross they intended saying in the course of January for her special intentions.

After going over all the news events of both the monastery and the town of Lacodere, Liz left the two young embryonic Benedictines with the promise that she would again visit them before Lent set in. They begged her to come earlier, but she declined their appeals telling them that she had to prepare for the adoption of her new little tenant. She told them that the Doctor and Glad Gerard would be up before very long and would have come for Christmas dinner, but for the doctor's sore throat, and carried the usual motherly and fatherly messages of love to the boys. The Gerards regarded Timmy as their second son and treated him on an equal basis with Gibby.

Even though Liz looked at Timmy while discussing the adoption, it never entered his mind that he could possibly be associated in any way with her proposition. He was not to know that he was the father of Madeline's unborn child until after he was safely ordained a priest of God. And only then by a queer coincidence of marked importance.

CHAPTER EIGHTEEN

The night of January 29th was cold and miserable. All through the day Frater Kevin felt strangely uneasy. Towards evening this uneasiness turned into physical pain and sickness. He went to the Superior to complain, but the Novice-Master was out at a nearby parish hearing Confessions. He took it upon himself to go to his cell and retire early. Gibby came to see him and offer assistance. For the first time in Timmy's life, he felt the need of solitude. When he was a child in Lacodere, he was afraid of storms that terrified old ladies and little children. Even as he grew in years, this fear of thunder never left him. He always thought of the little story Sister Mary Immaculata told her class when a great burst of rain and thunder would interrupt her teaching. She told them that God was awfully provoked at the people down here on earth who were committing sins at that very moment. And, to show how angry He really was, He commanded the clouds to bump each other with terrific force and create such a noise that the people way down on earth would get down on their knees and beg His forgiveness. The story had some merit for youngsters at the time, but as they grew older, they went right ahead and sinned despite the noise above, and if they did happen to recall the little reminder, they would only remember it as a story Sister Mary Immaculata dreamed up in her very vivid imagination.

But on this cold night with thunder raging and rain beating on the windows with a mighty force, Frater Kevin felt an illness creep over his body in the form of sharp pains about his stomach. He took warm water and some medicine that Gibby brought him, but it failed to relieve the burning sensation that ran through his abdomen. He threw himself on the bed hoping to fall asleep in a short time. The pains became more intense and forced him to cry out in agony, "Eli, Eli, lamma sabacthani?" No one heard his voice. At least no one apparently heard his cry for relief. The rest of the novices were on the first floor in the community room playing cards or reading the latest Catholic magazines.

In another section of the Southland in a room at old Hotel Dieu, the hospital on Tulane Avenue, Madeline Turrel was going through the agonies of hell in her labors. Her old mother was beside her bed trying to comfort her. Madeline had hatred in her eyes and heart as she screamed in blasphemous anger. She refused to see the priest and only tolerated her mother's presence because she had a message to deliver to her. All the beauty and charm had left Madeline's face. She looked much older than seventeen as she lay in the white-covered bed. In her hand, she held the Chain of Lacodere. Thrice she threw it the length of the room and each time, her poor mother went over and picked it up. She tried as best she could to comfort her daughter in this awful trial. She asked her to pray to the Blessed Mother to give her courage and strength to rally under the pain of approaching motherhood. All her motherly advice was scorned upon as she spit out words of hatred for ever being brought into the world. Never once did she mention Timmy O'Shea or the woman who patiently waited the delivery of her nephew's boy in a suite at the Roosevelt Hotel.

Mrs. Turrel walked up and down in the room imploring God to forgive her daughter's terrible conduct. Once, she knelt down by a statue of good Saint Anne and begged the grandmother of the Kings of Kings to "have mercy on my poor Madeline. She's very sick and not her real self." The nuns on duty in the hospital were afraid to enter the room lest they receive some venomous verbal attack that would cause a street-walker to blush with shame. The very devil himself was lodged in her soul and made her exterior countenance one of heinousness and recalcitration.

At eleven o'clock that night, the nurse came in to take her to the delivery room. Mrs. Turrel asked Madeline if there was anything she wanted her to do while she was giving birth to her child. It was a question prompted by fright rather than reason. There wasn't much anyone could do of a material nature while such an act was being perpetrated. Madeline ordered her mother to go straight to hell with all the speed she could devise and never show her ugly face again as long as she lived.

Mrs. Turrel swallowed her obvious hurt in her handkerchief. No mother deserved such treatment from a daughter when her only sin in life was giving up every enjoyment a mother could possess so that she could bestow the fruits of her labors and energies in the direction of her only daughter. No mother was ever created by an All-just God to suffer public abuse from the tongue of the child she bore in pain and agony. Most mothers can absorb the maltreatment of an ingrate child in the privacy of their own companionship, but to listen to a screaming girl in a hospital corridor en route to give birth to another soul, accuse her sick and aged mother of the vilest and most contemptible sins was too much for Mrs. Turrel to accept. She left her daughter to the care of the shocked nurses and found refuge in the dim lit chapel on the floor below, wherein resides a true and understanding friend, Who yearns for His loved ones to come to Him and pour out their most intimate thoughts, cares, worries and desires.

In a suite of rooms at the Roosevelt Hotel, Aunt Liz waited patiently for news from Mrs. Turrel. Together they planned to stay at the hotel until such time as the baby could be released to the care of its grandmother. Madeline shouted time and again that she never wanted to see the baby or hear its name mentioned. All she asked of her mother was the simple request that the child be given the Chain of Lacodere, without explanation as to its whereabouts or origin. Mrs. Turrel was to raise the child as best she could without looking to Madeline for any support or assistance. Further messages that were never delivered or given consideration as far as her mother was concerned, brought words of condemnation on Aunt Liz. It was Madeline's request that Liz never learn of the baby's birth or any knowledge of its father. It was impossible to keep this from Liz when she was the possessor of letters directed to Timmy, exposing the whole regrettable episode at the house on Fontaine Street that Thursday in April. Through Liz's clever manipulation, she was able to swing Mrs. Turrel over to her way of thinking and get her to move all her belongings into the O'Shea household. This was the first of several moves in the direction of acquiring Madeline's child. With such a friendly shoulder to lean upon as Liz's, Mrs. Turrel thankfully looked to her for that added advice when the news finally came to her directly from her sister in New Orleans. She wasn't hurt or shocked. She knew Madeline was after Timmy and knew the type of daughter she had brought up. She knew that a young boy with Timmy's fine character traits could fall very easily for her daughter's charm and resourcefulness without being totally at fault. She knew her Madeline would stop at nothing to secure her designs and satisfy her desires.

At eleven-thirty, the pain left Frater Kevin as mysteriously as it came about. The experience of that night came back to him with force much later. He closed his eyes for a night of complete rest, unaware that in the famous Hotel Dieu at the very moment the clock struck the half hour past eleven, he was the father of a crying, ugly, reddish mass of baby flesh with absolutely no apparent indication that it would ever grow to look as beautiful as its mother once looked, or possess the charm and handsomeness of its father.

Liz was notified immediately that the baby was born, and a very healthy little boy at that! She was beside herself with emotion. Her first impulse was to scream for joy and arouse the sleeping guests of the Roosevelt Hotel. How could she be expected to contain herself when within her heart she leaped like a child with a newly acquired doll? Liz forgot to ask about Madeline in her excitement, but Mrs. Turrell didn't forget to tell her that her daughter was doing well under the strain of being a mother so early in life and under the pressure of resentment.

The baby's nurse from Memphis was on hand at the O'Shea house days in advance of the arrival of the young lad. She was instructed to forward any news to the neighbors that Liz had adopted a boy baby and that if the inquisitive parties wanted to learn any further facts, they were free to come directly to the house for information. Even Father Joseph was led to believe that the child came from the New Orleans Orphan Asylum on Napoleon Avenue, and if it seemed queer that Liz wanted the baby baptized in Lacodere, well, Liz wanted it that way, and she wasn't one to trifle with, and Father Joseph knew it better than anyone else in Lacodere. Three weeks after Liz and Mrs. Turrel returned from New Orleans, they decided to adjust the matter of naming the little cry baby.

Madeline had been home with her Aunt Clare only four days when she told her guardian she wanted to go to Cuba with a friend. It was all the old lady could do to prevail upon her to remain quiet for a few more weeks before attempting any extensive trips or excitement. She refused to write to her mother, who had left with Liz as soon as the hospital released the baby. She wanted no mention of her child made in her presence. She told her Aunt Clare that it was a closed book, and she never wanted to be reminded of the fact that she was a mother.

Through persistent pleading, Madeline remained close to her Aunt's home and was agreeably pleasant. She received callers and often packages came to the house. One day a beautiful basket of roses with an engraved card bearing the name of Andre was delivered to the house. It was the introduction of Andre Bourdeau as a constant visitor, even to Madeline's bedroom! He was a very tall and dark sort of creature who talked mostly with his artistic hands. He vowed all manner of love to Madeline even in the presence of Aunt Clare. Bourdeau was older than Madeline, but very young in his ideas. His mother's allowance enabled him to dress in smart attire and give nice presents to young girls. His lady friends were members of the various musical circles about the French Quarter. Madeline, though, attracted him over and above her musical accomplishments.

Whatever possessed Madeline to seek solace and comfort in Andre Bourdeau she never deemed it necessary to disclose her findings to her Aunt Clare. On Washington's Birthday, she entered the Versailles Club with Andre at her elbow. Madeline always looked her best when before the public. It meant little to her what element of society the public happened to be. Andre suggested the Versailles Club because they featured a rare mixture of absinthe that tickled the soul and invigorated the mind. Many of the younger set found the Versailles a haven for forgetting the drudgery of final examinations and the burdens of specialized courses. In turn, the Versailles catered to the younger set, because they could mix the drinks to greater profit for the institution.

Skeets Malone eyed Madeline as she walked the length of the room and was seated in a curtained booth at the far end of the dance floor. Madeline saw Skeets, but refused to acknowledge his presence as being anything significant to her personally. After a few moments, Skeets asked leave of the woman he was with and walked over to the booth where Madeline sat alone. He looked at her and there was an exchange of smiles. There were words in these smiles that neither dared utter.

"Who's the twenty-five cent pimp you're sporting now, Madeline?" said Skeets, sitting next to the girl he once despised.

Before Madeline answered, she looked in the direction of Skeets' companion and then turned back to look directly at the awaiting questioner.

"I might add, Skeets Malone, by way of a like question, who is that ten cent prostitute you have over there?"

"Oh, that?" he said, indicating with his thumb over his shoulder, "that's your sister—if you ever had a sister."

"Still the same contemptible Skeets," said Madeline, reaching in her handbag for a cigarette. "How is it you never went away to become a priest with your other three friends? You'd made a fine Martin Luther or Judas Iscariot. Give me a light, will you?"

"As I look at you now, Maddy, I can't help wondering what Timmy O'Shea saw in you," he said, holding the flame close to her cigarette. "I guess one must give the devil his dues, though. You have a pretty fair chassis even from where I sit."

"Let's keep him out of this, Skeets," she said with burning indignation. "That's in the past, and I'm not living in the past."

"Honey, you're not living. That's what you really meant to say. If that long drink of ink can make you happy, sister, you're really up against it for some true happiness. Now, take me for instance. You and I could get together some weekend and ride up to Lake Charles and . . ."

"And just forget about the rest, Skeets. You're definitely the cheap kind. What you brought with you tonight is your speed. Why don't you go over and enjoy yourself while she's still in a receptive mood? From here it looks like her evening is about folded up. Goodnight, Doctor Malone."

Skeets stood up as he noticed Andre approaching the table. He asked Madeline if she still lived with her aunt on Pere Antoine Alley and if it would be safe to call on her some evening soon. He received a hurried affirmative answer and made his departure lest he become embroiled in some controversy with Andre and suffer eviction from the infamous Versailles Club. It wasn't uncommon for the premedical students to be asked to leave a night club of New Orleans.

Washington's Birthday was celebrated with a Gaudete. In all religious houses and monasteries, the brethren have a little extra rejoicing on the holy days as well as the holidays. Washington, as first President of the country, is no exception. The Southern religions may forget to give homage to the Great Emancipator, but never exclude Washington or Lee. The Novice-Master felt the novices were sufficiently guided by their established virtues to permit them to recreate "on their own" with a little ice cream and cake to add to the excitement. Little did he realize Frater Maximilian, better known as just plain Maxie, would tell one of his laugh-provoking tales about his Cousin George who was supposed to be a novice with the Franciscans in Buffalo. Frater Maximilian couldn't think of a name to take after his retreat in August, so the Abbot hung Saint Maximilian onto poor farmer Gienna. Sometimes it pays to think for one's self. At least, Gienna came to that conclusion.

"You know," Frater Maxie started out, "you fellows don't know how fortunate you are in having both a Gaudete and me on the same bill. They should only celebrate the big days of the year with the Gaudete, but because I'm here, they toss you a double deal of relaxation and mirth. But, that isn't telling you about my cousin with the Franciscans, is it?"

Frater Maxie listened to the chorus of, "on with the story" for a few moments, then began to entertain the novices with another of his mythical tales of a character who was merely a figment of his imagination. A character he had people actually believing existed and one who went through the trials of any normal novice of a Religious Order.

Timmy and Gibby sat close together as the story teller began his yarn. These interludes in the course of the Novitiate year added much pleasure and a release from strain placed on their nerves. Timmy admired Maxie for his ability to provide entertainment. He enjoyed Maxie most when he would play on the piano and fumble through his "Clair de Lune." The promise he received from Maxie that in a few short months of practice he'd know Debussy better than he knew himself tickled Timmy. There appeared just a short time later, when the "de Lune" caused Timmy to revolt within himself. Not that the immortal classic had changed, but the sensations it once caused in his heart turned to sadness rather than joy.

To tell a story successfully, one must insert the proper ingredients that tend to startle the listener. Maxie had the power and the qualifications of an artist in this respect. He was a comedian even in the most serious moments of monastic life. Just to look at him caused one to laugh. When he knew some certain inane expression brought laughter, he'd vie for the honors of provoking further hilarity by acting the clown either in conference or during Sacred Office. Without a Maxie in a Novitiate, the more staid novices would find life a boredom unexcelled.

"A lot of you fellows don't even believe I have a Cousin George, do you?" he started out by asking a rhetorical question. "Well, the whole thing boiled down only forces me to believe that you holy sons of Stain Benedict are just jealous.

"As a matter of fact, and you're free to believe this or not, I tried to get Cousin George to swing his spiritual carcass in our direction and become a "bene," but he thought I was mentally unbalanced. If I am, that's neither here nor there. Anyway, Georgie entered the Franciscans to be a beggar for Christ's sake. Don't laugh, I really mean it! Our Novitiate here is a breeze compared to his. The rules are about the same, but his Master is a first-class heel. He's always trying to catch a novice doing something contrary to Holy Rule. But, Cousin Georgie is too slick for the old Polish Master. You have to get up awfully early in the A.M. to catch up with Cousin Georgie.

One evening seven or eight of the novices were holding a session in one of the novice's cell. You know what a 'bear-cat' that is if you're caught. They really toss the book at you if you muff this one. But, you know how we all take chances—we're 'goofs' in that respect. Most of the boys were smoking and telling stories about past experiences, you know, the kind we tell—mostly damn fat lies! They had the lights out so nobody could detect anything going on up there. The window was wide open though, so they could let some of the smoke out and at the same time get a little fresh air. With stories like novices tell, you sure need fresh air.

"As quiet as they were trying to be, one of the novices started a fit of laughing over some remark that was made. Another followed suit and soon the whole group was beating their heads against the wall. In the excitement, one of the holy brethren had a direct call from Mother Nature. Because the window was open and there was no need to truck way down to the end of the hall, it was suggested to let fly out the window onto the court below. During the most humiliating session with all sorts of gymnastics to perform, with a habit as a means of further annoyance, the young friar balanced himself on the window sill and proceeded to render relief to his excited kidneys. In the act of gaining this so essential relief, a succession of quick knocks came to the door. "My God," said one of the boys. "It's Polonius, the eavesdropping Master! What in hell are we going to do?"

One of the friars who was older than the others said, 'Let the old bastard in. We might just as well ge it now as later!' One of the boys removed the chair that was leaning against the door as a bar of prohibition, while the unfortunate member on the window still had to frustrate his cell and leap to the floor, unable to complete his symphonic arrangement. The door was opened, and the Superior walked in with that 'ah ha' attitude written all over his face.

'So,' he said, looking around as if he missed someone or was looking for a friend in a crowded railroad station, 'I got you at last! In another man's room and breaking the rule of using tobacco. I see you are here, too, Friar George. This will go very hard with all you men!' The old man walked around the room sniffling here and looking under the bed there and then making a quick turn-about to see how the expressions on the boys' faces stacked up. He went to the window and looked out over the courtyard. As he pulled his head back in, probably in fear of someone pushing him out, he noticed stray drops on the sill. He gently put his index finger on one of the drops and then to his mouth as a chemist might do to taste some specific acid. As his tongue touched the liquid from his finger, he turned with a radiant expression and shouted, 'Ah ha and you've been drinking, too. So?' The last one-word question caused the friars to roar with laughter. It wasn't necessary to confirm the taste on the window sill. The Superior ordered the men to their respective cells and wanted no further reminder or mention of the experience."

The bell rang to end recreation as several young and tired Benedictines made for their own cells. They were still laughing as they slowly walked the stairs to the third floor. Maxie had again scored and added further zest to a group that needed humorous build-up every now and again.

CHAPTER NINETEEN

S hrove Tuesday, the day before Ash Wednesday, and the last day before the Lenten Season sets in, carries significance in several sections of the country. In the monastery, it meant burning the palms from Palm Sunday for the Blessed Ashes to be administered the following day. It wasn't a big task for the novices to perform, but it meant depriving them of their Tuesday walk through the countryside. These little excursions in the wooded area of the surrounding property afforded the young monks an opportunity to tear away from the routine of monastic life; to visit through forest lands and watch babbling brooks sing out with a merry tune, to examine trees and see if spring was really in the offing, to picnic under the nude trees and let the March wind blow through their hair, to return to the monastery refreshed with faces ruddy and exhilarant. These were but a few of the pleasures a novice derives in the course of his year devoted to prayer and recollection; a year that knows many trials and personal admonitions.

Because Ash Wednesday was late this year, it would force Easter to fall beyond the middle of April. March 1st was more than just Shrove Tuesday to many people. To Frater Kevin it was nearing the home stretch of a hard Novitiate year. At least to him, August 16th didn't look as distant as it did around Christmastime. In Lacodere, it was another day for Liz and Mrs. Turrel and their wild little baby boy, a day for bathing and seeing to his every need. Little Patrick was an over-favored little rascal. If his milk didn't show up at the exact moment when his first cry sounded, he would redouble his efforts to signal for his feeding. But, as much as he cried, he seemed to equally distribute his smiles. It was hard to determine at such an early date just who he resembled. He had an O'Shea nose and a Turrel pair of ears. He certainly would develop a Timothian smile and perhaps his father's beautiful disposition. If he were to develop talents, God alone at this early period chose to keep it a secret, and was the sole possessor of the knowledge from whence they would originate.

Mrs. Turrel was a stooge in the household. She was merely a means to an end. It was easy to understand why Madeline grew in recklessness. Her own mother gave evidence of being shiftless. The little things that were major problems to Liz were overlooked by Mrs. Turrel. It was extended charity on Liz's part to share the house with her. But, a secret must be cherished at any cost, and this was a means to its accomplishment.

On the twenty-seventh of February, Liz arranged to have Patrick duly baptized. Doctor and Mrs. Gerard acted as sponsors. The day before, she talked the matter over with Father Joseph in the library. Father thought it was very decent of Liz to give the child the name of her parish priest back in Ireland, even though the saintly priest was now enjoying the gifts of Heaven. So, it was decided on Saturday that Patrick should receive the name of Patrick Aloysius Dunne. Liz would have ample time to have a story ready when young Patrick became so learned as to want to know more fully the history of his progeny.

If the French-Irishman had any physical defects, they were so hidden that the profession of medicine knew nothing about them. Both Doctors Gerard and Jereau examined Patty only to shake their heads in disgust and wink at each other and say with professional dignity, "there's nothing here to cut up!"

Frater Kevin was duly informed of the administration of the Sacrament of Baptism in Saint Mary's Church in a letter written the following day by his Aunt Liz. She told him how young Patty cried and refused to take the pinch of salt on his tongue and how he nearly threw a fit when Father Joseph poured the water over his little head. All made good reading material, but served little to entertain Frater Kevin who handed the letter to Frater Ignatius in disgust. Gibby was even less interested. For young men away from the little excitements of home life, it is very difficult to describe via epistles the true meaning a baby can be to someone who is desperately lonesome. Had either Timmy or Gibby been in Lacodere when the baby arrived at the O'Shea house, perhaps the little tyke would have won them over as he did the two ladies. What little babies do in the form of entertainment can never be recorded successfully as it is actually seen by the witnesses. There is something purely personal about a baby's conduct that captivates the heart and makes the possessor swell with pride in being a part of that child's heart and soul. Frater Kevin would be impregnated with that impulse the first moment he held Patrick Aloysius in his arms. Patty's eyes would somehow reveal a story that he longed to forget, a story that brought memories of those last hours in April just a year ago.

As Liz splashed water over the white skin of a baby crying in a small tub, she knew whatever her Timmy took with him when he left for the monastery was restored in the voice of this child. Just because it was Shrove Tuesday and the day before Ash Wednesday didn't mean little Patty could dispense with his daily bath. Whether he liked getting soap in his eyes and having his ears cleaned out with warm oil and his tiny nostrils cleaned mattered little to Liz. She would be thoroughly rewarded when he would lay stretched out on the table and permit her to dry his fat little body with a soft towel. The smiles and laughter that would come when she powered him from head to toe always compensated her rough treatment of a few minutes of bathing.

In another section of the South, the great city of New Orleans was celebrating the last of the Mardi Gras. The three festive and merrymaking days preceding the advent of Lent were drawing to a close. The last hours were reserved for romancers. Beautiful costumes depicting the happy and the sad. Both men and women of all classes dressed to suit their particular moods. Little children raised in the atmosphere of the dramatic setting joined with the adults and ran the streets in wild excitement. Everybody should be happy on Shrove Tuesday. The ugly were made beautiful with gorgeous gowns of bright colored laces and satins. The masks hid the tell-tale story of weary and forlorn consciences. Men dressed as ancient Greek warriors and bandits of Sherwood Forest and Roman senators and gentlemen of the Court of Versailles all romped the streets of New Orleans or mounted the magnificent floats that paraded down the thoroughfare amid the excitement and screams of a city gone mad. But New Orleans went mad every year only to regain her sanity on the morning of Ash Wednesday.

A masked figure dressed as a wealthy Chinese merchant pushed his way along the swollen streets of humanity. He cared little whether the less sober women felt his arm dig deep into their sides as he forced himself toward Pere Antoine Alley. Girls dressed as French peasants danced in the streets in wild profusion. Little did they care of the exposé of their midriff as bare as the day they were born. The bolder girls, still in their early teens, cared little for the conventions of masks. Some bore the blue traces of abuse from rough hands, with hardly enough clothing to cover the essentials of decency.

It was difficult for Skeets to make time in such a congested area of the city. He had hopes of finding Madeline still at home and willing to share the evening with him. When he arrived at the apartment and inquired from Madeline's aunt where her niece intended to go, he received very little encouragement. All he learned from the old woman was the description of Andre Bourdeau and some excursion on the river. Clare said she was dressed as a Spanish senorita—black lace dress with red mask and shawl to match. The comb in her hair came all the way from France in the late Eighteenth Century, and Clare advised her to take the greatest care of it. It was the last reminder the old woman possessed from her homeland.

Skeets walked slowly in the direction of the waterfront. He could have enjoyed the company of many girls from the University that night, but his mind traveled in the sultry shadows of a tenant from Antoine Alley. He could never be guilty of being pensive or moody in the past. But, tonight he felt as if the bottom fell out of the well, and the abyss of loneliness usurped his very being. He didn't know what street he was walking along as he watched a crowd gathering a few feet from the wharf at the end of the street. He approached the scene with little concern. Excitement wasn't novel in New Orleans that night. No doubt some drunk was stabbed by a frenzied Frenchman who resented the passing remark made at his escort. The city's morgue wagon wasn't an uncommon sight in the lower quarters of New Orleans. Skeets remained in the outskirts of the crowd as interns bent over the frail body of a girl in a black Spanish dress. He listened with disconcern to the various hysterical buzzings of the women and their companions as the youthful doctors tried to render aid to the victim.

"I think she jumped off the ferry out there," one woman said. Another disputed this by saying, "She was pushed off, you mean." Someone said, "God, she's beautiful, isn't she?" a voice in the middle of the crowd said, "These girls that go out looking for trouble usually find it where they don't expect it."

Skeets couldn't see who they were talking about and cared less. He attempted to leave and found himself hemmed in by other late arrivals. He saw in the distance the driver and his assistant from the morgue smoking and leaning against a store window. They were prematurely called by some man who though the girl was dead. Someone else had the presence of mind to call Mercy Hospital and have an ambulance sent over.

A woman up front remarked about the comb in the girl's hair. "How could it stay in after such a fall?" the voice rang out. "It's such a beautiful comb, too, isn't it now?" the same voice echoed back to Skeets. There was something strange about the mention of the comb that startled Skeets. Why should he be interested in a French comb? Hundreds of girls wore them when they dressed for the Mardi Gras! His mind flashed back to Clare and the admonition she gave Madeline concerning the heirloom. He pushed his way through the crowd with no apologies till he stood behind the two interns. He bent over to get a better view and gasped as he recognized Madeline Turrel in a pool of water. Her beautiful Spanish gown was soaked and clung to her thin body. The interns didn't seem to know just what to do for her. They were mumbling something under their breath about the condition of her neck. Skeets overheard one say that it was broken clean and they'd better get her to the hospital for emergency treatment.

Skeets knelt down beside the intern with the bald head and told him he knew the girl, and they'd better get her to the hospital at once. If the interns resented this advice, they didn't show it. Skeets assured them he would accompany them back to the hospital and notify her relatives as soon as he could get to a telephone. He assisted the men as they lifted Madeline on to the stretcher and gave as much information to the police as he could in the short space of time he remained on the wharf.

In the ambulance as it roared through the crowded streets in the direction of the hospital, Skeets bent low over Madeline's body and whispered her name in her ear. There was no response to his mention of either his name or her own. One intern said, "She's about done for, Buddy," and lit a cigarette. But Skeets wanted to know what caused her to be "done for" and tried again to bring her to consciousness. It was no use. He was sure there was no response forthcoming.

A lot of things flashed in Skeets' mind as he listened to the wailing scream of the siren and the screech of brakes as the driver turned a corner. He thought of Timmy and that Christmas dinner when Madeline played with artistic beauty. He thought of the remark he made to Gibby about her virtue. He thought of her carefree and sing-song attitude as they grew up together. How he used to tease her when they were at the Academy and put gum in her beautiful black hair. All these thoughts raced through his mind as he looked upon her and bit his lip in shame.

If only she'd awaken so he could talk to her and let him make right the many wrongs. It would make them both feel better. "God, if she'd only come to!" he said over and over to himself. "This will kill Timmy if he ever learns about it." The interns heard mutterings of passengers before and gave little alarm to their meaning.

Skeets felt the movement of her hand under the green blanket and bent low to see if it was life or muscular reaction. He thought he saw her lips move in formation of words. His face was nearly meeting hers when suddenly her eyes opened very wide and closed again. He whispered in her ear that he wanted to help her and that all she need do was tell him how it all happened.

Madeline heard Skeets mention Timmy's name and opened her eyes and fixed her lips as if ready to speak. It seemed hopeless. She had sunk to the depths of despair. There was nothing left for her to live for in this vale of tears and sorrow. She had played her last concerto on the stage of life with the pathos of a Juliet. Her eyes opened again as the ambulance turned a sharp corner a few squares from Mercy Hospital. She saw Skeets' face so clear from those sad and tear-filled eyes. This time there seemed to be a sparkle of light glowing from them. She wanted to talk and speak out her soul, but life was quickly taking its hasty departure. The intern wasn't able to hear the whispered voice from the cot, but he knew there was conversation. He knew by the facial expressions of Skeets and Madeline that whatever was said was most intimate.

"Tell Timmy I still love him with all my heart. I'll always love him, Skeets. Tell him our baby is . . .". She couldn't find the words to express her secret, but changed to the short and final words, "please, Skeets, I need . . . I need . . . a priest!"

To any Catholic these are commanding words. Words that engulf strict obligations! When the ambulance came to a stop at the side entrance of the hospital, Skeets jumped out and ran to the attendant at the little office. "Get off your fat can, Joe, and get a priest down here quick! She's going out, and fast!" The men in the office had been called most every name in the book, so to be ordered by the name Joe didn't prompt hesitation.

The chaplain was at the side of the dying girl within a few minutes after Skeets asked for him through the attendant. She was never removed from the cot alive. The last words of the priest were intermingled with a sigh of thanksgiving that caused Skeets to make the sign of the Cross when he heard her voice. Something choked up within his throat that prevented him from saying, "Goodbye, Maddy."

After identification has been established and the usual routine set of questions were asked and answered, Skeets left the hospital office. No, he didn't need a bracer of a lift back to the frat house. He would walk. But, he appreciated the intern's graciousness, nevertheless.

How would he tell Clare? How would he ever have the nerve to talk to Timmy about such a horrible thing? When he found himself climbing the stairs of Pere Antoine Alley's Shuffert Apartment, he tried to make himself think that he heard wrong when Madeline mentioned the words, "our baby". He was in front of Clare's door ready to knock when an idea suddenly appeared in his mind. Timmy had wanted to talk to him that night when they were taking showers after baseball practice. But, then Timmy often had things to talk over with Skeets. Why should his evil mind think that Timmy could have been involved with Madeline to the extent that their association would or might produce "our baby".

"No," he thought to himself, "not Timmy and Madeline that way. It just couldn't be like that."

After the third knock, Clare came to the door in tears. She had heard the whole story just a few minutes earlier from the police. The hospital called her to inform her of Madeline's death. She needed comfort after such an ordeal. Skeets was too muddled himself to be of much assistance. He couldn't free his mind from these terrible words that ever appeared in constant whispered. He felt it wasn't for Clare's ears to repeat them and burden her further; not even for Mrs. Turrel's who would learn of the accident from her sister's account.

He sat in a stupor as Clare related the incident. When he left her apartment, he still didn't have it clear in his mind. He remembered something about Andre leaving Madeline for a few moments and some drunken man on board the ferry making advances to her. Clare went on to say that Madeline ran to the stern and lost balance and fell against the rail and then into the water. He couldn't remember what she said about the lifeboat and who took her to shore and the details concerning Andre's session with the police. All he kept asking himself while Clare sat reporting amid a profusion of tears was, "How will Timmy take this? Shall I tell him about 'our baby'?"

Liz accepted the wire handed to her by Mrs. Turrel. She read the brief account and looked into the sad eyes of the bereaved mother. There wasn't much Liz could say at a time like this. Mrs. Turrel didn't look for sympathy from Liz because she felt her daughter's hatred for her was keenly felt by the woman who befriended her in her greatest time of need. There were no words spoken as Liz returned the wire. She merely stood up and walked to the telephone and asked the operator to connect her with New Orleans.

CHAPTER TWENTY

L iz took care of all the arrangements for Madeline's funeral. At the old Cathedral of Saint Louis a low Requiem Mass was said and no panegyric was preached. That's the way Mrs. Turrel wanted it. It wouldn't have been the way Madeline would have liked it! But Madeline had lost forever her right to make decisions for herself.

A few nuns, too old to be otherwise employed, the usual number of elderly ladies and devout men who find themselves in Church every time the Church bell rings, were on hand to offer up the Mass for the departed soul who was resting in a casket in the aisle of the Cathedral. Skeets knelt with Mrs. Turrel and Liz. On her other side was Clare and her belching husband. It took a funeral to bring him to church and away from the sporting centers of the city.

After they placed Madeline's remains in the sealed vault and closed the outer door, the mourners left while the caretakers cemented the vault's door. It was all very simple and over with before eleven o'clock in the morning.

There were a few exchanges of meaningless conversation before Liz departed for the hotel and a session with Skeets. All seemed so cold and unaffected. Even Liz seemed more pleasant than usual when she ordered luncheon in her suite for Skeets and herself. She asked him how the studies at Tulane were progressing and complimented him for making a credible showing on the freshman team in basketball and football. If there was to be mention made of Madeline Turrel, it would find origin with Skeets.

She told him of their new addition in the home quite casually. But, it hit him like a bolt of lightening! Two and two really did make four according to his line of reasoning. The words "our baby" coupled with the news of an adoption in the O'Shea household not later than four weeks ago made him sit back and loathe the very food that was placed before him. It was quickly taken in its stride by the ever-observant eyes of Liz. She asked him point blank if he was ill. She knew she had spoken out of turn when she mentioned the word "baby." He must have had words with Madeline prior to her death! But, she was still too clever to permit herself to become involved with a young premedical student who was closer to the heart of her Timmy than any other boy with the exception of Frater Ignatius.

"As I sit here watching you struggle with something within yourself, Skeets," she went on, "I know in my heart you're too fine a friend to ever permit your thoughts to wander in the direction that may find themselves in words, and within earshot of ears that should never receive such a hurt from a friend."

"I understand what you mean, Liz," said Skeets, walking to the door with his head bent low, "but will he, or will she?"

The question was never meant to be answered as Skeets bid her farewell and departed down the corridor. It left Liz sitting near the window wondering to herself, as she watched the horse-drawn buggy pull away from the curb and disappear down the cobblestone avenue.

Lent passed with great rapidity. Easter Sunday heralded the Resurrection ceremonies after three days of prayer and preparation heretofore almost unknown to Fraters Kevin and Ignatius. It was more than just Maundy Thursday, and the thoughts of the Last Supper, followed by Good Friday and the Passion and Death of Christ. They were introduced to the depths of liturgical ceremony for the three days preceding Easter. They were happy to have gone through it all and to look in retrospect over the Lenten season. Much mail had accumulated over the forty days of fast and penance. Frater Kevin took his letters directly to his cell and sat at his desk sorting out the envelopes in the light of their exterior importance. Most of the mail came from Lacodere. A few letters with the Academy letterhead meant word from some young admirer or one of the nuns. A letter from Skeets in New Orleans, one from Father Joseph, another from Father Richard Brady in his new parish south of Savannah, and two from Aunt Liz. He favored Liz's letters and tore open the seal. It was sad to see a young boy go through the torments of that letter. The needle-like pain that must have shot through his heart as he read of Madeline's death caused him to break out in pronounced sobs. He read over the lines that told him how she received the Last Rites in the ambulance. He was surprised to learn that Skeets could very likely supply him with further news. Without a moment's delay, he took the letter from New Orleans, dated in early March and read the whole account. Skeets mentioned the affair on the ferry and how she wanted to protect her virtue, and met, through it all, her untimely death. Nothing was said about the last words and message from Madeline. It wasn't meant to be intrusted to the mails. Someday Skeets would see Timmy again and have a long talk, a talk that was supposed to have taken place the night of April 30th, a talk that Timmy wanted Skeets to be in on, but at the time, he had another date. In his letter, Skeets gently reminded Timmy of this engagement he had broken and told him they'd have to get together someday. Of course, Skeets assured him, it just came to his mind as he was writing to him that night, nothing to worry about. It could wait!

Frater Kevin didn't have the strong shoulders of a Father Joseph to lean upon during this trial and inward loss. He didn't have Auntie Liz to comfort him when sadness crept into his heart. He couldn't seek out Father Richard, who promised to be his friend forever. He wouldn't disclose his feelings to his Novice-Master for untold reasons. There remained only his ever faithful Gibby.

There are times in the course of a young man's training period when he realizes a spiritual dryness that causes him to look to the western sky and seek the unlimited array of gifts the world offers to his imaginative mind. He wants to throw aside the cloak of religious drudgery and painful humiliations inflicted upon him at every turn. The Religious Life looms up as a grotesque dragon that preys constantly on his nature and prods his intellect with desires of revolt. It isn't easy to dispel what appears to be gratifying. The older the man entering upon the life of a Religious, the harder will be his fight against these feverish and diabolical designs. Some fall, never to regain their former stance. For Frater Kevin, the trials were equal to those of the older man. He wasn't comparable in age, but he knew life in a different light than Frater Ignatius. This was a constant reminder, one that provoked his ever increasing desire to be fervent to the Rule and seek out only those in the Novitiate who could lend assistance rather than resistance to his noble ideals.

He never forgot Madeline Turrel. His mind never knew rest from her ever-present mental portrait as he pictured her seated at the piano and playing their piece, the haunting notes and chords that make up the "Clair de Lune."

Brother Francis MacDermott was a retired lay-brother in the Order of Saint Benedict. Because of his ninety-four years of healthy living, both in America and Ireland, and his ever cheerful attitude around the Abbey, he earned the right to do just about what he pleased. If he felt like calling the Father—Abbot to task for leaving the Abbey over a period of weeks, he never failed to take advantage of the opportunity. The Abbot would listen to the old man and smile. Everybody connected with Mounte Cassino loved Brother Mac. The students in the High School and College came to his room and listened to his wild stories of moving sheep four hundred miles across the Dakotas in the dead of winter. If he failed to mention certain incidents, the boys would remind him. He told the same stories over and over again with some additions or omissions. He chose to live on the first floor of the Novitiate because it was close to the Novice's chapel, and he like to be with the novices. It was contrary to the Rule to speak with the professed members, but exceptions had to be made in Brother Mac's case. He often referred to the Abbot by his first name, because he taught him how to hold a plow when he was a novice. Sometimes he was deaf and other times he heard too much. His sight was slowly leaving him. An operation a few years after the turn of the century failed to restore his vision in his left eye. The strain placed on his right eye was becoming a source of worry to everyone except Brother Mac. He loved to visit with the ladies who came on visiting Sundays to see either their novice-sons or the students in the school. When they would leave, he'd inform some novice that Mrs. So-and-So had a large rump or her legs resembled those of a piano. Little did he care that the Mrs. So-and-So might be the novice's visiting mother.

On a warm day in chapel when the novices would recite the Little Office of the Blessed Virgin, Brother Mac would join in the psalms and responses. He knew the Little Office from memory. Sixty-two years of daily recitation would enable any moron to memorize the Devine Office as well as the Little Office. The prayers that make up the Office are usually beautiful praises. Those who regard this obligation as an unpleasant task fail to understand the merit of prayer.

Sometimes in late May it becomes very warm in Georgia. Bodies kneel in choir with beads of sweat oozing out of their pores. The manual labor assignments don't cease in the late spring and early summer. There is much to do around a monastery to create tired muscles and provoke perspiration to flow. One day in the late afternoon, when the novices were reciting their prayers, Frater Maxie took advantage of the Superior's absence and sat directly behind old Brother Mac. He would reach over every now and again and tickle the old man's head with a chicken feather he always kept in the sleeve of his tunic. Brother Mac would make a wild slap at his head thinking the flies were unusually numerous that afternoon. Consistent tickling caused the old man to become infuriated and burst out with a loud, "God damn you stinking flies!" Of course, Brother Mac really wanted God to personally damn the infernal pests, but he brought hilarity into the House of God in so doing.

On another occasion, when the Master was away from the Novitiate over night, Frater Maxie caused another scene that nearly killed the old Benedictine brother. In the entrance to the Novitiate stood two life-sized statues of Saint Benedict and Saint Scholastica, the founder's sister. The latter was a beautiful replica of the saintly foundress of several convents. Artists could never depict the true loveliness, nor could sculptors chisel the sanctity of this holy Abbess. That all may be true, but Brother Mac entertained a personal abhorrence of nuns and statues that rendered them any degree of homage. He was sure that the Catholic Church could well afford to dispense with their services, that is, in many cases. But, he disliked nuns because he was jealous of their contribution to social and moral progress in the Church. More, perhaps, because he liked to hear himself shock the young novices. They'd be so cooperative in exclamations when he was doing his nightly bit of diatribe.

While the novices were having their recreation between eight and eight-thirty, Frater Maxie and Frater Alcuin left the Community Room and carried the heavy statue down the hall to Brother Mac's room. They opened the door and quietly stole into the old man's cell. He wouldn't be back there till after night prayer, and presently he was employed in telling another of his tall tales to the awe-inspired novices who were aware of the pending trick.

The boys placed the statue of Saint Scholastica in the middle of the Brother's bed and covered it neatly with his three Army blankets. They removed the crucifix that was in her hand and replaced it with a Confederate musket that hung on the old Brother's wall as a reminder of his youthful days under Nathan Bedford Forrest. The novices were in hopes that the semi-blind confrere would climb in bed and when he discovered he wasn't alone, attempt to shoot it out with the still form in a black gown, providing, of course, he could retrieve his musket from the hands of Saint Scholastica.

When the bell sounded, the boys went to night prayers. All during the brief meditation and nocturnal prayers, the novices giggled like convent girls. They were happy to be on their way to bed via Brother Mac's room and a few minutes of light comedy.

The old man walked slowly down the corridor humming an old refrain. He entered his cell, never realizing that he had a crowd of ten novices trailing him. He switched the light at the side of his door and walked over to sit on the bed and remove his shoes. As he sat there, he thought the bed seemed unusually low, and ran his hand towards the middle of the bed and jumped when he felt something foreign. He looked around and to his apparent horror, discovered what he thought was a live nun in his bed armed to the teeth as if protecting her Vows against the onslaught of some treacherous lecher. He left the bedroom with all due haste and went to the foot of the stairs, and with his loudest bellow called for help. "Will someone, for God's sake, come and help me remove this drunken nun from my bed. I can't reason with the witch. She's got my rifle all cocked and ready to shoot!"

The novices, hid along the corridor, couldn't contain themselves. There was a united burst of laughter as two of them hoisted their founder's sister out of the bed and returned her to the pedestal.

With spring cleaning on in both New Cassino Abbey and the house on Fontaine Street, many people were kept busy, and little time was left for correspondence. Fraters Kevin and Ignatius were assigned to the mountainous task of washing some nine thousand windows in all the Abbey's buildings. Other novices white-washed the chicken coops and cleared land beyond the cemetery. Some, with knowledge of horticulture, sprayed peach and pecan trees. Any novice who still remained idle found the small lake to be attended to. The months that followed the closing of the Novitiate year were busy. Everyone worked in the spirit of the Rule.

On Fontaine Street, Patrick Aloysius Dunne was growing gracefully into a fat and jolly five-month old baby. He still wailed for attention and began to recognize Robert as he tried to entertain him. Robert tried not to be rough with Patty, but his experience around six brothers and sisters taught him self-defense from the earliest days of his existence. Because of the vacation period, Robert was more than just a casual visitor. He took over Timmy's room nearly five nights a week. Mrs. Turrel occupied one of the guest rooms, and Father Joseph was staying at the house during the repairs to his own rectory. With Patty in a crib near Liz's bed, the O'Shea household was humming with activity. Father Joseph even took his breakfast after his Mass at the O'Shea home, because Mrs. Turrel knew just how to make his coffee.

With Jordan still occupying the basement apartments and telling Robert the weirdest of stories about the enchanting South of his youth, all forces moved in exciting activity. Liz never relaxed in her duty towards Patty. She would take him for a ride in the family car and let Robert hold him in the front seat as she drove to either Lake Tahoo or down to the church. Walking was only a necessary evil now that her abilities ran along automotive lines. She even planned the long drive to Cassino Abbey to watch Frater Kevin pronounce his temporary Vows of Poverty, Chastity, and Obedience. Only then would he be regarded as a real monk when he was licensed to sign his name with the included initials, O.S.B.

It would be a day of joy for the Gerards as they watched their brilliant son repeat after the Abbot his renunciation of the world, the flesh and the devil. They would sit in the chapel and listen to the annual sermon of the old Abbot instructing the young Fraters in their duties as members of a great Order of men. Mrs. Gerard would bite her tongue in an effort to avoid the mother's pride that shows forth in tears of gladness. There would be a host of mothers in that chapel with hearts bursting with admiration, as they listened carefully to the clear voices of their sons.

The summer passed very quickly. Robert learned to swim while he remained at the cottage with Mrs. Turrel. With the addition of weight and a body burnt brown, he was the picture of health when he took the front seat of the car beside Doctor Gerard. Liz and Mrs. Gerard remained in the rear of the car and let the men-folks hold sway in the front. Robert won the election to hold Patty nearly all the way to the monastery. There were times, though, when he shifted his responsibility to the back seat because of his ignorance of quick changes.

Doctor Gerard was never overly impressed with Gibby joining forces with the Benedictines. He thought his son should enter the Society of Jesus and be more active in the duties of the Church. The Benedictines were fine men as far as they went, but to Dr. Gerard, they didn't go far enough. He expected all men who entered upon the Religious State to come off the ecclesiastical assembly line just like Father Joseph. His knowledge of psychology should have taught him to deal with men in their respective moods and temperaments. Not all could be monks and not all had the ability to shift along pastoral lines. Some were, by nature, contemplatives and stayed in the confines of a monastery and prayed for their brother-priests who were assigned to the arduous task of preaching and serving their flocks in far-off towns and villages.

But, when he saw his son's face, with the ray of sunshine streaming in from the chapel window, as he knelt before the Abbot, his ideas for Gibby Gerard changed to conformity. Never as he knelt beside his wife, would he ever doubt the happiness Fater Ignatius, O.S.B. must be enjoying within his breast.

The Abbot closed his sermon by asking the parents to pray for their sons. Pray to God for continued perseverance during the hard road of College and Theology that faced the new recruits. He brought smiles to their faces when he released the ten professed scholastics to their parents for a vacation at home. They were to report back to the monastery on September 5th to start their eight years of travel along the path of intellectual supremacy.

CHAPTER TWENTY ONE

It was a car filled with happy people that made its destination into the Louisiana country.

The Novitiate stories caused Dr. Gerard to laugh like a boy again. Many of them reminded him of his days at Temple University and the pranks they pulled on the more timid students. Even the ladies laughed when Frater Kevin told how Frater Ignatius was commanded by the Superior to administer an enema to Brother Mac during the winter months. The old brother was very modest as senility crept steadily upon him. He resented medicine as a means of cure. When Frater Ignatius appeared at his bedside with the long tube and hose attached to an ordinary lard can, he received a vehement line of abusive and stigmatic defamation. In the world, Frater Ignatius never heard such language. As he attempted to comply with holy obedience, the ancient Brother Mac threatened to report his conduct to Rome and lay the whole story at the compassionate feet of Pius the XI. That was too much for Frater Ignatius. He knew there was no other means than the football tactics he learned at Lacodere. He sub-delegated his authority to three other strong members of the Novitiate, and a laughing quartet made up of Fraters Maxie, Alcuin, Kevin and Ignatius subdued the ferocity of the once self-acclaimed hero of Vicksburg in July 4th, 1863, and cowhand extraordinary a few years later, and produced the essence of humility in a soul that would gladly have undergone a persecution of Neroic infamy rather than subject his posterior anatomy to the gaze and ridicule of four ill-trained artists of the infirmary.

Three boys enjoyed Lake Tahoo more than ever before. It was a relief to be away from the supervision of the Novitiate and the assignments in Chemistry and Biology. Skeets, Timmy and Gibby took advantage of the cool water of the lake, and the well-prepared menu each day of their vacation. Mrs. Turrel acted as host to the boys, and Robert trailed the paths of the woods with ever-increasing admiration for his adopted monk-brother. The boy was growing each day, it seemed. The trunks Liz bought for his daily swim were going through the stages of outgrowth! He even slept in his swim suit to avoid the necessity of constant changing. Shoes were merely an evil that little boys hated. So, he avoided shoes! He tramped through the woods on those hot August afternoons trying to listen to the conversations of three young men. If he felt he was excluded, he could fix a special face for such circumstances. Frater Kevin knew what was running in his little mind and would invariably take him in his arms and carry him on his back. These little acts of assurance acted as a fidelity bond for young Robert.

No mention of Madeline Turrel was made throughout the three weeks of relaxation. Skeets deliberately avoided the Mardi Gras incident. On several occasions when the two found themselves alone on the raft sunning their bodies, it occurred to Skeets to play with words and direct them along the conversation that took place between him and Madeline in the speeding ambulance. Gibby or little Robert would appear on the scene to spoil the very carefully selected words Skeets had prepared. It never entered Timmy's mind that Skeets might have had something to tell him.

Although most of their vacation was spent at the cottage on Lake Tahoo, evenings found Timmy driving the car back to Lacodere to visit with Liz and keep Patty awake. Liz often found Timmy and Patty on the big bed in her room with the young monk talking like a philosopher to the uninterested child. Timmy couldn't even get the baby to give out with a "goo" for all his efforts. He would play with the baby long after his bedtime. Liz never scolded her nephew for this, but smiled contentedly in the doorway unnoticed by the youth, who loved children with all his heart.

Summer pleasantry soon passes to be replaced by fall and winter drudgery. Two young Benedictine Fraters left Lacodere to once more return to the monastery, this time as students in the college department. No longer would they be bound to the duties of a Novitiate. The new class of five young men was already learning the steps that lead to perfection in the Novitiate building. They would have their daily conferences and their times with old Brother Mac. The newly professed Fraters would take their regular college work and be able to assist with the duties of discipline in the various sections of the High School and College.

Although they were restricted to some extent, Kevin and Ignatius managed to at least get to the football games played on the home field. It was a hardship for Frater Kevin to sit by and watch the Abbey team being beaten by what he regarded as inferior material. Two boys sat in the stands in their full Benedictine habits wishing they could be in the battle. It all passed when the final whistle blew and the Fraters returned to their cells and the pleasant task of working steadily for scholastic attainment.

As the months rolled by, the new novices fell in line with routine requirements and assisted old Brother Mac as did the previous group. While in the main building, Frater Kevin and his class worked unceasingly to acquire knowledge. There were pranks committed by the inexhaustible comedian, Frater Maxie and his crew. But, the year passed by without the young men knowing where the time had flown. It was to them of little concern where it went, just so long as it didn't tarry.

The usual high scholastic average was maintained by Fraters Kevin and Ignatius. Through the year, though, each report showed Ignatius the better student by one or two points. This mattered little to the Fraters. There was no competition in vogue. All they wanted out of college was a commendable result for their expended efforts.

During the greater portion of their summer months, the two Benedictines helped out with the summer camp conducted by the Fathers near the little lake. The last three weeks were enjoyed at Lacodere and at Lake Tahoo. During those warm days of relaxation from studies and monastic rigors, the boys found much time to devote to their usual pleasures at the lake. Frater Kevin became more associated with the house on Fontaine Street and the little charge who was growing into a strong baby boy. Frater Kevin and Robert used to take Patty for long evening rides in the car and return with the child sleeping soundly in Robert's arms. Just to be with the baby seemed to be satisfactory evidence that Timmy loved him dearly. In his mind, he was planning the little lad's career. After the grades were completed, he would see that he made his high school training at Cassino.

It was always with a certain reluctance that Frater Kevin left Lacodere, now that there was real attraction in the home. He still enjoyed the companionship of Robert, who was growing fast into the spheres of boyhood. But, there was much left to be accomplished at Cassino, and when September of 1928 found itself ever apparent, two Fraters again set forth on their journey to Georgia.

The midwest in those days still suffered the ignominy of the notorious Al "Scarface" Capone and his henchmen. In the East, the Happy Warrior was campaigning for the Presidency of the United States. Little did he realize the once solid South would betray their party and switch to the Republican candidate, Mr. Hoover. If there was a national election that looked in September to be a heated session for the defeated Democrat, Alfred E. Smith, knew of a few supporters in the Southern area. At least, he thought he could count on the support of the Catholic Church. But, despite the national cry to keep the Holy Father out of the White House, and the other foul practices of the infamous Klu Klux Klan throughout the South, East, North, and West, two young Irishmen at the Abbey hardly knew the election took place. They had no vote to begin with, so there was really no vital interest to be expected. Frater Kevin's letters to Liz spoke only of the studies he was taking as a sophomore in college and of the welfare of his little Patty. He inserted the pronoun "his" through summer associations. But not one letter made mention of the fracas between the Democrats and the Republicans. On the other hand, Liz's letters were constant reminders of the efforts good Catholic women put forth to see their man make a showing at the polls. Liz, for the first time in her life, went hog-wild over a national election. She made local speeches to thwart the injustices others were throwing at Mr. Smith's fine character. She even spent money to show her intense interest in the beloved Catholic politician.

In December, after the Republicans won an easy victory, death hit the monastery. Old Brother Mac, who spent his last months in his cell fighting off the ravages of tenacious cold, gave up the ghost three days before Christmas. It was a sight to see the hundreds of men weep at the bier of their departed brother. Some of his most sympathetic mourners were the younger members who associated with him those last years. Frater Maxie could hardly control his emotions as they lowered the saintly brother into the cold ground of the little Abbey cemetery.

Another year and another summer passed by. Frater Kevin was learning to appreciate life as he celebrated his twentieth birthday in the monastery. He had to be reminded of the date by Frater Ignatius, who came to his room with words of congratulations. At the time, Ignatius made his entrance Kevin was writing a few words to Liz. He was also including a memento to little Patty and Robert. Now, he'd remind Liz that he was slowly gaining his majority, if that meant anything.

The four years of college work found Fraters Kevin and Ignatius both mentally and physically developed. Their thirst for knowledge seemed to show itself in the manner they accomplished each assignment. Unbeknown to them, they were watched during those last two years of philosophical training at the Abbey. The Abbot had plans for their future that startled the men when they were called to his humble office in the left wing of the Abbey.

It was a cool morning in June of 1931 when two twenty-one year old men knocked on the Abbot's door. They could hardly hear the response from within. The Abbot was getting along in years now and needed the patience of the rest of the Community. He had served the Abbey well for some twenty-two years, and he could see the candle of strength slowly melting away.

When a visitor came to his office, he always started his conversation by thanking the man for coming to see him. It sort of removed any ill-feeling that might have been in the mind of the caller when he made his initial knock on the door. Many times the Abbot entertained members of the Community who came solely to register some complaint. The Abbot's soft spoken voice and hearty welcome often subdued the visitor's wrath.

Today his heart was acting out of spirits. The pained look on his face gave the boys to understand he spent another of his miserable nights. They would let him start the proverbial ball rolling in the direction he thought wisest. His hands ran up and down the side of his scapular. Once in awhile, he would finger his gold chain and cross, lifting the latter and using it as a pointer to indicate a certain fact that may not be just clear in the minds of his listeners.

"By the expression on your youthful faces, Fraters," the old Abbot said, "you look worried, where, my dear, young monks, I should be the one who is the worry-bird. I have called you here to tell you how happy I am that you both rendered such a wonderful accounting in your college work. All your professors tell me you both are excellent students. Naturally, Fraters, I am proud of you. Especially, when I stop to realize what great athletes you were prior to coming to the Abbey."

The boys looked at each other and smiled. It was a chance for the Abbot to get his breath before telling them the big news he had in store for them. "What I'm about to tell you, Fraters, shouldn't be construed to mean that you are being rewarded. You know all good monks work for the love of God and the salvation of their own immortal souls. Their reward will come in the life hereafter. So, please, dear Fraters, look upon this appointment as a means to glorify God and bring greater riches to our little Abbey in a spiritual sense of the word. Look into the great future and say to yourselves, 'I have been sent on this mission to help bring souls closer to God.'"

The young men were on edge with excitement of their mission. They knew it was something very extraordinary because the Abbot wouldn't keep reminding them that it was a duty, first, and then a pleasurable undertaking, second. They wanted the old man to skip the fanfare and get down to the matter of the appointment or mission.

"Because of your ability along administrative lines and the logic which you displayed throughout your philosophical courses, Frater Ignatius, I am sending you to the Catholic University of America in Washington, D.C. for your Theology, and while there, you are to pursue in the direction of a doctorate in Canon Law."

While Father Abbot was getting his breath, he watched Timmy grasp his pal's shaky hand and swing him around in a whirlwind circle. Timmy loved to see Gibby appointed to something he liked. He knew his pal had to take second best all during their days at the Academy and at Lacodere Prep. Now, they were treated for what they were worth. The Abbot, too, was happy. He secretly admired Gibby over Timmy because of the latter's favorable reports in the papers, over and above those that Gibby received. What he admired most, though was the real loyalty these two Religious shared. They were truly brothers clear to the core.

"I am going to make you both sad," said the Abbot, with a smile on his face. "You see, Fraters, I must separate you for a few years. Frater Kevin, at the request of several members of the council, I am sending you to the Gregorian University at Rome to study your Theology and work for a doctorate in the field of psychology."

"Sad, Father-Abbot?" said Frater Kevin, bursting out all over with joy, "I've wanted to go to Europe to study ever since my first year of college. Didn't I, Frater Ignatius?"

Gibby acknowledged the question with a modest bow to the Abbot. He was happy for Timmy even though they would be apart for five years.

"Now, Frater Kevin," said the Abbot, pointing his cross at the young monk, "you're not going to find Europe a pleasant vacation period. It's very difficult to adjust yourself to Roman life. You'll be often tempted to come home and discouraged at your slow progress."

"I'm most grateful to you and your council for the opportunity, Father-Abbot. I'll do my best while away from the Abbey," said Timmy seriously.

Before their trip to Lacodere, Fraters Kevin and Ignatius visited Father Richard Brady in his new rectory in Hamlin, Georgia. They were treated royally by the priest and given a relic of their patron saints. Kevin took as his patron the great Dominican philosopher, Tomas Aquinas. Ignatius, on the other hand, bent his admirations in the direction of the founder of the Jesuits, Ignatius of Loyola. Father Richard gave the boys some words of advice before they departed for Lacodere. He warned them not to study to the point of injuring their health. No doctorate was worthy of a lost and un-regained health.

Two months of complete rest and pleasure were in store for the college graduates. They were even more than just college graduates. At the close of their Junior year, they were received into the Benedictines after their solemn and perpetual Vows. They were aware of their bond to Religious Life and to their ordinary obligations. Vows only meant that they did something more pleasing in the sight of God.

There was much to celebrate that summer. Young Patty was four years old and a very talkative little boy. Maybe he wouldn't grow up to be as smart in an intellectual way as Frater Kevin, but he certainly would be every bit as handsome and develop a pleasing personality. He wanted to go everywhere with Kevin. Even on Saturday night, when Timmy would visit the church for his weekly Confession, Patty wanted to go right into the confessional and listen to the stories that were told by repentant sinners.

And Robert was now growing steadily in the direction of being a real boy. He graduated from the Academy and promptly told Liz that he was now thirteen, and it licensed him to be the possessor of a girlfriend. Walks through the wooded sections of Lake Tahoo taught Frater Kevin that Robert knew a few more facts than his daily prayers. He at once commissioned Liz to have the adopted charge enter the ranks of the high school students in the solitude of Cassino Prep. This, fortunately, met with the youngster's approval. Any suggestion that found origin with Timmy met with kindness as far as Robert was concerned.

The people still admired their Timmy around Lacodere. He found the time to call on them and inquire about their petty ills. His Roman collar lent a certain pastoral air about his presence. Only his youthful face and glowing blonde wavy hair would indicate his years as some distance from the Priesthood.

Every summer, he would visit the cemetery and pray for his lost pal, Howie Forest. Even little Patty went on these excursions to the grave of the former teammate. As he returned from the cemetery and walked in the direction of his home, he couldn't restrain his thoughts as they centered around Madeline's departure from this life, and the Christmas Eve they walked to the cemetery together. He tried to dismiss her from his mind, but she often found herself in evidence.

Liz and Timmy talked over the European trip, and she assured him of enough money each summer to take jaunts through the principal countries near Italy. She insisted that one summer be spent in Ireland and gave him a list of his relatives who would certainly welcome a more wealthy member of the O'Shea clan. She told him to visit the seminary where his father attended college. There would be some priests who might still remember his father and the generosity he was known for.

But the greater portion of his summer was spent at the Lake Tahoo cottage. With the help of Mrs. Turrel, he was able to handle Patty, Robert, Gibby, and the occasional visits of Skeets Malone. But, usually, it would be just Robert, Patty and Timmy. The trio would take to the boat and either fish or just row around and let the heat of the sun tan their bodies. Timmy was taught caution around babies by his Aunt Liz. He had to make sure the child's legs were well oiled and a little towel jacket was ever about his shoulders. The annoyance of baby requirements mattered little to Timmy. What he failed to do according to the proper rubrics of child-rearing, Robert quickly informed him. There existed complete understanding with the trio at Lake Tahoo.

Frater Ignatius left early to attend Catholic University. He had to establish residence in Washington, D.C. and felt that the sooner he became adjusted, the better off he'd be. Skeets and Timmy bid him fond farewell at the station. They all promised to write to one another as they always did in parting. Skeets felt a little out of place at the station with two clerical students in their black suits. Although he was advancing in the realms of medicine with only a year of schooling at Tulane left for him to accomplish, he silently wished he had taken the road that led to the Priesthood.

As the two boys walked back to the car, Skeets asked Timmy if he thought he had made a mistake in his priestly move. When it was confirmed in his mind that Timmy was really happy about the ultimate goal he aspired to, Skeets pressed him no further. He told the young Benedictine he may see him in a year or two when he planned to do some graduate study in brain surgery in Paris or Berlin.

It wasn't hard for Frater Kevin to say goodbye to Liz and Robert when the time came to depart for Europe. Yet, it seemed like he was reluctant to leave little Patty who sensed the departure more than usual. Often he kissed Kevin when he left for the Abbey, knowing he'd be back again to give him "piggy-back" rides as well as automotive excursions. But, as he followed Kevin around in his room watching him place things in the large trunk, he just knew the tall man wouldn't be back for a long time. Patty's questions forced Kevin to take him by the hand and lead him to the window. There the two looked out over the same trees that seemed to be just as tall and stately as when he looked out over their lofty limbs so many years before.

Kevin tried his best to convey to Patty that his trip across the sea would be only for a few short years. Then he'd come back to Lacodere to a great big man of nine years. Together they would hike in the woods and climb the hills and camp out overnight in the warm summer months. Together they could visit the big cities of America when he had his vacations. Yes, together they'd always be, even though a huge pond of water separated them for a few years.

It wasn't easy for Kevin to watch the tears roll down the little boy's cheeks. He accused himself of forcing his attentions on the boy to the extent that parting was too great a sacrifice for the child to bear. It wasn't easy for Kevin to leave the lad who brought so much happiness to the house of O'Shea these last four years. No matter how hard he tried, he couldn't seem to make Patty believe that he would one day return to fulfill the many promises he made. Only for faithful Liz's intercession, Kevin would have seized the child in his arms and tell him he'd forget the trip to Europe. He was desperate in his desire to make Patty happy. Liz merely walked up to Patty and bent down on her knees and talked as only one with such experience can talk to a baby boy. Whatever power Kevin lacked, Liz had stored away in the chambers of her heart for such emergencies. She knew her Timmy could easily walk out of the European venture by merely calling his Abbot and making some false excuse. But, Liz also knew how much this experience would mean to her nephew and how short a space of time five years actually could be. No, not even the companionship of a few weeks each summer would stand in the path of Frater Kevin's success.

In late August, Liz drove Frater Kevin to Memphis where he was to take the American Airlines plane to New York City. All passage tickets from Memphis to Rome, Italy, were in order. His passports and documents signed by his Abbot were in tip-top shape.

Robert wasn't the sulky boy of a few years ago. He was filled with happiness that the young boys find in their hearts when they know they can now write letters to a distant country and perhaps receive some little gift from a foreign land. At least, Timmy often promised to send him a card from every big city he visited.

Liz wanted nothing but the assurance that he would take good care of himself. If there was anything he needed, he was to be sure and write. He wasn't to forget the visit to Ireland, but then, she said she would write before next summer the details of the trip to her old country land. All the way to Memphis, they discussed little Patty's future. He'd go to the Academy as did Timmy and Robert. By the time he was ready for the High School, he'd be with a man by the name of Father Kevin. They also talked about trips he planned to make into France and Germany. And, if time permitted, perhaps a trip to Moscow or Stalingrad. Although he didn't care much for the thought of going as a civilian into Communistic Russia, he felt such a venture would be a source of adventure as well as cultural training. Again, Liz assured Timmy there was sufficient money in his own name to do whatever traveling he so desired. If he wanted to return to America by way of the Orient, it would be acceptable to her as far as she was concerned.

At the Peabody Hotel, they took dinner in an engaged room because of Patty. Liz wasn't sure what he might do in a crowd and wasn't taking any chances on any outbreak of childish devilment. The plane left around midnight, so Kevin advised his aunt to secure a room large enough for the three to remain overnight. Driving back to Lacodere after the long trip wouldn't be very pleasant. Over their coffee, they talked about Ireland and how Timmy's late father once studied for the priesthood himself. Liz was so nervous, she couldn't tell the complete details, so Timmy didn't press her. Her anxiety was brought about because Timmy insisted upon flying to New York City rather than the slow process of the train. He told her he only wanted to fly because he'd have more time to visit in New York. Liz wasn't satisfied with this line of reason. Planes weren't safe, and if he met with disaster, she'd probably die of the shock. No matter how she pleaded with Timmy to take the midnight train to the East, the young monk stood firm in his desire to fly. He promised to wire her at the hotel the first chance he got in the morning.

Liz refused to go out to the airport. The mere mention of airplanes gave her a series of mental shocks. They kissed in their room and said their goodbyes with all the fortitude they could muster forth. Timmy couldn't joke through this parting as he did through previous goodbye ceremonies. There was little Patty to hold in his arms and swing around in a joyful prelude to a not-so-happy adieu. Lastly, he took Robert by the arm and together they walked to the elevator. Timmy wanted to say a lot to the little Frenchman, but words seemed to lodge in his throat never to come to his lips. They stood waiting for the red light to flash and the little bell to signal. It seemed like hours passed away in those brief and silent seconds. Robert stood by the large ash bowl and fingered the cigarette stubs. Timmy just nodded his disapproval, and the boy waved his arms around until they caught together behind him. He was growing, and his best suit should have been lengthened. The cuffs of his pants were high above the conventional style. Even his little coat sleeves matched the condition of his pants. But, there were more than apparel disorder as the two young men stood by the row of elevator doors that night. In the heart of young Robert, the blood was rushing in and out at rapid fire speed. He was nervous and uneasy those last moments with Frater Kevin. He wanted to tell him that he'd write to him every week and he'd always be his pal as long as he wanted him to be, and he'd mind Auntie Liz and do all he could to help her until he went to Cassino Prep, and then, the elevator gave its signal. Neither spoke their hearts out that night as they wanted to speak. Something went amiss with Frater Kevin that he couldn't explain. As the doors opened, a crowded car, filled with patrons descending from the Roof Garden, watched a young man in clergy attire pick up a lad of thirteen years into his strong arms and kiss his cheek with all the love and admiration of a father for his cherished child. As he placed him on the carpeted floor, he whispered in his ear, "I love you, Robert. Be a good boy. Write to me often. What I couldn't tell you tonight, I'll tell you in a long letter when you get to the Abbey." The little fellow couldn't say a word. All he could do as the doors shut between them was signal his farewell.

On the way down to the lobby, Frater Kevin didn't notice the redheaded woman who winked at him. He was still thinking of what he could have told Robert. What every man should tell his charge when he arrives at the crucial period of thirteen years. But, Frater Kevin was too choked up to remember what he had planned to say. He'd try and convey by letter what he wanted to say in person.

Back to his room walked a little boy trying hard not to show the feeling of his heart. He would bite his lip and cause a pain to forget a pain. But, Liz would know the moment she looked in his eyes. Together they'd have their cry and wonder off to drown their sorrow in sleep.

CHAPTER TWENTY TWO

Frater Kevin landed in New York City the next forenoon. He went to the Astor Hotel in the heart of Times Square. From such a location, he could visit all the places in the great metropolis that he had heard or read about. There was famed St. Patrick's Cathedral with all its splendor and art. He'd take the subway to Brooklyn, the ferry to Hoboken, walk through Central Park, visit Columbia University, hike over the campus of Fordham University, take in several shows of interest, not to exclude the many fine restaurants that offered unique fare. He knew he couldn't cover Manhattan in two weeks as thoroughly as he would have liked, but he promised himself that he'd return again with his little Patty and show him the wonders of a city of magical bliss.

Everyplace he visited, he noticed the courtesy extended to him. The Roman collar seemed to be more respected in the East than in his section of the country. This pleased Frater Kevin. To be referred to as "Father" at the hotel and the cafes caused him to blush with a certain fixed pride. Although he still had a hard grind ahead before earning the title, he appreciated the notice given to the dignity of the cloth.

In the middle of September, he sailed from New York's great harbor past the Statue of Liberty and into the great Atlantic. He cabled Liz at Locodere, Robert at Cassino Abbey, Frater Ignatius at Catholic University and Skeets at Tulane in New Orleans that everything was in splendid order. Many times in the course of his stay at the Astor Hotel, he would write a few lines to each of his friends. He didn't forget Buddy Feeley with the Jesuits or Mrs. Forrest or any of his many friends in Louisiana. All heard from Frater Kevin and from the tone and character of his little messages, all knew he must be the happiest young Benedictine in the Order.

The trip across the ocean was one of continual activity. No one knew he was a monk by the clothes he wore. In the morning, he'd wear a sport jacket of light tweed material with a silk kerchief around his neck. The rest of his attire might be of some fine flannel material with a pair of brown and white shoes. He'd play all the deck games and join with the youngsters for an afternoon in the pool. He couldn't find time to take a nap with the older passengers before supper call as he had to be with the children, either telling them stories or playing games with them. In the evening, he'd change to a dark suit with a polka-dot tie and perhaps a blue broadcloth shirt and walk into the dining salon to be pointed out by little boys and girls and their admiring parents. He was a striking figure as he walked between the tables bowing at this old matron and nodding at some young lady who might have walked the deck with him the evening before. One couldn't help admiring his manly features, his good looks and clean-cut complexion. Any of a dozen young ladies would have enjoyed his company during that dinner hour and on through the evening's concert or dance. Yet, he preferred a quiet table in a reserved section of the salon where he could watch the people talk and laugh or look out over the blue Atlantic with her white-capped waves dancing in angry turmoil.

Two days before the ship was to dock at Naples, Frater Kevin enjoyed a strange new thrill. It wasn't just exactly new, because men have experienced such sensations for centuries. Maybe it was new in its presentation, but rather ancient in the mode or character of its design.

The following night the Grand Ball was to be held. Partners were selected by a member from the steward's quarters who made a practice of looking over the ship's list to acquaint passengers early enough to establish a congenial arrangement for the Grand Ball. The name Kevin O'Shea didn't indicate any religious significance to the steward's man, so he coupled it with one which he thought should provide an interesting evening for both. If neither could dance, they could walk the deck and listen to the sweet strains of the orchestra and talk about places and people back in the United States.

It was all very simple. The night before the Grand Ball, the steward walked into the dining salon and publicly announced the couples his man had selected. If the arrangement wasn't satisfactory, the good people would signify their dislikes after the ship docked. But, for the present, all should try and make it the nicest ball they ever attended. There was no use mentioning the rudeness attached to objecting to one's partner. It was supposed to be all in the spirit of the trip. Nothing of a serious consequence should emit forth from passing an evening together even through it might be somebody's wife you happened to draw as a partner.

Frater Kevin listened to the names called out. He smiled as he heard the women scream when their partners were made known. It was to be a rather eventful evening to say the least. He sat at his solitary table playing with the piece of roast chicken on the end of his fork. He looked up when his name was called out and waited with hidden curiosity till the name of Mrs. James Everett Sloan, Jr. was announced as his partner. It was customary to stand when your name was called, so all could look with either awe or scorn on your countenance. It was embarrassing for Frater Kevin to stand waiting for his partner to come to the limelight. There was no acknowledgement forthcoming. An elderly lady with a profuse display of either costume or genuine diamonds screamed, "My God, if she doesn't want him, give him to me!" This was followed by like remarks from various sections of the salon. Timmy's face became flushed, and he tossed his napkin on the table and made a hasty retreat to the deck. On the way out, he heard remarks from members of his own gender. "Now, damn it all," said one middle-aged man, "if I were half that good looking, I'd have every old hen on this ship inviting me to her stateroom!" Another younger woman said, "Whoever Mrs. Sloan, Jr., happens to be, she'd better claim her prize, or I'll switch mine right now!"

Frater Kevin was a great deal more hurt than he gave evidence of being. He couldn't blame Mrs. Sloan if she didn't come to that particular dinner call, but he did hate the remarks aimed at him by a crowd he really didn't know. The past five years in a monastery hadn't socialized him to such conduct, and he decided then and there that he had made the best selection a young man could make. All sorts of thoughts ran up and around his mind as he walked the deck for his fourth or fifth turn. Starting his fifth or sixth (he didn't keep an accurate tally), a very soft and cultured voice forced him to stop suddenly and look deep into the shadows of the deck chairs near the outside walls of the staterooms.

He would have continued on, but the voice again came as a warning signal not to proceed. He walked over to the chair and as the ship turned to let the full moon shine forth in all radiance on the occupant, Timmy had to restrain a whistle that wanted to blast out his inward delight. There sat a woman as beautiful as anyone he had ever seen before. The blanket covered the greater portion of her body, but what Timmy saw pleased his sense of the beautiful and caused him to stare with fixed pleasure. He accepted her invitation to sit in the chair beside her own.

She apologized for interrupting his walk on such a heavenly night, but she had noticed him playing with the youngsters during the day and especially with her little son, Jimmy. Naturally, it was only fair that a mother should meet the companion of her five year old son. At least, that was her argument for having detained him. Frater Kevin still gazed into the large blue eyes of this gorgeous creature. He didn't hear a word she said about her five year old son, Jimmy. All he could hear was the thump of his heart and feel the flicker of his eye lids. Whoever she was mattered little. The way she looked at him when she spoke of her little Jimmy, or of the trip, made the Benedictine intoxicated with her charm and manner. He wanted to touch her lovely skin to make sure it was really flesh and not marble. The artistic features of her face indicated a class and culture Timmy had never known. Certainly, the husband of this rare jewel must be out of his mind to leave her unattended.

Frater Kevin might have been drunk with his infatuation for it was something quite new and different to him. Despite any inward call, he kept a buoyancy throughout the whole conversation. He recalled the little child he tried to teach to swim; the same little rascal that made him play catch in the gymnasium on the lower deck. He had spent many afternoons on their trip with Jimmy. He would have spent more had he known this child possessed such a charming and beautiful mother.

The last call to dinner was announced, and the lady asked Frater Kevin if he would join her for supper. Kevin accepted even though he wasn't interested in starting a second dinner. He helped her remove the steamer blanket of Scotch wool from around her waist and legs. Together they walked into the dining salon to be greeted by the announcer for the Grand Ball.

Several pairs of eyes watched the two take a table near the orchestra that was playing some Victor Herbert selections. Those eyes couldn't help admiring the striking beauty of the tall dark haired woman with the youthful blonde gentleman. Several social climbers knew who she was and had a fair idea of why she would take to this handsome companion. Kevin's name was buzzed around at all three dinner calls that night. When he appeared again, and with a woman, it was to be expected that many would have a few whispers to indulge in with neighbors.

Kevin ordered a scotch and soda after his hostess gave her selection to the waiter. While they were waiting for the results of their order, they listened to the music of the orchestra as it changed from waltz tempo to South American tango rhythm. Once she took a cigarette from a gold case and asked Kevin, who was momentarily looking in the opposite direction, if he'd give her a light. This caused him to fumble around in nervous anxiety only to have her hand him a match from the container on the table. His hand didn't appear steady as he brought the flame close to the end of her cigarette. She watched him, never taking her eyes off his face for a second. This situation never was quite understood by the man who not an hour before thanked God he was elected to follow in the footsteps of the chosen ones. She talked of places in Europe as if they were old friends. She asked Kevin if he planned a trip to the Rialto when he toured Italy. Kevin wasn't sure whether the Rialto was situated near Florence or Venice, but if she thought it was worthy of a visit, he would certainly make a point of seeing it. There wasn't a great deal Kevin could remember about his knowledge of Europe that would help him during this session with an apparent expert in the field of geography. The Sisters back in Our Lady of Lourdes Academy evidently forgot to include the hotels and resorts of the various large cities of the Continent. Kevin thought he would write to Sister Mary Immaculata some early date and advise her to include these important places as a means of broadening the student's cultural background.

The drummer gave out with a wild signal as the steward's handyman again appeared in the center of the salon. He had that awful list with him, the same list that caused Frater Kevin to exit from his dinner before he half finished. The man announced the name, then the accompanying partner. First, it was a man's name, then a lady's. They'd stand up for a short, but affected bow and then be seated. As the steward's man approached the list of names that started with the letter M, Frater Kevin leaned over, nearly upsetting his drink, and whispered to his lady friend, "Wait till you get a load of what I drew! The queen of the whole ship, I guess. She isn't even listed as a passenger in the dining salon. Must eat with the Captain."

Frater Kevin received a smile in return for this first real outbreak since they were together. Little did she know or care of the circumstances that caused his hasty retreat from the dining room a few hours before. When the name, Mister Kevin O'Shea was announced, Timmy winked at his friend and stood up. He was eying the whole salon in hopes that he'd get a good look at the woman he was to take to the Grand Ball. There was a moment of silence that lasted nearly an hour of Timmy's timing. He was feeling that same strangeness as at the earlier dinner when Mrs. James Everett Sloan, Jr., stood up beside her place and directly opposite Frater Kevin. Poor Timmy merely gulped and took the loud cheering and whistles in their proper stride. He was overcome with a certain feeling that made him speechless. He would have preferred that the ship take a sudden dive to the very depths of the Atlantic Ocean.

People who travel on large ships usually are carefree and unable to avoid the onslaught of a romantic night, the salty air from the ocean, or the soft strains of music from the ship's orchestra. They might leave New York with every intention of remaining aloof, but something creeps into their very soul that yearns for the sweet touch of companionship.

Vera Sloan felt the pregnable feeling of romance as she clung to Frater Kevin's arm while they walked on and on around the deck. They talked of little Jimmy like two young mothers might discuss the merits of their respective children. Kevin praised Patty and his alert mind. It was nearly midnight when the ship's whistle sounded a passing warning to a companion vessel. The two stopped and rested their elbows against the rail. They watched the passing ship in the distance. For want of something better to say, Kevin turned to Mrs. Sloan and asked her about Mr. Sloan.

"Well, Kevin," she began, "James is a publisher and broker. A sort of combination affair, I should imagine. We've been separated for two years now. I just received my final divorce papers three weeks ago. I'm going to Italy to spend the winter on the Riviera and then on to Paris for the spring. I'll probably do a little writing to keep busy. That's all I seem to be able to do with any proficiency."

Frater Kevin might have guessed Vera Sloan was a divorcee had he taken the pains to make some inquiries. But, he was content to know this creature just for her beauty rather than her domestic strifes. It didn't startle him when he learned she was husbandless. It seemed to make matters a little easier to handle. To be entrusted with the ship's most beautiful woman was an ideal commission.

They talked on and on about books and authors and irate publishers. Kevin cared little for the conversation because it did have a taint of the foreign about it all. In a sweeping turn of subject matter, Vera Sloan asked Kevin his purpose for leaving America and at such a time. He merely replied that he was going abroad to study. They discussed psychology till the subject became a bit boring for Mrs. Sloan. Then they switched to the ancient, but always modern topic of love and the attributes that go to make up the true ingredients.

"Kevin," she said, with a note that made him feel like he should pay every obligation to society. It's appeal lingered in his eardrums, I know you're very young, but at the same time, I can't help but think you've been very much in love during your short life. Oh, it may not have been with a woman, it may be with your studies or your work, or . . ."

"Or what?" said Kevin not meaning the sharpness of his question.

"Please don't misunderstand me, Mr. O'Shea," she said. "I certainly didn't mean to imply you're conduct is in anyway sub rosa relative to the matter of love."

"Well, Mrs. Sloan," Kevin retorted, still in a fog as to her unfinished statement, "when you state it wasn't with a woman, and it may be study or work, there isn't too much in the remainder one could find to love, now is there?"

"Your torrid exactness bores me," she said. "Please excuse me. I think I shall retire."

"You still haven't qualified your statement, Mrs. Sloan, and neither of us will rest comfortably through the night until its clearly analyzed," said Kevin, smiling directly in her bright face.

"I don't think I'm obligated to qualify any statements I make to you."

Kevin laughed his usual merry laugh. To him, all women were somewhat alike. They were just biological creatures that had redeemable assets over and above their fellow creatures. One may smile showing a set of perfect dental arrangement, whereas, her sister may never smile and show by her eyes a gleam of loveliness void in the countenance of the other.

Please don't leave as if you've sustained an unjust blow, Mrs. Sloan," said Kevin, gently holding her arm. "I assure you I meant no insult. You're too lovely to insult with words."

"How do you propose to insult me, then? Have you some device heretofore unknown to your peculiar sex?" was her sharp follow up. But, there was definitely nothing to become alarmed about in this remark. Both laughed heartily.

The stillness that followed was only the prelude to what would climax their evening together. Kevin was determined to kiss Vera Sloan under the glow of that moon. It wasn't that he really wanted to kiss her lips to fulfill any impulse, he just felt there was a moon above, stillness in the air and the most beautiful woman he had ever met standing right by his side, eagerly awaiting an embrace and the soft words that lull in the memory after the daylight of tomorrow awakens the mind to the harshness of reality. If it could be called a pseudo-romance without the obvious hurt that invariably must follow, it was only to be that and nothing more as far as Frater Kevin was concerned.

Vera sensed the stillness as any mature woman could. She turned when she felt his arm circle her waist. He smiled on her face as she melted into the awaiting arms. Their eyes closed as their lips met. It was over all too soon for the most beautiful divorcee and her very fraternal companion. Such a kiss belonged to the medieval parlors of the English courts. The selfsame kiss Essex might have received from Elizabeth for removing a disloyal servant. Mrs. James Everett Sloan, Jr. was thoroughly convinced that Kevin O'Shea was definitely not a romanticist, much as he may have given every exterior evidence of being such a character.

As they walked to her stateroom, she wanted to say, "goodnight, sonny," but her charity intervened. Kevin merely bid her an evening of restful dreams and slowly walked to his own quarters. He was smiling to himself as he opened the door. If he hadn't fooled Vera Sloan, he certainly hadn't fooled himself. He was quite contented to retire without the slightest pangs of worry beating against his conscience.

The following day found Kevin playing with the children and permitting them to jump on his back and pretend to feel the results of their "ducking" antics. On a deckchair, Mrs. Sloan watched her son enjoy the companionship of the hero of the pool. She knew in the daylight he was much too young and far too noble to seize. Ten years might make a vast difference, but she couldn't wait on time!

Most of the women on board spent their afternoon looking over the array of costumes. The men were satisfied with their evening clothes of either midnight blue or plain black. There was no need for masks because everyone knew his or her partner well in advance. All the Grand Ball seemed to signify was the final official get together of all the passengers. They'd dance, blow horns, and throw confetti. More would have headaches than heartaches the day they landed in historic Naples. But, if a few drinks enabled them to forget some of the past misgivings of their lives, who would dare stand in the path to suggest a degree of temperance? "Let all be happy," was the slogan that ran throughout the whole ship.

Even Frater Kevin would try and look his "worldliest," if one can put on such a disguise. He'd laugh with the rest of the passengers and dance as he never danced before. It would be the ultimate in festivities before settling down at the University for a grind of a fuller knowledge of God and His Commandments.

The grand affair was a success, if one can measure success by the happiness of the participants. Everyone joined with his neighbor as if they were long-established friends. The gowns worn by the ladies were resplendent in the multicolored lighting effects from the ceiling of the ballroom. Frater Kevin emerged from his stateroom with an ordinary evening suit. There was nothing outstanding about him that would distinguish him from any other well-groomed man at the affair. He was immaculate from head to toe. Not a hair on his head was misplaced or the slightest speck of dust on his clothes or highly polished slippers. He was still radiantly youthful in his every action and gesture. It was this above all else that made him so attractive and pleasing to the eye of the feminine members of the ball. But, he still seemed oblivious to all the outward signs of attraction. He retained that degree of modesty that would indicate his true qualities.

Frater Kevin danced the evening out with Mrs. Sloan. She enjoyed his company and found humor in his southern drawl. He would whisper something in her ear that often brought a smile to her face. At the intermission, he met several other prominent women of New York, Chicago and Boston society. He was able to withstand the shock of their personal remarks with all the candor his education afforded him.

On the deck were many couples holding on to the last breath of the evening. Some were holding their escorts close to their breasts and pledging all sorts of rash promises that would float with the morrow's dawn. It was difficult to find a spot that wasn't already inhabited by a cooing pair of lovers. They walked around the deck in hopes that when they returned, an opening would have been created. It was like waiting for a passenger to relinquish his seat on the B&M Transit around the morning or evening rush hours.

"Suppose we go to my stateroom for a drink, Kevin? That is if you're not afraid of me," she said with a deliberate coyness that seemed to rub against the grain.

"Aren't you afraid?" was Kevin's quick retort.

"I haven't been up till now. God only knows what may be in store for me if you do cross my threshold," said Vera, assuredly.

"What about young Jimmy? Aren't you concerned that he may awaken?" he said, trying to throw open an objection.

"If he did, what possible assistance could he render to his helpless mother, especially when he adores the assailant?" she asked, laughing.

"One drink, fifteen minutes without the usual fumbling through the family album. Okay?" said Kevin, curtly.

"As you wish, Mr. O'Shea. I'll try to abide by the dictates so carefully put forth."

Together they walked to AA3-4 where they found the lamp in the sitting room aglow. Her accommodations seemed to be more in keeping with her station of life than were Kevin's. He thought he had the nicest quarters on the ship. At least, they hardly resembled his monastic cell at Cassino Abbey. She sat down on a satin-finished settee. She told him where he could find the necessary ingredients for "one drink." But, Kevin tip-toed into the little bedroom of young James Sloan to see the tiny lad fast asleep with one leg uncovered and an arm hanging over the side of his bed. Kevin watched the child breathe in and out, and then walked over to the side of the bed and worked the leg back under the covers, placing his little arm by his side. He couldn't restrain the feeling that surged through him as he pushed the hair back on the boy's head. He didn't exactly remind him of Patty. He was just another little fellow who had a couple of strikes already registered against him.

The voice from the sitting room had a note of command about it. Kevin gave a last look in the direction of the child and left the room. He nearly fell over a teddy bear that was sitting in the middle of the floor watching its little master. The stuffed animal was every bit as large as its owner. Kevin left the door ajar when he walked out. That's the way he would have wanted it if he were Jimmy's age again.

Over a tall glass of bourbon and water, without ice, two extremely different persons sat side by side. Kevin had taken in every noticeable article in the room and was beside himself trying to locate something to fix his eyes upon. They discussed all sorts of books and their authors. After that session, they talked about Jimmy's future. Then came Kevin's. Till now he only told her he was a student. It was only fair to both that she be told what sort of student he was, and that he was a member in good standing in the Order of Saint Benedict, no relation to the Elks Club. He also told her he was the possessor of Solemn Vows and that if it didn't register a click in the direction of caution, he'd be better off in his own stateroom. If it did, they could safely drink bourbon and water the rest of the night together.

"These Vows, Kevin," she said, running her thumb over the glass, "actually how close to God do they make one? Certainly man shouldn't be forced to subject his will over and above the dictates of his own free will."

"Obviously, Vera, you don't regard the validity of Vows in the same sense as I do. You're contract with your husband didn't carry too much weight despite the fact that you and your husband made Vows as binding in the sight of God as mine happen to be," he said, placing his glass on the little table by the settee. "No one on earth forced me to take my Vows. No one could make me break them."

"That's very noble, I'm sure. But, you really haven't been tried in that respect, now have you? Do you know the acid test of gold? I mean how they used to test gold before the era of chemistry?" she asked, still thumbing her glass and mixing the drink in a circular whirl.

Frater Kevin knew very well the answer to this, but didn't answer. He looked at Mrs. Sloan and then around the dimly lit room. It was soft and comfortable. The time, the place, and the party was an ideal set-up. Thoughts raced through his mind as he again picked up his drink. Thoughts that once before entered his mind to cause him to let the dictates of his flesh charge through his mind until satisfied in the bedroom of his home on Fontaine Street. The words she just uttered resounded in his mind. He was determined to leave lest he hurt himself as he did before and bring disgrace on everything he stood for.

As he placed the empty glass on the table, he turned to Vera and started to say goodnight. She handed him the glass that was warm from her hands. There was an exchange of looks that needed no interpretation. He placed it next to his and turned to feel her hand slowly find itself around his neck. Her body was warm and soothing as if it were always meant to be near him. He felt her lips against his cheek and a soft hand run through his curly hair. He looked at her and brought his arm around her body. They were together in a closeness that admitted of wanton desire. Kevin could feel himself slipping deeper into the well of agreement. When her lips rested firmly on his, his heart beat a savage refrain. He freed himself by grasping her wrists and placing them by her side. The split second decision caused something to smart within her breast. She revolted as she watched him stand and arrange his hair with a sweep of his hand. The words, "You fool," still rang in his ears as he closed the door of AA3-4 and walked to his own stateroom.

CHAPTER TWENTY THREE

F rater Kevin didn't remain in Naples with the tourists who left the ship in a scramble. He was content to visit Vesuvius on another occasion. His first move after landing was a seat on the train bound for Rome, and the College of Saint Anselm on Via S. Sabina. Here he was to make his home for the next five years. From here, he would attend Theology with the students from the North American College until he was qualified for the higher requirements maintained by the famous Gregorian University.

The adjustment in a foreign country takes time and patience. There is little of either to be expended when one must acquire knowledge. Frater Kevin worked hard in Canon Law, Moral Theology and the Dogmas. With Church History, Chant, and the Sacred Scripture, plus courses in psychology, the young Benedictine found little relaxation or moments to write in answer to all his mail. There were those promised weekly letters from Robert, several from Liz, and Frater Ignatius who unfolded his troubles in long, hard-to-read missives. But, despite all his work, Frater Kevin did find time at Christmas and Easter to visit the famed Monte Cassino Abbey and its noble sister-in Abbey, Subiaco.

He also took short trips to Genoa, Milan, Florence and Turin. He listened to the stories the merchants told with great interest. He wasn't surprised to learn from a peddler in San Marino that bandits of the most fierce types roamed the streets of their city. For the meager sum of our ten dollars, one notorious cutthroat would kill his neighbor, and for a small additional sum, guarantee to exterminate him in the state of mortal sin. But, this happened centuries ago, so he said.

The summer in Rome is too intense to remain in the city. The Holy Father usually leaves in late June to escape the torture of the heat. Frater Kevin left for his first visit to Ireland long before the Pontiff moved to his castle in the hills. Timmy had places to see and people to visit. Ireland would only be the first of the British Isles. He'd travel through England and Scotland before the summer was spent. He wouldn't forget to send the promised picture cards of every large city he visited that would delight Robert and his friends.

Kevin arrived in Dublin in the middle of June. He went directly to Blackrock to see his Auntie Peggy. There, with a cousin, they traveled to Cork and back to Limerick then on to the Western Coast up to Sligo. They stayed at small hotels and joined in with the songs and dances. Kevin was greeted with hospitality wherever he stopped. His main objective was to see the homes of his parents and walk around the town where his father lived as a boy. Also, a trip to Saint Patrick's Seminary was included before leaving for an excursion of England.

While at Saint Patrick's Seminary, he met an old classmate of his father's. The priest was happy to see Kevin and invited him to his study where they enjoyed a long talk. There he learned of the real charity of Big Tim and the many donations he rendered to the Seminary back in 1911. He walked through O'Shea Hall where the Seminary housed some three hundred students in private quarters.

This, as well as many more gifts, was the result of his father's visit prior to his death.

In England, he was taken sick and was forced to seek confinement in the Benedictine Priory in Liverpool. Here the monks treated him as one of their own brothers. They nursed him back to health in a few short weeks and permitted him to go on to London. Another long session of visits took him to art galleries and historical places of interest. The thrill Westminster Abbey affords the London visitor is difficult to describe.

It was close to the end of August before he entrained for Glasgow. His first visit to the coal mines of Wales seemed an enormous event in his life. But, in Scotland, he found even greater pleasure in the people of Edinburgh and Dundee. They were large cities just as he found in England and in sections of Ireland. But, in the outskirts, he met the real Scots and loved their cleanliness and heartwarming reception. At Fort Augustus Abbey, he spent two weeks in retreat and prayer. It was far different than at his own Abbey back in Georgia. He could hardly refrain from laughing at many of their unique customs.

Back to Rome, a very refreshed monk sailed through his second year of Theology. He wrote his full experiences to Liz and asked her to forward the letter to his friends.

In his letter to Liz, Frater Kevin explained why he couldn't stop at either Portugal or the ports of Spain. His Superior at Saint Anselm's refused him permission to stop in those countries while they were at war or in sympathy with the war. Frater Kevin refused to disobey orders that might result in compelling his future vacations to be spent in Rome.

During the Christmas season, he always went to Saint Peter's for Solemn Mass. It was an impressive sight and one that lingered long in his memory. The great feasts of the Roman Church seemed ever to attract Frater Kevin to his duties as a Religion. He was growing strong in Benedictine fervor and was ever conscious of the awful demand made upon his soul. The priesthood wasn't far in the offing, and the terrible toll paid by an overtaxed mind often seemed unjust. To become a priest seemed in itself a mountainous performance without the added burden of working for a doctorate in psychology. At the termination of his second year, he was awarded a Master's degree. In itself, this was sufficient. But, his orders were clear in his mind. He was to return a doctor in his field. Frater Kevin often wondered if Gibby Gerard suffered the same pains of a tired mind.

The news of Mrs. Turrel's sudden death added further weight to Kevin's mind. Liz was so careless about particulars. All he could gather from her hurried lines was the short illness brought about by years of hard work, and the added account in the Lacodere Times. Together, they hardly seemed sufficient. The letter was filled with events of interest concerning Patty. Perhaps Liz felt this would tend to make up for the deficiency concerning Mrs. Turrel. The news that Skeets was a doctor and doing his internship at Saint Joseph's Hospital in Memphis made Kevin smile amid the tears. Liz also informed her nephew that it was Skeets' intention to be in Berlin in 1935 to do some research work.

Close behind Liz's letter came a confirmation from Skeets that he'd see his pal in some "booze hall," as he put it, in the middle of downtown Berlin. He told Kevin that medicine was still tough for him, and he had a great deal more he could learn before attempting to perform the much-promised operation on Father Quinn. He closed his letter by telling him that he intended to go to Washington, D.C. for Gibby's ordination prior to the sail across the ocean. He knew it would be a grand event, and he would like to be at Kevin's too. But, his internship would be over near the first of June, and the best he could do under the circumstances would be to make the Washington, D.C. ceremony.

Summer again bloomed forth after a glorious Roman spring. Kevin wanted to see France and the Shrine of Lourdes. Time, he felt, was drawing to a close, and each summer must be accounted for in due measure. He went through Switzerland and crossed over to France. He visited the Shrine after several weeks in Paris; on over to Brussels and then into Germany. He wasn't impressed with the German New Order or the way the children were regimented, any more than he smiled with favor on Italy's strange black shirt government. His studies prevented any real probing into the field of Political Science with any emphasis on German or Italian systems of dictatorial government. He did want to visit Russia, but it would have to wait till such time as he could visit the Balkan countries as well.

The third year of Theology was uneventful. Nothing happened at home except the steady flow of reports on a mischievous youngster. His correspondence was definitely falling off, with the exception of Robert, who remained his weekly contributor. Liz used Patty as an excuse for her failure to write more often. He was growing and required more care and attention. Without Robert around the house, it was a constant session with Patty. There were no signs of complaint, but a gentle reminder to Kevin that she was well-occupied. She did advise him against a trip to Russia, but left the matter for his own best judgment.

In the course of his third year, Kevin took Minor Orders at different intervals over the year. In his last year, he would come up for the three principal Major Orders, Sub-deacon, Deacon, and Priest.

When summer did arrive, he went directly to Moscow where he studied the people and the Five Year Plan that was in vogue for all the world to look upon with interest. Communism wasn't something to be looked upon lightly. Frater Kevin studied its peculiar traits so he could adjudge for himself its false concepts. It was then homeward bound through the Balkan countries and the fourth and final year of his Theological course of study.

Kevin made several interesting reports during his last year at the North American College and other seminaries around Rome. He had pictures to produce and only wished the sound could have been included. He made several long speeches before a host of Bishops and high-ranking clergy, and advised them to beware of the Red Bear's claws and artifice. His words were written up in several Catholic organs in the States and a copy sent to him by Frater Ignatius.

When ordination came, Frater Kevin was a tired man. He had worked very hard in the course of his four years in Rome. He wanted to return to his Abbey to be ordained by the Bishop of his own area. He was reconciled when he was informed that the Secretary of State would ordain his class in preference to the ailing Cardinal Bizanni.

Little did anyone realize at that early date Eugenio Cardinal Pacelli would reign as Supreme Pontiff in four short years. The honor of having a Secretary of State perform the Sacrament of Holy Orders was quite sufficient to ever enliven the memory of Kevin's stay in Rome.

The Superiors ordered Father Kevin to cancel all proposed plans for a second venture into the Russian territory. His reports didn't fall on happy ears in the Soviet Republic, and the action taken by his Superiors was prompted by their personal interest in the newly-ordained priest. Instead, they gave him permission to again visit Ireland, England, and a long rest at Fort Augustus Abbey. It was here during the hot summer of 1935, while making a semi-retreat and writing his doctorate thesis, that Dr. Skeets Malone paid him a call.

They talked of many things during the greater portion of his relief visit. Skeets described as best he could the beautiful ceremony at the National Shrine of the Immaculate Conception and Gibby's ordination. They discussed the year Skeets intended to spend at the University of Surgeons in Berlin. They walked along the beautiful Abbey paths that led one to tiny grottoes where monks prayed in silence. Skeets had matured in the course of the past three or four years. He wasn't the same witty rascal who pulled all sorts of pranks in school and depended on his friend to exercise some discrete move to free him. His knowledge of medicine was equal to that of the best in his profession. The fact that he wanted more and more knowledge convinced Father Kevin that Skeets would never be happy until he closed the medical books for all time.

"After a year in Berlin, I'm going back to Mayo's Clinic for a year or two," said Skeets. "Why don't you come to Berlin with me and get your degree in a secular university with some merit attached to it, Timmy?"

"I have the greater portion of my courses completed for transfer to the Gregorian, Skeets," said Father Kevin, looking worried. "I'm surprised that you hold the Gregorian in such disrepute."

R.G. Sommer

"Listen, Father Kevin, all Jebby schools to me are poison. So are the Domicans and Franciscans, and your own German outfit. They'll be years trying to catch up to Oxford and Heidelberg and our Harvard and Yale," said Skeets, rather hurt because Timmy failed to see his side of the issue.

"What do you mean by catching up? Financially? Did it ever occur to you, my learned physician, that the Dominicans, and Jesuits, and Franciscans, and our own Benedictines operated in the field of education long in advance of your secular outfits? Need I remind you further of one scientist by the name of Mendel? And, maybe you've forgotten history, Skeets, but those priests you've just taken a six inch punch at held chairs in the biggest universities of the world before they were ousted for unjust causes."

"What you mean to say, don't you, is they played politics the wrong way. They couldn't keep their noses clean and were tossed out so they wouldn't completely ruin the minds of their scholars," said the doctor. "Of course, though, you're in a position to defend the Church, right or wrong. It certainly would speak low of your character if you bit the hand that feeds you. To hell with it! Let's drop the subject and discuss something I've wanted to talk to you about for years, but always found a bit too delicate," said Skeets, motioning to a bench off the path.

"First, Timmy, you must promise me that you'll contain yourself throughout the whole story," said Skeets. "Okay?"

Father Kevin okayed the initial sentence and agreed to compose himself. But, he had to get a dig at Skeets before the latter could start.

"If you're planning to go to Confession, doctor, let me warn you in advance that I haven't the faculties to hear your particular yarn."

250

"Don't worry, Reverend, I'm not telling you my sins, faculties or no faculties," Skeets said, laughing.

With a quick turn to the serious side, Skeets again asked Father Kevin to analyze well the situation he was about to tell him in the event that he might be absolutely wrong and the whole story just a series of false ideas that worked itself into a plausible situation in his mind.

Father Kevin reassured him that he'd weigh the matter in the light of reason and to hurry along with his story before it gained unreasonable proportions in his imaginary mind.

"Let me start out by asking you a question that has bothered me for nearly ten years," said Skeets, looking directly into Father's blue eyes. "Remember the day in late April when we were in the showers back in Lacodere, and I gave you the business for playing 'lousy' ball? You told me you wanted to see me that evening to talk about something. You remember, you're Aunt Liz was due home in a day or so from Miami Beach, and I . . ."

"Yes, Skeets," said Timmy, looking very worried and complex. "I remember perhaps better than you do the whole circumstances surrounding my desire to talk to you. But the matter is cleared up now, and I prefer to forget the whole incident."

"That's what I thought! Well, I can't Father. I've been obsessed for years about that intended conference we were supposed to have and events later proved conclusively to my way of thinking that we should have had the talk, despite my previous engagement."

"I don't quite understand! I said, Skeets, I'd prefer to drop the matter," said Kevin, standing up and looking in the opposite direction.

"Sit down, Timmy. There's nothing to become all excited about. You're still closer to my heart than anybody I know of, even though you are a priest," said the doctor, standing beside Timmy and placing his arm around his shoulder. "All I want to do is clear your mind and my own befuddled reasoning powers. Now sit down, and let's talk sensible."

They resumed their former position, but it was clear to Skeets as he watched the expression on Father Kevin's face that the priest was worried. He didn't want Timmy to feel he was undergoing the Spanish Inquisition, but now that it took on the guise of a smile, he couldn't, in justice, back out.

"Suppose you tell me what happened that caused you to drop the idea of our get together that night, said Skeets. "Then, maybe I can complete the picture for both of us to gaze on."

"I prefer to forget all about it, Skeets, and if you persist in bringing up the subject that is obviously distasteful and definitely out of order here, I'll be forced to request you to leave. Please, for God's sake, don't ask me to review something that I've buried in the past," said the priest, looking strained and in a voice that denoted a plea of clemency.

"What the hell's the matter with you, Timmy. I'm not purging you. I'm only telling you something that may have been the result of an accident that you're not aware of, and should be," was his quick answer. "If you can't regard me as your friend in time of need, I'll accept your invitation to leave. Oh, come on, Timmy boy, snap out of it and tell me what the score adds up to."

Father Kevin looked at Skeets and then buried his face in his hands. There was no apparent use in stalling the persistence of his friend. He, no doubt, guessed something was amiss and probably had facts to back it up. He might just as well unload the story on Skeets as carry it forever in his heart.

"I don't know how to tell you, Skeets. Now that I'm a priest, I look upon life in a new light. We're no longer kids back in Lacodere, you know," he said, watching the serious expression on the doctor's face for some hope of encouragement. "I've made a terrible mistake that I've asked for pardon a million times. To you, it might have been just another passing event. To me, well, I really loved Madeline Turrel, at least I thought I did when it all happened." There was a brief silence and an exchange of looks. "My God, must I go on? Certainly you can at least speculate in your mind as to what happened."

"Go on, Timmy, let's have the works. You'll feel a lot better when you've cut loose," he said, taking a cigarette from a new package. He offered one to the priest, but received a negative nod in response to the offer.

"As you know, Liz was away for several weeks resting in Providence, Rhode Island, and down in Florida," Father Kevin said, starting at the very beginning. "The day of our outing at Tahoo ended with a dinner party at the house with only Madeline and myself doing the honors. She remained on and played the piano till very late. In fact, she remained all night." Father Kevin looked away for a few seconds, then turned his head to face Skeets. "I guess I should have been the stronger, but I proved the weaker. She stayed in my room with me, and . . . . the priest couldn't find words to express what raced through his mind. The friendly and firm hand of his friend gave assurance that it wasn't too shocking a revelation.

"Okay, Timmy," said Skeets, smiling. "I know what should have taken place. That is, I know just what I would have done under the same circumstances."

253

"I tried to see her again, but she left for New Orleans. I didn't have the nerve to write her and waited for her to write to me. I never heard from Madeline again," said the priest with a new outlook and a voice that seemed refreshed. "I went to Confession on Friday afternoon and would have told you all about Friday night if you had come to the house. Maybe it's just as well you had that date," said the priest, smiling.

"Do you think that's where the boat docked?" said Skeets, throwing his head back and blowing a series of puffs of smoke into the air.

"What on earth do you mean by that inane remark, Skeets?" said Father, looking at the doctor for a hurried explanation.

"I only mean this," he said, throwing the cigarette far in front of them. "Do you think the matter of duly performed Confession absolves you in toto from the whole matter when there could have been results of a serious consequence?"

"I'm fully aware of the intricacies of the Tract on Penance," said the priest indignantly.

"Then I need remind you of the obligation of the penitent to make due restitution. Your knowledge of Moral Theology covered that phase of the Sacrament quite thoroughly, I imagine." Doctor Malone was throwing all he had at the young priest.

Father Kevin burst into a rage. "Please, Skeets, have some compassion on the soul of the departed part in this case! Say what you want about me, but leave Madeline out of this. I take full responsibility for my conduct. I'm sorry. God alone knows I'm sorry. What further restitution is there?" Kevin was nearly in tears, not out of self pity, but his anger was brought to a head. "Why in the hell don't you leave for Berlin now?"

"The further restitution should be spent in the direction of the baby," said Skeets, coldly.

"In the direction of WHAT?" screamed Father Kevin, nearly beside himself with rage. "Get out of here! Did you hear me? Get out!"

"Compose yourself, Father. Compose yourself. Babies are being born hourly all over the world. Yours happened to be born the night of January 28th, 1927, at Hotel Dieu in New Orleans. That's according to the record, Father. Records don't lie!"

Father Kevin was speechless and seemed powerless to go on with any further conversation. He sat in a stupor trying to clear his mind of all that had just been laid bare. He didn't have to have Doctor Malone go into the matter, but he listened to the quiet words spoken so softly he had to strain his ears to listen.

"You've had enough psychology to fathom this not so perplexing situation. You needn't strike your breast and scream, '*mea culpa, mea culpa*' just promise yourself that you'll see that the child is given every advantage that you yourself enjoyed. Quit spending money traveling all over Europe and see that sufficient funds are put aside so the child can go on through school. Don't be so goddamn selfish and think of the body and mind you were a partner in creating."

These were stiff words to take. Coming from Skeets, they hurt even more so. When was Timmy O'Shea ever guilty of being selfish? Hadn't he always thought of the other fellow first? What prompted this terrible tongue lashing? He had a strange feeling of hatred for the man who told him this, let this creep into his soul. He didn't want to erase it from where it had lodged itself either. Father sat with his face in his hands. He would have preferred that Skeets leave him alone, but couldn't find the words to act as a restraint to those that followed.

"I told you in my letter about the ambulance incident. I didn't tell you everything. I was sort of bound by a solemn secrecy made to your Aunt Liz," said Skeets, turning to console the man he wounded. "Now that you're a priest, I feel you should know that she died with your name on her lips and mentioned the two words, 'Our baby' just before I got her a priest.

Father Kevin listened intently. So, Aunt Liz knew all about the whole matter. Her clever designs could be seen through the revelation made by Skeets. She engineered the whole adoption of his own child. It was she who wanted to protect her nephew's name at any cost. Patrick Aloysius Dunne was no other than Timothy O'Shea, III. He brought his fist down on the side of the seat with such force it nearly broke the old chair in two.

"I don't know what you're thinking about, Timmy, but you needn't become vexed. All I want, all any decent person could want, is to see that boy loved as any child deserves to be loved. You can say you hate yourself. You can develop hatred in your heart for me or Auntie Liz or anybody you goddamn please, but remember this. You owe Patty all the consideration in the world, and you can't hurt him like you hurt Madeline Turrel."

"You've made a mistake," Skeets continued. "God only knows how many I've made. There's been no repercussions as yet, but if there were, I'd carry the torch for the product of my own handiwork with pride, especially if it came out as beautiful a hunk of child as little Patty is growing up to be. Why, Tim, you should see that kid. He's really a clever youngster. You haven't seen him in going on five years. Everyone in the neighborhood loves him. Oh, I'm sorry,

Timmy, I didn't mean to make you cry. Hell, I only want you to keep ever before your mind that the boy deserving of your love, my love, everybody's love, but most of all, your love!

There was silence. A long drawn-out silence. Skeets didn't have anything to say now. He was waiting for Father Kevin to say something—anything!

"Tell me all you know about my boy, Skeets. Everything!"

Again the doctor unraveled what he regarded as theories that could make very good sense. The facts he had were undisputed evidence in Timmy's mind. He was a father in more than one sense of the word. He listened to the whole story, and when Skeets was through, he asked him to go. There were no harsh words when they said their goodbyes. Father Kevin assured Skeets he was quite in agreement with the major portion of his ideas. He'd hold nobody at fault, nobody, but himself.

Back at the Abbey of Fort Augustus, Kevin told the Abbot he had to leave for Rome. Nothing the old Abbot could say would stay the guest from making his departure that very night. His idea was to return to work as soon as he could and hasten his trip to Louisiana and the little lad he loved who lived in the house on Fontaine Street.

CHAPTER TWENTY FOUR

Doctor and Mrs. Gerard had a lovely reception for Father Ignatius. All the old friends were invited. Timmy's cable of congratulations was handed around to all who came to pay their respects. The new priest was a sober and calm-appearing young man. The difficult studies just completed and the thought of a year further at the Catholic University made a very studious character out of Mrs. Gerard's little Gibby. She was truly proud of her son's accomplishments. The doctor invited all his friends from far and wide to be on hand at the First Mass. Any thoughts about the boy entering the Jesuits were obliterated when his son gave out Communion at the rail before all the parishioners. In his Mass, he was assisted by the now aging pastor, Father Joseph and his old chum, Mr. Buddy Feeley, S.J. The latter wasn't quite near the priesthood, but was able to act in a sub-deaconate position on the altar.

Even little Patty helped with the ceremonies. Although he was only eight and didn't know all his Latin prayers, Father Ignatius insisted that he be clothed with a surplice and a red cassock. He told Patty he could be his little Monsignor. They never did anything on the altar anyway!

Father Ignatius received about as many gifts as his friend in far off Rome. Although Father Kevin was waiting a homeward trip before saying his real First Solemn Mass, he wasn't forgotten in the least by his many friends.

Aunt Liz sent him a beautiful set of breviaries with his name inscribed on the red leather binding. She also told him to use the enclosed check to buy himself a chalice. She was told by Father Joseph they were of better quality in Europe. Similar presents were bestowed on Father Ignatius by Aunt Liz.

The summer passed very quickly and found Father Kevin and Father Ignatius once more working to obtain their doctorates in their respective fields. It was most laborious for Timmy to work and concentrate in his difficult field. He had to master the Italian language and work several hours a day at the various mental hospitals about the city of Rome. He intended to make a last session of research at Paris before returning to his Abbey in late September of 1936. While he was working like a Trojan to obtain all the required material, he was ever thinking of his boy, who was nearing his ninth birthday. He often stopped suddenly and placed his pen on his ear and thought what a boy nine should look like in size and general appearance. The wound created by his friend had sufficiently healed. He wasn't going to return to Lacodere and create a scene. No, he was satisfied that Liz was doing her noblest to make the situation a most pleasant and agreeable one. He should thank God for all that He had rendered him these past twenty-seven years. If Patty never learned his father's identity, Timmy would be his father, brother, uncle and pal, all rolled up into one lovable heap.

The degree of Doctor of Canon Law was even more difficult than the Doctor of Philosophy in the field of Psychology. But, Father Ignatius had the mind of an attorney and could analyze cases with unheard of rapidity and accurateness. He loved study as difficult as the matter was to master. He also assisted at a Benedictine Church in Washington, D.C. to help out his Abbey with the stipends. Personal donations from his father were always turned over to his monastery, unbeknownst to Doctor Gerard.

On February 1st, Liz planned to celebrate Patty's birthday. They moved the date up a few days to be able to have it on a Saturday. The little fellow wanted a night birthday party so he could be like real grown-up people. Liz was getting along in years and felt there was no reason to waste precious hours in argumentation. The party would be at night, and all the little eight and nine year olds in his class would be on hand to celebrate. As usual, Doctor and Mrs. Gerard and Father Joseph, after his Confessions were heard at Saint Mary's, and Robert's brothers and sisters, would be there to eat the cake and ice cream. Robert would have loved to come, too, but certain restrictions had to be placed on Benedictine Novices so they would fully understand the import of the Holy Rule.

On the afternoon of the big party, Patty went to Confession. It was more of a Saturday duty, like taking a bath or getting a haircut or cleaning that back room. What could a little child of nine do that would hurt his soul and place it in a state of disgust before an All-merciful and All-just God? But, Father Joseph said all little boys and girls, and many big ones, too, should confess their little sins as well as the big ones every Saturday. That's all Patty had to have. Father Joseph's word was still dogma with the children.

On the way home from Confession, Patty, who developed a great admiration for the Armed Forces through books and the radio, spotted his first, real live Marine. It was a thrill only a very small boy could enjoy. In books, he read about the great battles these fearless leathernecks fought and died in. The Marines were his favorites.

Every night he said an extra Hail Mary to the Blessed Virgin to make him big and strong so he could be like the Marine Sergeant on the poster in the front of the post office. Whoever the hard and determined-looking member of the Marine corps was who posed for the poster, he had an admirer in little Patty. He used to deliberately go out of his way to visit with his chesty friend on the poster. He even talked to him with all sorts of facial expressions, knowing full well the sergeant would never let his big gun down and leave the parade to talk to this little insignificant child of nine. He had a long time to wait till he had a chest like his friend's on the poster. No matter how much he practiced, it would never quite stand out as far as the sergeant's. And those medals! He often stood by the poster just counting the ribbons and awards the marine displayed. Most of all, Patty was in love with the colorful uniform. Those light blue pants with the long red stripe, the white officer's cap and belt to match, the deep blue coat with the shiny buttons. Yes, the Marine Corps was Patty's only outside love. Others could have their football and basketball and even baseball, but Patty wanted to be a Marine, a Marine just like the big, tough, hard-faced and determined fighter on the poster in front of the post office.

To see a Marine was an event. But to see one on your birthday, well, that was just the best present anybody could give a little boy. Here, not a half a block away, was a member of the famed Corps who police the Navy and guard the foreign interests of the country. Patty was elated beyond words. He wanted to run up and touch the man who wore the beautiful uniform and ask him a million questions about the life in the Marines. Little did he realize not all Marines are as easy to talk with as the friend on the poster. There are some who have fought bitterly abroad and know little about the desires of a very small boy. They have different things on their minds. They sometimes get quite peeved when they are molested with trivial questions, and it's not always easy to find a Marine in a happy mood, especially when he took the wrong bus for Monroe, Louisiana and found himself dateless in a place he never heard of called Lacodere.

Patty walked up to the Marine and asked him if he lived in Lacodere. That was evidently the wrong approach for his initial introduction to a member of the U.S.M.C.

"Live here! My God, kid, I wouldn't even come here to die!" said the tall, young fighter, looking down on Patty with a sneer.

"Are you mad at someone here?" asked Patty, sitting down on the curb and looking up into the face of the Marine with pride. "I'll be your friend if you want me to!" said the little boy, hopefully.

"Listen, kid, you'd better run along home to your old lady. I can't be bothered shooting the breeze with some half-pint kid. Now, beat it!"

These were cruel words, and even if said in jest, would have been unkind under the circumstances. When Patty loved someone or had an ideal so firmly rooted in his heart, he didn't want anything to blemish the avowed love he expressed. Patty stood up and looked at the Marine in hopes he would tell him to remain. He turned slowly and started to walk up the street, unable to swallow the hurting remarks that dug deep into his heart. The Marine seemed unconcerned until he heard the sniffle from the little boy's nose. He let out an oath and walked up to Patty and asked him to "drop his anchor."

The boy smiled amid the tears and tried to hide the fact he was moved by these harsh words of a few seconds ago. It was a thrill to feel the strong hands of this sailor-soldier around his own thick arms.

There, right before his face were the Marine's medals and ribbons. They denoted service in far-flung areas of watch and duty. They looked like sterling silver shining in the late afternoon's sun. To be so close to someone you've admired only through picture books or posters was better than any party of ice cream and cake.

Patty wanted to touch his face and feel the day-old beard so rough and coarse. He didn't dare, though, enjoy this familiarity with someone so sacred as a member of the Marine Corps. Yet, he couldn't help thinking how nice it would be just to touch him so he could tell his Auntie Liz of the experience.

"I'm sorry I blew my whistle so loud in your ear, sonny. But, I had a date with my woman in Monroe for tonight and the witch will probably throw a wingding if I don't get over there," said the Marine without flinching or tying to avoid the child's stare. "If you want to be my pal, well . . ." he looked Patty up and down from an arm's length distance and continued, "I think it can be arranged without too much trouble."

What a birthday present! To be able to say to the other fellows at school that you were the possessor of a real, live Marine for a pal. It was just unbelievable such a thing could happen to Patty, and on the day he was celebrating his party.

The next bus left for Monroe early Sunday morning. There was no sense leaving then for Monroe because he'd have to spend all day Sunday explaining how he happened to get on the wrong bus at the station in Memphis and landed in Lacodere. Too, he'd have to confess breaking his promise that he would never touch the bottle again only to be properly ousted from the front room of the Methodist house in complete disgrace. They decided to go back to the local bus station and find out when the next "rattletrap," as the Marine called it, would rumble its way to Memphis.

Hand in hand, the tall Marine and little Patty walked up the main street. Patty was really proud to hold the Marine's big, calloused hand. Oh, how he wished some of the boys who were coming to his party could see him now! It was an effort for Patty to keep step with the serviceman who hurried along the street in hopes there'd be a bus to Memphis in a short time.

Together they walked into the station. The attendant greeted Patty wit his usual, merry, "hello, handsome" and then turned to the Marine and asked what he could do for him. When he was told the next bus left at midnight, his face dropped. It brightened a little when he was told there was one at seven, but it fell right back again when the ticket agent told him he made a mistake. "That one leaves in the morning at seven," he said.

Two men, one very small, and the other very tall, sat dejectedly in the station. They were told there was a train leaving for the North at one in the morning. All the Marine could say to the agent was, "Helluva lot of good that does me, now!" He turned to Patty and apologized for the use of his language, but found himself using it quite incessantly in the course of the evening.

"By the way, sonny, what's your name?" the Marine said, looking down on Patty, who was always afraid he'd be told to go home by his newly-acquired friend.

"My name is Patrick, but everybody calls me Patty," said the little fellow looking up into the brown eyes of the man for a smile of approval. "What's your first name?" he said turning the tables on the Marine.

"My first name is Garrett, but so help me God, if I hear you call me by that name, you and me is washed up for keeps! The fellows in my Company call me Garry. That's what I want you to call me," said the big fellow, patting the smiling boy on his mass of curly black hair.

"Gee, Garry, that's a swell name. If it was a Catholic name, I'd take if for confirmation," said Patty, not caring what religion his friend professed.

"What the hell do you mean, if it were a Catholic name you'd take it for Confirmation? Ain't you never heard tell of Saint Garrett? Why, in our Sunday School, all the kids learned about him. He's the big shot that came down to Earth and told Mary she was to be the Mother of Jesus. You mean to tell me, Patty, they don't teach that in your church?"

"Sister Mary Immaculata said Saint Gabriel told the Virgin Mary that she was to be the Mother of the Baby Jesus. That's really what she told us, Garry," said Patty, not wanting to doubt the Marine or hurt his feelings in any way.

"Oh, she did, did she? Well, maybe Sister Mary Inaccurate, or whatever you just said her name was, had a point there. I'm not up on my Bible like I used to was. But, that doesn't mean she's one hundred percent right just because I'm not batting in the three-hundred class myself, now does it?"

Patty would rather agree with his friend than doubt for a moment the wisdom of his words. He was quite convinced that the Marine was a mountain of strength and beauty in his colorful uniform. If he wanted him to believe he was also endowed with Socratic intelligence, that, too, was all right with Patty.

The two left their seats in the bus station and walked through the swinging door that led to the street. It was getting close to six o'clock, and Patty knew his Aunt Liz would be pretty put out if her little boy wasn't home by six and in the tub bathing. If Patty was aware of the hour, he was also sure that he didn't want to leave his buddy in distress. He would even lie, just a little, even after coming from Confession to keep his hand in his.

"I don't suppose you know any good-looking women in this town? Of course not, what would you be interested in women for? That was a crazy question to ask you, wasn't it?" The Marine really didn't think it was so crazy, but instead, was in hopes that maybe Patty had a big sister or a cousin, or anything with a little youth and some fire still operating in her burner.

Patty thought a minute, then made a quick discovery. "You could see my Aunt Liz. She's pretty, and I've always liked her, and I think you'd like her, too."

"How old is your Aunt Liz?" said the Marine, looking down at Patty's hidden face, "and do you think she'd go for me?"

"Go for you where?" said Patty innocently.

"Oh, that's just one of them damn expressions. What I meant to say was, do you think she'd like my style? You know, Patty, a lot of women are funny as hell. They don't seem to trust us Marines for some reason or another. But, I'm strictly different. Really I am! I wouldn't make a pass at no dame the first time I met her!"

"What do you mean by a pass, Garry?" said the little boy, looking up into the bewildered face of the Marine, as they walked down the street to the corner where Patty should be turning off for his home on Fontaine Street.

"A pass? Oh, you mean a pass! Well, Patty, that's not easy to explain to little fellows. You see, when you get big like me and go to school and pass from grade to grade, that's it. You pass from grade to grade," said Garry, running his freehand over his face to hide his embarrassment. "Understand? You move in on the Eighth Grade stuff after polishing off the Seventh Grade stuff. Clear, isn't it?"

It wasn't clear to Patty, but he found himself agreeing, nevertheless. Maybe his friend's line of talk was peculiar only to his fellow Marines. Why should he try to understand thoroughly something he really was only vaguely familiar with? It wasn't of prime importance anyway. The fact that Garry was willing to hold his hand and walk down the same side of the street was sufficient for him. The cup of satisfaction was filled, verily, to overflowing!

"Where does your Aunt Liz live, Patty?" asked Garry.

"Where I live," said the young partner, quickly getting in line to turn the corner. "Do you want to come over right now and see her?"

"By the way, Patty, how old is your Aunt Liz?"

"Oh, not very old," said Patty, trying to think of a figure that might meet with the Marine's approval.

"Not very old! For God's sake, pal, don't tell me she's around your age!" said the Marine with a note of anxiety.

The little boy laughed heartily. The thought of Aunt Liz in her upper fifties being associated with his own tender years.

"Well, what the hell struck you so funny all of a sudden? Come on, out with it!" demanded the Marine indignantly.

"I was just laughing when you said Aunt Liz as around my age. Why she's lots older than me, Garry," said Patty, still laughing.

"Okay, okay, so your aunt is older than you. The point is how much older—just in round numbers, please."

"How old was the girl in Monroe you were going to see?" asked Patty, ready for the real catch.

"She was nineteen or twenty, damn if I can remember. She lied so much about everything, maybe she was forty for all I know!" said Garry, trying to think back on his date's age.

"My Aunt Liz is twenty," said Patty, wishing he could bless himself for such a terrible lie. He wasn't clever enough to think in terms that could get him out of the lie once it was perpetrated. But, Liz would have loved him for placing her back in those tender years, now so fully relegated to the days of yore.

"Patty, my pal, let's start operations in the direction of Aunt Liz. You lead the way, and I'll fortify the rear!" said Garry, releasing his hand to enable himself to button the top button on his coat and arrange his hat at the cocky angle.

The little lad couldn't be happier if he tried. This, to him, was complete heaven. At the same time, he couldn't have elected a more unpropitious hour of the day to race home with a guest. At the foot of the stairs, he screamed at the top of his voice for Aunt Liz. In the bathroom off her bedroom, Liz never looked more harassed, her long, grey hair falling carelessly to her hips. An application of Elizabeth Arden's line-removing cream was still in evidence all over her face, giving one a vivid description of the grotesque. She was trying on the new foundation garment that just arrived from Gerber's in Memphis. It was the latest two-way stretch affair that guaranteed to eliminate the bulges and bumps so noticeable in the corsets of bygone days. It was a sacrifice for Liz to modernize her figure at this late date.

Normally, Patty didn't scream as if the bottom fell out of the guestroom toilet. He was taught never to run in the house and the other manners well-behaved youngsters are so thoroughly schooled in before they reach the age of nine. But, this occasion demanded his highest pitch, and he rendered it with all forcefulness. The second summons brought Liz to the middle of the staircase before she was able to realize she was neither modestly clad nor appealingly beautiful. As she stood looking in bewilderment at the two popeyed males at the foot of the stairs, she couldn't explain what power forced her to remain so dumbfounded and unable to escape their stares. Liz, with her dark blue brassiere that would admit of no traces of glamour, her disheveled array of grey hair, and the creamy substance all over her face, with the added novelty of a garment from Gerber's that just wouldn't cooperate with her figure, made Liz look every one of her fifty-seven years with a few thrown in to make sure there'd be no error.

Patty witnessed this sight many times before. It was neither new, nor breathtaking. But to his visitor, of only twenty-one years of life on this Earth, it was something distinctly out of this world! On his bus ride to Lacodere, a mistake he was ever becoming conscious of, he found the current copy of Weird Tales. In it, he remembered a like creature that predominated in one of the stories. In the advertisement on the subway car in Boston, there was the grape juice ad that had a woman in similar circumstances with the bold caption, "Don't You Get Like This, TOO." To the Marine, in hurried mental comparison, the subway car's advertisement depicted rare beauty.

When Patty made his introductions, Garry bowed like someone in fright. Liz, in turn, acknowledged his sheepishness and begged

Patty to seat his friend in the living room till such time as she could both dress properly and talk to him secretly.

Within a short lapse of time, Aunt Liz appeared in the living room. She was interested in the way Patty took the Marine by the hand and showed him the house. Anything the hero of the hour wanted to know about the history of the house or its contents, Patty was able to supply him with the answer, in detail! The Marine, in turn, was spellbound by the rich appointments the house afforded. Everything seemed so much nicer than he was used to either at home or in the Corps. He played a few bars of the Marine Hymn for Patty until he caught Liz's much more pleasing appearing body in the doorway of the room. She was dressed in a long evening gown of black material. There were no signs of fifty-seven years. Her hair was neatly put up in the conventional knot at each side of her head. Gary saw some traces of his own mother in the expression of warmth on Liz's face. But, he certainly wouldn't make any mention of this trace.

The Marine left the piano and walked over to the entrance of the living room. He asked Liz to accept his apology for accepting the child's invitation to come to the house. He would be glad to leave now that he fulfilled what he regarded as a good deed. Before Liz could say anything, the Marine told her the story of their meeting. He was so honest and sincere about his designs to make little Patty happy, he received the never-to-be-refused command to remain for supper and the party. The Marine smiled his acceptance.

Patty was ordered to the bathroom for a much-needed workout in the tub. He refused to leave till the newly-acquired pal forfeited his blue coat with the buttons and medal and ribbons. Patty took this prized possession to the bathroom where he could watch it with admiration, and at the same time, hold his friend from any desire to escape the house in his absence.

In the living room, Garry and Liz had much to make conversation about. His exploits in China and the Canal Zone. Women of the jungles he had seen and taken pictures of in those rare poses! Liz, in her usual quiet manner, told him about Father Kevin and his studies in the Eternal City. Together, they had much to discuss for such a brief acquaintance. It wasn't a difficult task to make the Marine comfortable. Within a short time, he was calling her Liz, and she forgot about including a "mister" to his family name of Palmer.

Patty was singing a few lines of each of the hymns Sister Immaculata taught her class. But, he always ended the hymn with something noteworthy about the Marine Corps, regardless of the fact it should have terminated with some praise to Our Lord or His mother. As he splashed in childlike fashion in the tub, he didn't even think of the boys and girls who would soon be in the living room listening with awe to the wild stories of the China Costal towns and the furious battles of the lower Shanghai district, after dark, so dramatically narrated by Garry Palmer. All Patty could think of, as he threw a bar of soap at a ducking foot in the extreme end of the bathtub was the beautiful blue coat so majestically and reverently hanging on the locked door of the bathroom. For those precious minutes while he washed his little body in haphazard fashion, his eyes were focused on the medals that hung so gallantly on the breast of the coat. He was as proud of them as the man who earned them.

After the quickest bath any boy ever took, Patty went to the closet and brought out a large towel. He spent the usual amount of time getting the major portion of combine soap suds and visible water off his body. Anything he couldn't see or reach was never meant to be dried. The thrill that forced him to lock the door was now to be experienced. He stood up on the stool and took the Marine's coat from the hanger. Before the full-length mirror, he carefully watched himself place a small arm in each sleeve and drape the coat about his nude body. It could easily have passed for an overcoat on his little frame. As he was standing before the mirror humming the "Stars and Stripes Forever," a knock came to the door to interrupt his boyish emotion.

He recognized at once the voice of Garry Palmer. "Hey, pal, what's the big hold up? Some of your kid friends from your school are downstairs. Shake it up! By the way, where's my coat? I look like an usher from the Gem Theatre in East St. Louis with these pants on. Give me the coat so I'll at least look like a Marine."

Patty was petrified as he stood in front of the mirror listening to Garry's voice through the door. He had to obey his command lest he offend the man who so kindly consented to come to his home. When he unlocked the door, the Marine walked in to see Patty unbutton the last of the shiny buttons and slip the coat from his shoulders. He was more ashamed of the liberty he assumed with his friend's beautiful coat than his juvenile nudity. He couldn't look Garry directly in the face. He stood waiting for a severe chastisement.

"So, this is what's keeping you from getting on with the party. That's okay, Patty. I used to be just like you. If I had two dress uniforms, I'd be glad to give you one. But, with the kind of dough I make, you're plenty lucky if you can keep one out of the hock shop."

Patty was elated with the joy this message brought. He stood in the center of the bathroom watching the husky Marine fix his hair and put the coat on his massive shoulders. He didn't care how many people were waiting to wish him the greetings of the day. He was content to be right there in the bathroom watching the idol of his dreams brush the imaginary lint off the spotless coat, arrange the white belt with the large shiny buckle, and then touch his finger tips to the end of his tongue, and in two or three brushes, arrange the out-of-place hairs on his eyebrows. To Patty, this was a necessity completely foreign to his particular toilet routine.

"You'd better get your best duds on, Patty, or I'll back out on your Aunt Liz's offer," said Garry taking a last and admiring look at himself in the mirror.

"You mean you're going to stay for my whole party?" said the child, wild with the thought of such a bestowed favor.

"Better than that, Patty, I'm going to stay all night," he said, patting the excited boy's wet head. "Now, get off the dime, pal, and let's make this a real party."

"Are you going to sleep with me in my bed?" the boy yelled as he ran into Timmy's room and started to dress himself with all earnestness.

"I'm afraid you'd kick me to pieces," was the voice from the bathroom. I'll just flop any place your Auntie Liz wants to put me. Any bed in this house should be a dream-bender compared to some I've slept in. Come on, Patty. Hurry up! I'm getting a little on the hungry side."

At the table in the large dining room filled with happy children, Patty sat at the head of the talkative group. At his right was the hungry Marine who kept the children and the adults in a fit of continual laughter with his war stories. Anything he seemed to suggest was taken as a command by the youngsters. After the dinner, he took them into the living room and played party games and assisted with Dr. Gerard in awarding the prizes.

He kissed each little girl goodnight and shook the hand of every little boy. Doctor Gerard and Father Joseph were impressed by this young man who was so gifted with a rare talent. Never did they think, as they walked to their cars, that a Yankee could be so friendly and such a source of enjoyment.

After early Mass on Sunday, they would drive Garry to Memphis. It would be an extended birthday present for Patty if he'd go to bed real early. Such a treat couldn't be trifled with, so Patty hurried off to bed without a moment's delay. Only once did he return, and it was touching to see the little fellow boldly walk up to the hardened Marine and throw his arms around his neck and kiss him firmly on the cheek. If little boys who dream with a pleasant smile on their faces could only reveal their subconscious pleasures, what a beautiful fantasy it would make for the ears of tired men. The Odyssey of a child lives but once. How painful it must be to outlive its grandeur.

Somewhere in the course of the night, Patty awakened from his little world of make believe to feel the chill of loneliness. In his sleep, he must have bid goodbye to his Marine. He must have watched him sail again the oceans that separate the lands. In his excitement, he rushed to the guest room to make sure his dream didn't work itself into a fearful reality. There, on the soft, high bed with a chest exposed to the winter's air, was the man who upset his dreams. He softly crawled into the side of the bed and lay motionless beside the hero of his day. Sleep overcame his tired eyes and when morning dawned, Garry awakened with a start to find the arm and hand of his little admirer firmly around his neck and chest. He smiled on the sleeping figure as any man would who knows children.

CHAPTER TWENTY FIVE

After the conference at Fort Augustus Abbey with Doctor Malone, there was no real rest or pleasure for Father Kevin to be enjoyed in the shadows of the Vatican. Letters to Lacodere and his Abbey only made the young priest homesick for the States.

He was tired of Italy and its coarse food. He was tired in his heart and soul with the people and their customs. He wanted to return to America and see Patty, Gibby, Liz, and everyone who missed his cheerful personality.

Only one letter did Kevin receive from the busy doctor in Berlin. It contained the little card that he kept in his wallet. The little German the priest knew helped him to translate its doctoral meaning. Often he'd take it out and be reminded of his obligations to his boy. They were words of heavy import on his soul. He would never discount their intense worth, but often wondered why Skeets should have thought it necessary to remind him. He read the card on a rainy and cold day in late February. The words were the same, but the command seemed to be ever more poignant: *"I shall pass through this world but once. Any good therefore that I can do or any kindness that I can show to any human being, let me do it now. Let me not defer or neglect it, for I shall not pass this way again."* He returned the card to its place in the wallet on the desk. He looked at the three letters on his nightstand that must have been placed there by the mail collector earlier that morning. He was void of his usual ambition to open with all haste the epistles from the States. The last few days were days of extreme loneliness for Father Kevin. He didn't want to read those letters till his spirits were lifted to the peek where he could sit down and enjoy their contents.

The letters remained untouched on his nightstand for a full week. Others arrived and were tossed on his desk. He never reported to the Gregorian during his mental siege, but walked through the streets of Rome contrary to all the dictates of the latest Vatican announcements. Something was radically wrong with the young priest. He ate very little and slept less. It was becoming quite an obvious malady, and at the first opportunity in the beginning of the week, he was called to the Abbey's office.

The usual routine questions were put to him. No, he wasn't sick. He wasn't disgusted with his studies. He would remain till June and finish if he were temporally left to iron out his own affairs. But one in Religious Life isn't left to harbor thoughts that pain his soul and being. He must be able to share his sorrows along with his joys in Community Life. Father Kevin confessed to the Abbot that he wasn't sure he was happy in the state of Community Living. He was most happy when he was left by himself; society of both genders were showing their cruel scorns, and it was difficult for the priest to understand why he was the butt of them all.

The break and turning point in his shadow of doubt came when he went to the American Church in Rome conducted by the priests of the Congregation of Saint Paul and talked the matter over with the Paulist Father. In Father Kevin's analysis of the Paulists, he was little impressed. He felt they were founded on a deliberate act of disobedience and shouldn't have received approbation from Rome. But, today he didn't come to discuss the break between the followers of Hecker and the Rule of the Redemptorists. He wanted to talk to an American and tell him his troubles.

In his room at Saint Anselm's, he was jovial and freed. Whatever the abortioned son of Saint Alphonsus offered by way of consultation, it met with concord and spiritual delight. Father Kevin opened his first letter from Patty with eager hands. He read the scribbled lines and smiled like a child with a new toy. He was happy that the medals Garry Palmer handed to his little son made Patty so thrilled. He was happy, too, that someone was assisting him with his grave responsibility and thereby making his load even easier to carry.

The second letter opened came from Buddy Feeley. He told of his teaching assignment at their high school. He mentioned frequent visits to the house on Fontaine Street and the little "question box" who resided there. Everybody who met Patty couldn't help being attracted to him. He made such a big ceremony out of the most trivial incident. A visit from Buddy Feeley was just as important in rank as Father Joseph's frequent evening calls. Buddy told Father Kevin he wanted him to be home for his ordination and assist him with his First Mass. To Buddy, four more years wouldn't be so very long after he spent so many in training en route.

The third letter provoked tears of gladness. It was a late Christmas letter from Robert. He expressed his sorrow for failure to write, but he was sure when Timmy knew he was now Frater Martin and no longer known as Robert, he'd be forgiven. Yes, he joined the Novitiate at the Abbey and made Aunt Liz promise not to tell his little secret till he was able to write to Father Kevin himself.

All the letters, coupled with others of less importance, lifted Father Kevin to new heights. He would return to his studies with that renewed effort and fond hope of one day soon seeing those builders who helped construct the new Father Kevin.

CHAPTER TWENTY SIX

When Father Kevin returned to Lacodere on September 2nd, he wanted to see his little Patty alone. Together in his old room they sat and talked like two old friends. There was no need for introductions. They both remembered each other despite the long separation. It would take a little time for Kevin to get used to Patty again, but for Patty to shower his love on the priest, it was only a matter of an afternoon's visit. The child had much to tell him and more little trophies to show off. Patty wasn't too big to sit on Father's lap on the old rocker in the corner. There they sat looking into each other's eyes with a fondness and deep understanding. The priest wanted to whisper his secret into the child's ear, but something in the innocent expression on the boy's face wouldn't permit it. Another day, perhaps, he'd be better situated to discuss his relationship that would meet with approval rather than misunderstanding.

Long after Patty's retirement and in the early hours of the following morning, Father Kevin and Liz discussed the child's future. She wasn't able to argue with her Timmy now. He was a doctor in a field that understood the mind as it really functioned. He was versed in all sorts of problems unheard of by Aunt Liz. How could she be expected to lie in defense of a truth that her Timmy was fully aware of its implications. Father Kevin refused to spare his aunt with questions relative to Madeline and himself. He wasn't nearly as shocked as she thought he'd be when she disclosed the matter of the letters she intercepted while he was at the lake. All he wanted from Liz was the story as she alone could tell it. Strangely enough, there were no tears at this conclave. It was conducted just like any psychologist might tear a story from the heart of his client or patient. With the tools of his profession so cleverly applied, Liz wasn't qualified to operate with her former decisive mandates. She had to submit no matter how much it hurt her pride and years of experience.

Father Kevin's First Mass was celebrated the following Sunday at the high altar of Saint Mary's Church. Father Ignatius, who came over from the Abbey where he was elevated to the post of procurator, acted as deacon. Mr. Buddy Feeley, S.J., took over the duties of sub-deacon, and the pastor, Father Joseph, preached the sermon. In the sanctuary, in the robes of arch priest, was Kevin's friend, Father Richard. The post of master-of-ceremonies was taken over by Frater Martin Duseaunault, O.S.B., in honore. Even Patty again put his red cassock and white surplice, with the long white sash, on his little frame and knelt with all the dignity of the minor office he held.

Father preached a sermon that touched the hearts of every parishioner in his crowded church. To all but the celebrant, it was heartwarming. Father Joseph praised Timmy's fine accomplishments and acknowledged to the world that the Church was proud of the character of Her clergy. But, in the chair between his two friends, Father Kevin sat looking directly at his boy. Patty heard those words so eloquently preached by Father Joseph and smiled his approval in the direction of the celebrant's seat. Little did he realize those piercing stares were prompted by a burning love from father to son.

Father Kevin had to be reminded by a touch from Father Ignatius that it was time for the Credo. Yes, there was much he really believed as he spoke those words of Faith. There was much more running through his mind as he raised the Host at the elevation of the Mass. The Holy Sacrifice of this Mass would be one of many he would offer on the altars of time. Personal and heart rendering sacrifices that would lacerate deep and lasting wounds in his heart. Sacrifices that he must bear with the noble carriage of his office.

In the front pew of Saint Mary's Church, Liz knelt as she watched her nephew sing that First Mass. She watched him in that same church make his First Holy Communion. She listened to his prompt answers to the Bishop's questions at Confirmation. Now, after so many years of patient waiting, she watched him reach the goal she prayed so often he'd attain. She was happy amid her sorrow. What they discussed a few evenings before she thought would never come to light. Any happiness she enjoyed as she watched her Timmy and his Patty on the altar seemed surpassed by the affliction of her own admission.

The reception at the house on Fontaine Street was attended by all. No invitations were necessary. All knew Timmy O'Shea and wanted to be on hand to welcome him back to the States after so long an absence. He stood in the center of the living room shaking the hands of old friends and talking to each and every guest. He was tired when the last of the crowd bid him happiness in his life as a priest. Tired as he was, he still was rested enough to spend many minutes talking to Patty as he prepared for bed.

Kneeling side by side in front of the large crucifix, Father Kevin and Patty prayed for their special intentions. When Patty had asked God to bless his Aunt Liz and keep his Timmy a good Father, the child felt the hand of the priest slip around his little shoulders and his hand firmly grasp his arm in a tight embrace. The boy looked up into the smiling face of the priest as his father bent low and kissed him goodnight. Father Kevin didn't laugh as the lad jumped into bed and then out again. He forgot one very important request of his Heavenly Father. "And please, God, make me a big, strong Marine like my pal, Garry!" Then the happy youngster let Father Kevin cover him and tuck the loose ends of the blanket under the mattress. When he switched the light out and started to walk to the door, the priest heard his name called. There was something Patty forgot to whisper to him after such an exciting day. The priest sat on the side of the bed as the boy picked himself halfway out of the covers. "You're the best Father in the whole world. Even better than Father Joseph!" Father Kevin gently pushed the child to the pillow and ruffled the curly locks of the lad's hair. He was content to be the best father in the world, and he'd do his best to live up to those laudable expectations.

In the library, Father Kevin found Liz reading on the large, red davenport. She put the *Lives of the Irish Saints* on the mantelpiece as Timmy took a chair on the opposite side of the room. His expression told her that he wanted to talk.

He discussed his appointment at the Abbey as new junior Dean of Men and the various classes in psychology and philosophy he would teach in the college department. They talked of many things that night and the morning that followed. Anything he or she omitted in their letters abroad was fit subject for conversation. He described the many countries and cities he visited. He included the visit Skeets paid to the Fort Angustus Abbey in Scotland. The subject of Patty again became the important topic of discussion. His future and the planned summers the priest had made while he was in his post graduate studies in Rome, all just for Patty, would be the reality of their next six years together. Father Kevin told Liz he would take Patty on long trips throughout the United States and make him thoroughly realize that he loved his boy with all his heart.

At the Abbey, Father Kevin proved a good dean can also be a better teacher. The students liked his honest appraisal of their difficulties and found him an easy man to talk with and unbend their trying uncertainties before his keen sense of good judgment. He always had time to take a little walk to the lake-pond with a student who found it hard to believe some of the complicated situations of life. If Father was tired after these sessions, he never showed the slightest signs of his weariness. The first year as assistant to the Dean, he helped many young men find themselves and redirect their steps on the path of righteousness. To his fellow Religious in the Abbey, he was ever a source of inspiration. Frater Martin enjoyed his class in Logic and Introduction to Philosophy. The clear lectures made the theories and propositions with their strange terminology clearer to the bewildered Frenchman.

But, above all, Father Kevin lived those fall and winter months with the thoughts of the summer he was to spend with his little ten year old boy. Anything the little child wrote about in the weekly letters was a major consequence. He sat up till the wee hours of the morning composing letters he felt would be of interest to his Patty. The child, in turn, cherished these as treasured keepsakes and read them over and over to himself in the quiet of the library, or stretched out on the large sofa in the living room before the fire in the grate that lent sufficient light, as well as warmth.

June of 1937 ushered in the first of a series of grand trips for Father Kevin and little Patty. He was told to select a district he thought would be of prime interest to his youthful imagination. Wherever he was to decide to roam, the priest would be happy to be at his side, sharing in his joys and juvenile happiness.

It didn't take Patty long to pack his bag for the long-awaited trip. A few pairs of hose, a handful of handkerchiefs, a pair of swimming trunks, some shirts, and an extra pair of pants with his toothbrush and paste carelessly tossed in the compartment for incidentals. He was up long before six o'clock waiting for Father to arrive from the Abbey. He decided a visit to Chicago and the surrounding area would be the nicest vacation a young boy could take.

The only exterior evidence of Father Kevin's priestly station was in the manner in which he drove on the highway. Time was something that shouldn't be wasted in idle day dreaming. Several times he was halted by the State police and produced his license only to be warned that he wasn't operating a fire truck. But, the faster Kevin drove, the happier Patty seemed to be. He was like any other small boy who loves to get places irrespective of the manner of safety.

In St. Louis, they stopped over for a week. They registered at the Jefferson Hotel and appreciated their comfortable room and shower. There was plenty of time to see St. Louis in their week of relaxation. The beautiful parks and picturesque churches were visited along with a day at the ball part and an upset victory for the Browns.

Chicago made Patty gasp in admiration. It was the busiest place he had ever seen. Here they stayed at the Drake, and Father Kevin felt he should insist upon his boy's very best manners. Together they visited the boys' department of Marshall Field's grand store and bought several little gifts to be sent back to his little friends in Lacodere. Also, a new summer outfit that would make the lad a bit more presentable in such a fine hotel as the Drake.

While in Chicago, Kevin took Patty to the campus of Notre Dame University. In the small town of South Bend, Indiana, he introduced his boy to the memory of a great man. A man who built character in men. Knute Rockne was always the inspiration of the young Benedictine. On the campus of Notre Dame, they visited the chapel and buildings that make up the famed University. Summer school was in session, and Patty was amazed to see the number of various Orders of nuns streaming out of this building and that one.

Before they made the drive back to Lacodere, they took a boat ride on the large lake that borders the city's north side. Patty thought his little Lake Tahoo was great until he saw Lake Michigan.

The time devoted to make a boy happy and carefree enabled Father Kevin to look with new hopes to his coming classes in the fall. He knew he was becoming a real part of this boy.

CHAPTER TWENTY SEVEN

The following summer saw two figures sitting side by side in the Chicago and Southern Airliner bound once more for Chicago. Patty was growing now and gave every indication that he'd be very tall before many years. He could very easily pass for a boy of thirteen despite his immature face. It was his first ride in an airplane and the thrill lasted long through the winter months. In Chicago, they met Joey Roys who was associated with the Eastern Airlines Company. He insisted that Father Kevin accept a pass for the two of them to visit New York City, but Kevin wanted to forestall the visit till the World's Fair. He declined his friend's offer and the two took a train for Canada. They visited the major cities of their neighboring country and attended the devotions at the Shrine of Saint Anne and Brother Andre. Everyplace the two traveled, they found something of interest to write to Auntie Liz. Little gifts of pottery and linens were sent along from the quaint shops.

Homeward bound with little time to rest the weary priest and his companion traveled. Steadily moving from city to city not only usurped time, but vast stores of energy. Kevin wasn't as young in spirit as little Patty. He couldn't keep up the pace to see what was around each corner. While on their second trip, the priest found time to outline courses for the following year. The college coach resigned to take a position with greater remuneration and left the post to be filled by a man who was already overworked with classroom assignments. But, Father Kevin knew he could make the time, if through this summer, he prepared in advance a detailed outline of the first semester's work.

Back in Lacodere, Patty enlisted in the eighth grade. He was very young for the class, but had a fair mind and could adapt himself to work with some degree of ease. This was to be his final year with the good Sisters of the Academy. The next year would find him in the ranks of high school and in the confines of the Abbey Prep.

The season that followed proved a disappointment for the coach. With a ten-game schedule, he was only able to win two games and tie one. He attributed the losses to his own inability to produce winning material from raw recruits. No matter how much Father Ignatius tried to encourage his friend, the priest refused to believe the men on the squad weren't football "timber." He told the Abbot to replace him and let him return to the classroom in full standing as a teacher.

Patty remembered his twelfth birthday in 1939 because he received from his aunt Liz the beautiful Chain of Lacodere. He was told how hard Father Kevin worked to earn the medal and chain, and it was a rare honor to have it bestowed on such a youngster. He promised to prize it above all his possessions and only take it off when he was in the shower. During their trip to the Pacific Coast that summer, Kevin learned for the first time that the medal and chain was on the boy's person. While they were washing before breakfast in the Pullman car, Father Kevin watched the boy remove the top of his pajamas. There before his startled eyes was the gift he gave Madeline Turrel so many years before. He was happy that

Liz thought to turn it over to Patty, and let the child have something personal belonging to his father. Father Kevin was amused to watch his son take such precaution with his prize.

On their first trip West, the priest and boy were awe-struck by the Dakotas and the long trip through Montana. In Butte, they stopped to visit a priest who made his studies at the North American College with Kevin. The young assistant pastor took his guests down the mine shaft and into the earth that produced great tons of copper. After a few days spent in the wilds of the West, heretofore only read about or seen on the movie screen, Kevin and Patty left for Seattle. The beauty of the Cascades seemed to surpass that of the Rockies. In the observation car on the rear of their train, they sat and marveled at the giant Evergreens of the great Northwest. Never had Patty seen such beauty and freshness so vividly depicted before his startled eyes.

In Seattle, they were guests of an Irish family from the same town in Ireland as Kevin's parents. Here the priest was reminded of Rome's many hills. On the summit of Queen Anne Hill, they looked out over the beautiful Lake Washington, saw the two main ranges of mountains, the Cascades and the Olympics, watched the boats and ships in Elliot Bay and Puget Sound, admired the greenness of the grass and the beauty of the homes of these Far westerners. Kevin didn't want to leave this paradise of beauty. He wished many times on his trip to Mount Rainer that his father had never moved from the city of his birth. Why couldn't Big Tim have left his child in this Garden of Eden and taken his wife alone to the South? Such a city built so close to the great Pacific and proud of its cleanliness made Kevin sad to bid it farewell.

They thanked their host as they took one of the Alexander boats to the city of the Golden Gate. Here, as elsewhere, Kevin gave Patty the run-of-the-town. They stayed at the Mark Hopkins Hotel and visited the then reigning San Francisco Exposition on Treasure Island. This was the first, but not the last big fair Patty was to visit. The museums of interest and the various amusement centers were all attracted by the two travelers. They found time to walk through Golden Gate Park, see Telegraph Hill, Chinatown, and the Ocean Esplanade. Never had bridges appeared so gigantic as the famous Golden Gate and Bay Bridge.

In late August, the priest and his excited little Patty entrained for Los Angeles. Through another North American College classmate, they received passes to visit the studios. They watched Mr. Crosby and other celebrities go through their daily routines before the camera. The priest-friend of Father Kevin's took them over the course so often traveled by tourists. They visited the homes of the Gables and Barrymores, and other notable characters of celluloid fame and fortune from a respectable distance.

Time wouldn't permit a trip to Mexico or even further enjoyment in the City of Makebelieve. At the famous May Company Store, Father Kevin bough Patty his complete school outfit and had it sent along to the Abbey. After a long, lingering look at the Ocean and a swim together at Malibu Beach, they took the plane at the Los Angeles airport and flew over Arizona and Texas and finally back to Memphis, Tennessee.

Father Kevin was determined Patty should be as happy at Cassino Prep as the many other boys who traveled from far and near to attend the Benedictine School. Everything was done to make his stay a most pleasant one. His courses were mapped out, a small private room was equipped with all the conveniences of his own room at the O'Shea home, including a small radio. He also enjoyed the continual visits of Father Ignatius and Frater Martin along with the oft-enjoyed pastimes of his own Father Kevin.

When the close of school in late May of 1940 arrived, Father Kevin noted a change in his thirteen year old son. He grew irritable and wanted to be left to his own company. Being a brilliant psychologist, Father Kevin was able to analyze the situation without too much trouble. A recent letter he found on the lad's dresser indicated the boy's intimate thoughts.

With war raging in Europe and another National election looming before the American people, Kevin's thoughts were more mature. He wanted to abandon the summer trip with Patty, but the boy's condition demanded a change. The letter Patty received from Garry Palmer told in bold print the adventure for those who joined the ranks of the Corps. It livened the boy's imagination to do big things in the uniform of his country. He wasn't content to be a schoolboy and read about Caesar's Gallic Wars and the dullness that went along with problems in geometry. He wanted to be like Garry and see life from a soldier's eyes. True, it worried poor Kevin and upset Auntie Liz. The boy's marks in class gave every evidence to his various teachers that he was definitely in a terrible mental slump. Something must be done to lift his mind from battles un-fought and yet to be won.

The Abbey needed Father Kevin for many important assignments around the monastery that summer. But, Kevin knew his son needed him now more than ever before. Patty wasn't of an age when mothers hold sway with soft words of advice. He needed a man's voice and a man's understanding counsel.

Although Patty was only thirteen and quite a distance away from fourteen, he could easily pass for sixteen. He was tall and muscular. Throughout the course of his freshman year at Cassino, he refused to play football. In its stead, he went out for the boxing team and made a mild showing every day that created his physique, as it was the arduous task of daily exercise and leg and arm work. He ate everything that was placed in front of him. There was no reason why a healthy, normal boy of thirteen shouldn't gain weight and make the Fairbanks scales register a neat one-forty. The only thing that really bothered him was the changing notes in his voice.

Once more Father Kevin and Patty entrained for a vacation together. This year they left the Abbey and went directly to Florida. Here they spent a week swimming and tanning their bodies on the beach at Miami. It was here that Father Kevin noticed the major transition in the physical make-up of young Patty. Each day on the beach, they were as friendly as they had always been. When it came time to dress and return to the hotel, Patty balked. He was very gracious about it, though. He would tell Father Kevin to go on ahead, and he'd follow later. The fact only became apparent towards the end of their stay at the beach when the priest also decided to balk. He knew something must be amiss, and it was his duty to find the quirk in his boy's machinery. They walked silently to the bathhouse off the beach and in the dressing room, the priest noticed Patty had departed to another and more secretive section of the bathhouse to take his shower and change. Father Kevin remained alone in the showers thinking of a possible pep talk he was going to administer to a boy suddenly overcome with chastity of false concept. It dawned on him then and there that Patty was acting anything but his usual carefree self. In the hotel room, he was the same as in the bathhouse about his dressing habits. When the priest returned to his locker, he found the surprised boy standing before the locker door trying vainly to dress himself with a towel about his waist. Father Kevin watched this adolescent peculiarity and laughed out loud. It made matters worse for the boy. Whatever had come over him in the course of twelve short months? The priest told his son, then and there, to prepare for a good session that night on the subject of moral tactics.

Father Kevin was a pretty fair judge of boys, having been one himself. Patty wasn't any different from the general run of lads in his class. Yet, he became affected by the retreat given by the priest in January of that year. He confessed to Father Kevin quite honestly that the retreat-master gave a severe conference on the virtues with special emphasis on chastity. It so impressed Patty that he changed his whole mode of personal conduct. Father listened to the boy's version of the priest's little talks. He told Patty there was such an evil as punctiliousness or scrupulosity that had a tendency to thwart the ideals the good retreat-master was trying to impregnate in their youthful minds. He told the boy that he admired his wonderful ideas of personal living and conduct, but he was also quick to point out to him that he could become over-zealous in this respect and find himself suffering from and doctoring the dreaded disease of a child with a phobia all of his own. He concluded by telling Patty to be his own natural self. If he had problems that bothered him, and what boy hasn't, he was free to come to him and together they'd iron them out.

Father Kevin knew this talk would bring the lad around. It was just one of the maladies that youth suffer in the artless task of growing up. Not all have the good fortune of growing in the same degree of wisdom and prudence. The priest was content that an evening away from a good Wally Berry movie rewarded the child in the years to follow. They went to bed as they had done on their previous excursions, refreshed with the thought that both accomplished more for their cinematic abstinence and the encouraging words of a man who was more than a priest.

When the lights were out and sleep was about to entrap two tired men, Father Kevin felt Patty's hand slip into his own, and the soft words of a grateful boy rang deep in the recesses of his mind, "Thanks for wising me up, Timmy. I was sure heading for the 'jerks' seats, wasn't I?" Father Kevin didn't answer. He merely closed his hand a little tighter on the hand of his boy. It was the first time he could recall that Patty wanted to be this close to him. He went to sleep smiling, and still holding the hand that wanted to be in his.

Never again did Father Kevin witness the slightest change in young Patty. They took the train to Washington, D.C., where they spent another joyful week touring the greatest city in America. Every building was important enough to visit. From Washington, they made a three-day stop-over in the friendly city of Philadelphia. Here, Independence Hall and the huge Liberty Bell and the historic surroundings of a great old city enthralled and charmed the two wanderers beyond words. When they arrived in the Penn station in New York City, Patty wanted to go directly to the Empire State Building and have a bird's eye view of Manhattan. But, Father Kevin felt he must secure a hotel before they start the rounds of a large city with a World's Fair in progress. He tried four of the leading hotels in Manhattan until Patty advised him to put his Roman collar on with his gabardine blacks. It worked so successfully they didn't have to go beyond the Taft Hotel in the heart of Times Square.

Three weeks of their grand vacation were spent in New York City and Brooklyn. A short trip to Newark and Jersey City meant very little to Patty. They were just two more cities that could use a little air conditioning in the heat of the summer. In Times Square, they went to the Astor Theatre and the Roxy, and, of course, Radio City's Music Hall. Patty saw a review the like of which nearly made his dazzled eyes pop out of his head. The beauty of the stage and the art of the performers was incomparable.

Through New England with a final resting place at the Copley Plaza wandered the two men. There was much they wanted to see in Boston, but their time was drawing to a close. They wanted to visit the historic places so enriched with cultural background. They took in the birthplace of Franklin, the Boston Massacre Monument, along with a score of other monuments of interest and Harvard University, where Kevin would soon be enrolled again as a different kind of student, the many other colleges and universities in the area, along with the Natural History Museum, a phase of their culture unwanted in their previous travels.

The priest overlooked Providence and Hartford and the many more cities they planned to aimlessly and listlessly visit while they were making out their itinerary in mid-December of the previous year. They were forced to take a plane from Bangor, Maine with connections out of Boston, for the Southland. The two were a little frightened when they reported late to the Abbot, but Irish explanations are easily provocative of forgiveness, even by the staunchest of Irish disciplinarians.

Patty's sophomore year proved a little more practical for the boy. He forgot a lot of his silly ideas and decided he must begin the task of real study. The improvement was noticed by all who tackled this pleasing personality either on the grounds or in the classroom. The visits from Frater Martin were just as numerous as those of Fathers Ignatius and Kevin. They were all vitally interested in the little boy who was prone to regard himself more in the status of a man than a child.

Father Kevin cast his first vote for Mr. Roosevelt in the November elections. When asked why he didn't favor the Republican candidate, he merely said he wanted to give Roosevelt his first vote. Although there were many things Kevin disliked about the Democrat from New York, there were many more he admired in the man. While assisting in a parish at Christmastime near Columbus, Georgia, he visited the famous resort spot, built in a large measure by the President's aid. Kevin went to Warm Springs to see a student who was sent to the hospital for the cure in infantile paralysis. While there, he met Mr. Roosevelt. The President talked to Kevin for over an hour as they laughed together. This meeting forced a sincere respect to awaken in the mind of the young priest for the Commander-in-Chief of the Army and Navy. He at once appreciated the President's true qualities.

Father Kevin knew he would again become entangled in foreign affairs. He hated war purely out of psychological reasoning. The loss, economically, was of little concern when matched against the human toll of American youth. Blood sprinkled over soil where Americans found no haven, would be felt in the years to follow, yes, even through generations of American people.

The October sixteenth's registration meant war was certainly eminent. It carried its implications to the youthful attention of young Patty who again thought of war and Garry Palmer. This time it was to be a lasting blow to both Liz and Father Kevin.

The summer rolled around to greet an uneasy world. All Europe was suffering tremendous losses at the hands of the Axis Powers. Hitler wanted the whole of Europe for his domain and was willing to include Japan's Tojo and Italy's Il Duce to support his cause. The trio made advances that were costly to all involved. Nothing save a miracle could keep the United States from one more coming to the support of a haughty Britain. The so-called Isolationist was, in truth, a moral realist at heart. In American circles speculation was running high. There was no time, now, for idle vacationing. Let Patty stay the summer with Auntie Liz and enjoy the quiet of Lake Tahoo and the little blue and white cottage. It served as the nucleus for many vacations in the past. Let it now suffice with the shadows of war dimming the hopes and prayers of American mothers and fathers.

Father Kevin was most severe in his remarks to Patty after the close of the school term. He demanded in no uncertain terms that the boy belonged near Aunt Liz while he was assisting with the development of several projects to better Cassino College. With Father Ignatius raised to the office of Prior and acting Superior of the Abbey, Kevin found little time for sociability with his friend. There was no doubting the matter, Father Ignatius was an administrator of the finest character. What Gibby was to his office, Timmy was to his many assignments.

If Patty was restless when classes resumed in late September, he was not alone. Father Kevin was now thirty-two years of age and losing some of his blonde waves. He exercised and kept in the best of condition despite all the classes he was assigned to teach. The Abbey rocked with the news of the fateful destruction of Pearl Harbor. Something rocked within the breast of Father Kevin as well as in the heart of Patty Aloysius. A grave transgression had been committed against a great country. It must be reckoned with in the mode the transgressor chose, arms, ships and planes!

Through the remainder of the month of December and the rest of the scholastic year of 1942, Patty had ideas of mountainous character. He kept them in his heart pondering over the possibility of their enactment. While in his cell on the second floor of the Abbey proper, Father Kevin was negotiating with the United States Navy and the Military Ordinary concerning a commission as a Chaplain in the Service of his country.

The summer of 1942 found a fifteen year old boy very restless. He remained at the Abbey to assist with Fathers Ignatius and Kevin in conducting the camp for the little boys of the area. Here, it would seem, Kevin found some degree of rest. He could watch the anxiety of Patty grow steadily. He knew what was running through the boyish brain. Everyday the papers disclosed the names of Lacodere youths who were called to defend their Country's rights. Everyday Kevin and Patty pondered while they read and reread the list of names. It was during one of these literary sessions with the morning or evening paper that Patty told Timmy he was going to enlist. The priest gulped! He couldn't believe what his ears kept ringing. In his mind, he was reviewing those short years ago when he was a novice and Patty was a mere baby. No, he couldn't make the sacrifice and watch his boy slaughtered on some unknown land. He tried to reason with Patty, but it seemed useless. It was even difficult to argue with the boy when he knew that it was common talk about the campus that Father Kevin may be made Chaplain. What was right for one wasn't necessarily correct procedure for another. But, Patty wanted the uniform of the United States Marine Corps if it meant gaining it in fraud.

CHAPTER TWENTY EIGHT

Father Kevin O'Shea received his notification from the Military Ordinary in New York City. The Abbot gave him a send-off party with the blessings of the Community. His first assignment was to attend the Chaplain's School conducted at William and Mary College. From here he graduated to a special and further type of study at Cambridge and Harvard's School for Chaplains. While he found time to write to his Abbot and the others who waited his interesting letters, no word came to him from Patty. Even Liz found Patty's letters were falling into decline as far as interest and even intelligence was concerned. When he arrived in Lacodere for the Christmas holidays, she gave the boy a verbal "going-over" for his failure to write Father Kevin. He gave an apology that lacked some of the prime requisites for sincerity. All he said to his Aunt Liz in answer to her request was a faint, "I'll try to do better when I get back to Cassino."

Shortly after his sixteenth birthday, he wrote to Father Kevin to thank him for the shock and waterproof wrist watch. It was something he wanted and expressed his desire after seeing an advertisement in Life Magazine. Liz thought it best that Father Kevin buy the watch for Patty. She wrote him after Christmas to inform him of the boy's desire, and it was promptly taken up by the priest.

In early February of 1943, the letter that shook the foundation of the O'Shea house arrived. Patty left school to enlist in the Marine Corps. He told Liz not to worry about him and not to tell Timmy till he had completed his training at Paris Island. There was something about secrets that were abhorrent for Aunt Liz. She felt it was her duty to tell Timmy what his boy had done. She dispatched a wire to the priest and received an answer of but a few short words. There was nothing for him to say to Liz but to join with her in solemn prayer that God would spare their little Patty.

Before his training was completed, Father Kevin paid Patty a call. The priest had a full lieutenant's rating in the Navy, and his orders were to report to the Pacific Fleet. The few days of grace that were granted the priest were spent with his Aunt Liz, his son, and the kind old Abbot. While he didn't approve of his boy's enlistment, he had to admit there was peace and contentment in his every expression. The road of training was tough with the marines, but Patty loved every minute of it. He was no longer swayed by the bright uniform of peace days. The olive drab suited his fancy to the letter. In the few short weeks of service as an embryonic Marine, Patty gained weight and still more height. He was toughened to the talk of his Company and learned too fast the stories that pass from tongue to tongue.

In May, he was released to active duty. The action lay in Sandpoint Naval Station, a few miles outside the city limits of Seattle, Washington. It disgusted the boy to be assigned to such a dull position. Walking in front of a gate and asking car owners their business seemed like Boy Scout work at best.

He learned from Aunt Liz that Doctor Malone received his commission as a Captain and was sent immediately to the European theatre. Although he only met Joey Roys once, he was shocked to learn that a Nazi picked him off in his return from a mission over occupied France.

During the summer, Patty found little to entertain himself in the growing city of Seattle. With the other members of his Company, he found the "dives" of First Avenue and the "joints" of Washington Street merely places to venture when the rest of the city slept. He refused to enter the "rooms" around Blanchard Street with his companions, who felt the need of sociability. Something within him repelled against such behavior. When a free Sunday would fall his lot, he went to the little brick Church of Assumption where he could attend Mass at the Benedictine Church and talk with the monks from Saint Martin's Abbey.

And it wasn't uncommon for him to ride to the top of Queen Ann Hill and look out over the Bay and admire the scenes he and Father Kevin enjoyed so much a few years before. Even Woodland Park with its zoo, and Volunteer Park with its beautiful gardens running over with summer flowers attracted the youthful Marine.

On the battleship, Nebraska, Father Kevin saw war and the horrors it brought. His confessional was situated wherever someone stood ready to reveal his faults. He was as attractive for the Jews and Protestants as he was for the Catholics. The men had him compose letters to their wives and sweethearts. He was especially concerned about those young sailors and marines who failed to write often to their mothers. He'd prod them on and spell out words for them and assist in every way possible. He attended to the recreational activities and supplied a small library for the men. Each Sunday, he offered his Mass on the open deck and preached a straight from the heart sermon to his boys.

The Nebraska was hit twice before it took refuge in a repair dock in San Francisco. A much needed rest was afforded the Chaplain who accepted it with thanks. He was flown to Seattle where he met Patty in a grand reunion. They had dinner at the Olympic Hotel and took in a movie at the Fifth Avenue Theatre. Patty was radiant with pride as he walked the streets of the city with a Lieutenant-Commander of the Navy. In his white uniform, the priest was quite attractive as the Private First-Class by his side in a green marine's outfit.

Kevin and Patty found themselves walking endlessly and talking of old times. They stopped to make a visit to the Sacred Heart Church and light two vigil lamps at the Shrine of the Mother of Perpetual Help. Father talked for a few minutes to the Redemptorist priest who was saying his Office in the aisle of the church. The two men walked out to the sidewalk and Father Kevin gave the Redemptorist a bill and asked him to remember the young marine in his Mass. Patty joined the two priests on the sidewalk in front of the church and told Kevin he thought it was time to get back to his base.

CHAPTER TWENTY NINE

It was January of 1944 when Father Kevin received word from Patty that he was assigned to real action on board the destroyer Omaha. When he read the boy's letter, he stopped and renewed his prayers for his son's safety. The letter also told of several encounters with Jap destroyers and battleships. Kevin felt his son was like the child who witnessed too many newsreels at the local theatre. He was beginning to realize that his Patty was really in earnest about the war and its complications. Patty's letters to Liz described none of the horrors of war she read about in her morning *Commercial-Appeal*. He told her he was happy and well, and he'd be home before very long. There was no thought of homesickness in his letters, but one could read between the lines that the boy was getting fed up with the sea and the tropical islands of the Pacific.

In early June of the same years, Robert was ordained a priest of the Order of Saint Benedict. Again, Saint Mary's Church enjoyed its fourth First Mass ceremony. The people who attended the Mass were not the same happy flock of parishioners who knelt in prayer while Gibby and Timmy offered the Sacrifice. A war-torn people knelt and asked God to bless this young priest, and in the same breath, protect their sons and daughters who were flung in various theatres of the world fighting to preserve a peace that their parents engaged in not quite twenty-seven years previously.

Father Feeley, of the Society of Jesus, and newly appointed Principal of his old High School, assisted Father Martin Duseaunault along with Father Ignatius. Again, Father Joseph preached a sermon that touched the hearts of his congregation. He implored his good people to renew their prayers and storm heaven with an earnest appeal to ask God to bring about an early victory and just peace.

Robert failed as a teacher in several starts. He tried teaching a class in Latin. The students were in constant revolt. He switched over to a mathematics class. If he knew his subject matter, it never became apparent. The period was spent largely in trying to maintain order and discipline. The Abbot took counsel with several of the monk-priests, and it was decided that Father Martin would be best suited in a parish with some older priest to teach him the "ropes."

So, after his First Mass, the young priest didn't have far to go for his new appointment. He was assigned to remain in Lacodere with his old pastor and devoted friend, Father Joseph. He heard Confessions and said his daily Mass and visited throughout the parish. Mothers loved this young and friendly priest.

Father Kevin heard about Robert's inability to teach and his appointment to Saint Mary's Church. He wrote his "adopted" brother a long letter of encouragement. "Someday," he said, "we'll be together in a parish of our own." The words pierced deep in the Frenchman's heart.

At the Abbey, Father Ignatius had little time to communicate with Timmy. He was taking over all the duties of the old Abbot, who was now unable to attend the Devine Office or say his daily Mass. Every action taken by Gibby had in mind the best interests of the

Abbey and the development of the college and high school. The war took the major portion of their regular student body and through his diplomatic dealings made their little college into an Army Intelligence School. Father Ignatius was credited with building a separate high school department and a large combination gymnasium and indoor swimming pool. This called for money in large quantities. Gibby knew who possessed money and took it from them gently. The old brick gymnasium was converted into a large auditorium where he engaged prominent members of various professions to speak to the student body. The Abbey building housed the monks and college students in private rooms. The high school department enjoyed private quarters for seniors and three large dormitories for the three other classes. All the classrooms were situated in this one building and the only association the high schoolers had with the collegiate was at mealtime.

The war prevented the building of greenhouses and huge barns that Gibby felt should be replaced. He wanted to do something about the Novitiate building and the Sister's house. He had the plans formulated and set before the Abbot and his council. Only the termination of hostilities awaited his action in this regard.

With the advent of his march to monastic superiority, there came with it a decided divorcement from things in Lacodere. He only came home to visit when there was something urgent to be accomplished in the vicinity. If he was to be regarded as frugal, it certainly must be contributed to his intense love of the Abbey and his duties. The war to him tied the hands of progress for Cassino Abbey. He very rarely read the papers and found himself becoming old in his office. Yet, he was young in his ideas of advancement and would not relinquish his two classes no matter how heavy his schedule appeared.

When September rolled around, he was made coadjutor-Abbot with the right of succession. Father Kevin sent his vote when he learned of the Abbot's desire to have an assistant with power to act in his stead. The Abbey was aglow with purple and red-robed members of the hierarchy. His mother gave him the Abbot's ring of authority and his fellow monks presented him with the pectoral cross and chain. He was the youngest monk in the history of modern Benedictineism to be elevated to the perpetual office of Abbot. Gibby took the honor in his stride and used it wisely.

CHAPTER THIRTY

September wasn't all joy to everyone. To the Gerards, yes; to the O'Shea's, no. Two major transfers of prime concern to Father Kevin and Patty took place in early September of 1944. Patty left the destroyer, Omaha, and Father Kevin transferred to the transport, Sharbroock. When the two met on the large transport, they weren't too surprised, just extremely happy.

The war progressed favorably for the Japanese government during these heated months of battle. Every major fracas from Guam to Guadalcanal resulted in terrific losses for the Allies. Now, in the turning period, and before the utilization of atomic bombing, the Allies wanted Peleliu, as did the Japs, who held it.

From the Solomon Islands, the transport made top speed with its load of men, guns and ammunition. A number of destroyers paved the road and kept a good eye out for enemy U-boats. The priest in his quarters knew the importance of this mission about as thoroughly as the officers who conducted it. Patty only knew it meant adventure and a real crack at the fiends of the Rising Sun. The morning of the fifteenth, the Commander gave his orders in rapid-fire decision to hundreds of men with packs on their backs and guns in their hands. The Catholics knelt while Father Kevin bestowed General Absolution of all their sins. Even the Jews felt, at this critical moment, there could be no harm in kneeling for a priest's blessing.

Over the side of the transport climbed sailors and marines into the waiting LSTs that would take them to the shore for their bloody assault. The battle of Peleliu was in full swing! From the transport rang the fire from stationary guns in answer to the whistle and screaming noises from the Peleliu ridge. The Japs had the ridge fortified with deathly armaments, and snipers were incased in every hole in the fortress. It was sheer suicide to attempt the storming of such a fortification. The marines were used to suicide tactics and proceeded on and on through the rain of fire and exploding shells.

Patty wasn't reading *The Adventures of Tom Sawyer* while the LST moved toward the beach. In the flash of battle, he remembered where those Rosary beads were hidden. It was all very clear to him now. War was the essence of hell on earth as he heard the screams of men shot and wounded on their first landing barge. He was crouched in the third LST as it moved swiftly to the shore, and when the gate fell with a loud splash, he saw before his youthful eyes the bodies of men from the number two boat, as well as the initial landing barge, strewn along the beach in pools of fresh blood. There wasn't time for consolation. The dead were dead, and the dieing would be picked up by the medics. Their orders were to advance at any cost. "Get those yellow-livered bastards and blow their guts all over the goddamn island!" It still rang in Patty's ear. He was well-trained in the art of linguistics as well as battle tactics while at Paris Island. He could expect this. He even looked forward to experiencing its thrill.

Patty felt the cool water of the shoreline and waded onto the beach. It would appear from a sweeping glance of the beach that there were thousands of bodies moving slowly across the sands. Some never moved, but lay crouched with blood oozing out of a series of large holes. It was a most frightening sight to behold. Once Patty looked back to see others coming out of LSTs that were held fast in the mud beach. He got up on his knees to make a run for a hole just created by a bursting shell when the sniper's aim found its mark in the chest of the seventeen year old boy. It spun his body around with terrific force. The hole in his chest burned with the pain of fire. Why it never shattered his life then and there will never be known. In his agony, the boy called out one name and tried to advance gunless through the flames of fire and bullets. He was beside himself with pain as he fell in the mixture of coral, sand, and blood. He was muttering a name that meant his only love, and Timmy wasn't there to hear him call. The boy dropped into unconsciousness with a fighting spirit.

Still the battle raged onward through the late afternoon. Youth fell never to move again or be picked up so wounded their torn and massacred bodies that were poor representations of human strength and endurance. Boys who only a few months before lived normal healthy lives. Boys who went wild when a Bob Feller pitched a no-hit game, or dad would come through at the last minute with the car for that big date, or those same kids who sat around Al's Hamburger Shack polishing off "double-deckers" and talking about their Mary's and Bessie's. The same youthful faces that scorned on tough "trig" problems and equations in "Chem" were now dead to all the experiences so memorable of days spent in growing into maturity. The future Van Johnson's and Tyrone Powers who wanted only the decencies of a free life that yielded the fruits of a generation to come. They suffered and died dreadful deaths for a cause that was never made clear to their befuddled minds.

The Medical Corps worked incessantly to find and care for the wounded. The dead, for the time, were in the hands of the Supreme Caretaker. Improvised surgeries were established as the roar of guns and the hellish brimstone rocked the tents. Doctors and their aids operated under conditions of great peril to their safety and well-being. It was here in the shadows of war and unearthly noise and screaming, Patty was carried to a table to have plasma shot into his blood stream and prepare for what the doctors hoped would be a "chance"—the removal of three Jap shells from his chest.

Father Kevin was crawling on the beach behind the boys, asking God to spare them from the torments of a lingering death. A dispatch was handed to him of those taken to the hospital units. He quickly scanned the list of Kelly's and Polowski's and Goldstein's, along with that all-American institution, the Joneses. Beads of sweat fell on the sheet as his hands shook in nervous anticipation. He read the names of the reported dead and offered a quick, but sincere De Profundis for the repose of their souls. On to the near-dead and mortally wounded. In letters that stood out in bold, stencil-like prominence, was: PFC PATRICK A. DUNNE. Something came to the priest's throat that refused to wash down. He tried to swallow, but it remained steadfast as a reminder of what awaited him at the hospital tent.

As the priest rushed into the tent where several patients were stretched out either waiting for operations or recovering or slowly dieing from their inflictions, he heard the Captain say, "The Dunne boy is just about sitting up there with God!" Father Kevin asked the sergeant where they had Private Dunne, and upon learning that he was at the far end of the tent, rushed past the row of stretchers of maimed and wounded to fall on his knees at the side of the suffering boy.

"Patty, Patty!" cried the priest, nearly falling on top of the sleeping boy's body, "please wake up. There's something I . . . there's something Timmy has to tell you." The boy's eyes opened with a little effort and then closed. The priest called his name again in a loud whisper.

Outside, the roar of guns stilled for a brief moment while Timmy listened to the groans of the suffering boys. He again turned back to Patty who met his eyes with a forced smile on his lips. The priest knew he recognized him and began to talk.

"Don't say anything, Patty. Please try to listen to what I have to say. I know you've been to Confession this morning and your soul is fit for the sight of God. But, don't go, Patty. Please stay with me!" The boy shut his eyes for a second while Kevin spoke. He opened them again when the priest asked him to come back.

"I must tell you something that you should know. When you see God, face to face, maybe you can tell Him how sorry I've been for all my sins, especially . . ."

Again, Patty's eyes shut as he tried to move his hurt body. The pain that ran through him was a torture. He opened his eyes again, and in a soft, but clear voice said, "Go on, Timmy, you're the best pal a fellow ever had. Don't leave me now!"

"Don't ask me to explain how it happened. There isn't time. But, please believe me, Patty, it's the truth, and I can't say what joy you've brought to me. You've been everything a son should be. Don't die knowing that I was your father and ever felt ashamed about it. It may have been a mistake many years ago for a boy to make, but the results of that can't be sin when they produce a boy as fine as you've been. Yes, Patty, I'm your real father! Liz never told you because she thought you may never understand. I didn't even know it till Skeets told me in Scotland the year I was ordained. Your mother and I loved each other madly. She left never to return to Lacodere. You were born in New Orleans and adopted into the house on Fontaine Street by Liz. Mrs. Turrel was your grandmother."

The first real smile came to the boy's face. In his heart, he was happy. He was always in love with Timmy from that first time he remembered him playing with him as a mere baby.

"I feel like I'm going . . . Timmy. It's getting awful dark, and I'm thirsty. Will you get me a . . . a drink of . . ."

Unconsciously, the priest reached for his canteen on the side of his hip. He opened the top and gave his boy a few drops of water. Patty smiled his thanks to the priest. There was something he wanted to say as he opened his mouth to start to speak. Then he closed his lips together and turned his head towards Timmy.

Father Kevin bent low to catch the sound of his son's heart. It would beat fast, then slow, then fast again. Yes, Patty was still alive, but slipping into the chasm of the Great Divide from whence no man has yet returned to suffer.

The boy opened his eyes again and smiled. His lips parted, and he tried to raise his arms. He seemed to rally for a few seconds and want to speak. The few drops of water revived his spirit and the smile remained on his face till Father Kevin was called away. Before the priest left his boy's side, he felt Patty's hand grope on the blanket as if in quest of some lost item. When the priest took Patty's hand in his, there appeared a broader smile of satisfaction on his countenance. The boy's lips parted, and he spoke the words that were magnificent to his ears.

"Timmy . . . stay with me . . . I feel like the bottom is falling, and I'm sinking . . . I'm sinking into . . ." His voice faltered for a moment and then he continued, "I'm happy that I learned I have the best dad a guy could ever have. Tell Liz I didn't cry, and I just had to be a marine . . . and, is anyone looking at us, Timmy?" Patty said this with much hesitation. It wasn't easy to say goodbye this way when you should be saying hello to a new life with someone you just met. He was assured by Timmy's soft whisper in his ear that they were alone and together despite the tent full of groaning and suffering sailors and marines. "Would you . . . would you think me too big a baby if I asked you . . . if I asked you . . . to kiss me goodbye, dad?"

These were moments of tenseness for a priest who loved a child he wasn't allowed to call his own. He couldn't contain himself as he burst out in tears and pressed his lips firmly against his son's. The tears mingled with the salty sweat, and the noise of thunderous applause from the guns of fighting men acted as the finale in the most sacred drama of two people. Patty spoke no more as his head turned, and his hand reached to his throat to firmly clasp the Chain of Lacodere.

A corporal in the medics came up to the priest while he was bent over the body of his boy. The non-com tapped the shoulder of the weeping priest and with a look of bewilderment at the scene he was witnessing asked him to come at once to another section of the unit where a boy was screaming for "the priest."

Duty knows no personal feelings. The priest left his son and followed the corporal. He administered the Last Sacraments to the crying sailor and tried his best to comfort him in his agony. He promised to write his mother that he died bravely and with the Last Rites according to his Church.

After a hurried call at the bedside of still another suffering human being, Father Kevin arrived in time to see the corporal pull a sheet over the face of his Patty and mark a notation in his scorecard of "men no more," which was too much for Timmy to take. His nerves broke, and he had to be held up by the strong arms of the medical corpsman. In that flash of time, he recalled the beautiful scenes of his own childhood and his growth to manhood made more pleasurable by the association his Patty brought.

CHAPTER THIRTY ONE

F our days later the fighting ceased for a breather. The commander of the transport knew it wouldn't be for long. He knew the Japs too well for that. He ordered the dead to be draped in the flag of their countries and made ready for sea burial.

Father Kevin, in his quarters, held the gold medal and chain he removed from the neck of his son. While he was writing the account of Patty's death to Aunt Liz, he stopped several times to hunt for the proper words to express his own deep sorrow. He knew well how she would take the Navy Department's wire with its trite and seemingly insincere note of condolence. But, could she feel nearly as sorrowful as he felt when writing those lines?

They were ready for him to officiate. At least the knock on his door made him jump with startled expectation. He walked out on the deck with a surplice and stole of purple and white. The officer called out the name of Private Jordan. Father read a few lines from the New Testament, and the body was released to the jaws of the ocean. Then Sergeant O'Hara followed his brother sailor into the depths of the calm Pacific. After O'Hara, there were several others before the name of Private Dunne came to the ears of the priest. He bit his lip to avoid the sorrow that engulfed his being. Slowly he read a passage from Saint John, a passage he loved and knew Patty would have enjoyed hearing if he could be there alive and his happy self. As they lifted the plank to permit the body to slide swiftly to its watery grave, Father Kevin's voice broke, and he spoke nearly in hushed whispers the Latin phrases that ofttimes came to his mind when he retired for the night, "In manus tuas, Domine, commendo spiritum meum!" He heard the body of his boy hit the water with a resounding splash. It was the end, but only the beginning of his memories of Patty Dunne. Father Kevin fainted away in a slump on the deck of the transport. Some said, "The Chaplain is killing himself with work!" But Timmy knew what caused him to lose hold of his senses. It was the sound of Patty's voice and the way he smiled up at him, the memories of those many trips they made together. All hit with terrific boomerang velocity. The thought of never seeing his boy again shut out the light and life from his soul. For a few moments, these terrible thoughts cut off his desire even to live. He swooned to the deck with overpowering grief and emotion.

In Lacodere, Father Martin found himself being comforted by Aunt Liz; ever faithful Aunt Liz. She read the telegram, which had been delivered several days after the fifteenth of September, to the young curate of Saint Mary's Church. For one who grew in the same sunshine, played with the same toys, and entertained himself with the company of the child, it was a blow that would find its wound ever apparent in the mind of the priest. Father Martin loved Patty as he loved his own little brothers and sisters. Perhaps more so! He was there when he took that first tumble down the long winding staircase. He listened to the first words and went screaming to Aunt Liz. He took him on walks through the town and presented him as his little brother. Their Christmases were happy in the thoughts of each other's happiness. It was the priest's place to console Aunt Liz, but she was acting in that capacity.

When Liz heard from Timmy, she felt more pain for his grief than her own loss. She knew he was trying amid great trials to make it sound as if it were a glorious thing to be admitted into heaven. God only knew the suffering Father Kevin underwent to write those lines.

Patty wasn't the first to give his life to his country from the little city of Lacodere. There were others in Italy, France, and over Germany. But none received the touching words in a sermon prepared by Father Joseph as did Patty Dunne. The old priest's voice quivered as the words fell from his lips. Patty to him was another Timmy. And his love for Timmy was outwardly spoken by his constant praises of the lad with the perpetual smile.

Close to the end of September, the fighting continued with losses mounting into the thousands. No war in the history of mankind could ever be so costly in the blood of men who loved life. Father Kevin received his orders from the Department of Navy Personnel to take a furlough until further orders were forthcoming. Little did he realize this order came at the request of Commander Jake Murphy, the Fordham Ram of earlier gridiron years. Murphy could see the priest's vitality slowly leaving his big body. He knew, too, the priest would continue till something cracked. He sensed something when the priest passed out during the burial service. He associated nothing of a personal nature. The priest could just as well take the dive when he was reading over Corporal Johnson. He knew Chaplain O'Shea needed a long rest, whether Chaplain O'Shea liked the idea or not.

Orders were orders. Father Kevin didn't feel like returning to the States. There were too many reminders back home of things he had to forget. His nights were restless with the jumbled-up version of the music that once was soothing melody to his ears, "Clair de Lune." Why should it come now to him when all these years it lay dormant in the recesses of his brain? It wasn't the beautiful notes played with the heavenly rapture of a Madeline Turrel on Christmas night. These were harsh and laughing chords that sounded like a saw scraping against steel; notes that scorned a beautiful memory with mockery and derision taunting him through the night.

On the first of October, he looked out of his window in the guest quarters of the Bishop's residence in the coastal city of Madras. Located as it was in the Southern section of India and facing the Bay of Bengal, it afforded the young priest to find rest and change from the severity of his chaplaincy duties. The old Jesuit Bishop, who remembered Chicago back in the late nineteenth century, pumped him with questions irrelevant to things of war, things about Rome, the Jesuits, and the old Chicago White Socks. He knew a sick priest when he saw one. He knew when to leave Father Kevin to the garden and the quiet of his room overlooking the bay.

After Timmy was thoroughly rested, he asked leave of the Bishop of Madras. The Bishop declined to let him leave knowing in his heart this man was still sick and unfit to return to the grind of warfare. He begged him to stay until the middle of December, if not the New Year. Father Kevin knew it was useless to argue with a Jesuit, so he remained and accepted his invitation to accompany him to the leprosarium on the Island of Polonia, where he would Confirm several lepers the nuns had prepared for months for the Sacrament of Confirmation.

The small craft that took the Bishop and priest down the Indian Coast past Pondichery and Cuddalore turned its nose to the deeper waters of the Bengal Bay. Less than thirty miles from the mainland, they were greeted by the inhabitants of the Island of Polonia, who stormed the little dock to greet their annual visitor. All were natives with the exception of an old, a very old, Jesuit Father, and three Sisters of Charity. Father Kevin helped the old Bishop out of the boat and met the ancient member of the Society of Jesus. His face turned white when he met the shy little sister who stood behind Mother Josephine. Before his eyes was an exact replica, a perfect double of someone he once loved very dearly. He walked over to her and extended his hand. The poor thing could only dream of meeting a priest so young and handsome after five years of working among the dead. With downcast eyes, she bowed from the waist and placed her thin, long hand in his. Father Kevin wanted to say something about her resemblance to someone else, but the Bishop intervened and took his arm.

A special feast was prepared for His Excellency. They also wanted to show him the improvements made to the main building. There was a nursery built for the little children from the money which the Bishop had found for the good Sisters. All the little exciting events of the year were retold by the old Jesuit with the help of Mother Josephine. Sister Rose Monica sat silently by the end of the table and blushed when she found Timmy's eyes fastened on her. How could something so beautiful find itself lodged in a place so defiled with human stench and corruptibility? Father Kevin ate very little. He was afraid to touch the napkin so pure and white.

Sitting in the crude living quarters of the Sisters brought back the "Clair de Lune" in its hellish version. Father Kevin wasn't listening to the conversation of the Bishop and his hosts. His mind started wandering back to his youth. He asked the Bishop to excuse him as he wanted to look around the colony. Alone with his thoughts as he walked aimlessly down the manmade roads of the island, he counted ten boys around the ages of fifteen to twenty pass him with only one warning, "UNCLEAN." It was never Timmy's intention to touch one of them, but he was happy that they thought enough of his dignity to leave the road completely when he passed. Father Kevin didn't realize where he was walking. It seemed that he was going up, up into the very heavens. The night was beautiful and the summit of the hill he climbed gave a commanding view of the bay and the blue-green water around the island. Below, he could see the buildings of the leper colony, the only buildings on the Island of Polonia. He knew these couldn't house the five hundred members who composed this horrible community of both sexes. Where did they live? Who fed them? What in God's name did life have in store for them?

Timmy heard footsteps of someone coming up the road in the darkness. He couldn't make out who it could be. A fear crept over the soul of the man who saw death and destruction surround him but a few short weeks before; a strange fear that knew no weapons to ward off the oncoming attack. In his nervous anxiety, he screamed at the approaching figure, "Stay back, stay 'way from me. Go to your own!"

"May I talk to you, Father?" came the soft voice in the darkness. "I just want to talk to someone from home," said Sister Rose Monica, standing in the shadows of the brush that hid her face and body.

"You're a leper. You belong with the rest of your diseased people. Get away from me," shouted the priest, hysterically.

"Father, I'm not a leper. I'm just Sister Rose Monica. Please forgive me for such an intrusion on your private moments. Won't you talk to me?" said the nun with an appeal of loneliness in her every word.

Father Kevin ran to the place where the voice came from. Before he knew it, he placed his hands on the tiny nun's shoulders. He could see two big, blue eyes looking deeply into his own.

"I'm terribly sorry, Sister Rose. Please forgive me if you can," said the priest, trying to say something that would erase the awful words he spoke to the figure in the darkness. "But, my nerves are so upset. You know I'm resting from a siege at Guam and Peleliu. Of course, you wouldn't have known that! I'm just trying to make excuses for my conduct when there isn't any excuse. I'm really not as mean as I sound, Sister. Why, back home at the Abbey they think I'm . . ." He stopped short when the sister turned her head and freed herself from his hands. "Now, I've done it again! You'll never believe me when I say I'm sorry. I keep saying it so often."

The sister turned to look at the priest. She was about to say something, but hesitated. Maybe he'd laugh and think she was mentally diseased, if he was at least sure she was physically clean.

"You were about to say something, Sister," said Timmy, trying to get her face to turn. "Please don't let my gruffness of a few minutes ago frighten you."

"When you mentioned, 'back home in your Abbey' I couldn't help feel a strange sense of loneliness creep all over me, Father. Oh, don't misunderstand me, now. I really love my work here. But, there's something about meeting someone from the United States that holds you spellbound. When I first saw you with the Bishop this afternoon, and when you walked through the buildings, I wanted to scream out, 'Hi, America.' You see, I haven't seen home in five years, not that I ever expect to leave Polonia, nor do I want to, but . . ."

"I understand, Sister. I was in Rome for five years. I know how it is to want the comfort of a United States bed and some good old American food," said Father Kevin with a laugh that rang out over the hill.

"You're very young to be a priest, aren't you?" said the nun, for the want of something better to say.

"Gosh, Sister, thanks a lot. I'm a priest nearly ten years. Don't I look every single one of my thirty-five years? Now, come on, tell the truth, Sister," said the priest, making the smile reappear on her face.

Kevin looked deep in her eyes while she blushed and tried to find words to keep pace with the priest. He noticed when she smiled, her face shone in a different light than her ordinary expression. He imagined she had a beautiful head of black hair under the white linen and black veil and would have loved to touch the soft skin of her cheeks if he wasn't sure she'd scream for shame and run back to her Mother Superior. He couldn't ever forget the expression in her eyes. They told a story with every twinkle. She couldn't have seen too much of this world out of them, either. Perhaps twenty-three, or at best, twenty-five years. Nuns couldn't be too deceptive about their ages, not all nuns anyway.

They stood on the side of the hill for hours that seemed like minutes. To them, their conversation together was like a passing parade of wonderful floats with pompous pageants in a never-ending procession of grandeur. They talked of people and places and events. They laughed and were happy in their brief association.

When it was long past Sister Rose Monica's time for night prayers and retiring, they strolled down the path and watched the little lights from passing boats and ships signal their approach, and listened to the weird whistle of their warnings. It was then Sister Rose told Father Kevin of their need. No, not the vast material needs of the colony. Those were obvious. Their need was the need of a young priest like Damien to come and teach the lepers to love God and serve Him as best they could so they could be happy with Him forever in an everyman's heaven.

The priest drank in the words of this sincere nun. He knew too well what a sacrifice a man would make to come here and preach, build, teach, and die for a cause so forgotten by the modernism of a century that wanted less of sacrifice and more of greed and selfishness. He saw the picture clearly in his mind. The old Jesuit could hardly get around to even speak words of advice and encouragement to his flock. He was at the evening of life with nightfall closing in from every side. He remembered another Jesuit priest who spent years in the Indian mission fields. He wondered where Father Cerveneau was that night.

He saw the Sisters of Charity working day in and day out with little rest to care for the vast colony's needs. All were strong and healthy in November of 1944. Would they be able to nurse the horrors of the dreadful disease in ten years hence? Three women without even a doctor to encourage them by an occasional visit to the island. Funds from the Propagation of the Faith Society in Rome kept them in the bare necessities. Their Mother-General could send some money, but money wasn't enough. These Women of Charity wanted associates—ten, or even five more would help. The priest could see how discouraged they'd become after prayerful years in asking God for help, and His answer was still in the negative.

The two twenty dollar bills Kevin pressed into the nun's hand was every cent he possessed on the trip to the island. He promised to write to the Sister Rose, who brought him so much happiness in their few hours together. He didn't promise ever to come back and see her, because he wasn't able to make his mind think in that sacrificial direction.

The next day brought rain to spoil the outside ceremonies. The old Bishop couldn't stand the stench of so great a gathering of decadence in one small hut. He insisted the Confirmation would proceed as planned outside! The three nuns stood drenched as they watched mothers assist their leprous sons to the alter; sons who had legs or arms eaten away, and assisted by fathers and mothers without ears or eyes; masses of humanity with the scourge of hell written on their abyssal faces.

Try as they might, they wanted to be clean and looked upon as others. They realized they were the earth's damned with hopelessness their only beacon.

Timmy watched this sight. He saw, though, not suffering man, but creatures composed of body and soul who were moved to religious fervor not only because God was intact, but souls which were clean and pure as the lilies that bloom to welcome the Risen Savior.

After a modest luncheon, the good Bishop McGuire spoke to the assembled people of his desolate diocese. He told them to renew their faith in God and to pray for continued charity, one for another! This was the same sermon he preached every year. The people knew it. So did the Bishop.

Father Kevin sat on the Bishop's left and watched Sister Rose Monica's face change expressions. There was something about this noble, little woman Kevin found pleasing. To leave her home and country and devote her life for the welfare of suffering humanity seemed an awful sacrifice to make. Yet, she appeared very happy, and her happiness showed forth on the faces of those unfortunates, which caused Father Kevin to think of the Lord's strong words learned during those days in preparation for his First Communion: "For what shall it profit a man if he gain the whole world and suffer the loss of his immortal soul? For what exchange can a man give for his soul? The angel of death shall appear in the night . . . and . . ." Father Kevin thought of this many times in the course of his youthful life. There was no particular reason for him to think of it now as he looked upon the face of the innocent Sister Rose Monica. Surely, he knew there was no thought of this child of God exchanging her soul for anything the world had to offer. And, why should he think of it himself? He certainly had no designs on the world or the accomplishments it afforded. The more he thought of the depth of its forcefulness, the more he began to realize its meaning had far reaching proportions. He wondered as he silently listened to the Bishop, if he could construe from this sudden thought that he was called to the Missions of Polonia. He thought of those opening words again: "What does it profit a man . . ." and clenched his fist. Surely God wouldn't want him to don the robes of another Damien and live for the balance of his life in the perpetual stench of rotting bodies, with only the hope that one day he would die and be buried alongside a "fellow leper." The thought caused his head to swim with the current of the picture his mind was painting. Man wasn't called to leave his monastery, the prospects of his career as a Doctor of Psychology, the good he could do for his fellow healthy beings. No, these were fiendish thoughts! Thoughts that ran through his head to make him think he wasn't even worthy for the office he now held.

Sister Rose could see Father Kevin was having a mental fight. Her thoughts were of his work and the trials Army and Navy Chaplains encountered. She never associated Father Kevin with the Island of Polonia.

On the dock, the old Jesuit priest with the Sisters of Charity and the lepers standing afar off, came to bid their visitors safe passage to Madras and God's graces. There was something Timmy had to say to Sister Rose before he left the island. A little something he thought would make her charming face smile with joy; smile those smiles that appeared the night before on the hill overlooking the great Bay of Bengal. He walked over to the extreme left of the dock and asked the nun to free herself from the listening ears of the Sisters.

"Last night, Sister Rose," he began, "you said you played the piano as a girl. As a matter of fact, you said you loved to play the piano as a girl. Isn't that right?" Father smiled when the blush appeared in her cheeks and continued, "Would it make you happy if I made arrangements in Calcutta for you to have a piano? You could play those beautiful fingers till your heart sang again, and these," the priest made a gesture to the lepers, "would be a little happier when they heard your music."

"That would be a wonderful gift, Father, but I couldn't expect you to do that for us," she said, looking directly into the eyes of the priest.

"Who said anything about us. Is it contrary to your Rule to be happy? I only want this little gift to be a source or medium of your happiness here in this cesspool of human stench," said Father Kevin. "It isn't as if it were something so great that would make Mother Seton toss with anxiety in her grave," said the priest, trying to be humorous by making light of the founder of the nun's community.

"I think Mother Seton would be equally as happy if she were right here," said the nun. "But, if I could be assured of your prayers and an occasional remembrance at your Masses, and . . . ," the nun looked down on the rough planks that made up the dock before she continued, "a letter from you now and again, with a few clippings from the Catholic papers. If it wouldn't be too much trouble, well, that's what you could do for me."

The priest took the Sister's hand in his. He held it for a long time as he gazed into her eyes. The little sister hadn't enjoyed this familiarity with a man in so long, she wasn't used to the sensation it caused in her heart. There were other things she wanted to tell Father Kevin up there on the hill in the cool of a November evening, but they suddenly disappeared with the conversation about the war and his Abbey. Now, here he was leaving. She thought of those little forget-me-nots that bloom in the heart of an excited woman, but the time and place seemed so irreverent.

As the priest stepped into the waiting craft, he waved his goodbye to the Religious and lepers who started the beautiful hymn, "To Jesus Heart All Burning" at the signal from Mother Superior. It was touching to watch and listen to the mixed voices of the unfortunates sing their praises and only expect the smile of their visitors as a token of thanksgiving.

Father Kevin threw the rope to the dock and watched the expression on Sister Rose's face. He called back to her with the excitement of a schoolboy, "I'm going through with the piano deal, Sister, and . . . and . . . you'll hear from me with a long letter, too."

Timmy was too far out to see the tears form in Sister Rose Monica's blue eyes. Those were tears mingled with joy and sadness.

Joy brought about by meeting someone who stirred you from within, and sadness expressed by saying farewell all too soon.

He looked back as the boat tugged through the rough waters. The Sisters and priest still were waving their hands with voices in the background dying out in competition with the waves that splashed against the sides of the boat. Father watched the little huddle on the dock till it became a speck against the hilly island. He listened to the old Bishop relate the story of the colony and how he came to invite the Sisters from far off Covent Station in New Jersey to operate it for him. He lamented the fact that he couldn't replace Father MacKay with a younger man, as his own diocese was sorely in need of priests in urgent posts in the main cities.

Father listened to the Bishop as he spoke, but his real thoughts wandered back to Polonia and the happy face of the contented Sister of Charity.

CHAPTER THIRTY TWO

W ord, received from Washington, D.C. removed Father Kevin from India to the States. He was assigned to assist at Halloran General Hospital in New York. He wasn't as disconsolate about the transfer as he thought he would be when it came in the form of a removal to the Home Front. He accepted it as another duty to speed victory and peace for his boys.

After a short visit and with a mission fulfilled in Calcutta, Father Kevin flew over Arabia to the seaport city of Alexandria. There he awaited a Navy plane to fly to Lisbon. After some delay in Portugal, a plane took him to the enchanted West Indies. He remained in Jamaica for three days before he was able to again set foot in a large bomber bound for Pensacola, Florida.

It was the twenty-second of December when Father Kevin reported to the large hospital in New York. The weather was a contrast to the Pacific and Indian climate. His blood was still thin from the months spent on the islands and hardly able to adjust itself to the Eastern winter.

Christmas Eve Father Kevin heard Confessions until after nine o'clock. Another priest took him to the heart of Manhattan and left him in front of the Algonquin Hotel. The priest walked down to Forty-second Street to watch the people rush for that last minute present and hurry home to their families. It was a much different Christmas Eve than any he had ever experienced. In the largest city in the United States, he felt alone among millions of people. He couldn't help thinking of Patty in his watery grave no matter how many times he promised himself to only think of him for the duration of a prayer for his soul.

As he walked over to Fifth Avenue and started to return in the direction of the Algonquin Hotel, his thoughts went back to Madeline Turrel. He wondered if she was as happy tonight as she was that Christmas night in his home in Lacodere. As he passed Forty-third and walked steadily on, his mind contrived the meeting in the great beyond between Madeline and Patty. How she must love him, he thought! In so many ways they were alike. He possessed many of her expressions and little mannerisms.

Before Kevin knew it, he was in front of Saint Patrick's Cathedral. So absorbed in the thoughts of the past, he hardly was aware of the blocks slipping past. He walked into the Cathedral and watched the people standing in rows of forty or fifty waiting to have their sins absolved. Kevin knelt in a pew close to the rear of the beautiful church built from the pennies and nickels of poor Irish "work-in" girls. There was hardly a sound in the large Cathedral that night. The occasional shifting in line as one would come in the box and another would leave managed to upset his train of thinking only for a few seconds.

It was here in the silence of his loneliness, the Debussy strains of "Clair de Lune" haunted his soul. Why did it follow him even to the sanctuary of the Lord? It passed away when his thoughts reverted themselves to the Island of Polonia and the memory of a nun who held his hand on a hill overlooking the rough Bay of Bengal in the coolness of a November evening.

As time passed on, his thoughts turned to Father Ignatius and the curate at Saint Mary's. He wondered what Aunt Lis was doing in that big house on this Christmas Eve. He looked at his watch. The priest promised to pick him up to return to Halloran by eleven o'clock. It was ten-thirty, and the people were crowding the front of the Cathedral, most of them members of the Armed Forces. Soon they'd be coming in for Midnight Mass and fill old Saint Patrick's to the doors.

He was disturbed by the multitude that swarmed on Fifth Avenue. He had to push his way along the busy avenue as he answered the greetings of passers-by.

Back at Halloran, he offered his own Midnight Mass before those men who were unable to come to the room set off for the priests. He remembered all his friends, but especially his Patty.

The year cruised to an end and ushered in 1945 with hopes for an early settlement of peace throughout the world. Father Kevin worked very hard at Halloran and was called upon to preach at various camps in and about the New York area. During the months to follow, he failed to write as regularly to his Abbey as he was wont to do in the past. When the announcement of the death of the old Abbot came to his desk and the notification of the elevation of the Assistant-Abbot to full authority, Father Kevin answered the letter three weeks later. It was a source of disturbance to Abbot Ignatius, and he telephoned the hospital in hopes of talking to Timmy. When Father Kevin was informed he was wanted on the phone and that the call came from Cassino College, he walked away with a strange smile on his face.

Father Kevin worked hard for the first six months of 1945. He worked too hard many asserted. His only correspondence was an occasional letter to Aunt Liz and Sister Rose Monica. Even these letters bore no traces of real news. He showed signs of constant and irritating repetition. There was nothing classical in his treatment of events; random notes hurriedly scratched out with meaningless interpretation for the reader.

When the armistice was signed in Europe, Father Kevin asked to be changed to the Pacific theatre of war. His answer was in the form of complete discharge. The Navy thanked him for his services rendered, but advised him to rest and avert a complete nervous breakdown.

In June, Timmy arrived in Lacodere, Louisiana. He was welcomed at the station by Aunt Liz and Father Martin. They noticed his tired and worried expression and attributed it to the scenes of hell he witnessed throughout his term as Chaplain. A letter from Abbot Ignatius informed him that he was free to take the summer and rest up before returning to the Abbey in the fall. The post script to the Abbot's letter foretold a heavy schedule for the returnee.

Timmy tried to rest and prepare classes in his field for the coming semester, but the memories of Lake Tahoo were too pronounced. He sat on the little porch of the cottage and every tree and path reminded him of Patty. Often he had to check tears that formed in his eyes as he could mentally vision the little boy running up to him and asking for a ride in the boat or the car. He seemed to feel the child's legs dangle on his chest as he carried him around the cottage. It was difficult for Aunt Liz to find words of comfort. Only when she sent for Father Richard, who was extremely busy in his little parish and entertained no thoughts of a vacation that summer, did Father Kevin seem to show signs of normalcy. The two priests played cards and talked of parish work. The war was an excluded subject, and even when Father Martin wanted to know the real Japanese treachery, he was told in no uncertain terms that he could derive whatever version he pleased from the current reports of overseas correspondents.

Aunt Liz noticed how old her Timmy had grown in the past few short years. He wasn't the same Timmy she raised in a happy house on Fontaine Street. He was touched now by some strange magic that caused a fire to burn within his breast and scorch all those he came in contact with by his harsh and snappy remarks.

He never once acted discourteous to her, but something had gone amiss along the road that caused him to be sullen and unfriendly. She found him happiest when they talked of the old Bishop of Madras. A letter from the old Jesuit made him smile again and show his former happiness. The letter requested help for his diocese in the form of material aid. He needed men to fill the vacancies. He wanted Timmy to make the supreme sacrifice to come and re-establish the Island of Polonia. Whatever the old Bishop said in his letter restored Timmy to his former self. Aunt Liz read the letter in her room in hopes it would introduce her to some thoughts or ideas to make this sudden burst of joy continue throughout the summer. She gasped with a sickening fright at the word "leper." If this was in the mind of her Timmy, she was going to do everything within her power to uproot it regardless of how he felt about his life.

In a session in the library after his Mass at Saint Mary's Church, Father Kevin sat silently waiting for his coffee, reading a letter from Sister Rose Monica. There were smiles and once or twice an outright burst of laughter. Aunt Liz asked Timmy to read to her the part that caused the youthfulness to return to his saddened face. Father Kevin accepted the cup of coffee with a nervousness that wouldn't leave his hands. He smiled and put the letter in his tunic and refused to speak. He knew too well how Aunt Liz would react to any proposition of returning to the leprosarium to offer his life and the remaining estate of Big Tim's fortune to such a work. After listening to her pleas, he told her, in full, the story of his visit to Polonia and the thrill of meeting the gallant little nun who worked only for God and the salvation of these outcast souls.

He told Liz, in confidence, that he wanted to return someday to the island. She argued with him that it was totally unfair to his Abbey and Abbot to want to devote his life to a work as he was neither trained for, nor qualified to perform.

She told him the Jesuits were established in the diocese and the Jesuits could better afford to relinquish men than the Benedictines. She tried to make him understand that the Benedictines educated him far beyond the normal training of their men for a very definite purpose. He was only thinking of a small fraction and not the whole.

Timmy was defiant in his intention to one day leave his Abbey. He told Liz he wasn't made to settle down in a classroom and grow old in a monastery. The world he lived in wasn't the same five years ago. He was changed by a series of unfortunate circumstances, circumstances his Abbot knew would arise to foster a change in his outlook on life as a Religious.

The fact of facts lie hidden in the passing of Patty and Peleliu. Everything he touched around the house or cottage had an imprint of his boy's memory. If he were to return to the Abbey, even there he'd be accosted day and night with thoughts running feverishly through his mind of the boy he loved so dearly, doing the little acts of kindness and making the other students happy to be associated with him. No, he had to get away and be in places where Patty's shadow never appeared. He had to have freshness of life even if he must seek the deadness of Polonia.

CHAPTER THIRTY THREE

In late September, Father Kevin was introduced to the student body as a former professor returning from a duty performed in the various circuits of the late war. V-J Day had come and undergone its national celebration. The actual signing was only another event. The students greeted the psychologist with warm welcomes. Stories were told and retold about his former classes and pleasant associations with the collegiate and high school students. He was Cassino's real hero, and every boy would have tried to register for his classes had they been permitted to do so.

A certain percentage of the old Father Kevin returned. The new Abbot, and real friend of the priest, did everything to make his readjustment as pleasant as possible. A radio-phonograph was placed in his cell and more comfortable furniture installed. Students were allowed to come to see him and discuss their problems. By Christmas, he wasn't having nightmares and sleepless intervals. The Debussy classic never rang in his ears or haunted his tranquility.

November found a change in Father Kevin for the better, but it was Christmas that caused him once more to slump into a mood that was unbearable for both students and Religious.

Father Joseph called the Abbey to report directly to Abbot Ignatius the horrible news of Aunt Liz's death. Father Joseph and Father

Martin were playing a game of three-handed bridge on Christmas night with Aunt Liz. At that time, she felt well, or appeared so and only expressed sorrow that Timmy wasn't able to be there to join in the get-together. Timmy was helping out at Father Richard's parish in Nlen, Alabama—a week of real work.

Abbot Ignatius knew what sadness this meant for all who were associated with Aunt Liz's charm and goodness. He wired Timmy to report home at once not mentioning what caused the sudden change of plans. According to his first notice of parish work, he was to stay for the duration of New Year's Day and then report back for classes on the third of January.

Father Kevin called the Abbey and received the news direct. He heard Gibby crying over the phone and could hardly make out what his Superior was trying to tell him. Taking the train for Mobile, he hastened to Lacodere where he was met by Father Martin. Here he was greeted by a weeping priest who could neither control himself, nor inform Timmy what had happened. Father Joseph told him as much as he could about the strange death. She was apparently all right before they left her the previous night, but when she failed to report for Mass in the morning, he sent Father Martin to inquire if she felt ill. The house was open and the lights burning. Evidently, Aunt Liz never left the living room, because only in that room was there light. Father Martin found her on the floor by the fireplace holding Patty's picture.

Timmy was grief-stricken and sick. He walked alone to the house on Fontaine Street and entered the parlor of his home. He stood as a stranger looking at the walls and pictures. Tears were streaming down his cheeks as he slowly walked into the living room and through to the library. He was standing in the center of the room when his eye noticed a letter on the desk. He walked over and picked up the envelope and read his name. With one hand wiping the tears from his eyes and the other holding fast to the letter written by Liz, he turned to walk to the living room. With head bent towards the floor as if he were looking for some lost article, he walked into the room to meet Father Martin, who stood by the fireplace. Father Kevin looked at the priest and nodded his greeting. Both men sat down as Timmy read the letter:

Christmas Night

Timmy dearest,

I feel very low tonight as I write these lines. Fathers Joseph and Martin have just left. We had a pleasant game of bridge and a light supper. They were so nice to come over and spend the evening with an old lady. I'll miss them when I go.

Dr. Jereau was over this morning when I called him about my heart. He told me the truth, although I was better able to tell him than he was to tell me. I haven't long to live, Timmy, and I wanted you to know that it was through you that I was able to live so long on this earth and to be so happy in my state. Every moment I ever lived from the time I arrived in Lacodere, I have lived because you were a part of that life.

When you were a little child, I felt you were my child, my little baby. When you were sick during that awful siege in the last war I prayed as I never prayed in my life that God would spare you for me. When you sat with me in the evenings before the fire and listened to my stories of Ireland with those sparkling and exciting eyes of yours, my heart burned within me for the joy the Lord bestowed upon me.

When you grew, I also knew my love for you was steadily growing. I continued to pray that God would grant you all the graces necessary to make you a good priest. When Madeline stepped into your life for that brief spell, I thought all my efforts to hold you were in vain.

The day you and Gibby left for the monastery, I was as happy as a child again. The thought of losing you forever never occurred to me until I didn't hear your goodnight in my ear that first night you were away. Oh, Timmy, how I missed you. Miss you as I miss you now.

Those letters Madeline wrote to you making all sorts of demands upon you were met by me. I destroyed every letter that came to you from the woman I knew was only bent on destroying your noble character. Please forgive me, Timmy, if I entered your life during those hectic months of your last summer here, and intervened in what I thought was for your best interests. I formulated plans to adopt your child because I felt I was partially at fault for not watching you closer during those months when I might have known something would go wrong. I blame myself for becoming ill and requiring a rest away from Lacodere.

Patty meant every bit as much to you as he did to me. This I know! But never have I loved you as you loved your baby. I watched you and was envious of the love Patty gave you. I was jealous because I loved you so much I couldn't even force myself to have even a child love you as a son should love his father.

Timmy, my heart aches tonight. Not the ache of one who is alone and sad. It's a physical pain that I've had since you went to war, since Patty went to war, and since Patty failed to come back to me as he promised!

In closing these hurried lines, let me assure you again and again, Timmy, I love you with all my heart. If you feel you must join the cause that the Little Sister of Charity is carrying on in the island off the Bay of Bengal, take what we have left, sell this home and all it has meant to us, the bonds we have, the stock your father left us. Take it all and do what you think God would be most happy in having you do. But, remember, my boy, my little Timmy, I'll pray for you until we are in heaven together. Never will I cease asking God to grant you an abundance of graces and to bless your work, which I know will be His work. I'll pray for Gibby, Buddy, Skeets and all the little boys who were your playmates, and for my dear little Robert, who has never been anything but a constant source of joy and happiness. I'll ask God to protect him, and in this note beg of him to watch over and remain with you for all your days.

Pray often for your old Aunt Liz, Timmy, and remember how much I'm going to miss your voice and pleasant smile. God love you always and keep you ever close to his Sacred Heart.

Your loving Auntie Liz

Father Kevin didn't feel ashamed to cry in front of Father Martin. He placed the letter on the table by the fireplace and buried his face in his hands. His whole body seemed to vibrate with the emotion caused by Liz's passing. The letter didn't surprise him. He went to the house in hopes of finding something like that. Father Martin came over to him and put his arms around Timmy's shoulder. He was the same lovable Robert who only wanted to be near his "big brother." He felt Timmy's hand pat him gently as a thanksgiving for the continued loyalty he expressed. Robert would have cut off his arm to help Timmy out of some difficulty. Most people say they'd do something as drastic, but when called upon for the acid test, find the arm looks better as it hangs from the shoulder uncut!

The arrangements having been settled and the funeral a week past, Father Kevin made an appointment to visit the Abbot on business. This was really the first time Gibby could remember receiving Timmy as long as he was the new Superior. Each time it was Gibby who went to Timmy's cell for a conference or to make some suggestion. Now, Timmy was coming, like all monks, to the door of Father-Superior for a very grave reason.

Saturday, January, the fifth, Father Kevin knocked on the door to receive a very business-like "come in" signal from the Abbot and knelt to kiss his ring.

"Well, Timmy," said Gibby, with his best smile of diplomacy beaming on his face, "we can dispense with all the formality and get right down to the matter of your business. I've several calls to make and must go out to attend the banquet with His Excellency tonight, and . . ."

Timmy cut his friend off very short and curtly, "What I came here about, Father-Abbot," said the priest, determinedly, "won't be pleasing to you or your council members. In fact, the lowliest novice in the Novitiate will probably comment on the validity of my decision. Nevertheless, here it is!"

Father Kevin related the whole story of his association with Madeline and its resultant factors. He told him of his experiences at Madras and his present desire to return to do something constructive. He wanted his release from the Abbey to foster the work started by the Jesuits, and to all appearances, left in that state by their desire to abandon the work.

Gibby stood up and gave a speech that really hurt him more than it did the listener. He told Timmy he couldn't release him now or ever. He had plans for him right at Cassino that didn't include any further jaunting around the world. He reminded him of his vow of stability, and the amount the Abbey expended on his education and his obligations to his students and possible future priests. Under no circumstances would he release him to rot away in a work that was neither started by the Abbey, nor to be encouraged in the future by their monks.

Father Kevin bowed gracefully and walked out. He went to his cell and prepared to pack his belongings. The door was left ajar as he busied himself with papers and books. His bags were taken down from the top of the clothes closet. He was just about to open the large "two-weeker" when the Abbot walked in and stood at the doorway.

"Son, this is all monastic life means to you, Timmy!" said Gibby, looking at his subject. "What does the Vow of Obedience mean to you? Don't answer me, Timmy, your actions speak for themselves. As God is my judge, Father Kevin, much as I love you as if you were my own brother . . . I'll . . . I'll have you silenced if you leave this Abbey as a fugitive."

Timmy stopped short. The word fugitive burned. He had met some priests who were unhappy in the world because of their inability to "take it" from Bishops or Superiors. It never dawned on him as he walked out of the Abbot's office a few minutes before that he was going right into the footsteps of those he pitied in the places he traveled. The priest knelt down in front of his Abbot and kissed his ring. In a whispered voice, he told Gibby he was sorry, but made haste to say, "At least, Gib, you know I'm not happy here, don't you?"

Father Kevin taught his classes and continued to be a source of happiness for his students. Each evening he'd help one or two over the difficult hurdles of definitions in psychology. The students knew they could worm a story out of him regarding his experiences in the battle zones. They knew if they stayed long enough, he'd "go off again," as they put it, on the trip to Polonia.

On Ash Wednesday, he received another letter from Sister Rose telling him of the death of the Jesuit priest. She described the funeral at great length. But, between the lines, the priest could read how much they needed a helping hand from someone who was young and energetic.

When Easter made its glorious appearance, Father Kevin went to Lacodere to close the deal on the sale of his house and the cottage at Lake Tahoo. He received the permission from his Abbot to appropriate the money left to him and the results from the sale of his possessions to whatever source he so desired. Timmy knew that Gibby would have been pleased to receive the check for well over a hundred thousand dollars after the disposal of all the stocks, bonds, and property holdings. But, Timmy had other plans for the spending of this small fortune.

The cash in the Southern National Bank amounted to very little. Perhaps three or four thousand dollars. This he donated in full to

Father Joseph's Church and for a trip to his wrecked homeland. The old priest often wanted to see Germany, but not under the regime of Hitler and his henchmen.

During his stay at Saint Mary's Church, he helped the two priests on Holy Thursday and Good Friday. On Easter Sunday, after three Masses were celebrated, Father Feeley's parents entertained the four priests with a large baked ham dinner. Father Feeley was told about Polonia as was everyone else who came across Timmy's path. He wasn't too concerned with the duties of the Chicago Province of the Jesuits, but confined his interests to the New Orleans Province, and the development of vocations to their Society in the Southland.

While he was telling Father Feeley of the grand work the Jesuits "used to do" in Madras, Father Martin sat very attentively in the group. Never did he feel he should interrupt the two while they were discussing the laxity of the Jesuits, at least, Timmy's thoughts ran along those lines even if Buddy's didn't find words of agreement. Robert sat unnoticed in the living room of the Feeley home thinking along the same subject as Father Kevin was discussing so forcefully.

On the way back to the rectory, Robert turned to Timmy and nearly knocked the priest over with his proposition. "Why can't you and I go to this Polonia and help these people? Your money could build a nice little hospital and church, and maybe a little school with a playground for the children, and I could . . ."

"Look, Robert, I can't even get the Abbot to release me. How in the name of God could he ever turn both of us loose? We might just as well forget about Polonia. That is, we can only talk about it, not let it go beyond the yardstick of dreaming," said Timmy, patting Robert on the back.

"We'll see, we'll see," said Father Martin, engrossed in deep thought.

The stress of renewed work, preparing debate teams for extensive trips to other colleges in the South, the coaching of the high school baseball club, the five courses in philosophy and psychology, all were a constant wear on the disposition and strength of Father Kevin. By May first, he was forced to decline an offer to preach a novena in honor of the Blessed Virgin in Memphis, Tennessee. He wanted to spread devotion to Mary, the Mother of God, but it just seemed the other tasks that enveloped him usurped his whole strength and time.

The night of May twenty-ninth found the priest in a broken spirit. All day he heard the mournful reminder of "Clair de Lune" and the days of his past. It was ever thus when his spirits were low. Everyone knew when Father Kevin wasn't feeling too well. They could tell by the amount of food he'd take at the evening meal. They would know something was amiss by the very expression on his face as he sat watching the reader during mealtime, never taking his eyes off the young novice who seemed to remind him of someone he wanted to forget.

All day he had given examinations. The night he reserved for correcting and recording the results in his notebook. But, tonight was going to be vastly different. He was going to set himself on a deliberate excursion of dreaming in fond hopes of settling once and for all the matter of the past. He would play "Clair de Lune" for the last time!

Father Kevin's head was slumped on his chest and the medal and chain he held in his hands fell to his lap. He was a picture of peace and contentment when the Abbot touched him gently on the shoulder.

"Another night without the aid of your bed, huh, Timmy?" was the Abbot's only address.

Timmy awoke with a startled look in his eyes. He rubbed his face and remembered the Chain of Lacodere. He picked it up and looked at it before turning to his Superior and saying, "There was a lot I wanted to sit here and remember about. I guess I'm ready to go back to the grind and accept your proposal to act as Dean of the College and settle down to the life of a monk. By the way, Gibby, how late am I this time for my Mass?"

The Father-Abbot looked at the priest and smiled. "I've been a fool, Timmy. I should have realized it was too much to expect that you'd be able to settle down after a life such as you've been exposed to. It took poor Robert's tears to bring me around. The letter he received from the Bishop of Madras convinced me of my own selfishness. Don't look at me that way, Timmy! It's true, Father Martin came in late last night, and we talked the whole matter over. He's willing to go as your helper and . . . and I'm willing . . . now . . . to give you both my heartfelt blessings." The face of the tired Abbot worked a smile for his friend in the leather chair. He knew this news would make his lifelong pal restore himself to the fullness of his capabilities.

Timmy stood up and shook Gibby's hand. He couldn't speak. Words just wouldn't come out or even formulate in his mind. He had been happier before in his life, but those days were snowed under with the sadness of the last few years. Today, the Memorial Day of departed warriors was his greatest Memorial Day. Today he was free to do a real work at a cost few men were willing to pay—one's very life.

Father Kevin kissed Gibby's hand three or four times and bolted out of his cell down the slippery corridor of the monastery to the room in the far end of the Abbey, reserved for visiting bishops and distinguished visitors. At the door, he looked down at his feet to notice for the first time in that long run he hadn't stopped to put on his shoes. He burst into the room to find Father Martin sound asleep. With one dive, he landed on top of the sleeping Robert and planted a resounding kiss on the astonished face of the monk.

"You're the best politician I ever met, Robert. Get up! Time's moving too swiftly to rest. We're headed for the Island of Polonia. That is, as soon as I flunk a few potential psychologists," said Father Kevin, pulling the young priest completely out of bed.

Robert watched Timmy make his hurried exit. At that early hour, a verse or two from Longfellow came to his mind as he started to dress. Sister Mary Immaculata made him memorize it back in the early grades. It didn't mean much to him then, but it's significance began to portray something to him now. He ran over the whole poem and then returned to repeat:

> I remember the gleams and glooms that dart
> Across the school-boy's brain;
> The song and the silence in the heart,
> That in part are prophecies, and in part
> Are longings wild and vain.
> And the voice of that fitful song
> Sings on, and is never still:
> "A boy's will is the wind's will,
> And the thoughts of youth are long, long thoughts."

There are times of which I may not speak;
There are dreams that cannot die;
There are thoughts that make the strong heart weak,
And bring a pallor into the cheek,
And a mist before the eye.
And the words of that Matal song
"A boy's will is the wind's will,
And the thoughts of youth are long, long thoughts."

END

A SINCERE THANK YOU TO THE FOLLOWING FOR ALL THEIR TIME AND EFFORT IN BRINGING THIS STORY TO LIFE

FATHER DONOHOE

FATHER GIANOLA

CHARLES SEEMS

JILL KAMIN

JOHN MYLES